MISSING IN MIAMI

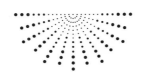

KATHRYN LANE

Copyright © 2022 by Kathryn Lane

ISBN: 978-1-7354638-1-0

Printed and bound in the USA

Tortuga Publishing, LLC

The Woodlands, Texas

Editor: Sandra A. Spicher

Cover Design: Heidi Dorey

Interior Design: Danielle Hartman Acee, authorsassistant.com

Expert Readers: Dr. Joseph Burckhardt, David Hart, Pattie Hogan, Jorge Lane, Ann McKennis, and Nancy Miller

For my husband, Bob

My son, Philip

And in loving memory of my mother, Frances Lane

LIST OF CHARACTERS

(This list is provided for the reader's benefit. Characters are loosely listed in order of appearance. A few minor characters are omitted.)

Nikki Garcia – Private investigator at Security Source, a firm in Miami, Florida

Eduardo Duarte – Nikki's husband, a Colombian citizen and medical doctor

Floyd Webber – Nikki's boss and owner of Security Source, a firm in Miami, Florida

Milena Webber – Floyd's wife

Charlotte – Office manager and computer geek at Security Source

Andrea Rodríguez – Sixteen-year-old daughter of Delfina **Morales and Yoani Rodríguez**

Dr. Yoani Rodríguez – Medical doctor and Andrea's father

Dr. Delfina Morales – Medical doctor and Andrea's mother

Dr. Urbano Barriga – Rodríguez's partner, Andrea's Godfather, also called Uncle Urby

Dr. Corrado López – Andrea's primary care doctor

Pepito – Andrea's dog

Raquel Álvarez – Urbano Barriga's wife

Jack Smith – Medical Examiner; also called Smithy

Lila – Evidence Technician
Sergeant Maldonado – Miami police
Ms. Hale – School principal
Spider Candella – Man with no identity
Alejando Álvarez – Raquel Álvarez's father
Carolina Castillo – Raquel Álvarez's mother
Hamilton Estrada – Agent at Security Source
Dr. Da Silva – Voodoo expert
Peterson – Security guard at Deep Sea Cruises
Nancy Rivas – Chief of security at Deep Sea Cruises
Santiago Téllez – Security guard Deep Sea Cruises
Benjy Ávila – Raquel's cousin
Yésica Fernández – Nurse who works the night shift
Victoria – Manager of the Cuban clinic; also called Vicki
Sonia – Barriga's sister, also called Mama-Sonia
Oliver Ortega – Tour guide
Terri Acosta – Case worker from Child Protective Services
Frank – young CIA operative
Sam Huerta – Seasoned CIA field operative
Mrs. Ballesteros – Child Protective Services' supervisor
Jordan – University student

GLOSSARY

alebrije—Folk art from Oaxaca, Mexico, that originated in the 1930s. Fantastical, imaginary, and whimsical animals sculpted in wood and painted in elaborate and colorful patterns. They represent anything from spirit guides to figures intended to ward off evil spirits. Today, they are considered an important form of Mexican Folk Art.

amor mío—My love.

bandoneón—Musical instrument that is essential for tango music.

bisnero—A person involved in an illegal business.

Boyeros—Where the Havana airport is located. In English, the word means *oxherds*.

buen provecho—Bon appétit.

coño—All-purpose cuss word used by Cubans, meaning "holy shit" or "wow" or "damn," though in other parts of Latin America, it can be considered derogatory sexual slang.

cuentapropista—Slang Cubans use to denote a self-employed person.

economic espionage—As used in this novel, one country steals trade or research secrets from another to benefit its own economy.

¡Ese hombre es tremendo mangón!—That man is so hot!

diplomáticos, hombres de negocio y turistas—Diplomats, businessmen, and tourists.

gordita—Term of endearment for a loved one, such as a daughter.

Habana Vieja—Old Havana.

habas saladas—A salty, fried Peruvian snack.

jama—Slang for food.

jinetero—Street hustler.

La Yuma—Cuban street expression for the United States.

Me están pagando por la izquierda—They are paying me under the table.

Necesito jama—I need food.

No entiendo—I don't understand.

pisco—Peruvian brandy. Unlike cognac, whiskey, brandy, and rum aged in oak barrels, pisco cannot be aged in wood at all. Instead, pisco is distilled in a copper pot still. A well-known Peruvian distiller, Johnny Shuler, has said that "cognac is made by oak, whereas pisco is made by the gods."

regulados—Cuban citizens who are not allowed to travel abroad due to their dissident political activities, human rights advocacy, or practice of independent journalism.

resolver—making do with what one has available and/or making ends meet.

Si eso es lo que quieres—if that's what you want.

tremendo paquete—someone who lives with heavy drama as in a drama queen.

CHAPTER ONE

C arefully moored yachts glistened in the late afternoon sunlight. Nikki Garcia sighed. "It's spectacular! I could stay here forever." She snapped some pictures of the marina with her smartphone, then looked up at Eduardo. His sunglasses reflected miniature versions of the graceful white vessels.

Her husband smiled. "Think what you'll miss when you leave for Hong Kong."

"I'll miss *you* much more."

Nikki opened her phone's browser and read a description she'd brought up on the drive to Miami Beach Marina. "Victoria Harbor is a natural landmark, where the sky kisses the mountains and skyscrapers accent the greenery over the blue waters of the Hong Kong harbor."

"I'm jealous," he said playfully. "Your boss always makes offers you can't refuse."

They were here to meet Floyd Webber, Nikki's boss, and the founder of Security Source. He was also a former CIA operations officer.

"You know I'm more effective in foreign countries. And I'm going to ask Floyd if you can join me after your exams." She saw a speedboat approaching and recognized the man at the helm. "Speak of the devil."

Floyd slowed the speedboat to a crawl, angling into the dock. Then he reversed the engine, halting the boat and making little waves. A black-backed gull that had been walking along the pier stopped to watch.

An attendant ran to secure the boat and the bird retreated. With a burp from the outboard, the stern settled against the slip. Floyd and his wife, Milena, took off their lifejackets. The attendant helped them onto the floating walkway.

"That was great docking," Nikki said. "I hope you enjoyed the trip over."

Milena hugged Nikki. "I haven't seen either of you since Barcelona."

Eduardo and Floyd bumped elbows, then they all followed Eduardo to the car. It was just three miles from the marina to their borrowed condominium with its gate and camera-secured subterranean parking.

Once in their living quarters, Milena exhaled. "This is lovely."

"Eduardo will show you around and serve drinks while I get hors d'oeuvres ready." Nikki headed for the kitchen. She nestled sea scallops on twelve clam shells she'd cleaned earlier in the day. She dribbled lime juice, butter, and Peruvian Pisco over them before generously sprinkling Parmesan cheese on each half shell. Using an oven glove, she pushed the platter under the broiler.

After a brief tour of the condo, Floyd took a seat by the marble countertop that separated the kitchen from the great room.

"Nice place," he said.

Nikki faced Floyd. "I have a favor to ask. I'd like Eduardo to join me in Hong Kong after his medical board exams." She glanced toward the beige sectional sofa, where Eduardo was talking quietly with Milena.

Before Floyd could respond, his phone buzzed. He glanced at the number. "Gotta take this." He slipped outside to the balcony.

Nikki cut two limes in half, wrapping each half in cheesecloth and tying it with a green ribbon. She sprinkled salt and a spice blend over a bowl of habas saladas. The crunchy Peruvian snack's texture would complement the soft sea scallops.

Floyd returned to the marble countertop and leaned against it. "We need to rethink Hong Kong." He studied her face.

"Why?" she asked, hoping her blank expression didn't change. Floyd had been coaching her on keeping a poker face. "Showing emotion can be deadly for a private investigator," he'd advised her.

"I need you for a case here in Miami," Floyd said now.

"Miami?" she repeated, disappointed.

"A teenage girl has vanished."

"Kidnapped?" Nikki felt her stomach churn. Cases involving kids reminded her of her twelve-year-old son's tragic death several years before.

"All I know is that she's disappeared. That was the mother who called —Delfina Morales. The father is Yoani Rodríguez. She said they haven't yet reported her missing."

"That's strange. It's the first thing they should have done."

"If you take the case, you can follow up with the parents tomorrow and ask them."

"If a child's missing, I should go right now," Nikki said.

"I offered. I told the mother how important the first few hours are. But she insisted on tomorrow morning at nine. Said her daughter might return home tonight."

"Let me call her from your phone." After several rings, it went to voicemail. Nikki left her number and asked the mother to call her.

Her chest tightened at the thought of working on a missing teenager's case. "I'd rather take the Hong Kong job. Can't Hamilton do this? Or one of the junior investigators?"

"Your work on missing children is exceptional. Think about it and give me your answer at the marina when we—"

Nikki grabbed the glove and yanked the oven door open, coughing as she pulled out the platter.

"Burnt Parmesan!"

Floyd covered his nose.

"That smells awful," Eduardo muttered, approaching the kitchen. "Scorched scallops?"

"Like rubber," Nikki said, flipping on the exhaust fan. "Change in plans. Take the wine, cheese, and crackers to the balcony while I bag this for the garbage."

"Good thing the fire alarm didn't go off," Eduardo said.

"I just hope security doesn't tell the owners I'm stinking up their beautiful condo." Nikki ran cold water over the burnt scallops and dumped them into a plastic bag, then put the sealed bag in the freezer.

Eduardo showed their guests to the balcony. The condo, in the Faena District of Miami Beach, boasted a wraparound terrace from the primary bedroom all the way to the great room. Glass walls extended the indoor-outdoor feel of the living space.

Nikki could see Milena outside on the balcony, holding onto the railing. With her own fear of heights, Nikki could never get that close to the edge, not twelve stories up, not even if she grabbed the railing for support. She picked up the bowl of habas saladas and joined them, taking a seat on a chaise longue. A fresh, warm breeze blew a wisp of dark hair across her face.

Milena peered down at the white sand beach. "What an incredible view."

"It's gorgeous all right," Nikki said. "But it's not us. I feel like an intruder."

Eduardo refilled Floyd's wine glass. "I keep telling Nikki we should enjoy it while we can."

"How much are you paying in rent?" Floyd asked.

"Nothing. We're house sitting," Eduardo said. "They wanted to pay us. Can you imagine? They insisted so much that in the end, we let them pick up our utility bills. Even that makes us uncomfortable."

"And the owners—"

"Off on a world tour for one full year," Nikki said.

"Milena and I can take care of it if you don't want to." Floyd chuckled.

"Then we'll move out tonight," Nikki said, getting up from the chaise longue in an exaggerated manner.

Taking a seat, Milena suggested Nikki relax and pretend to be on vacation for a year.

"A vacation in Hong Kong sounds more exciting," Nikki said, hoping she sounded calm. She took a seat again. Just because she'd been eaten up by anxiety from the moment Floyd told her about the missing teenager was no reason to ruin everyone else's evening. "I was supposed to fly out next week."

Eduardo dabbed Stilton on a cracker. "When my surgeon friend offered us the condo, we thought it'd be a great idea. Let us get to know the city before we buy our own home. We didn't realize the stress of living in a picture-perfect place. We're afraid of chipping the paint or spilling coffee and staining that Italian marble countertop." Eduardo gave his wife a devilish glance. "Or god forbid, Nikki burning the place down with Parmesan scallops."

Nikki laughed. "From now on, we'll order pizza every night."

"That'll work while I'm studying for my exams." Raising his glass, Eduardo toasted his wife's upcoming trip to Hong Kong.

"I may not be going to Hong Kong after all," Nikki said.

"In that case, we can invite Floyd and Milena for Peruvian conchitas next week. With luck, they won't be charred." Eduardo lifted his glass again.

Milena took a sip of wine and glanced toward the beach, in the direction of candy-cane-striped umbrellas at the beach club. "You'll soon love it here. You won't want to leave when the owners return."

"That's the next issue," Eduardo said, nibbling on habas saladas. "We'll fall in love with it and we'll have to leave. We can't afford a property like this. I haven't worked for over a year and I still have to take my exams to get my medical license."

"Yeah, I'm supporting him." Nikki laughed and winked at her husband.

As the others helped themselves to habas or cheese and crackers, Floyd told them he'd asked Nikki to take the case of a missing Miami teenager instead of working in Hong Kong. He apologized for disappointing her.

"I wouldn't burn this place down if I were in Hong Kong," Nikki said, laughing.

Nikki wondered how she could hide her unease about working on the missing teen case in Miami. She would have loved the Hong Kong job. Anything would be better than a kid in danger. Her gut twisted at the thought.

———

"Tomorrow is a workday," Floyd said. "It's time we leave."

Eduardo and Nikki drove their guests back to the marina.

It bustled with people. Couples pushed baby strollers, children darted here and there, and singles walked their dogs along the brightly lit street near the waterfront. Eduardo parked and the four of them headed toward the dock.

"We must plan an outing in the boat," Milena suggested.

Eduardo responded with enthusiasm.

Floyd asked Nikki what she'd decided on the Miami assignment.

"If a girl is missing, I'll give it everything I've got to find her."

He nodded. "Are you sure?"

"I'm committed," she said. "There's no turning back now."

"That's great." Floyd was not one to waste words. Motioning to a dock attendant for assistance, he handed him a tip. He took his wife by the elbow, and they boarded the boat, then put on their life jackets.

Floyd started the engine and the attendant untied the boat.

Before he cast away from the dock, Floyd joined Milena at the gunwale and waved to Nikki and Eduardo.

"Must be nice to own your own boat," Nikki said.

"Let's walk that way." Eduardo pointed toward three anchored yachts. "And dream about owning one of those." He took her hand.

"When I met you in Colombia, you told me you were not wealthy. They're beautiful, but it'd take real money to own one."

Ignoring her comment, Eduardo stopped and turned her to face him. "What happened to Hong Kong? You'd told me you're more effective in foreign countries."

Nikki looked into her husband's eyes.

"A teenager is missing. How could I possibly not try to find her?"

CHAPTER TWO

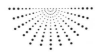

Early the next morning, Nikki stopped by Charlotte's office to chat about the change in assignment.

Tall and thin, Charlotte never had to diet. Her outdoorsy lifestyle and organic, vegan cooking kept her in shape, she claimed. A computer expert, she handled online research to support cases for Security Source. She also supported the team of investigators. Her work frequently provided breakthroughs in tough cases. The firm depended on Charlotte to dig up information that they would not have even known how to access online.

Besides the huge computer monitors dominating the walls in her office, the geeky young woman displayed a collection of elephants. One was an elephant alebrije, whimsical folk art from Mexico that Nikki had given her. Charlotte claimed it warded off evil spirits.

"Andrea Rodríguez is the missing girl," Nikki said, giving her the few details Floyd had mentioned the night before. "Her father dropped her off at school but she never made it to class. She simply vanished. Apparently, the mother was so distraught when she called Security Source that Floyd's not certain when she actually disappeared."

Charlotte keyed the name into her computer. "That's weird. No missing person report."

"Not good. I'll tell them they must file one. Look up the parents, Yoani Rodríguez and Delfina Morales."

"Here's the parents' residence," Charlotte said, tapping on the keyboard.

Nikki looked over Charlotte's shoulder to check the map on the screen while her assistant texted her the address on Paradise Point Drive in Palmetto Bay.

"It's a couple miles south of Coral Gables, in a frou-frou neighborhood." Charlotte's typing speed was impressive despite the green and yellow acrylic nails on her fingertips. "Interesting, there's nothing on Yoani Rodríguez," she said. "That's the wife's house. The county records list Delfina Morales as the sole owner."

"Please get all the information you can on the parents. Where they were born, educated, and their employment records—both past and present. Are they separated? Divorced? Any issues? Arrests, criminal records, financial difficulties, bankruptcies, DWIs, whatever. You know the drill," Nikki said.

Twenty minutes later, Charlotte sent Nikki an electronic file containing her research. And she followed up on the intercom. "I can't find much on the father. He must pay to erase his digital footprint. No social media on either parent. Andrea did have postings. Nothing unusual, typical teenage stuff. Though she doesn't seem to have a lot of friends. Her last post was six days ago."

Nikki studied the information before calling Delfina for an appointment. On her way out, she let Charlotte know she was meeting with Andrea's mother at the home address. She always felt more secure if someone knew where she was.

Nikki took US Route 1, the longer but more scenic drive. Her GPS chirped instructions to take SW 152nd Street east until it narrowed and became Paradise Point. Stopping at a guard shack, she provided her driver's license and signed the roster of visitors.

She glanced at the map on the navigation system. It showed a single street, Paradise Point Drive, meandering on a narrow stretch of land resembling a finger pointing to Cutler Channel in Biscayne Bay. Studying the map, she realized she'd passed over a small bridge right before the guard shack. Paradise Point was actually an island.

Getting clearance from the guard, Nikki left the window down as she drove toward the bay to get a feel for the neighborhood. The first section had expensive-looking condos to her left. Beyond the condos, boats were anchored at a marina along the canal. On her right, a wild and densely wooded area appeared to have been untouched since the days of Ponce de León. She deduced that developers had left the mangrove forest on the south side of the finger-shaped island to keep storm surges from damaging the community.

Despite the mangrove forest, the air smelled like citrus and ginger. Driving on, she encountered a huge cul-de-sac with magnificent homes. Each mansion overlooked the channel. She slowed to a crawl. Big and impressive, the showy places sprawled across manicured lawns. She wondered how they fared in hurricanes. Storms didn't care whether a community was gated, a home simple or lavish.

Spotting Delfina's address, she pulled into the driveway. A white-crowned pigeon was perched on a weathervane on the roof. It flew off when Nikki closed the car door.

A petite woman, casually dressed, invited her into the two-story great room. Nikki sat on an extra-long white sofa with decorative throw pillows in navy blue and bright orange. Delfina sat in a black leather and steel Barcelona chair angled toward the sofa.

Nikki detected a faint aroma of vinegar. Maybe coming from the rug under the sofa and chairs. An attempt to get rid of pet odor? Or perhaps it was a scent diffuser. In any case the architecture was far more interesting. It seemed like a hybrid of two distinct styles. An Acapulco geometric design, accented by a curved staircase, contrasted elegantly with the simplicity of open interior spaces in cantilevered construction, creating the illusion of modern architecture reminiscent of Mies van der Rohe.

A gigantic rug in orange and black hung from a vertical white marble partition, the only solid wall in the great room, added color to the sparse décor. Natural light filtering through wall-length windows fell on the monochromatic furnishings, casting sharp-edged shadows that generated a tapestry of angles.

"You spoke to Floyd about your daughter. Is that right?"

Delfina nodded. "Only by phone."

Other than a rhythmic Cuban intonation further emphasized by a nasally accent, Nikki noticed her client spoke excellent English. To a casual bystander, the woman's swollen eyes might have appeared to be defined with red liner, but Nikki knew tears had caused that illusion. "Tell me about your daughter's disappearance."

"My husband dropped her off at school."

"Which school?"

"Everglade Academy. It's excellent. My daughter always calls me from the cafeteria to tell me she's there. As usual, she called that morning. She's a responsible student, so I was shocked when the principal's office called me around ten to ask why Andrea was not there."

"Your daughter called you every morning. Why?"

"It became a ritual for us. I wanted to make sure she was okay."

"Okay?" Nikki asked, surprised. Then she remembered Floyd's advice not to show her emotions. "Okay from what?"

"A mother's reassurance is all."

Nikki took another angle. "What day did she disappear?"

"Friday."

"Five days ago?" Nikki inhaled. Today was Wednesday. Most abducted children and teenagers are killed within the first twenty-four hours after they're taken. "Have kidnappers contacted you to request ransom?"

Delfina shook her head, pursing her lips together.

"Why haven't you reported it to the police?"

Delfina looked away, glancing out the windows to an enclosed patio with several flowering Buddleia bushes against a stone-veneer wall.

"We thought she'd return by now, but it's a long story."

"I have time," Nikki said.

She turned and looked straight at Nikki. "We're Cuban. We have green cards now, and Yoani does not like to rock the boat."

"When did you arrive?"

"In 2012. We'd tried to come here for many years. We decided it was then or never. We had a six-year-old. Coming by raft was too risky. We flew to Nicaragua on business, knowing they had a friendly policy toward Cubans trying to get into the US. Once there, we thought it'd be easy to fly to Mexico, and then cross the border into the US.

"We miscalculated. At the airport, we learned we needed visas to Mexico and special migratory documents to pass through that country. After we were denied legal entry to Mexico, we traveled overland with a smuggler from Nicaragua. Grueling trip. Our daughter got very sick."

Delfina's knuckles grew white. She choked as she started to speak. Sounding distant, she recounted the toll that the hazardous journey had taken on the six-year-old. "Dizziness, headaches, and exhaustion—they all seemed normal under the circumstances."

"I can imagine," Nikki said in a comforting manner.

"It got worse," the woman said, taking a deep breath. "She developed an infection and ran a fever. Lost weight. It impeded our progress. We had no money. The smuggler had demanded so much cash to take us to the US border, we could not afford to take her to a doctor. Plus *I am* a physician. I still get angry at myself for not recognizing the symptoms.

"After three horrendous months, we crossed the border at Laredo, Texas. A nightmare, all of it, but the smuggler gave us the name of a clinic that would take care of her. She was diagnosed with leukemia."

"How is she now?"

"The irony is," Delfina said, looking pained, "we'd left a country where medical treatment was free. Here, doctors gave us professional courtesy, so we didn't pay them, but we had to contribute toward the therapy. Both of us started working. I'd found a good job and my husband started managing our friend Urbano's business. That was before Yoani became his partner. We asked Urbano to take Andrea to Cuba for stem cell transplantation. He stayed with my gordita until she could travel again. Andrea was cured."

"That's wonderful," Nikki said.

"Yes, but there was another issue. Stem cell transplant is only as good as the cells that are used. There can be side effects."

Glancing at Delfina, Nikki was unsure what to say.

"At fourteen, she developed lupus. Now she's on medication all the time. Even heavier doses during flareups." Delfina looked away. "And eighteen months ago, she had chest pains. It took several months to diagnose. It turned out to be primary spontaneous pneumothorax, PSP for short. It's also called blebs. I'm convinced she also developed these from the stem cell therapy."

"I'm sorry to hear that," Nikki said. "I know about lupus, but I've never heard of PSP or blebs."

"It's genetic. Neither Yoani nor I have ever had it. It's the abnormal accumulation of air in the chest cavity between the lungs and the pleural sac. Air pockets form in the lungs. When the blisters, called blebs, burst, the air builds up in the chest cavity and can cause partial or complete collapse of a lung. One of Andrea's collapsed."

"I can't imagine what you're going through. We'll do our best to bring her back."

Delfina nodded mutely, looking miserable.

Nikki paused a moment before asking questions she hoped would elicit useful information. She took notes on her mobile. Inquiring about doctors who treated Andrea, she keyed in their names, marking the primary care doctor, Corrado López, with an asterisk.

"Is there any reason Andrea may have run away?"

"None that I can think of."

"Have you checked with her friends?"

"All of them. More than once."

Surprised the school had not involved the police, Nikki wondered if the principal had informed the parents of their obligation to report Andrea's disappearance. "Why didn't the school call the police?"

"My husband handled it. I'm not sure how he convinced them not to call law enforcement. You'll have to ask him."

Nikki had been surprised not to see Yoani Rodríguez at this meeting, but she'd follow up with him later. "Does your daughter have a boyfriend?"

"Once boys find out about her medical condition, they dump her," Delfina said. "In fact, she doesn't even have many friends. She's very studious."

"Do you have her cell phone?"

"No. She had it with her when she disappeared from school."

"Have you tried calling her?" Nikki asked.

"It's either turned off or the battery is dead. It goes directly into messages. Do you have an expert who can examine her computer? I'm not savvy enough to make the type of search required in this situation."

"As her mother, you can access her computer. Surely you know how to access email, social media sites, check her search history. It's basic stuff."

"We don't have her passwords."

"Federal law prohibits us from doing it," Nikki said, not mentioning that Charlotte had already accessed Andrea's social media sites. She could not disclose that. "The police can search her computer once you file a report. Plus they can add Andrea's case to national crime databases."

"As I said earlier, Yoani is reluctant to get the police involved."

"If you don't, you can get into trouble for failing to report it. What specific reason does Yoani have for not reporting it?"

"We came here as undocumented foreigners. Only recently we received our green cards."

"Did Andrea have any disagreements with her father? Or you?"

Delfina shook her head and looked down at the floor. "Well, three weeks ago, my husband and I had a terrible fight. She may have overheard, but things had calmed down. So there was no reason for her to run away."

Seizing on Delfina's openness, Nikki asked her what the fight had been about.

"All marriages have issues."

"Did this fight involve Andrea?"

"Indirectly." Delfina stared at the floor and ran her hands through her hair.

"Can you share it with me?"

Delfina paused, as if searching for an answer. "It concerned her medical treatment, about having stem cells for the lupus. I did not want to expose her to PSP again. I'm always involved in decisions on her health issues."

"What about Andrea's father? Is he involved?"

"He has to take care of the business. He handles the travel agency."

"Is that why he's not at this meeting?" Nikki asked.

"I'm on a leave of absence until we find our daughter. But Yoani has a partnership to manage."

"Who is your husband's partner?"

"Our friend Urbano, who came from Cuba years before we did. The one who arranged our flight to Nicaragua. He was instrumental in our decision to come here."

"What's the company called?"

"SunNSand Getaways."

"And his partner's full name?"

"Urbano Barriga."

"You said Barriga? Like in belly?" Nikki asked.

Delfina glanced down and half smiled for the first time. "We Cubans are known for our unusual names, but it's normally our given names. In Urbano's case, Barriga is his family's surname." She glanced at Nikki. "You may be aware that our country controls everything. The one liberty every family has is to give their children distinctive or one of a kind names. That's the reason Cubans have memorable names."

Nikki thought about the name Delfina, the feminine form of dolphin. An actual name, but definitely unique.

The questions continued, with Nikki asking about the travel agency's business address. When she requested Andrea's photo, Delfina invited her to a study down a hallway past the curvilinear staircase.

"Your home is beautiful," Nikki said.

"And it comes with a monstrous mortgage. To my husband, this represents our success in America."

The study was cozy. The lower ceiling and the glass wall looking out to the enclosed patio gave it a charming feel. Nikki noticed a table with three chairs on the patio near a built-in grill. A half-hipped roof provided cover over part of the patio, sheltering a large-screen TV hanging on the opposite side of the stone-veneer wall from the grill. Butterflies flitted from one Buddleia shrub to the next.

Nikki turned toward three silver-framed family photos on the desk.

Delfina opened the desk drawer and pulled loose photos out. Smiling, she handed Nikki an eight-by-ten glossy of a pretty teenager with brownish shoulder-length hair falling on a lavender blouse.

"This is my gordita."

"Tell me what she was wearing the day she disappeared."

"A tan outfit, pants, and a matching sleeveless blouse. Sandals, beige."

"Any jewelry?"

"Yes, the necklace she's wearing there," Delfina said, pointing to the picture in Nikki's hand. "For her sixteenth birthday a month ago, I took her shopping and that's what she selected, including the lavender blouse. She loved the ruffles around the collar and down the front where it buttons up. It had matching pants you cannot see there."

Glancing down, Nikki noticed a "Be Happy, Be Me" pendant with two medallions on a gold chain. Andrea's name was engraved on the outer edge of the larger one.

Nikki took a picture with her phone. "May I also keep this copy?"

Delfina nodded and Nikki slipped the photo into her purse.

Looking on the desk, she saw Andrea's photo in the same lavender outfit, holding a Chihuahua puppy. "Does your daughter have a dog?"

"Oh, that little munchkin. Another one of her birthday gifts, from Urbano. It's at the kennel right now. I can't deal with him. Reminds me too much of Andrea. Plus Pepito is not house trained."

"Is there anything else that might be important to our investigation?"

"Nothing I can think of," Delfina said. Her voice broke and it trailed into a whisper. "Please find Andrea."

"We'll work hard to find your daughter. But the best advice I can give you is to report her to the police. She's been gone five days. The longer she's unaccounted for, the more serious her situation."

"You mean she could be dead?" Delfina lost her composure. She wiped away tears, took a deep breath, and looked into Nikki's eyes. "Because of our green cards, Yoani does not want to involve the police. Besides, he's positive Andrea will return on her own."

"Let's hope he's right," Nikki said, trying to be reassuring. "But now that I'm involved and aware of her disappearance, the law requires me to file a missing person's report."

"My husband will be upset." Delfina uttered an anxious, almost tormented sigh.

"If he'd taken time to be here, I would've explained it to him. I recommend you file the report. If it's not done within four hours, I'll have to do it." Nikki pulled a card from her purse and handed it to Delfina. "Call me anytime, day or night."

CHAPTER THREE

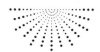

After driving back over the Paradise Point bridge, Nikki looked for a place to stop and text Charlotte. A sign directed visitors to the Deering Estate, so she pulled into the museum grounds and parked. An oversized welcome sign advertised environmental lectures, kayak rentals, and a nighttime ghost tour. She made a mental note to schedule a moonlight kayak outing. According to the sign, Charles Deering had been an art collector, philanthropist, and one of the first environmentalists of the early twentieth century.

Unfastening her seatbelt, she sent Charlotte a text asking her to find the address for SunNSand Getaways. Then Nikki took a few minutes to review her interview notes on her mobile. As she went over them, the gnawing sense that Delfina was hiding something grew. *Why was Delfina's husband so distrustful of the police? Could he have a criminal record in Cuba? Or in the US? Did his mistrust of authority come from his years in Cuba?* Yet Charlotte had not found his name connected to any crimes.

Charlotte smiled as she dialed Nikki. "I've sent you the address you wanted. And I had time to do some quick research on the firm. It's a travel agency owned by Yoani Rodríguez and his business partner, Urbano Barriga."

Nikki thanked her for the address.

Charlotte continued. Something about the firm was odd. "The travel company moved recently to its current location. It seems to move at least once a year."

"Maybe they keep upgrading their offices. Delfina's house is damned expensive. Someone is making a lot of money," Nikki said.

There was another thing Charlotte had to tell Nikki. "Just so you know, I set up an alert for missing people in Miami."

"Delfina said they haven't filed a report."

"Right, but I thought they might," Charlotte said. "A notice came through that didn't mean anything until now, but it can't be a coincidence. Looks like Barriga's wife was reported missing. Her parents filed earlier today."

"How long has she been gone?"

"Unknown. Her parents estimated several days, maybe a week. Her name is Raquel Álvarez. Married to Urbano Barriga."

"Look up Barriga's home address," Nikki said. "I'll swing by later and try to find out why he didn't report his wife's disappearance."

Charlotte texted the address and looked back at her monitor. "But wait, there's something else. Raquel rented another house a few weeks ago. Maybe she and Barriga split up."

Nikki was silent.

"Are you thinking Andrea's abduction is connected to Raquel going missing?"

"I think I have to act quickly on Raquel's disappearance now that the police are alerted. Once they start investigating, I won't have as much access. And yes, I think the two cases are somehow related. Send me Raquel's new address."

"Texting it now," Charlotte said.

"I'm off to Raquel's first. Call me if anything important comes up. Oh, and please dig up whatever you can on Dr. Corrado López. He's Andrea's primary physician. I'll visit him tomorrow."

Charlotte grinned. She was on the hunt.

Nikki headed south on Old Cutler Road and arrived twenty minutes later at the address on Blistering Street. She pulled into the driveway, facing a medium-sized house with shrubs and trees lining both sides of the drive.

She knocked on the front door and rang the doorbell three times. No answer. She tried the front door. It was locked, so she walked to the street. A canal bordered the property. There was no fence between the yard and the canal. Through the bushes, Nikki could see a path along the waterway and a small dock. She took the path around to take a closer look at the backyard. But a large bundle, trapped under the wooden dock, caught her attention.

Walking on, a rotten odor assaulted her senses. A corpse. She jumped back. Pulling the phone from her purse, she speed-dialed Floyd.

"Oh my god, I've found a body. Under a dock."

"Where are you?" he asked.

"Charlotte found a missing person's report on the wife of Rodríguez's business partner. I came to check it out. I'm in the Cutler Bay area, near Southland Mall on Route 1. It's a house on a corner lot with a canal running along two outside boundaries. Charlotte can give you the exact address and details."

"I'll call the medical examiner. His office will coordinate with the investigations bureau and get the police out there. Take pictures. Document anything unusual."

"I'm already on the pathway and I'll wait for the first responders. I advised our client to file her daughter's disappearance with the police. Told her to do it within four hours or I'd be forced to do it myself."

"Good," Floyd said. "Call me after you leave."

Nikki documented the scene in the canal. She snapped pictures from where she stood to avoid disturbing any evidence. She didn't want to risk falling in, either. Alligators could be lurking under the surface. Stories of them in the canals often appeared on the news. After taking a few photos, she felt as if someone was watching her. Looking around, she saw nothing.

Nikki walked the pathway back to the street. Two vehicles drove up.

As the first car parked, Nikki noticed its license plate—4N6— phonetically spelling forensics. *Cute*, she thought.

The medical examiner introduced himself. "Call me Smithy," he said.

"So you work with Floyd. Good man. We've worked a few cases together over the years."

He gestured at the house and surrounding foliage. "The house is a bit isolated. It could be a crime scene." He didn't usually come out to the scene of an accidental death. He was here because Floyd had asked him.

A middle-aged woman with a huge camera dangling from her neck walked around the car. "I'm Lila, Smithy's evidence technician." She and Smithy were fully suited up in forensic clothes. "We always come prepared."

Nikki assumed Lila was referring to their forensic outfits.

Two men in their thirties got out of the second car. Over their suits, they wore vests that said they were crime scene workers.

"Show us where you found the body," Smithy said.

With a slight jerk of her head, Nikki indicated the rear of the house. "In the canal under the dock."

The medical examiner asked everyone to follow him. He talked to Nikki while he led the team around the bushes and shrubs on the side of the house toward the waterway. "I suppose you took care not to trample any evidence."

"If anything's tampered with, it happened before I got here," she said.

Everyone stopped to take in the overall scene.

"The smell indicates this body's been here a few days," Smithy said, walking closer to the dock. "I'm surprised it wasn't found sooner."

The guys in the vests taped off the area. Lila took photos while Smithy put on his gloves and approached the dock. He pointed to an object wedged between a couple of boards at the edge of the dock. Lila put her own gloves on and nudged it free. Holding a woman's shoe up for everyone to see, she placed it in an evidence bag.

Nikki wondered if the victim could have fallen in accidentally, perhaps after drinking too much. Someone unable to scream or whose screams were not heard.

One of the vests, the one who appeared to be the crime scene manager, headed for the street and Smithy suggested Nikki go with him.

She introduced herself to three police investigators, two men and a woman, who had just arrived.

"I'm Sergeant Maldonado," a stocky man said. "You found the corpse?"

Nikki nodded.

The crime scene manager and the other male police detective told Maldonado they would check the perimeter of the house.

Maldonado waved at the female investigator. "Please record our witness's statement and get her contact data before she leaves." Turning to face Nikki, he asked why she had been on the pathway.

Nikki hesitated, wanting to protect her clients. "I'd come here to talk to the woman who rented this house. When she didn't answer, I walked around to the path. Her parents had reported her missing. I wondered if she was simply avoiding them."

"Did they hire you?"

Nikki shook her head.

"So you're an ambulance chaser?"

"Private investigator." Nikki pulled out her wallet and showed him her license.

As he turned at the edge of the house, the sergeant stopped and glanced around the small backyard and the canal. The young female officer continued scribbling Nikki's responses on a paper pad.

Smithy's guy in charge of the crime scene and the other male police detective returned to report they'd found two dead alligators on the patio.

"Left near the back door," the male detective said.

Maldonado told them he'd get to it when he completed his interview with Nikki.

"Did you notice anything unusual?" Maldonado asked Nikki.

"Other than the body, no," Nikki said. "You can see for yourself. It's an isolated street, new construction, three empty lots to the closest neighbor. Could be an accident, but probably not. It's an easy place to access without being noticed."

"Did you walk the perimeter of the house?" he asked.

"No. Only the path by the canal."

She glanced toward the canal and saw the body had been retrieved from the water. Lila, taking photos, obscured most of the corpse. She bent down to bag a couple of small items. Nikki couldn't tell what they were.

The technician moved in for more photos, partially obscuring her view. Nikki stepped toward the corpse. The sergeant stopped her, informing her he'd finish taking her full statement and then she'd have to leave.

Still taking pictures, Lila moved to the opposite side to photograph the human remains from that angle.

With the body in full view, Nikki gasped.

Alligators or other predators had severely damaged the corpse. The skin was blotchy. An arm was missing, the face was mauled, and the pants were shredded where the legs were mangled. Yet it was not the mutilated remains that had made Nikki gasp. It was the blouse, which looked lavender under all the filth. A torn ruffle ran down the front. The resemblance to the one Andrea wore in her birthday picture had stopped her cold.

CHAPTER FOUR

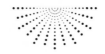

After leaving Raquel's place, Nikki called Floyd and told him about Smithy, his forensic team, and the police. Once she'd seen the blouse on the corpse, she'd had no choice but to inform the police about the missing girl.

Floyd suggested she call Delfina. She could explain to their client why she had to report Andrea's disappearance to the police.

"I was planning on that, but I really hate to tell her about that blouse. When the police took my statement, I had to tell them why I'd been there."

"We have to tell Delfina the truth too."

Nikki cringed. "Right. Of course. I'll do it."

Looking in the rearview mirror, Nikki saw a white Honda Accord with tinted windows behind her that she'd first noticed a street past Raquel's house. She shuddered, thinking how killers often revisit the scenes of their crimes.

To make sure he wasn't following her, she took a right turn. At the next intersection, she took another right. Checking the mirror, she didn't see the car. She'd been so preoccupied rehearsing, in her mind, the conversation to have with Delfina that she forgot to take the license plate number. She chastised herself for such a foolish mistake. Probably being paranoid, but she still couldn't shake the sensation someone had been watching her at the canal before the coroner arrived.

Pulling into a Walmart parking lot, she turned the engine off. Delfina answered immediately. Nikki explained about the missing person report that had prompted her to check out Raquel's house. Then she dropped the bomb: she'd had to explain about her job to the police investigator.

Silence.

"Delfina?"

"You should have left us out of this."

"I understand," Nikki said, "but I was a witness and once we called the medical examiner, there was nothing for me to do but tell the truth. And there's something more you need to know. You might be called to identify the body."

"Why me? Urbano should do it. Didn't he file the report?"

"Her parents filed it."

"Then they should be the ones to identify her."

"I'm so sorry, Delfina, but there's more. I'd prefer to tell you in person, but I don't want the medical examiner's office or the police to be the ones to inform you. And keep in mind until an autopsy is performed, we won't know the identity, but the body had a lavender blouse with a ruffle—"

"Oh my god, it's Andrea—"

Nikki heard a scream. And something hitting the floor. After a few seconds, she realized the phone had gone dead. She decided to drive to Delfina's. On the way, she called Charlotte to let her know where she was going.

"Do you have protection?" Charlotte asked.

"My Glock. It's in my purse, like always."

Nikki reversed the route she'd used earlier to get to Raquel's house. All she could think about was her own son. Her chest tightened as she recalled the worst moment of her life, at Abbott Northwestern Hospital in Minneapolis, when the doctors informed her of Robbie's death. He'd been twelve. His death still felt as if it'd happened yesterday. Whenever she dwelled on it, she'd get nightmares and couldn't sleep.

She reminded herself to think about the present, about the case she was working. Two women were missing, a teenager and a woman in her forties, and there was a chance this body was not Andrea's. Maybe Raquel had a blouse similar to Andrea's birthday outfit. And if that were the case, the teenager's mother was being put through unnecessary hell. *But what was the chance of two similar blouses?*

A flashy new gold Mercedes coupe filled the driveway. Before getting out of her own car, Nikki snapped a photo of the license plate. She'd ask Charlotte to check it out.

A man answered the front door. Wearing a stern expression and expensive-looking athleisure, he asked if she was the private investigator his wife had hired.

"I'm sorry to bother you, but I've given Delfina bad news. I came by to make sure she's okay." Nikki noticed that Yoani's accent was much thicker and harsher than his wife's.

"As okay as anyone in these circumstances. Come in. I'm Yoani."

Delfina stood in the entry, a few steps behind her husband, leaning on a console table.

Nikki apologized to Delfina for the way she'd delivered the news. "And it's important for you to understand that until an autopsy is performed, you won't know for sure."

Those words set Delfina into another bout of grief. She bent over, holding her stomach, and cried out in heartbreaking anguish.

"If an autopsy is needed, then the body must be in bad condition." Rodríguez moved back a few steps to get near his wife.

"Unfortunately, that's correct. It's been in the canal a few days."

Delfina stood straight again and wiped her nose with a tissue, making a visible effort to regain a bit of her composure. "I haven't heard from the medical examiner yet. Of course, I've met him, though he wouldn't remember me."

"One bit of information gives me hope," Nikki said. "I thought you told me she was wearing a beige outfit the day she disappeared."

"That's what I thought, but she could have changed. The lavender blouse was her favorite," Delfina said, turning to face her husband. "You drove her to school. Do you remember?"

"I have no idea what she wore," he said.

"Since you're both here, let me remind you to report this to the police."

"You're forcing us to." Rodríguez sounded angry.

"State law requires it, not me," Nikki said.

Rodríguez's lips tightened before he spoke. "Well, as soon as we report it, she *will* show up. Trust me. That won't be her body."

"Why are you so certain she'll return?" Nikki asked.

"I can feel it in my bones," he replied.

"Listen, Yoani, when I tell you that the longer she's gone, the less likely she is to return, I mean it. Those are the statistics on minors," Nikki said. She could feel Delfina's anguish as she pronounced those words, words that caused the bereaved mother to turn away.

Rodríguez opened the door, suggesting it was time for Nikki to leave.

Nikki had one more point to discuss with the mother. "Now that the police are investigating, Security Source will refund the retainer you paid. If you have any questions, please call me."

Delfina looked at Nikki. "I don't want a refund. There's still work I need. The police are not trustworthy. In fact, you *must* continue investigating. I need to know what happened." Her voice faded to a whisper.

"I don't think this private investigation is necessary any longer," Yoani said to his wife.

"Yes, it is," she responded resolutely.

CHAPTER FIVE

Nikki pulled into the parking garage behind the travel agency. She hadn't called in advance, preferring a surprise visit. A visit while Rodríguez was away. Her gut told her the corpse did not belong to Andrea, even though she couldn't explain the ruffled lavender blouse. She wondered if it was wishful thinking, like that fateful evening she'd been awaiting news on Robbie at the hospital in Minneapolis. When it finally arrived, that news had been tragic. But for this case, she would continue the investigation as if the teenager were still alive. Unless the autopsy proved her wrong.

The receptionist acknowledged Nikki as soon as she entered. The foyer was upscale and tasteful, not over the top as she had imagined. She asked to see Urbano Barriga.

"Mr. Barriga is traveling."

Nikki raised her eyebrows. "Gone? When did he leave?"

"A week ago."

"When do you expect him back?"

"He hasn't mentioned his return. Can I have someone else meet with you?" she asked with a friendly smile.

"Where is he traveling?"

"Latin America. He's taken clients on a tour."

"Can you call him and ask him to contact me? It's rather urgent."

The receptionist offered to have the other partner, Mr. Rodríguez, speak with her. She also offered to answer questions.

When Nikki declined, the woman asked tentatively if her health issues could wait until the traveling partner could return to book a tour for her.

"That depends," Nikki said, realizing this was no ordinary travel agency. She kept a straight face to confirm her suspicion. "If my health requires it, can something be done sooner rather than later?" With a compassionate expression, the receptionist suggested a private tour. "It's more expensive than going with a group, but it's worth it."

Asking for all the options for treatment, Nikki looked straight at the receptionist. The woman glanced away slightly.

"That depends on whether you want to go to Cuba or elsewhere. We recommend Cuba. They've been on the forefront of stem cell research and deliver excellent results. We also have a first-class clinic in Grand Cayman. May I take your name?"

"Let me talk it over with my husband and I'll be in touch," Nikki said, keeping her expression neutral when the receptionist mentioned stem cell research. She picked up a business card from the desk and stopped on her way out to help herself to brochures at a side table.

Back at her car, Nikki glanced at the clock on the dashboard. She sent Charlotte the photo of Rodríguez's license plate. While she waited for Charlotte's response, she studied the brochures. They had normal travel destinations: Cuzco, Machu Picchu, and the Sacred Valley in Peru; the Lake District in southern Chile; Buenos Aires, the wine area of Mendoza, and Patagonia in Argentina; Rio, Iguazú, and island getaways in Brazil. Nothing about medical tours.

Next, she input Corrado López's address into her navigation system. Again wanting to pay a surprise visit, she did not call the doctor's office for an appointment.

Charlotte rang. Nikki listened as her assistant told her a missing person report on Andrea popped up on her screen a minute earlier. "You intrepid private eye, you forced her parents to file."

Nikki felt a release of tension at the news, glad to learn that the parents had come to their senses. Though they didn't have much choice.

"About the license plates you sent," Charlotte said, "the car's registered to Delfina, not her husband."

"That's weird. The house is also in Delfina's name. Why record the assets that way?" She had Charlotte confirm that the travel agency was in the two partners' names. "See if you can find photos of both partners and send them to me."

"I'm searching now. Wow," Charlotte said. "Is Rodríguez that handsome in person?"

"He's good looking, all right. And probably charming, but under the circumstances, it's hard to tell. And I guess you know I found a corpse behind Raquel's house?"

"Floyd told me."

"Just so the office knows, the mother requested I continue my investigation. I'm going to proceed as if the girl is still alive. My decision, not the mother's."

Nikki headed into early rush hour traffic.

"This concerns his patient, Andrea Rodríguez," Nikki explained to the nurse at Dr. López's office.

"That's confidential information."

"Right. I'm not requesting anything confidential. I'm working for Dr. Delfina Morales and I only need fifteen minutes."

"Let me check with the doctor." The nurse left Nikki standing at the front desk. The sound of her heels hitting the tile floor echoed in the hallway.

Returning to the desk, the nurse escorted Nikki to the doctor's office.

Nikki showed her private investigator license to Dr. López. He appeared to be updating patient records on the computer.

"You know I can't reveal anything," he said, hardly looking at Nikki.

"I know. I'm only here to connect the dots on Andrea. She disappeared from school last Friday."

The doctor turned and eyed Nikki.

"Is there any reason she might have run away?" she asked.

Looking pensive, he shook his head. "Have you questioned her teachers? Her friends?"

"Delfina has covered those areas. I plan to visit her school tomorrow. I know you can't tell me about her health or specifics about her medication, but are there any issues that put her in further danger?"

The doctor appeared perplexed.

"I'm asking what kind of danger she'd be in if she's not taking meds for her lupus."

"Severe stress could be detrimental without her medication. Both her parents are medical doctors. Her mother practices at Mt. Sinai in Miami Beach. It's very prestigious. Her father is a research fellow in stem cell therapies. They've both been involved with her treatment, especially Delfina."

"That does not answer my question."

"Her lupus is severe. If untreated, she could suffer a heart attack. Even at her age."

"It'd help if you tell me the name of her medication. My assistant can see if that could give clues to where she is."

"I did not give this to you. Understood? One is an antimalarial, available everywhere, but the other is an expensive biologic."

He scribbled a couple of names and dosages on a pad, added the pharmacy used by the family to fill the prescriptions, and handed the sheet to her.

Nikki glanced at the paper, noticing Benlysta and hydroxychloroquine. "Thank you. Would you have any reason to think she's been kidnapped?"

He shook his head.

"What about issues at home that would make her run away?"

"They seem like concerned parents. I'm not aware of their marriage being troubled, if that's what you're alluding to, but then I don't socialize with them."

Nikki laid a business card on his desk, asking him to call her if anything came to his attention that he could share. She left the office, wishing she had time to visit the school, but it was too late in the day.

Nikki left a message for Charlotte to research Andrea's medications or shipments of those meds to get clues about where the teenager might be.

CHAPTER SIX

Nikki tiptoed into the study and found Eduardo deep in concentration, studying for his exams. Glancing at her, his face lit up. His smile melted Nikki's heart. Standing up, he kissed her. In the kitchen, Eduardo popped open a bottle of champagne and grabbed two crystal flutes off a shelf while Nikki laid out Stilton and crackers left over from Floyd and Milena's visit.

"Hard day?" Eduardo asked, following Nikki outside to the balcony. He filled their flutes, handing one to her. He clinked his glass against Nikki's.

She nodded. A rough breeze touched her cheeks. Sipping champagne, she glanced down at the shoreline, noticing the wind stirring the seawater into prominent swells. The waves, larger than usual, formed whitecaps that crested before dissipating into white froth that hit the beach, washing the grains of sand before the receding wave scooped them back to the moody sea.

Peering up at the sky, she saw wispy, feathery cirrus clouds, the kind that usually meant another storm front would be on its way. "My latest assignment might be over," she said, taking another sip.

"Over? You just started today."

"I found a body, so the police are now in charge. The mother wants me to keep going. She insists I find her daughter. Or provide closure."

"Body? Like in a corpse?"

"That's right, trapped under a jetty in the canal. So badly mangled, alligators probably found it days ago. But I'm not so sure that's our missing girl. It may not even be related to the case. But the wife of a close family friend is also missing."

"So much for Floyd's easy cases," Eduardo said. "I sensed the other night that you'd rather be jetting your way to Hong Kong."

"That's for sure," Nikki said, holding the flute up high. "To Hong Kong!"

"My precious wife does love exotic places."

"True. And I like it when we work cases together. You should get a private investigator license."

"Sure, right after I get my medical license." Eduardo stretched and rolled his shoulders.

"I'm serious." Nikki set her glass down and rubbed Eduardo's shoulders. She could feel his tension dissipate.

Over a second glass of champagne, she highlighted the full day's activities. She described how she'd found the corpse, the police interview, and her agreement to continue on the case.

"The parents' reluctance to involve the police bothers me. If she were my child, I would've filed a report the minute she failed to show up for class. But I'm investigating this case as if the girl is still alive."

Eduardo looked at her skeptically.

Nikki snuggled closer to him. Savoring champagne as the strong breeze whipped her hair into her face, she was glad for the partial roof over the balcony.

"You should join the team. There's a medical angle to this case." Nikki continued, telling him about the parents' flight out of Cuba, the child's leukemia, stem cell therapy, and the onset of lupus and PSP. "Let's head to the kitchen. I'll start dinner."

"I've ordered pizza."

Nikki glanced at him in surprise. "You really are afraid I'll burn this place down."

Eduardo looked at her playfully, his face breaking into a tender smile. "I thought we'd polish off the bottle before dinner arrives."

"You devil," Nikki said, giving him a mischievous glance. "You know champagne puts me in an amorous mood and I still have to write a report for Floyd."

"Amorous is the plan." He moved in closer, took her in his arms, and kissed her.

Nikki kissed him back with passion. Then she suggested taking the champagne and fancy flutes to the bedroom.

Eduardo slipped the precut pizza onto a serving platter and took it to the dining table where a robe-clad Nikki smiled.

"Champagne and pizza—the last of the romantics." She giggled uncharacteristically.

Eduardo chuckled and slid a slice of pizza onto her plate. "I've never seen you so buzzed."

"Comes with not eating lunch. I'm starving." She stopped talking and devoured the slice of pepperoni and cheese.

"I wonder why Delfina mentioned the travel agency but failed to tell me about the stem cell tours?" Nikki was thinking out loud. "Especially since she didn't seem particularly happy with the treatment her daughter received. Neither did she mention her husband is also a doctor and a fellow at the research university in Miami. Could that have been intentional?"

After taking another slice of pizza, she pushed the platter toward Eduardo, tipping over her flute. It hit the floor and shattered.

"Oops! No wonder you don't trust me in the kitchen!" The glasses, like everything else in the condo, belonged to its owners.

"Not to worry. I'll buy a replacement." Eduardo put his own flute down and swept the fragments up. He cleaned the floor with damp paper towels.

Nikki wanted to know about stem cell therapy. "It's available here, so why offer tours to Cuba and Grand Cayman?"

"A great question." Eduardo dropped paper towels crusted with glass fragments into the trash can. "Current FDA-approved stem cell applications mainly treat cancer and arthritis. Desperate people will entrust their lives to promises made in countries where these treatments may be unregulated. India, China, Latin America, the Caribbean, and

Russia attract potential clients over the internet. They sell stem cell as a cure-all."

He dampened more paper towels to make sure the floor wasn't sticky.

"So people with health issues the FDA hasn't approved for stem cell therapy succumb to wild promises on websites in other countries?"

Eduardo nodded.

"Can you explain how Andrea's leukemia treatment could have contributed to her lupus?"

"Theoretically, yes," he said, "but keep in mind I haven't seen her medical records."

Sitting down again, Eduardo described how Andrea's immune system may have rejected the original transplant, causing her system to turn against itself. That, combined with a genetic predisposition, could have brought on the lupus. "There's so much we don't know about lupus. Environmental factors may trigger its onset. But another stem cell therapy, mesenchymal stem cells or MSC, is showing promise in treating it."

"So the treatment that caused her lupus in the first place could now be used to cure it?"

"There's no cure for lupus, not yet anyway. But MSC often reduces inflammation in patients." Eduardo toyed with his empty flute. "Basically, it provides more effective therapy with reduced side effects. But medical use of stem cells is fairly new and needs far more research to prove its efficacy."

"Is there anything else I should know?"

Eduardo looked across the room while considering the question. "Several types of stem cell therapies exist. The law allows stem cells to be used as long as they are collected from adult cells and are used in patient treatments the same day."

"Changing the subject to blebs, is it a hereditary condition?"

"Known in medical circles as PSP, it can be a genetic disease," Eduardo said.

"Oh, and I almost forgot. Andrea is taking an expensive biologic."

"Probably Benlysta," he said. "For lupus."

"Exactly. See why I need you on this case?"

"You said the case might be over."

"True, but I hope not. I want to save this child."

"With the evidence you talked about, don't get your hopes up. Besides, what makes you think she's still alive?"

"Intuition," Nikki said. "I have a gut feeling."

"Intuition is good." Eduardo stacked the dishes and the remaining champagne flute on the empty platter. "But what happens if the case closes? Will Floyd send you to Hong Kong?"

"Intuition also tells me I'm still needed to find Andrea."

CHAPTER SEVEN

Floyd paced around his office as he dialed Nikki. He caught her on the road. She asked him to hang on until she could pull over. He could hear that she was on speaker, but maybe she wanted to take notes.

"I hope you have good news," she said.

"The body's not Andrea's," he said. He heard her exhale.

"That's great news. Do her parents know?"

Floyd told her the medical examiner's office had notified the mother.

Nikki wanted to know if they'd identified the body.

"The dental records matched Raquel's. Smithy is certain she was murdered. There's evidence of blows to the head. Her parents were notified, but the husband hasn't been located yet."

"He's traveling in either South America or the Caribbean."

"I read that in your report this morning. The police will find out soon enough about Barriga's travel, though I did mention it to Smithy. He told me the police took dogs to Raquel's house to search for Andrea."

Floyd heard motorcycles vrooming by Nikki's parking spot. He stopped until the noise subsided.

She asked him to repeat what he'd said.

"They didn't find Andrea. Or any other bodies, for that matter."

"Thank god," Nikki said.

Floyd heard her exhale again and asked her if she was okay.

"I'm releasing tension is all," she said.

"So what's your plan for today?" Floyd asked.

"I'll visit the school. Interview the principal and maybe a couple of teachers. I want to get the layout of the buildings and the grounds. And I need to ask Charlotte to research the stem cell tourism industry."

Floyd said Charlotte was on another line.

Nikki asked him to have Charlotte call her back.

Charlotte could barely contain her excitement. She dialed Nikki. "I've got a little surprise for you."

As Charlotte expected, Nikki demanded to hear it.

"I traced a shipment of Benlysta from Andrea's pharmacy to a post office box. I can't trace a credit card payment, but I checked the PO box. It's been closed. Rented for one month to a Spider Candella. I can't find any credible leads to that name." Charlotte thought of making a wisecrack about a spider and a belly, but she knew it'd be in bad taste and let it go.

Nikki thanked her and asked if she had other ideas.

"They paid by cash or check, which means whoever rented it visited the pharmacy in person, even though they had it sent to a post office box. I thought I'd drive there on my way home and talk to the pharmacist."

"What about PayPal or the like? Wouldn't you lose track of the credit card?"

"I checked for PayPal, cell phone payment, and debit cards. It was definitely cash or check and it's the only time they've been sent to a post office, according to the pharmacist. Someone went out of their way to get her meds."

"And to hide their identity," Nikki said. "If we could figure that out, we'd know who took her."

Approaching Andrea's high school, Nikki saw gorgeous brick homes, gracefully set back on large lots with lush landscaping. *No cookie cutters here*, she thought. *Homes from a bygone era.* On the other side of the street was a trilevel townhome complex that seemed out of place in the exclusive community. A block further down, she pulled into a lane leading to the high school's robust gate. Beyond the guard shack, the school grounds were enclosed by a tall, sturdy wrought-iron fence. Nikki stopped to hand her credentials and ID to a guard.

The high school's campus, set out on several acres, resembled the grounds of a state capitol. The main edifice, red brick with a white cupola, dominated the middle of the property. Well-tended grass, bushes, and flowers covered everything that did not have asphalt. The guard cleared her, handed her a pass for the dashboard, and told her where to park.

She took her time walking to the central building for her meeting with the principal. Security personnel had been very cooperative, and she hoped to get the same collaboration from the educators and administrators. She arrived early and waited. At last another uniformed guard ushered her into a spacious conference room with large windows overlooking the school grounds. The principal, a teacher, the counselor, and the school nurse were already seated.

The guard introduced Nikki.

The principal, Ms. Hale, expressed the school's concern about Andrea's disappearance. Once she finished, she asked the nurse to take over.

"We called Delfina Morales when Andrea failed to show up for class last Friday. The mother indicated she'd call her husband to find out what had happened and she'd get back to us, which she did, about an hour later. Andrea had taken ill unexpectedly and the father had driven her to the emergency room instead of bringing her to school."

"The mother said that?" Nikki asked, trying to hold her poker face. "Delfina told you Andrea was taken to the ER and never came to school that morning?"

The nurse nodded. "That's what I noted in my records."

"Yet she's a good student and stays at the top of her class," Ms. Hale said. "Given Andrea's history of illness, we never considered anything beyond what we were told."

Andrea's home room teacher said Andrea was one of the best students she'd ever taught. Since she was the oldest person in the room, Nikki figured she had lots of experience.

Glancing at the counselor, Nikki asked if there was evidence of any emotional issues or abuse in the home.

"None that we ever detected." The counselor shrugged. "She's very pleasant. Seems like a well-adjusted teenager, though not overly social. I only talked with her after a couple of long absences when she'd been ill. Our counseling policy is to interview students after an illness to ensure they don't fall behind academically and to make certain they don't feel uneasy when they return."

"I called her home on Monday morning to see if she was improving," the nurse said. "When no one answered, I called Dr. Morales's office. They told me she was on a leave of absence. I had a similar response from the father's side. He was not available."

"When did you discover Andrea had disappeared?" Nikki asked, shifting in her chair.

"Late yesterday afternoon," the guard said. "A detective from the police crime unit came by after a decomposed body had been found in a canal. Saying it could possibly be Andrea, he asked what we knew about the missing girl."

Nikki wanted to check the school grounds and move on to another interview with Delfina to get these discrepancies explained. But she reminded herself to relax and gather all the information she needed while she was at the school. She glanced at the guard. "How could Andrea have been abducted from here?"

"We don't think her father dropped her off that morning. The detective and I checked the video feeds. We never located her or her father in any of the feeds."

"The mother told me Andrea had called her from the cafeteria that morning," Nikki said. "Can you view any security videos from there and let me know if she's in any of them?"

"After the detective left yesterday, I went back over all the videos," he said. "She's not in any of them. I'll check the cafeteria ones again and call you if I find anything."

"One last question. Have any of you heard the name Spider Candella?"

Everyone in the room said no.

"Is he a person of interest?" the guard asked.

"I'm not sure. It's just a name I came across, so I thought I'd check."

Thanking everyone, Nikki rose and glanced at the guard. "Can you give me a tour of the grounds?"

Outside, Nikki brought up an interactive map of the campus on her phone that she'd already studied over breakfast. To refresh her mind, she glanced at all the entrances and exits on the streets. Two major thoroughfares bordered the north and south sides of the property, but neither one had access. The other two streets had several accesses, all with gates that were probably locked at night.

"That service road at the back of the campus," Nikki said, pointing. "Does it have security videos?

"Absolutely," the guard responded. "It leads to the athletic fields and tennis courts. We always keep the gate locked, except when we sponsor sports events. And then it's policed."

"Did you have an event on Friday morning?"

"None."

"If you were going to abduct a kid off this campus, how would you do it?"

"From another location," he said gravely. "We have very tight security."

From the car, Nikki dialed Charlotte. She reported her findings at the school and said she'd visit the travel agency again to question Yoani Rodríguez.

"Be careful," Charlotte said. "It scares me that there's already one corpse."

Nikki turned right on the side street out of the school grounds. She'd thought of something else. "Check the airlines to see if Urbano Barriga flew out of the Miami airport in the last three weeks," she said.

"That may take a while, but I'll get it for you."

CHAPTER EIGHT

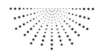

The receptionist at SunNSand Getaways greeted Nikki as warmly as she had the day before.

"Luck is on your side today. Dr. Rodríguez is here."

She announced Nikki through a diminutive cordless headset and accompanied Nikki to the hallway, opening a door for her.

Yoani rose from behind his desk to greet her.

"How are you today?" Nikki asked.

"How would you think I'm doing?" With a wave of his hand, he signaled for Nikki to take a seat.

"Sorry, I didn't mean it that way." Her voice sounded both defensive and apologetic. She needed to get a grip.

"So you were the one who came snooping here yesterday?"

"Snooping? Hardly, I came to interview your business partner," she said.

"Didn't you pretend to be a prospective client?"

Nikki took a shallow calming breath. "Your receptionist assumed it. I knew nothing about your stem cell trips until she brought it up. So when did you last see Urbano?"

"Two weeks ago, maybe."

"Where is he now?"

Rodríguez glanced at Nikki and then looked out the window. "By now, he'd be in Cuba."

"Do people take vacations before they receive treatments?"

"Some do." He cleared his throat. "If the condition is not critical, a few might tour Mexico or parts of South America before flying to Cuba. We accommodate our clients with the type of service they want. They sign a waiver acknowledging that stem cell therapy can be dangerous, even life threatening, though we provide excellent doctors and facilities. But there are no guarantees."

"So they travel before the treatment? Get that last bucket item in just in case they die."

Yoani smiled. A killer smile, the kind that melts women's hearts and their resolve. Charlotte was right. This man was terribly handsome, and probably accustomed to using his charm. Not that he was doing that today.

"When is Barriga returning?"

He shrugged and said that each partner acted independently, like doctors in a practice. "We substitute and help each other out, but I have my clients and he has his."

"You're both medical doctors?"

"That's right. Both of us did stem cell research in the early days. Then I turned to surgery and performing transplants. When I came to this country, I vowed I'd take it easier."

"And Barriga?"

"Stem cell research mostly. He was a pioneer in Cuba's development of it." Rodríguez stared into Nikki's eyes, his gaze so intense it could almost bore holes. "What does this have to do with finding Andrea?"

Nikki shifted in her seat but held the doctor's gaze. "Your daughter's missing. Barriga's estranged wife is dead and he's unreachable. I'd like to speak with your partner. The two incidents might be related."

The doctor shook his head. "I doubt it. Urbano and Raquel had a difficult marriage." Rodríguez lowered his voice to a whisper. "She was a most unusual woman. Her religious beliefs were infused with Voodoo. Venezuelan, you know. They're like that."

"I gather you weren't fond of her," Nikki said.

He flipped his hand. "When they married a few years ago, our relationship with Urbano changed. She changed it."

"In what way?" Nikki studied his expression.

"She was a suspicious woman and didn't like our friendship with him. Poisoned his attitude. Jealous, perhaps. Her Voodoo practices cast a spell on him. He became distant."

"You don't really believe that, do you?" Nikki asked, watching him skeptically.

He raised his eyebrows.

"That she could cast a spell on him," Nikki clarified.

"All I can tell you is that others saw the change in him, not just us. Other Cubans here in Miami."

"So when is Barriga returning?"

"I don't know."

"Does your receptionist know?"

"I doubt it. When Urbano needs something, he calls. He will change client itineraries on a whim to please them. We charge top dollar and we try to delight our travelers."

"Can you give me his phone number? And the address to your clinic in Cuba."

He retrieved a business card from his desk and handed it to her. "This has all our numbers. The addresses are on the back side."

Was this man leading her on? Or did he genuinely not have a clue where his business partner was? Feeling she was not getting anywhere, Nikki decided to change the course of her questions.

"I visited the school today."

Rodríguez's eyebrows lifted ever so imperceptibly. "I would expect you to."

"They claim Andrea was not taken from the school."

He shuffled papers on his desk. "I never said she went missing from there."

"Tell me what happened when she disappeared."

"I'd taken her to the emergency room at Coral Gables Hospital. On Douglas Road. We had to wait. I had a slight headache and decided to get coffee from the cafeteria. Andrea told me she'd wait in case they called her. When I returned, she was gone. I thought she'd been taken in, but the nurse at the check-in desk said no. I told her I had to check for myself with the triage nurse, so I went back there. She hadn't seen Andrea."

His face reddened. He stood and walked toward the window.

"I know this is hard, but if I'm going to find Andrea alive, I need answers. What did you do next?"

Returning to his desk, he sniffled gently and reshuffled the documents he'd already arranged.

"I called her mother and explained Andrea had disappeared. She drove to the hospital and we both looked for our daughter."

"Did you think of calling the police?"

"I wanted to leave them out of this. Law enforcement could cause more problems than we already had."

"Why would that be?" Nikki asked, perplexed.

He reached down to open a desk drawer. She held her breath, ready to hit the floor. For a second, Nikki thought he might be pulling a gun. She felt relieved when he tossed a green card on the desk. Picking it up, she checked the name and date and looked at the photo.

"There's your answer. We don't want to mess up our status in this country. It's citizenship we're after. But thanks to you, the police are involved now. In fact, they took a couple of dogs to Raquel's house to see if they could find our daughter."

"So who do you think may have killed Raquel?"

Rodríguez's eyes flashed as if Nikki had hit a nerve.

"I did not kill her." The skin around his eyes tightened. "If that's what you're asking."

Looking at him calmly, Nikki told him that her question, normal under the circumstances, was about who he suspected in the woman's murder. "What about your partner? Nobody, not even the police, can find him."

"I don't think Urbano would have done it. Besides, he left before this happened. Probably a lot of others thought of killing that witch, but I wouldn't know who. We didn't have much to do with her. Or Urbano once he married her."

"Do you think Raquel's death is related to Andrea's disappearance?"

"Coño! Not at all. People hated Raquel."

In her car, Nikki added Barriga's contact info to her phone. When she was done, she texted the contact data to Charlotte. Driving out of the parking garage, she noticed the gold-colored Mercedes coupe in a reserved spot. She was already on the hands-free updating Floyd on the case.

"Delfina needs to come clean. I'm on my way to see her. Looks like they're both lying about their daughter's disappearance. If I don't get straight answers, I can't work for her."

Floyd agreed, though he suggested there could be a legitimate reason Delfina had given her a different story. Once they understood, they could decide.

"If we remain on this job, I'm seeing the possibility of a trip to Cuba," Nikki said.

"Why?"

"I'm fairly sure that's where Barriga is hiding. Unless the police have located the traveling widower."

"You want to go all the way to Cuba to interview the man?"

"He may have Andrea with him."

Floyd pointed out it would be a waste of time if she got over there and couldn't even find Barriga, let alone Andrea, but he listened as Nikki laid out her theory.

"If Delfina and her husband trusted Barriga to take their child to Cuba for stem cell treatments when she had leukemia, it makes sense he could have taken her there for a round of treatment for lupus."

Nikki felt Floyd considering her words.

After a few seconds, he told her he'd wondered the same thing, but he'd concluded the parents would know if Barriga had taken their daughter to Cuba. "Can't believe we came up with the same theory. If you go to Cuba, you'll need someone with you. Either Eduardo or me."

She immediately reacted to the suggestion. "You'd be tagged as former CIA, so it makes more sense for Eduardo to go with me."

Floyd agreed and asked about Eduardo's board exam.

"The final portion is scheduled for this coming Friday. After that, he's a free man. At least for a few weeks. Since he's a doctor, he can get into Cuba easier."

"How do you figure that? Cuba has tons of doctors." Floyd sounded confused. "They even export them, like a commodity, to other countries."

"They also promote medical conferences all the time. I've already checked one out for later this month at the Palacio de Convenciones in Havana. On regenerative therapies using stem cells."

Floyd seemed to be digesting her reasoning. "That takes care of his entry. So how do we get you in?"

"As the trailing wife," Nikki said. "Remember, relations with Cuba these days are nearly normal."

He took a few seconds again before responding. "Hmm, Cuba could be ripe for turmoil with the resignation of Raúl Castro, but I'll ask Charlotte to check into it. I'm not convinced going to Cuba will crack this case."

"I'll have to talk with Eduardo first. I haven't discussed the conference with him. Though I did tell him I could use his medical expertise on this case."

They both remained silent for a few seconds. Then Nikki suggested that Floyd leave Barriga a message on his mobile phone, asking him if he knew about the urgent matters in Miami.

Floyd asked for the man's phone number.

"I shared his mobile and the Cuban medical center phones with Charlotte."

CHAPTER NINE

After ringing the doorbell twice, Nikki reprimanded herself for not calling to ensure Delfina would be at home. She gave it one more try. Slowly, the door opened a slit. Delfina, red-eyed and wearing a white terrycloth robe, pulled the door wide enough for Nikki to enter.

"I haven't slept since Andrea disappeared," Delfina said. She ran a hand through her tousled hair. "I took something last night to help me sleep and I sort of passed out, I guess. With my leave of absence, I can get up late."

Nikki caught a whiff of stale alcohol breath, like the day after a binge.

"If we can sit and talk, I'd appreciate it," Nikki said.

"Follow me to the study. The light is more subdued there."

Glancing at her watch, Nikki noted it was almost noon. She followed her client into the cozy study she had seen during her first visit.

Delfina rubbed her temple. "I need coffee." She headed straight to a side table with a shiny steel coffeemaker complete with a bean grinder sitting on top.

Taking in the scent of freshly ground beans, Nikki felt her senses awakening, alertness spreading throughout her body. Her head cleared, anticipating the first sip.

Delfina opened a compact fridge behind her desk. She pulled out cream cheese, smoked salmon, and a wheel of soft, ripened Brie. She set it on paper plates with some crackers and cheese knives. Returning to the coffeemaker, she filled two porcelain cups and passed one to Nikki.

"I'm out of napkins, but these will do," she said, pushing a box of tissues toward Nikki.

"Thanks. Looks like a feast. But I'm here to ask a few questions." The coffee gave her the pleasant jolt she needed. Nikki suppressed her disappointment at finding her client hung over. By the second sip, she'd placed herself in the woman's situation and felt a resurgence of empathy.

Swallowing coffee, Delfina turned to the snacks. "Forgive me. I'm hungry y necesito jama."

Delfina's Cuban slang made Nikki wonder. Was the woman just hung over, or was she more comfortable with Nikki now? Studying her, Nikki noticed a faint bruise on her left cheek.

Nikki cleared her throat. "We need to clarify a few issues."

"I was hoping you were here to give me good news." Delfina bit into a cracker and chewed. "I just want my daughter back."

"I know you're suffering. And I hate to ask again, but I need honest answers. You said that Andrea disappeared from school. But the principal told me this morning that Andrea was taken to an emergency room."

Delfina stopped eating.

"To do my job effectively," Nikki said, lowering her voice to avoid sounding threatening. "I need the truth. You can't keep secrets from me if you want me to find your daughter."

"My husband does not want to jeopardize our citizenship here. He's so scared now that the authorities are involved." She looked out the glass wall to the enclosed patio and sighed heavily. Glancing back at Nikki, she started crying. After a few seconds, she dabbed her eyes with a tissue. "Yoani asked me to say that. After you saw me the first time, he realized the school would involve the police. That's when he told me to say what really happened."

"And what is that?"

"Andrea wasn't feeling well on the way to school, so he took her to the emergency room instead."

"And that's the truth?" Nikki asked.

"As far as I know. I wasn't with them."

"Why is your husband making this so difficult?"

"I've already told you, he's nervous about the authorities."

Nikki stared at her client. "Can you tell me what your husband is hiding?"

"I don't get involved in Yoani's business so I don't know. He's always been secretive." Delfina rubbed her cheek. "Ever since I've known him."

"Do you understand that misinformation only hampers my ability to find Andrea?"

Delfina nodded.

"Who do you think may have killed Raquel?"

Delfina frowned. "I wish I knew. If you find out who did it, would that give you a clue about Andrea's disappearance?"

"Could Barriga have done it?" Nikki asked, ignoring Delfina's question.

"Urbano is one of the most kind and considerate people I know. No one understands why he married her."

"What do you mean?"

"She was movie-star beautiful. I guess that's why he fell for her. But coño, she was a tremendo paquete, and scary as hell."

"¿Tremendo paquete?" Nikki raised her eyebrows.

"Sorry. Heavy drama. Raquel was a drama queen."

"Tell me about her background."

"Raquel was into Voodoo. She supposedly had revelations in her dreams."

"Tell me why she was scary."

"Her psychic power." Delfina's accent had become more pronounced.

"What do you mean?"

"She could read people's minds. Dig out the most guarded family secrets no one could have ever known. It was uncanny."

Nikki thought about the little she knew about Voodoo. "Did Raquel practice the occult in a negative way? I understand there are good witches and bad ones."

"That's not for me to say. She had patients who consulted her for healing purposes. Beyond that, I don't know."

"Did people like her?"

"Not in our circle of friends."

"Who would want to kill her?"

Avoiding Nikki's gaze, Delfina seemed to be choosing her words carefully. "An unhappy patient or someone she'd slandered. People considered her a rumormonger."

"Why would she be wearing clothes similar to your daughter's?"

Delfina looked shocked. She pressed her hands to her temples. "I've been so worried, I forgot."

"Forgot? Such an important detail?" Nikki had to focus on keeping her poker face.

"The stress. Also the sleeping pills."

Nikki suggested they check Andrea's room to see if the lavender blouse was missing.

Both women walked upstairs. Reasonably tidy, the bedroom looked like a typical teenage girl's room. Colorful posters hung on beige walls. On a small desk, a set of maracas lay next to a laptop computer. A doll collection lined bookshelves along the wall opposite the bed.

"Tell me about the doll collection," Nikki said.

"Some are from Latin America, like that one." Delfina pointed to one in a colorful outfit with a flared, long skirt and an embroidered top. "It's Peruvian. And this other one is from China. Then there are these three Japanese—"

Delfina stiffened.

"Oh, my god. No! No!" Delfina recoiled and dropped to the floor with a scream.

Nikki looked at all the artefacts on the shelf. Then she saw it.

A Voodoo doll. An effigy obviously representing Andrea was clothed in a lavender cape with a ruffle. Two pins were stuck in the doll's chest, right and left, puncturing the ribcage. Nikki shuddered.

"That Voodoo witch cast a spell on my daughter." Delfina, on her knees, pounded her fists into the floor.

Could Raquel have broken into the house to steal the blouse and plant a Voodoo doll in Andrea's collection? If so, either Delfina or Rodríguez could have seen her, murdered her, and disposed of her body. But if that were the case, why hire me?

After Delfina let out her anger and grief, Nikki brought the woman's focus back to the reason they were in Andrea's room, to search for the ruffled blouse. She helped her client stand up.

Nikki opened a closet swollen with clothes. Shoes tumbled out. The bureau drawers were equally crammed. Not seeing the lavender blouse,

Nikki also took dirty clothes from a hamper and spread them over the floor.

"This gives me the creeps," Delfina said, staring at the Voodoo doll in her hand. "How did she plant this awful thing?"

Nikki asked Delfina to put the doll back on the shelf for the police to examine. "That's important evidence. About the blouse, think where else it might be. At a friend's? Or at school?"

Delfina shook her head and told Nikki that her daughter could not have left it at someone else's house since she hardly ever stayed with friends. And certainly not since her birthday, when they'd purchased the outfit.

"If you don't mind, double-check with her friends," Nikki said. "I'd appreciate it."

"It's that woman who did this. She somehow orchestrated my daughter's abduction. Worse yet, she broke in here and hid this diabolical image in plain sight with the dolls. I can't believe how evil she was."

"Did Andrea ever spend time with Raquel?"

"No way," Delfina snapped.

"Are you sure they were not in contact? Young women Andrea's age can be impressionable." Nikki threw dirty clothes back into the hamper.

"I'm positive. She knew her, but that's all."

"What about Barriga?"

"If you're asking if he and Andrea shared a friendship," Delfina said, her voice softening, "he's her Uncle Urby. He's wonderful to her. But our friendship with him cooled after he married that Voodoo witch. Raquel was always jealous of Urbano's relationship with my daughter."

Nikki wanted to know when Delfina had last spoken with Barriga.

"Maybe two weeks ago. Then when Andrea went missing, I called his mobile phone several times, but his message box was full. I couldn't even leave voicemail."

"If you haven't already, I'd suggest you look for a diary."

Pointing toward the computer, she told Nikki that if her daughter kept a diary, it would be there. "When do you think you'll have news on my daughter?"

Nikki smiled ever so slightly. "I started this job yesterday. Give me a little time. And accurate data." Nikki emphasized *accurate data*.

"Please find her." Delfina breathed deeply. "Or find out what happened to her."

"We'll do our best," Nikki said, turning toward the stairs. "I should leave now."

When the women entered the two-story great room, Nikki noticed a box of baking soda tucked under the outer edge of the sofa. The vinegary odor she'd smelled during her first visit was gone.

By the door, she stopped and faced Delfina. "Can you tell me what happened to your cheek?"

Delfina's hand went straight for the bruised area. "This? I reached for a book on a shelf and it slipped and hit me."

Nikki nodded sympathetically. "How's Pepito?"

"You remembered." Delfina seemed surprised. "He'll stay at the kennel until Andrea returns."

"Thank you for the coffee. And for answering my questions. Call if you think of anything that might help in the investigation. Or if you simply need to talk." Walking toward her car, Nikki turned to Delfina one more time. "Please. No detail is too small."

Climbing into her car, Nikki decided her next interview would be with people who could help clear up the traits, or lack thereof, on the mysterious Raquel. The same people who had reported her disappearance —her parents.

CHAPTER TEN

"Raquel's folks live in Doralzuela," Charlotte said. "That's what they call Doral now because so many Venezuelans have moved there. It's only a mile north of the airport. I've texted you the address."

Nikki exited the Ronald Reagan Turnpike and continued onto Northwest Forty-First Street. She was pleasantly surprised at the neighborhood. Chastising herself for thinking she was going to a poor immigrant barrio, she found the community thriving.

Miami was vastly different from Minneapolis, where Nikki had grown up after her parents left Mexico in search of a better life. Other than the summers she'd spent visiting her grandparents in Oaxaca, Mexico, Nikki had lived in Minneapolis until Floyd asked her to join his firm. Then she and Eduardo had moved to Florida. Still acclimating to her new city, she realized this assignment was giving her the opportunity to experience districts reflecting different Latin American cultures. She was liking the Magic City.

In the rearview mirror, she saw the white Honda she thought had followed her the day she discovered Raquel's body. It had the same tinted windows, making it impossible to see the driver. She called Charlotte and read off the license plate. Making a right turn, she lost the car.

The GPS guided her to a gated community. Sweet-talking the young

Spanish-speaking man in the guard shack did not get her in. She showed him her investigator badge. That opened the gate for her. She drove to a two-story, double-garage home in creamy yellow stucco with a red tile roof. A cluster of palm trees in the front yard gave the house a serene quality, and the shrubbery was neatly trimmed. Three cars claimed the driveway, forcing Nikki to park in the street.

A petite woman in her early sixties—attractive, with snow-white hair —answered. Nikki introduced herself and explained the purpose of her visit.

Without changing her expression, the woman stared at Nikki and called someone named Alejandro.

A man, unshaven and balding, with wisps of frizzy hair, came to the door.

"Esta señora nos quiere preguntar sobre nuestra hija," the woman told him.

"Questions about our daughter?" His tone and demeanor were unfriendly. "Can't you see this is not a good time?"

"I realize you must be experiencing overwhelming grief. But I found your daughter's remains."

"We've already talked to the police," the man said gruffly.

"Of course, but they have a huge caseload. I'm devoted to one case only. Maybe I can tell you something the police would not."

The woman looked at her husband with begging eyes.

"Fine, Carolina, si eso es lo que quieres." He turned back to Nikki. "I'm Alejandro Álvarez and this is my wife Carolina Castillo."

Nikki gave the man her business card. "My contact data."

He glanced at the card. Sighing, he asked Nikki to step inside. She followed them into a study adjacent to the entry. One wall had a built-in bookcase with drawers in the lower portion. A shelf had a computer keyboard sitting on it. Above the keyboard shelf was a blank computer monitor. Alejandro turned an ergonomic desk chair around to face the room. He motioned for Nikki to take a seat on one of the brightly upholstered wing chairs. A large, framed photograph of a beautiful young woman in a tiara and a pale blue dress adorned with rhinestones hung on the wall in front of her. Carolina took the other wing chair, at an angle to windows overlooking the front yard.

"I'm a private investigator," Nikki said, pulling her license out to show them. "I'm looking into the disappearance of Andrea Rodríguez, and I'm sure your daughter's death is somehow related."

"Related to the disappearance of that girl?" Carolina asked. Her expression changed to confusion.

"I respect your privacy, so I won't take much of your time. If I uncover information in this case that might be important about Raquel, I'll pass it on to you. That is, as long as I can do it legally."

"You're not working for us. Why would you do that?" Alejandro asked.

"As a courtesy."

"The police will give us information," he said bluntly.

"Yes, they will. I often provide information that can fill gaps in what law enforcement delivers. If you want it."

Nikki briefly explained why Yoani Rodríguez and Delfina Morales had hired her. She told them her questions might be painful for them, but she was trying to find out what happened. That way, she emphasized, the person responsible for their daughter's death could be brought to justice. Though the autopsy was not yet complete, it did appear Raquel had been murdered.

Alejandro asked her to get on with the interview.

"Do you know of anyone who might have wanted to harm your daughter?"

Carolina and Alejandro both shook their heads.

"Do you know of anyone who wanted revenge for something Raquel might have done?"

Again, they shook their heads.

"What about someone from Raquel's work?"

"She worked at Deep Sea Cruise Lines, right here in Doral," Alejandro said. "At headquarters, in management. Everyone liked her."

Deep Sea Cruise Lines, Nikki thought. She worked to keep the surprise from showing.

"I thought she was a practitioner of—"

"Voodoo? Is that what you heard?" Alejandro's face twisted in disgust. "That bitch. She hated our daughter. If anyone wanted to harm Raquel, it was that damned woman."

"Raquel was a very spiritual person," Carolina said. "And a healer. She believed in performing rituals where people could feel good about themselves so they could live happier lives."

Carolina told of Raquel's counseling and the people who'd found purpose and peace of mind from it. Her daughter's work provided healing, both emotionally and physically. That was Raquel's motivation, to make people feel better. She'd developed a program of meditation and prayer. For nonbelievers she used music and chanting instead of prayer. Depending on the person's needs it could include praying out loud to communicate with God and the saints in the Catholic pantheon. She taught people how to ask for forgiveness if they felt guilty toward a deceased person.

"But it was not Voodoo," Alejandro said. "Not at all."

"What do you know about her relationship with the Rodríguez-Morales family?" Nikki asked.

"They knew each other. After all, our son-in-law, Urbano, and Rodríguez are business partners." Alejandro looked at the floor.

Nikki pressed on gently. "Would you say the two families liked each other?"

"Delfina, being a medical doctor, always made snide remarks about Raquel's counseling," Carolina said. "Especially in front of others. It hurt our daughter."

"Did Raquel have a close relationship with Andrea?" Nikki asked, looking at Carolina.

"Not really, but she knew the girl had a difficult home life. Raquel tried to help her after Rodríguez killed Andrea's cat. The girl reacted by running away from home."

"Rodríguez killed Andrea's cat?" Nikki tried to suppress her emotion. "Why would he do such a thing?"

"Raquel didn't know. Maybe he's hateful, maybe he doesn't like cats." Glancing nervously at her husband, she continued. "Before her death, Raquel told us she found a couple of dead baby alligators at her back door. Nails driven into their heads had killed them. That's why we think—"

Alejandro cleared his throat and interrupted, saying that Carolina would like to blame the Rodríguez family, especially Delfina. He also thought Delfina could be capable of murdering their daughter, yet he told

Nikki he kept reminding himself they should not speculate until the police performed their investigation.

Nikki had forgotten about the dead alligators the detective had mentioned to Sergeant Maldonado at the crime scene. She hadn't realized the alligators had been killed, nails driven into their heads.

Carolina covered her face with her hands.

Attempting to return to a less emotional topic, Nikki inquired when Raquel had tried to help Andrea.

"About two years ago, maybe a little less," Carolina answered, sighing as she took her hands to her lap.

"How many times has she run away?"

"No sé," Carolina said. "I don't know, but it's been at least three times since Raquel married Urbano. The other times, she's returned to her parents after a couple of days. I think she mostly stayed with friends. The other parents thought she had permission."

"Do you know if the police were ever notified?"

Carolina shook her head.

"Was Andrea a difficult child?"

"Not at all," Carolina said. "According to Raquel, her parents were controlling, mostly her mother. And to some extent the father. He has a bad temper."

"Why did Raquel and Urbano separate?"

"First they dated. Then they lived together for ten years. And they had an exceptionally good relationship. They finally married three years ago," Carolina said. "Our son-in-law helped the Rodríguez-Morales family come here. Strange as it sounds, trouble started shortly after our daughter married Urbano. She couldn't point to one single thing that caused the rift, but pressure from Delfina and Yoani on our son-in-law certainly didn't help."

"Yet Yoani is in partnership with Urbano."

Carolina rubbed her hands together and appeared uncomfortable. "Having a business together is difficult, you know. Our daughter begged her husband to leave the partnership and return to a sole proprietorship. Like he'd had before Yoani arrived."

"Did the two partners get along well?" Nikki asked.

Carolina looked at her husband and cleared her throat before responding. "Our son-in-law needed someone to run the business. After years of working together, Urbano trusted Yoani to do that, but it was Urbano who took the clients to Cuba. You see, Yoani can't return to Cuba because he's in exile."

"How did your son-in-law get here if not by arriving as a refugee?" Nikki asked, perplexed.

"He pioneered the idea of taking patients to Cuba for stem cell therapy. That lucrative business also happens to raise much-needed cash for Cuba. He specialized in stem cell research before arriving in Miami, and Cuba is on the forefront of stem cell therapies. So the government over there cooperates with Urbano. He comes and goes as needed."

"It sounds as if your son-in-law could run the business himself, with the help of an office manager."

"Urbano has a client list separate from his partner, so they should have split up the business." Sadness showed on Alejandro's face.

Nikki fell silent for a few seconds. Then she asked if they knew how Raquel had pursued the issue for her husband to leave the partnership.

"Urbano kept giving excuses why he couldn't do it, like earning more money through a partnership, about being able to travel when he needed to," Alejandro said.

"Was that it?" Nikki asked.

"Raquel felt Yoani had something on her husband. Finally, our daughter rented a separate house, thinking that would make her husband come to his senses."

"If Raquel worked in Doral, why did she move to a house on the south side?" Nikki wondered why she'd moved so much closer to the Rodríguez family.

"We don't know. She may have wanted to get far away from Urbano," Carolina said, "that's my guess."

"And your son-in-law travels a lot?" Nikki asked.

"Quite a bit." Alejandro shook his head. "For the first year of the pandemic, not at all. But this year, it's picked up."

"When did you learn your daughter was missing?"

"Her office called. Raquel worked from home on Fridays and Mondays. When she didn't come to work on Tuesday, they contacted us. We called and texted her. Nothing. On Wednesday, we drove to her house and she wasn't there. We panicked and filed the report."

Nikki asked them if they had walked the backyard.

Carolina shook her head. "If we'd found her, the way you did, I don't think I could have . . ." her voice trailed off. She covered her eyes with her hands.

Nikki told them the coroner had estimated the time of death to be last Thursday, between five and nine p.m. "When was the last time you saw her?"

"Two weekends ago," Alejandro said. "She joined us for dinner and spent Saturday night here."

"What about your son-in-law? When did you last see him?"

"About two months ago. Before Raquel left him." Alejandro stared at the floor for a few seconds. Looking up, he frowned. "His wife is dead and we can't find him."

"Where do you think he'd be?" Nikki asked.

Alejandro grimaced. "Havana. Taking clients for stem cell treatments. But when I called Vicki at the Havana clinic, she denied he was there."

"I only have a few more questions." Nikki glanced at her phone. "Do you know anyone by the name of Spider Candella?"

Carolina nodded. "We've heard of a Spider, but I can't remember his surname." She asked her husband if he knew it.

"I remember they mentioned him," he said. "But they always just called him Spider."

"Our daughter helped him with a crisis he had. I don't know any details other than it had something to do with the death of his son."

Nikki caught her breath. "Did he hold a grudge against your daughter?"

"As far as we know, he was a good friend to Raquel and Urbano. They both spoke highly of him."

"Where can I find him?"

"Do you think he did something to Raquel?" Alejandro asked.

Nikki told them she'd like to ask him some of the same questions she'd asked them.

"We never met him," Carolina said. "Raquel and Urbano mentioned him a few times. The name is so unusual, I could not forget it."

"What do you know of Andrea's illnesses?"

"Illnesses?" Alejandro asked. "She had leukemia, but she was cured, I thought."

Carolina looked at her husband, turned away, and stared out the window. "Raquel told me, about two months ago." She hesitated before continuing. "The child suffered from chest pains and a collapsed lung about a year ago."

"Didn't Urbano have the same thing a while back?" Alejandro asked.

Carolina stared outside. Nikki wondered about the Voodoo doll in Andrea's room. *Was that symbolic of collapsed lungs? If so, what did it mean? Could whoever planted the doll with pins in its chest in Andrea's room also have planted baby alligators with nails driven into their heads outside Raquel's house?*

The silence became unbearable.

Nikki looked over at the framed photo. "Is that Raquel?" she asked, wanting to end the conversation on a high note.

Carolina's eyes glistened with accumulating tears. "That's when she was named Miss Venezuela, two years before we moved here."

"She was beautiful," Nikki said.

"And more so in person." Alejandro's eyes were brimming. "Her death breaks my heart."

CHAPTER ELEVEN

"My head's spinning," Nikki told Charlotte over the speaker. "I don't know who's telling the truth and who's lying."

Charlotte suggested everyone was probably reshaping reality to fit their needs.

Nikki elaborated on the description the mother provided of Raquel's spiritual work and the different picture painted by Delfina who called the woman a Voodoo witch. "And get this! Andrea has run away from home before. Raquel's mother says she's gone missing at least three other times. Check if the parents ever contacted the police about it."

"Will do," Charlotte said. "That'll be easier than finding airline tickets for Barriga and Andrea. I've checked several airlines and I can't come up with anything."

"They may have traveled under assumed names."

Charlotte agreed that made sense. "I'll keep trying on the tickets to see if I can find something plausible."

"And please send me the address to Deep Sea Cruises in Doral. I want to talk to somebody in HR. Also, send me Barriga's address. It's apparently in Doral too."

Charlotte texted the cruise line's address on Northwest Eighty-Seventh Avenue. Nikki activated directions on her GPS.

Charlotte's next text was Barriga's address.

A jovial man welcomed Nikki at the cruise line's guard shack. Nikki told him in Spanish that she needed to interview someone in human resources about Raquel Álvarez. He smiled broadly and held his hand up.

"Lady, I'm sure your Spanish is excellent, but I can only speak English and Haitian Creole."

Nikki laughed and passed him her ID and PI license as she repeated her request in English. He studied her ID while he made a call.

The large, colorful lobby broadcast a merry atmosphere, just right for a company in the vacation business. Lively background music made her want to sway to the beat. At the guard desk Nikki mentioned her appointment with human resources. Within five minutes, a young woman from HR arrived and ushered her down the hall into a small office. Nikki again described the purpose of her visit.

"Raquel Álvarez worked here for fifteen years," the HR person said. "She was a responsible employee and received several promotions. People who knew her were shocked about her sudden death."

"It was murder," Nikki said. "Did she have issues with anyone here?"

"We've spoken to the police and we have nothing further to say," the woman said. "Let me show you out."

"Answering questions about Ms. Álvarez might help solve the case of a missing teenager. The two cases seem to be connected."

"Ms. Garcia, we are through here."

When Nikki stopped at the guard shack to pick up her ID, the jovial man introduced himself as Peterson. "I guess you were investigating the parking-lot incident?"

"Tell me about it," Nikki said.

"Some jealous woman came here and accused Raquel of shacking up with her husband."

"Did you say the woman's name was Delfina?" Nikki asked.

Peterson's jovial smile evaporated. "No. Never mind. Pase yon bèl jounen. In Haitian Creole, that means 'have a beautiful day.'"

Nikki handed him a business card. "If you have something more to say about who might have wanted to kill Raquel, please call me." As she prepared to drive away, she said cheerfully, "Que tengas un hermoso día. That means 'have a beautiful day' in Spanish."

Nikki activated Barriga's home address. Again, she arrived at a gate with a guard shack. This time, the guard spoke Spanish. He was friendly but firm, refusing access to the community.

"His wife has been found dead, probably murdered," Nikki said, holding both her investigator and driver licenses for him to see. "We've been unable to find him, so I need to leave a message on his front door."

"Write one and I'll deliver it."

She wrote a note on a business card and handed it to the guard. Driving off, she thought that everyone in Miami must either work as a guard or live in a gated community. The building where she and Eduardo lived seemed impenetrable. She'd taken that for granted, given the prominence of the owners who had loaned the condo to them.

That damn Honda is following me again, she thought, looking in her rearview mirror. It was three cars behind, so she couldn't verify the license plate. Instead of taking the direct route to the office, Nikki decided to cross the Venetian Causeway to Miami Beach, the area of the city she knew best, to see if the car was tailing her.

When she took the exit for the causeway, the Honda continued straight on the freeway. Heavy traffic made it impossible for her to turn around, so she continued into Miami Beach. She'd felt jittery when she'd spotted that car, but it could be a look-alike. *How many white Hondas with tinted windows does Miami have?*

Now that she was on the island, she'd decompress. Consider the case so far. For one, Delfina's telling her that Barriga had taken Andrea to Cuba for leukemia treatment. Had it happened again, without the parents' consent this time? Either Barriga was in Cuba, or worse, he too was dead.

Gazing ahead, she saw buildings she passed every day going to work. South Beach was becoming familiar. The art deco style of the city fascinated her. When they first moved into the Miami Beach condo, she and Eduardo had taken the bus to the historic center. She'd always loved to run, but hadn't since they'd returned from Barcelona. *Eduardo and I have to start running along the paved pathway from the condo to the historic center.*

From Collins Avenue, she turned right on Fifth Street and continued onto State Road A1A. Looking across Biscayne Bay to the Miami mainland, the white buildings on the shoreline sparkled like diamonds and were reflected in the bay's sapphire water. She felt lucky to live in such a splendid city.

CHAPTER TWELVE

At Security Source, Nikki slipped into a chair in Floyd's office. She found him eating a sandwich.

"Looks tasty," Nikki said.

Floyd finished chewing and swallowed. "Cuban."

She glanced at the plate on his desk. "Appropriate, since I may be going to Cuba soon."

"Any news?"

"I had an interesting meeting with Raquel's parents. They described her as a wonderful person, much loved by all."

Floyd put the sandwich down and wiped his mouth with a napkin. "That's understandable. She was their daughter."

Nikki nodded. "From Voodoo witch to saint."

"After death, even the worst people take on saintly qualities. Did you get anything worthwhile?" Floyd took another bite of his sandwich.

"I'd say so," Nikki said. "Apparently, Andrea's run away from home before. To her friends' homes. Overnight. Charlotte checked, but nothing was reported. No wonder the father keeps insisting Andrea will return home."

Floyd took a sip of coffee. "Interesting. But she's never been gone so long. What else?"

Nikki mentioned the Voodoo doll with pins stuck in the chest. "It must have something to do with Andrea's collapsed lung last year, don't you think?"

Floyd gave Nikki a look of disbelief.

"Come on, Floyd, a lot of people are superstitious." Nikki shook her head. She'd planned to mention the dead alligators, but given Floyd's skepticism, she decided to forgo that conversation. "How about a trip to Havana for me to check out the stem cell clinic."

"Why?"

"To find Barriga. My guess is that he's either there or he's dead."

Floyd shook his head. "That's not enough reason to travel. We're looking for a teenager, not him."

"We've talked about this." Nikki stood. "I think Barriga took Andrea with him. He knew stem cell therapy might help her lupus, and her parents wouldn't take her."

"I'm not convinced," Floyd said. "Why would he take her without the parents' permission?"

"He took her the first time Andrea had stem cell therapy."

Glancing sideways at Nikki, he looked surprised. "Really?"

"I'd mentioned that to you. The parents asked him to take her. Apparently, they couldn't go because they're exiles."

"Hmm." Floyd shook his head. "If you take the trip, let's suppose you find Barriga and he has Andrea with him. What would you do?"

"First of all, I'd talk to him. Find out why he'd done it. Then we'd take it from there."

Floyd sipped more coffee and appeared to be thinking. "If you fly over, you'll need Eduardo with you. Is he willing to work with us on this job?"

"As soon as he completes his board exams tomorrow."

"Cuba could get complicated."

"If we're going to solve this case, one of us needs to go. You and Hamilton can't. The junior staff isn't ready. That leaves me."

"You need at least three days to prepare, preferably five. Hamilton can provide the latest information on getting around in Cuba. And I'm not saying you're going, but if you do, you'll both need new identities. For extra safety, you'll both need a change in appearance. Tell Eduardo to let his facial hair grow. A mustache and a few days of beard would be good."

Nikki thought for a few seconds. "Disguises? I've done disguises before. Isn't that too much?"

Floyd scratched his head. "There's a big difference with Cuba. These people are the spymasters of the world. They rank right up in the top three countries. I hate to say it, but Fidel outwitted the US many times. His presumed defectors joined the CIA and were double agents, secretly sending intel to Cuba. They also recruited and turned people already in the agency, like Ana Montes."

Nikki was mildly confused. "Fidel is dead. With Raúl's resignation, the Castro family is technically out of the government. Cuba is changing."

"And that's the unknown factor. The Castros and the Cuban Communist Party have always been obsessed about a Gorbachev moment," Floyd said.

"What's that?"

"Gorbachev changed Russia almost forty years ago by instituting reforms. The old guard in Cuba will want to prevent reformers from gaining power." Floyd ate the last bit of his sandwich.

"Change is inevitable," Nikki replied.

"That's the issue. With Cuba out of the Castro family's control, the hardliners are afraid they'll lose their power."

Nikki bit her lip. "I get it. You think the upheaval will make them paranoid."

"Exactly," Floyd said. "In times of strife, it can go either way. They may be so concerned about losing control that they'll strike at anything."

"On the other hand," Nikki said, "they may be so busy watching each other internally that they would completely miss us."

"The current president is a hardliner. We'd have to prepare for the worst-case scenario. I'll ask Hamilton to start training you right away, just in case. And I'll line up other details to be prepared." Floyd looked at his empty plate. "That was the best damn Cuban sandwich I've ever eaten."

On the way to Charlotte's office, Nikki stopped by the coffee station and served herself a cup. Charlotte had texted her about the owner of the white Honda. It belonged to a student at the university. She'd also pulled his address and phone number. He had a part-time job as a messenger for a law firm and drove all over Miami. Charlotte suggested that was why Nikki might have noticed the car several times.

"I stopped by to thank you. I get sensitive about cars that might be following me. Thanks for checking him out so thoroughly."

"Any time." Charlotte smiled. "I'm happy to be your remote bodyguard."

"I've been wondering about something. Raquel's mother told me two dead baby alligators, with nails through their heads, were left at her daughter's house the week before she was murdered. The day I found the body, the police detective mentioned dead alligators, but I didn't see them. What do you suppose that's about?"

"Ahh, it sounds like Voodoo," Charlotte said. "Usually headless chickens are used. It's supposed to be like a sacrifice to ask the spirits for help. But I'm no expert. Maybe you should consult with one. I'll find a reference for you."

"Headless chickens? Sounds creepy." Nikki shrugged. "Alligators with nails through their heads is unnerving too."

CHAPTER THIRTEEN

Nikki kissed Eduardo goodbye, wishing him good luck on the board exam. She took the elevator to the basement garage and walked to her car.

A scream died in her throat, leaving her chest aching. Running to the stairs, she climbed two at a time to the lobby. She saw the valet who parked and retrieved cars for residents, a service they had declined, and demanded to know how a dead alligator got on her car.

"A dead alligator?" The valet took a step back. "It must be a joke."

"Hell no! It's a dead alligator on the hood of my car." Nikki knew Floyd would not approve of the look of indignation on her face. "How the hell did someone get into the garage and put it there?"

A young guard joined them in the stairwell. He offered to take a look. The three of them walked to Nikki's car.

"It's just a baby." The valet reached out as if to remove the alligator.

"Don't touch it!" Nikki realized she'd shouted. Quietly, she added, "I need to get it analyzed for fingerprints and DNA."

"Just trying to help," the valet said. "I thought maybe it was a prank. It sort of reminds me of the woolly mammoth skeleton at the hotel next door. Know anyone with a weird sense of humor?"

"This is no joke. I need to check the surveillance videos. But first, one of you get me a clean paper bag to put this thing in." Nikki was relieved when both men hurried away.

She snapped a couple of photos. If she hadn't known about the alligators left at Raquel's, she might think the little alligator was resting. She called Charlotte to let her know she'd be late and why.

Eduardo got off the elevator.

He saw Nikki and sauntered over.

"I thought you'd be gone by now," Eduardo said.

Nikki gestured toward the dead alligator.

Eduardo whistled in surprise. "My god, Nikki. We must tell Floyd immediately."

She explained she'd already called the office. Floyd would send it in for testing of fingerprints, DNA, and anything else that might identify who had placed it there. "Go to your exams. That's more important. I can take care of this."

"You're the most important of all, amor mío," Eduardo said. "What about the video surveillance in this place? How could someone get around that?"

"I'll check that next."

Eduardo opened the trunk of Nikki's car and pulled out a new set of nitrile gloves, handing them to her.

The guard returned with two large brown paper bags. Nikki took them with gloved hands. The valet looked on.

She carefully set the dead alligator inside one of the bags. She folded the top tightly around the body to prevent it from shifting. Then she double bagged it and placed it on the floor of her car.

"Let's see the videos now," she told the guard.

"Hmm, I don't think I can do that," he said.

"Look, she's a detective." Eduardo towered over the young guard. "If you don't run the videos for her, she'll get someone who will. As residents here we have every right to see who did this to our property."

The valet's phone beeped and he left.

That reminded Nikki. She turned to Eduardo. "You need to leave. You can't be late for your exam. I'll talk with the guard and catch up with you later."

They kissed goodbye.

The guard walked Nikki to the security office behind the elevators. He fast-forwarded through videos from the afternoon and evening before. Once they saw where Nikki's car entered the garage, he slowed the video. After ten minutes, Nikki asked him to speed it up until they found someone setting the dead reptile on her automobile.

When a hooded figure appeared at her car, she asked him to back the video up to catch details. The hood covered his head almost completely. The guard brought up another angle. Nikki quickly realized it had the same problem. Besides the hood, the perp was wearing a surgical mask. His gaze must have been glued to the floor.

"That guy either knows where the cameras are set, or he has a lot of experience at this, always looking down and keeping his head well covered," the guard said.

Nikki asked the guard to back up until the man entered the garage carrying a package. He must have followed a careless driver into the secure garage.

They viewed the videos from two cameras on the outside of the entrance. They saw nothing unusual.

"I'd like to see the log for people that came into the building yesterday." Nikki said.

"I can't show you that." The guard shook his head. "I shouldn't even have shown you the videos."

She asked him to check the log and take note of all delivery people, making certain they were properly checked in and out. At what times? He should verify that every delivery person left the building through the lobby. She asked him to look for anyone using the lobby bathroom and then bypassing him or the concierge to access the stairs or the elevator to the parking area.

"If you find someone," she said, "I'll need the name. If I have to get a warrant, I will. Or you can save me some time."

———

Driving to the office, Nikki called Charlotte. "I want to talk to that Voodoo expert today," she said. "Maybe you can set up a Zoom conference at 9:30 today for Floyd and me to speak with him."

"It's actually a her," Charlotte said.

No sooner had Nikki entered her office than Floyd came to see her.

"What's this about dead alligators?" he asked.

"One was planted on the hood of my car. I need to take it seriously. That's why I requested a conference with an expert. According to Charlotte, the woman works with the police when dead animals show up on doorsteps, cemeteries, or public places."

"Charlotte told me two alligators were at Raquel's back door."

Nikki nodded. "It sounded too crazy to report. Until they left me one." She opened the Zoom app on her computer. She and Floyd had time to grab a cup of coffee if they rushed down the hall.

Dr. Da Silva was on the screen when they returned. She introduced herself and gave her credentials, a PhD in Caribbean religions. She explained that her particular emphasis was on Voodoo and other practices that incorporated elements of Catholicism, such as Santería. Her consulting experience included work for police departments around the world, she assured Nikki. She could probably determine what religious practices had sacrificed the animals and what it might represent if anything.

Nikki told her about the alligators at the murder site with nails in their heads, the Voodoo doll at the home of the missing teen, and the alligator on her automobile.

"Alligators?" Da Silva repeated. "That sounds like someone who doesn't know anything about Voodoo or Santería or any Caribbean religion." She inquired if the alligator on Nikki's car had nails in it.

"Not that I found," Nikki said.

"The nails in their heads lead me to believe someone with evil intent is leaving them. It could also be, as I said, someone using the idea of sacrificed animals without knowing what animals they should use, whether it is meant to be black magic or white."

Nikki shivered. "If I understand correctly, you're telling me I'm being threatened by someone who intends to kill me."

"In your case, no nails were in the alligator. Right?"

Nikki nodded.

"Someone is probably giving you a warning to mind your own business. You should exercise extreme caution. Don't go anywhere alone. And notify the police."

"That's reassuring," Nikki said with a hint of sarcasm.

"Now for the so-called Voodoo doll. Despite their name, the dolls are

European. They're called poppets, used in witchcraft and folk magic. They're not African Caribbean Voodoo articles, although they have come to be considered as such. In the missing teenager's case, they were most likely used to scare the parents. But police should be involved there too."

After discussing Raquel's spiritual practice, Dr. Da Silva gave the opinion that at best, someone believed Raquel was borrowing ideas from Santería and giving her a dire warning to stop it. Nikki and Floyd thanked her and ended the conference.

"Sounds like someone believes Raquel practiced Santería or is trying to portray that she did. That person is using that idea to send a message," Nikki said. "Even sending the message that she was killed for her beliefs."

"The fact remains," Floyd said, "she was killed."

Nikki agreed.

"One thing is certain," Floyd said.

With trepidation, Nikki asked what he meant.

"We need to get you away from Miami."

"Cuba?"

"That's a possibility," Floyd said, "since everything is ready for you and Eduardo to leave as soon as Hamilton gets you trained."

Nikki raised her eyebrows in an unspoken question. Floyd had vacillated about the trip to Havana.

"Dead alligators changed my mind," he said. "Cuba will be safer for you. And Barriga may hold the key to finding Andrea."

CHAPTER FOURTEEN

The air conditioning blew relentlessly from the ceiling ducts. Nikki pulled a shawl from her desk and draped it around her shoulders. Was the AC making her shiver, or was it the prospect of the next steps in her investigation? The curly tresses falling over her shoulders felt frizzy to her touch. Must be the humidity. The tight curls felt strange, so different from her normal straight hair.

Today, she and Eduardo would start the crash course on Cuba with Hamilton Estrada, her colleague that she suspected was either former or current CIA. Security Source might only provide a cover for him. How little Nikki knew about Hamilton. He was charming, witty, and fun to be around. He had left Cuba as a child when his parents took him, in a homemade boat, across the Strait of Florida to Key West.

Hamilton worked Security Source's high-profile cases involving famous people or sensitive politics. He was hardly ever in the office. Nikki often wondered about his relationships with Interpol and agencies such as National Security, Defense Intelligence, and the Office of the Director of National Intelligence. Floyd also had contacts that amazed her, but he was open about the years he'd worked for the CIA.

Eduardo stepped into her office. Floyd and Hamilton followed shortly behind.

"So you're going to Cuba," Hamilton said, speaking to Eduardo.

"Looks that way." Eduardo glanced at Nikki with a broad smile. "All part of what I do for this woman."

Hamilton led them to a small soundproof conference room. Two packets of disposable masks were on the table. Charlotte had spread out ten books, mostly mysteries.

Nikki spotted one hardcover among the paperbacks, *Klara and the Sun* by Kazuo Ishiguro. An upright card "So you don't go nuts during quarantine!" had Charlotte's signature and a hand-drawn smiley face.

"No more incidents I need to know about?" Floyd was obviously alluding to the alligator incident.

"Nothing new," Nikki answered, reading the book titles and sorting them into two stacks.

Floyd laid out the general plan for Cuba. The five-day quarantine would take place in the same hotel, just a different floor. Charlotte had already coordinated the hotel reservations, airport pickup, and Eduardo's registration, under his assumed name of Carlos Ramírez, for the stem cell conference. She'd also prepared an envelope that held their round-trip tickets with open return dates, travel insurance with medical coverage, proof of COVID vaccinations, and passports with the green visitor cards that served as visas.

"If we're going in clandestinely, how could Charlotte make all our reservations?" Eduardo asked.

"I called on a friend for a favor. Someone who's stationed at our embassy in Mexico City," Floyd said. "Charlotte provided all the information and my friend has a contact that makes these documents look authentic. So everything is in good order. Your backstories are also good. If anyone checks on your employment, it will be confirmed."

Eduardo wanted to know what story Floyd had given the Rodríguez family about Nikki's absence.

"She's in Canada following up on a lead that we can't discuss at the moment. Canada has a two-week quarantine, not just five days like Cuba."

Nikki opened the envelope and pulled three airline tickets out. One was for Valentina Ramírez, an alias for Andrea. It was the same first name as Nikki's cover and Eduardo's assumed surname.

Floyd asked Nikki if the passport and other documents for Andrea looked correct, reminding them to bring her out of Cuba only if it looked feasible.

She mentioned to Floyd that Andrea's visitor card was already torn in half.

"The other half is already in Cuba and will be planted in their system the day you arrive. That way, it looks like she went in with you. Otherwise you won't get her out."

Floyd pointed to a plastic bag containing what looked like a mouthpiece.

"It's custom made according to Andrea's dental records. Pop it into her mouth and it will change her appearance slightly."

"But what about face masks? Cuba is requiring them."

"As you go through immigration at the airport, you must remove face masks. That's when you need her wearing the mouthpiece."

Nikki muttered an okay.

"Use the wig to change her hair color and style. If you find her, get straight on a flight out. Don't take her to the hotel room with you."

A chill ran down Nikki's back. "What happens if the hotel keeps our passports at check-in? How could we get out in an emergency?"

"Good question. Cuban hotels no longer take passports upon check-in," Floyd said.

Nikki relaxed.

"Cash is king in Cuba, but beware the pickpockets," Floyd continued. "Merchants don't take US debit or credit cards, and physical bitcoin is too heavy to carry."

Eduardo chuckled. "I thought we could transfer cryptocurrency online."

"If you could use the internet, yes. But the government limits sites and surveils app connectivity." Floyd's tone was serious.

He handed each of them a pouch containing Canadian dollars, Euros, and Mexican pesos. They could exchange a portion of the money for Cuban pesos, he said, but warned them against Cuban convertible pesos. "That currency is no longer valid. A few Cubans still holding it have been known to pawn it off on naïve tourists."

"It'd make a great scam. Like the Iraqi dinar," Nikki said.

Hamilton handed them each a card, telling them to memorize the number in case they needed out of the country. It was only for an emergency.

"Above all," Ham said, "don't get yourselves arrested."

"These are long-range two-way satellite radios." Floyd opened three small boxes and made it clear the radios were to be used only if absolutely necessary.

Nikki was amazed. The radios were watches, not handheld as she'd envisioned. One was large and clunky, the second a bit smaller. The third box held a pendant, which she assumed was for her.

"Now let's go to work," Hamilton said. Picking up the pendant, he showed Nikki where extra lithium batteries were hidden. Then he taught her how to use the watch for communication. In the final step, he demonstrated where to change the batteries.

"They're rechargeable, but we don't want you to risk carrying chargers," Floyd said. "The radios work off a satellite, but you each have two channels. We've blocked all others."

Hamilton cautioned them that Cuba's surveillance might pick up the signal. He opened another box with two mobile phones. They had an encryption app for all messages. Nikki and Eduardo spent the next fifteen minutes learning how to use the spy gadgetry.

"Use this equipment in an emergency only," Hamilton repeated. "And don't expect communication from us unless it's critical."

"Visiting Cuba throws you into a different era," Floyd said. "It lulls you into thinking you've gone back in time. The antique cars and Old Havana are only one small part. It's important not to forget the advanced spy apparatus Cuba has built."

"And the people are friendly," Hamilton added, "which puts visitors at ease. Scams to get money from tourists are abundant. Think of every single Cuban you encounter as a potential spy, agent, informant, or snitch. Especially taxi drivers. You can assume they will report any unusual behavior by tourists to the Intelligence Directorate."

"The DI, also called the G2, is the entity responsible for collecting all foreign intelligence," Floyd said. "It employs fifteen thousand people on a full-time basis. And these are no ordinary people. They study languages, sociology, and communications. Then they undergo extensive foreign intelligence training. Over the years, Cuba has placed DI agents in diplomatic positions all over the world."

Floyd said the two of them must go dark.

"We get it," Nikki said. "We'll be careful. But China's spymasters are brilliant, recruiting in plain sight through social media."

"We'll worry about China if you ever go there," Floyd said.

Hamilton spent the morning explaining to Nikki and Eduardo they would be surveilled no matter where they went in Cuba. He started out by telling them live feeds from their hotel room would be transmitted directly to the DI.

Nikki and Eduardo shared a glance and groaned.

"That ends any notion of a romantic trip," Eduardo grumbled.

"When you return," Floyd said, "you can take a week and go somewhere romantic."

Hamilton suggested focusing on their case. "You're going in to find a kid and bring her back. It's life or death."

Floyd sat through the first part of the training but left after the morning session.

The three of them spent the afternoon reviewing and working on Nikki and Eduardo's new identities. Hamilton pointed out what they would need to be conscious of. He reminded them that if they got in trouble, real trouble, Havana could be officially locked down within ten minutes. The city wouldn't reopen until the authorities found what they were looking for.

"We should never be in that category," Nikki said.

Hamilton nodded. "Today's lesson is don't get into trouble. My favorite quote by Dostoevsky is 'the degree of civilization in a society can be judged by entering its prisons.' My dad was imprisoned in Cuba when I was a kid. When they finally let us in to see him, he told us about the deplorable conditions. They had no running water, for one thing."

"That's surely changed," Nikki said.

Hamilton scoffed. "Not really. There's still no running water, except for prisons they showcase to the world. Holding cells are different. The DI uses them to interrogate people. Trust me, you don't want to end up in one of them either."

Eduardo put his arm around Nikki. "There will be better things to see than prisons, right?"

"If you lovebirds will listen, we can continue." Hamilton shook his head. "It's imperative not to let your real identities slip."

Then Ham asked Nikki to share her background: her parents, where she grew up, what interests she had, and what kind of work she did.

"I'm Valentina Archuleta. I grew up on a farm in central Mexico, in the state of Aguascalientes. My father and grandfather were both farmers. Eventually they sold the land to larger companies that have mechanized agriculture in the region."

"Are you still in the farming industry?"

"No. I went to the university in Mexico City."

"What did you study?" Hamilton asked.

"Business."

"How did you meet your husband?"

Nikki explained. Her company had sent her to a conference. The hotel had other conferences going on, and she had a chance encounter with a handsome Colombian medical doctor. The next day, they happened to see each other at breakfast. He asked to join her at her table. "That's how it started. We were married a year later."

Hamilton drilled Nikki for two hours. Then he covered cultural mores, like not spitting on the streets and not blowing their nose in public. Littering was against the law, though they would find plenty in certain sections of the city.

Then it was Eduardo's turn to talk about his new identity. Hamilton picked up on topics Nikki had mentioned and asked him further questions.

At the end of the day, Hamilton summed up the training. Preparing together for this assignment should make them more comfortable with their new identities. "Not all agents have to use covers when working, but this job is best done in your new personas."

"Why?" Nikki asked. "I know people who have visited Cuba without any issues. In fact, they thought the country and the people were lovely. Though they did mention crumbling buildings. Oh, and the food. They complained it was pretty dismal."

"Your friends did not go on a secret assignment."

"True," Nikki said.

"Neither one of you is CIA nor FBI, so you won't be on their radar. But it's best to keep separate identities in case anything goes wrong. So they won't find you easily after you return. That's another reason we've changed your appearances."

Eduardo tugged on a lock of Nikki's curly hair.

"Yeah, it's always my hair that takes a beating when I change appearances. I've had to cut it, dye it gray, and now I'm all curly."

"Curly is good in Cuba," Eduardo noted. "You'll blend in unnoticed."

"And you'll blend right in with your stubble and those outrageous glasses." Nikki laughed.

Eduardo adjusted his glasses and ran a hand over his chin. "Yeah, it's stubble, but I'll have a full beard when we return."

"We can still equip you with the latest appearance-altering device for spies—a fake beard. You could wear it for a full month before it has to be removed," Hamilton said. "In a pinch, it works great to change appearances." He told them they'd pick up again tomorrow, and turning to Eduardo, he asked him how the board exams had gone.

"Great," Eduardo responded, "though I don't know yet if I passed."

Nikki punched him. "Don't be so modest."

"I'll see you both tomorrow," Hamilton said. "And for the rest of the week."

"This is more intense than studying for my exams," Eduardo said as they left the conference room.

On the balcony, Nikki and Eduardo were eating pizza again. No champagne this time. They were flying to Mexico City the next day. Much as Nikki liked to cook, she did not have time to fix evening meals. Preparing for Cuba had consumed all their leisure hours during the past week. So busy they hadn't been able to invite Floyd and Milena back for Peruvian conchitas.

Her mobile rang.

Not recognizing the number, Nikki answered with a simple hello. A melodic accent greeted her.

The caller identified himself as Peterson, the security guard who had wished her a beautiful day in Haitian Creole at the guard shack last week. He told her he could lose his job for mentioning Raquel's parking-lot scuffle.

Nikki assured him she would not tell anyone.

"Ms. Garcia, I've debated about calling you. You must understand I liked Raquel Álvarez very much. Only when you were here that day did I learn she'd died. That's why I'm calling. I will talk if you swear to keep my name out of this."

Nikki promised.

He said the other woman accused Raquel of stealing her husband. Three security guards had intervened. None of them thought it was serious, though they had seen the intruder yank Raquel's hair, and in turn, she'd kicked the other woman's shins. They yelled obscenities at each other until the guards separated them. The guards had laughed about it for days.

"Do you remember the woman's name?" Nikki asked.

Peterson explained that the woman must have been waiting outside the property for Raquel, and when she saw her going toward her car, the woman climbed over the fence in a flash. The guards separated the two and planned to question the intruder. Raquel intervened and told them to let the other woman go. No one saw any identification. "Two guards escorted the woman off the premises, all the way to the street. Raquel left and the next day she laughed with me about the incident."

"Did the men get her license plate number?"

Peterson explained the woman had walked to the corner of the block. A few minutes later, one of the guards saw her get into a bus.

"Do you think she was capable of killing Raquel?"

Peterson sighed. He'd lain awake wondering the same thing since he'd learned of Raquel's death. He said his intuition told him that woman would not have murdered her.

"She had motive, though. Didn't she?" Nikki asked.

"Her jealousy, yes. I'd never forgive myself if she did it and I'd failed to speak up about it."

"Can you describe the woman?"

"Small, with blond hair. Could have been dyed."

"Age?"

"Maybe late thirties."

Nikki asked if he'd gone to the police.

"No ma'am. I'd lose my job."

Nikki called Floyd with the news. She offered to stay in Miami instead of leaving the next day, thinking she might get more information by locating the blonde woman. She also explained she'd learned of a parking-lot fight from Peterson the day she'd gone to the cruise line and had become distracted with talk about Cuba and forgot to mention the fight when she debriefed him.

"Let's stick with the plan," Floyd said. "We'll add security guards to the list of follow-up we already have. As a starting point, I'll have Charlotte trace the parking-lot brawler. Somebody who pulls that kind of nonsense is not going to keep her identity a secret."

Finishing the call, Nikki sighed and glanced at Eduardo. "As they say, the plot thickens."

CHAPTER FIFTEEN

Boarding the Aeroméxico flight in Mexico City bound for Havana, Nikki squeezed Eduardo's hand. "I'm sure it's going to be a big adventure," she said in Spanish. She and Eduardo had worked out hand-squeezing, finger tapping, and finger writing on each other's palms to communicate silently. One squeeze let him know she was okay.

Eduardo pocketed the passports and green visitor cards. "You've always wanted to visit Cuba." Leaning in to whisper in her ear, he added in his soft Colombian Spanish, "There are no alligators near Havana."

From the time they left Miami, they had spoken only Spanish and called each other by their assumed names. They settled into their seats in first class. The flight to the José Martí International Airport in Havana would take less than three hours. Eduardo made sure the medical conference registration packet was visible in his shirt pocket. Immigration and customs officials could easily see it and confirm the business purpose of his trip. After takeoff, he leaned his seat back and, much to Nikki's chagrin, fell asleep.

Upon landing, Eduardo opened his eyes. "That was a good flight."

"You slept the whole way." Nikki glanced out the window at the small airport with five separate terminals. Ham had said they'd likely arrive at terminal 3, recently renovated and by far the most comfortable. He'd also suggested exchanging money there.

Following passengers ahead of them, Eduardo showed their passports, green visitor cards, and proof of vaccines and medical insurance to the immigration official. The man tore the visitor card in half and handed it back with Eduardo's Colombian passport, insurance card, and COVID-19 card. He looked at Nikki's Mexican passport and asked her a question in English.

Nikki stared at him. "No entiendo."

The official handed the packet back to her and waved them on.

They waited a half-hour for their checked baggage. As they waited, they watched a large closed-circuit television monitor advertising the country's medical tours. Smiling doctors greeted patients, then the video showed patients surrounded by state-of-the-art equipment, lab technicians were shown taking patient's blood and testing patient's blood pressure. In the final scene, before the ad started over again, personal trainers worked with recovering patients, and physical therapists meticulously massaged patients. Their luggage finally arrived and they headed for the exit doors to find their limo service.

Nikki tried not to ogle the beautiful two-tone vintage Buick.

Their driver left the airport grounds in Boyeros. The area they were driving through looked poor, apartment complexes in need of repair and dilapidated old factories. Right away Nikki compared what they were riding in with the old cars they were passing that were not sparkling clean or polished to perfection. She assumed they belonged to local residents. Whiffs of fumes surprised her.

A world without catalytic converters. She stared at passing vehicles—old Russian Ladas and Czech Skodas. In amazement, she mentally counted the number of recent models. All the photos she'd seen of Havana showed mostly the grand old American cars. As they approached the city, she could see the skyscrapers she'd noticed from the plane. She squeezed Eduardo's hand to signal that she was doing okay. She glanced at her husband. With the mustache and stubble he'd grown, and his heavy glasses, he looked older. But his facial hair was hidden under the face mask. Smiling, she tapped an "I love you" message on his wrist.

The driver cleared his throat and interrupted their silent play.

"Where do you come from?" he asked.

Nikki wanted to cover her ears. She'd grown accustomed to Eduardo's soft Colombian pronunciation. This man's loud voice and staccato words, even with his mask, were unexpected.

"We live in Mexico," Eduardo answered. "I'm originally from Colombia, but I married this wonderful Mexican woman and now live there."

The driver became very talkative. He drove up historic avenues and past monuments. Nikki suspected this served not only to increase the taxi fare but also to show them the best aspects of Havana. And he was surely working for a better tip. He slowed as the sports stadium came into view.

"That's the Estadio Latinoamericano. Locally, we call it the Colossus of El Cerro, the hill." The driver laughed. "It holds the second biggest crowd in the world. And be careful in this area of town. Cerro is not a safe neighborhood."

"Cuba is famous for its baseball," Eduardo said.

"It's the Cuban national pastime. We love the game."

The driver took them by the center of power, Revolution Square. Built under Batista, it consisted of eleven acres. He pointed out the various ministry buildings and took them past the granite José Martí memorial. The last building he showed them was the Palace of the Revolution, a plain, rectangular edifice with an unadorned colonnade. Before the revolution, it housed Cuba's supreme court and the attorney general. Fidel repurposed it as the seat of government.

"We may be a small island, but we have grand monuments," he said with pride.

On Fifth Avenue, they passed gorgeous prerevolution mansions. The driver said many of them now served as embassies or homes to high-level Cuban government officials.

Finally, they entered a circular driveway to the porte-cochère extending out from the glassed-in lobby of the Meliá Habana Hotel on Third Avenue. It was a modern facility, close to the beach and within three miles of the convention center. It was even closer to the clinic Nikki would visit.

The hotel receptionist was friendly, young, and beautiful. Not wearing a mask, she informed them that she was fully vaccinated.

She took time to enumerate the hotel amenities, mentioning the restaurants, the exercise room, the conference and banquet rooms, and the swimming pool. Most of all, she emphasized the first-class spa. All of these would be available after the quarantine period.

"During quarantine," she went on, "food is to be ordered from the restaurants once a day. You can always change your mind if you call two hours before the time you've requested a meal delivery."

Smiling at Eduardo, she added, "the spa offers the best massages in the world. Your quarantine suite comes with a view of the ocean and free Wi-Fi. You'll move to a regular suite in five days if you pass the COVID test. The bellman will take your luggage up in a few minutes." Still smiling, she handed key cards to Eduardo.

"¡Ese hombre es tremendo mangón!" As they walked toward the elevator, Nikki heard the receptionist tell the other person behind the counter. *That's right. My husband is hot, even with the face mask.*

In the room, Nikki looked out the panoramic windows toward the ocean. "It's beautiful. And I'm glad I'm here. That receptionist could not stop flirting with you."

Eduardo put his arms around his wife and gently tapped her shoulder twice, signaling for her not to say anything out of turn.

"Let's call the hotel restaurant for dinner tonight," Nikki suggested. "Right now, though, I need a shower."

She entered the bathroom and flipped the switch on, then turned it off. But she had to act normal, like someone who didn't know about the room cameras. She put the light back on. She pulled off her blouse, careful not to drop the two lightweight wigs in special pockets sewn into her blouse under each sleeve.

CHAPTER SIXTEEN

FIVE DAYS LATER

The second COVID test since their arrival was also negative. The nurse who administered it told them they were now free to roam Havana. Though she cautioned them to be careful and urged them to wear masks despite their vaccinations.

The regenerative medicine conference started that day. Nikki walked with Eduardo to the Palacio de Convenciones to get her bearings. Miramar, where their hotel was located, was not crowded. Walking let them talk without fear of being overheard or recorded.

"The hotel's not bad," Nikki said. Her curly black hair whipped into her face with the ocean breeze. She took a band out of her purse and tied it into a ponytail. "I'm glad we had books to read. The lobby is lovely, the views are wonderful. But I was hoping our second suite would be better than the isolation one. Neither is as nice as I expected of a Meliá."

"I read that the Meliá has several properties in Cuba, but doesn't own them outright," Eduardo said. "So they maintain them but they don't invest in a complete renovation."

At the beach, Nikki took her sandals off. Waves slapped the sand with rhythmic energy. A dozen teenagers walked ahead of them, their hair tousled by the ocean breeze. One of them carried an old boom box belting out Camila Cabello's song 'Havana'. She asked Eduardo to listen to the lyrics.

He stopped and turned toward the expanse of ocean. They listened to the Cuban American's song about missing the city of her birth.

Before returning to the street, Nikki stepped into her sandals. Across from the convention center, Eduardo asked her to be patient and only get a lay of the land today.

She kissed him, his whiskers tickling her lips.

Nikki waited until he went into the hall before she retraced her steps back along the oceanfront, taking in the buildings as she strolled. Once in a while she turned to view the ocean and make sure no one was following her. The area matched the study they'd done. Google Earth provided scant information on Havana compared to other places. Regular maps she'd seen seemed fine, though according to Hamilton, they were far from accurate. She guessed she'd find out in the next couple of days how precise they really were.

Presumably, the maps had not been updated much since the start of the revolution. Map services in various countries adjusted details wherever they could. Floyd and Hamilton also said that some maps of Cuba might be digitally altered deep fakes.

CHAPTER SEVENTEEN

The drive to Deep Sea Cruises had Floyd mulling over Raquel's death and Andrea's disappearance. By the time he arrived at the guard shack, he'd concluded they needed more information. He wasn't at all certain the missing teenager was in Cuba, although he'd facilitated a passport, dental appliance, and other paraphernalia in case Nikki did find her. And even if she located the girl, getting her out would be a big deal. But if anyone could do it, Nikki could.

A possible new suspect sparked hope they'd get a break in the case. That was why he was here. Floyd gave the guard his name and said he had an appointment with Nancy Rivas in security. The guard checked his driver's license and input it into the computer. Judging from Nikki's description of Peterson, today's man could not be the guard who had called Nikki. When the guard gave him a parking pass, Floyd noticed his name: Santiago Téllez.

Nancy was petite, with short blond hair. At her office on the third floor, Floyd explained in full what information he needed.

"You can't just come in and ask to see our surveillance footage. You're not the law, so you wouldn't have a warrant."

"No, but I represent Raquel Álvarez's husband." Floyd wasn't above lying. "He's desperate to know what happened to his wife. A friend mentioned something about a scuffle here a few days before Ms. Álvarez was murdered. Finding that woman might lead us to solving this crime."

"You know I can't tell you anything."

"My company is also handling the case of a teenager's abduction," Floyd said. "I have reason to believe the two incidents are related. The minor has been missing for over two weeks."

"I'm sorry to hear that, but I can't help you."

"Then let me speak to the guards who saw the woman who assaulted Ms. Álvarez. We have the life of a teenager to consider."

"Mr. Webber, I'm truly sorry I can't help you."

"You're tough." Floyd put on a winning smile. "Let me know if you want to run for attorney general. I'll be the first to back you."

Nancy laughed. "Then you'd hound me for special favors after my election."

Floyd started his SUV and dialed Charlotte. "Work your magic to find out where Santiago Téllez, a guard from Deep Sea Cruises, goes for drinks after work, coffee in the morning, or to play baseball on Saturdays. The sooner I can talk to him, the better."

"On the double," Charlotte responded. "I'll get it even if I have to go out there and talk to him myself."

CHAPTER EIGHTEEN

Nikki circled a large sculpture of an elephant and checked to be sure no one was following her. She left the Miramar Business Center and its statues and headed toward the clinic where Urbano Barriga brought his stem cell tourists. Turning right at the intersection and right again at the next corner, she looked back to see if anyone was trailing her.

Nothing.

The streets were a kaleidoscope of colorful cars. She noticed a jalopy packed with people. She smiled, thinking it was a group of friends having fun, until she saw it stop. A couple of people got out at the intersection and three others climbed in. *It must be a form of public transportation.*

A street vendor prepared café con leche. Nikki enjoyed unexpected details on the streets of Havana, like the coffee vendor. She looked around for anyone following her before standing in line at his battered steel cart to get a cup of the sweet, rich-smelling coffee. Sipping the aromatic brew, she headed for a vacation home rental agency across the street.

A woman about forty with dark, curly hair greeted her.

Nikki introduced herself as Valentina, telling the woman she'd be in Havana for only a couple of days and wanted to plan for a future vacation.

"I'm María." The woman smiled widely. "You must be Mexican!"

"How did you know?"

"Your accent. Your Spanish is Mexican. We get a lot of people from Mexico City. Back to your question. Our island is changing so quickly, I cannot possibly tell you what will be available six months or a year from now, but sit down and we'll talk. How much do you know about Cuba?"

"Not much," Nikki said.

"I'm proud to say this is my business. I'm a cuentapropista."

Nikki congratulated her.

"Fidel himself would not recognize Havana today. After his brother Raúl took over, he encouraged entrepreneurism to help the economy. Now that Raúl has resigned, we have a new president."

"The Castro brothers were in power for a long time," Nikki said.

"Sixty-two years." María asked Nikki if she'd like a malta.

Nikki asked what it was.

María smiled. "It's the best nonalcoholic drink in the world. Made from malt, a bit like a beer without the alcohol. It's not just Cuban. All the islands drink it." She left the room and returned with two tall glasses.

Nikki tasted it and found it sweet and spicier than beer.

"Now where was I?" María asked.

Half an hour later, Nikki felt like she'd been in a current events class. María had filled her in on the island's political developments since Fidel's death.

"Now, let's get to business. How many people do you plan to bring to a vacation rental?"

After Nikki told her it'd be four adults, María used her laptop to show pictures of different towns and districts. Nikki sipped malta as María spoke. Handing Nikki an info packet, María told her to call two months before the trip to get good rentals.

Nikki thanked her and said goodbye. María wished her a good stay and invited her to come back anytime.

The malta had refreshed Nikki, but now she was hungry. She had to check out one more place before lunch—Urbano Barriga's stem cell clinic.

As she turned the corner on Lázaro Cárdenas Avenue, she expected to see a cozy one-story building. Surgery and therapy would be administered to patients who recovered at hotels that coordinated with the clinic to provide round-the-clock nursing, special meals, and massage in a caring atmosphere. To her surprise, the clinic was a large three-story edifice.

Business must be booming, she thought.

A sign near the front door said the clinic catered to diplomáticos, hombres de negocio y turistas looking for the scientific advances and the excellent health services Cuba offers. Nikki sniffed. *Apparently, they don't cater to businesswomen.*

It appeared to be a full-service clinic, offering various specialties. Tempted to enter, she decided to wait until the next day. After she checked once more that no one was following her, she continued along Thirty-Seventh Avenue until she spotted a restaurant.

Eduardo enjoyed the emcee's jovial banter. He welcomed the participants, all doctors, primarily from Latin America and Canada, with snippets of humor that warmed up the crowd for the first speaker of the day.

In the afternoon session, the emcee announced a change in speakers about autoimmune disease treatment with stem cell therapies. He told the audience they were indeed lucky to have such a distinguished and knowledgeable physician, one who had been a pioneer in Cuba's stem cell research, take over for the planned speaker.

"I'm thrilled to introduce Dr. Urbano Barriga," he said.

With that, a man stood up from the front row and joined the emcee at the podium.

Eduardo almost jumped out of his seat. How could Barriga be here, presenting at a conference, when his wife had been murdered? Maybe he killed her and was hiding on the island. Cuba doesn't extradite to the US. *A perfect place to avoid prosecution.*

But Eduardo found him an eloquent and knowledgeable speaker. He sounded passionate about stem cell therapy's potential for better treatment of autoimmune disorders and illnesses such as rheumatoid arthritis. When he spoke about lupus, Barriga's enthusiasm about advances was palpable.

After questions and discussion on autoimmune diseases had ended, Eduardo approached Barriga. He asked about treatment for young patients and listened, nodding his approval, before asking Barriga about his practice in Cuba.

"I used to be a researcher in stem cell therapies here, but I don't work on the island anymore. I own a travel agency in Miami. We collaborate with clinics here, bringing people for surgical and therapeutical procedures that they can't get anywhere else."

Nikki and Eduardo strolled along Third Avenue looking for a place for dinner. She asked about the conference.

"I was wondering when you'd get around to that." Eduardo smiled. "Barriga was brought in to address us."

Shocked, she stopped immediately, almost getting hit by a pedestrian walking behind her. "I didn't know he was on the program."

"He wasn't listed," Eduardo said. "They introduced him as a pioneer in Cuba's stem cell research. Apparently he was attending the conference and when the scheduled speaker was unable to make it, he substituted."

"And you're sure he's our Barriga?"

"Positive."

Needing more time to talk, they dismissed the first restaurant they passed and continued walking. Traffic seemed heavy and exhaust fumes permeated the air.

They crossed the street and walked down the block, turned right and then right again. Stopping near the entrance of a restaurant, Nikki checked to see if they were being followed while Eduardo studied the menu.

"It's early. Let's find another place," she said.

As they continued walking, Eduardo shared the details of his conversation with Barriga.

"How was your day?" he asked.

"Boring by comparison. I think Hamilton and Floyd exaggerated. People here are friendly, I wasn't followed, and I found the clinic. I almost went in, but decided to limit myself to exploring today."

"Any surprises?"

"Nothing earth-shattering like yours. I ventured into a travel agency and the owner, a woman, gave me a lesson in Cuban politics."

"Didn't Hamilton and Floyd tell us to stay away from that topic? It could be dangerous."

"Yes, but I acted very naïve so I don't see any harm in it."

"Anything else?"

"The size of the stem cell clinic surprised me. It's much bigger than I anticipated. Plus it handles all sorts of medical procedures, not just regenerative therapies—but just for men. A sign clearly stated *businessmen* could seek Cuba's advanced medical procedures. Can you imagine?"

Eduardo chuckled. "I'm surprised you didn't storm the place."

CHAPTER NINETEEN

Floyd entered El Toro Corrido, a loud club apparently well known to tango lovers. He looked around the bar and noticed people on the patio. It was early, and Floyd hoped Santiago Téllez would show up.

After ordering a beer, Floyd sat on a rickety bar stool. On his second beer, he asked the bartender to close his tab.

"Don't leave yet. El Toro starts singing in about half an hour. He's amazing!" the bartender said. "That's why I work here. To listen to him."

Floyd thanked the man and slapped down a twenty-dollar bill. "Keep the change." Headed for the exit, Floyd saw Téllez come in. He approached him.

"Hey, you're the guard from Deep Sea Cruises."

The man looked surprised, then recognition settled across Téllez's features.

"Let me buy you a beer," Floyd said.

They sat on bar stools and Floyd ordered two pint glasses of Gunfighter Blonde, a German-style hefeweizen. Floyd engaged Téllez with small talk about local beers he liked.

"By the way, I heard you had a blonde who started a parking-lot brawl," Floyd said, holding up his beer as if to make a toast. "This

Gunfighter Blonde is appropriate. Good thing that woman didn't have a gun on her."

"Yeah, quite a fight. It's such a shame. Raquel is, well, was a good person. I can't imagine anyone having an issue with her. At least not like that," the guard said. "How do you know about it?"

"Remember I went by to talk to security? I'm working for the widower to find out who murdered Raquel. The police are slow in their investigation and whatever solid evidence I find, I'll share with them."

The guard sat up a bit straighter and looked uncomfortable.

"I keep my sources confidential," Floyd said.

"How's that possible?"

"For one, I don't name the people who give me information. Sort of like a journalist who'd rather go to jail than reveal a source. I only provide data that can't be traced back to my sources."

"This is good beer," the guard said. "I've never had it before."

Floyd stopped pressing him. The man was purposely changing the subject. Taking the conversation in another direction, he asked if Téllez was from Argentina.

"Most people think that, but I'm Uruguayan."

"You like tango?"

"It's why I'm here. El Toro, the owner of this place, is one of the best tango singers I've ever heard."

Floyd glanced at his watch, knowing the show would start soon. He ordered two more beers.

"Do you think Raquel knew the woman who attacked her?"

"Either she knew her or she pretended to know her." The guard swirled the beer inside the glass.

"None of you asked for identification?"

"Not after Raquel told us to let the blonde leave."

The patrons erupted into enthusiastic applause when a heavyset man took to the stage. He resembled a young Pavarotti. An ensemble of violins, string bass, and the wailing melancholy of the bandoneón played the introductory piece, emphasizing melody over the underlying rhythm.

El Toro took the microphone and again the crowd clapped and whistled. Floyd listened to the singer express emotions from hopeful and joyous to sorrowful and nostalgic. El Toro belted out his song with passion, but tango was not Floyd's favorite.

CHAPTER TWENTY

Sunlight filtering through the windows at the Meliá warmed Eduardo. Without moving from the bed, he watched Nikki dress slowly and deliberately. Folding a wig into her clothes to get it positioned correctly without hidden cameras picking it up took patience on her part. He knew she carried it in case she needed to change her appearance during her work today. An extra blouse, long and loose-fitting, to give her a complete makeover was probably already folded in her handbag. Eduardo contemplated the tough assignment facing him today, yet he did not minimize the work Nikki had to carry out. Pangs of worry overwhelmed him for a few seconds. An unpleasant feeling arose in his stomach.

Last night, they'd discussed how he would approach Barriga about Raquel's death. If all went well, perhaps in the evening, they would meet him at a restaurant for dinner. They had agreed she would return to the hotel by five-thirty that afternoon in case he came by to take her to meet Barriga.

He sat up on the edge of the bed and continued observing his wife. She turned to face him as if she'd felt his gaze. She said good morning with a smile and hugged him. Normally, he would pull her into bed, but today they had work to do. Plus they wanted to avoid sending video feeds of their foreplay to the DI.

"I'll forgo the hotel breakfast," he said to Nikki. "The conference has croissants on the breakfast buffet and the best coffee I've had since we arrived."

She told him she planned to eat at the restaurant downstairs and then go sightseeing.

Despite showering and shaving the top line of his beard and freshening up his mustache, he got dressed and was ready to leave before Nikki. She blew him a kiss and wished him a good time at the conference.

Eduardo served himself a cup of coffee after he'd eaten two croissants. He saw Barriga arrive. He watched as the Cuban doctor stopped to speak with a couple of people before hitting the breakfast buffet. Eduardo looked away so Barriga wouldn't think he was being monitored. To his surprise, Barriga headed in his direction.

"I liked your presentation on lupus yesterday," Eduardo told him.

"A terrible disease. It deprives young people of a normal life. Now we have hope for many of them."

"You don't think it will provide false hope?" Eduardo asked.

"Not at all. This really works. Of course, the stem cells have to match if they come from a donor. That's the biggest issue. Often it's relatives who provide the stem cells."

"I think we may have a mutual acquaintance," Eduardo said.

Barriga looked at him with a quizzical expression.

Eduardo was glad for the opportunity to have a frank conversation with him.

"This acquaintance asked me to tell you something if I saw you here. It's quite a coincidence that you spoke at the conference yesterday."

Barriga frowned. "Who might that be?"

"I was asked to relay sad news to you." Eduardo took a breath. "Your wife was murdered."

The man stepped back, away from Eduardo, shaking his head. "That cannot be, that cannot be."

Barriga staggered, losing his balance. Reaching out with one arm to steady himself against the wall, he leaned against it. "She was perfectly okay when I left. This cannot be."

Thinking the man might still fall, Eduardo stepped toward him, took his arm, and walked him away from the crowd of doctors in the lobby to the hallway, near the restrooms, where they could talk privately.

"And now you're here to kill me," Barriga said, his voice quavering.

"I'm not a killer," Eduardo asserted.

"Benjy Ávila, he sent you."

The lights blinked, notifying the conferees it was time to return to the auditorium.

Eduardo looked straight into his eyes. "I don't know anyone by that name. I'm not here to do any harm. I'm actually here to help you."

"I don't believe that."

"Believe what you want. Since Raquel is dead, there are several people concerned about you. Some thought you might have also been killed. Your office assured us you had left Miami more than three weeks ago."

Barriga looked around. "I thought you were from Mexico."

Eduardo kept talking. "We tried to find you here. Your mobile phone doesn't work and your voicemail is full. We called the clinic where you bring people for treatment, and we were told you had not arrived in Cuba. So I was hired by friends to find you."

He scoffed. "Friends, eh? Friends like Ávila and Rodríguez?"

Eduardo said he'd heard of Rodríguez but did not know him. "And Rodríguez's daughter is missing. Andrea disappeared about the same time as your wife was murdered. Some people think that's not a coincidence. I'm here to try to help you."

The two men stood in silence. Eduardo thought the doctor was assessing the information he'd given him. Likewise, Eduardo was analyzing the man's response.

"I'm sorry to give you such terrible news. I considered inviting you to dinner and telling you there. But bad news is terrible no matter when, where, or how you receive it."

Barriga's face contorted, as if he were holding tears back.

"How can I believe you?" he asked.

Eduardo pulled two pieces of folded paper from his pocket and handed them to him.

"The top one is Raquel's death certificate," he told Barriga. "The second one is a missing person report on Andrea."

Eduardo studied the man reading the documents. The self-assured doctor who had spoken about stem cell therapies the day before was barely recognizable in the slumped, sad-looking human being standing in front of him now.

CHAPTER TWENTY-ONE

After Eduardo left the hotel, Nikki fidgeted in anticipation of his confronting Barriga. Now she set out to do her own work.

After a light breakfast, she took a taxi to Old Havana. Her purse, flung over her shoulder, felt light without her baby Glock. But carrying a gun here would be far more dangerous than going around unarmed.

Her first item of business was making sure she was invisible. Her word. In the lingo of spies, the word is clean: unnoticed and not followed by anyone.

The driver dropped her off in the park in front of the national capitol building. Everything looked immaculate. The capitol building resembled the one in Washington, DC. Armed with a street map Charlotte had printed for her, she ambled from street to street, enjoying the prerevolution architecture. Surprised by the beauty of the area, she found it in complete contrast to the dilapidated, gray neighborhoods they had seen close to the airport.

A man about her age, casually dressed like most Cubans, stopped her, introduced himself as José, and asked her if this was her first time in Cuba. Sticking to Hamilton's training tips, she replied it was her third visit.

"You have a map in hand. Where are you going?"

"The Museum of the Revolution," she said.

"It's closed for renovations. Instead, allow me to walk you to a good place for breakfast."

Maybe he was just trying to get a free meal, but Nikki suspected he was a scammer who'd get a finder's fee from the restaurant for bringing her in.

"I'll take my chances on the museum," she said, quickly walking away.

Arriving at the museum, she found it perfectly open for visitors. She bought her ticket and entered. When she left, Nikki wondered what it meant that the revolutionary history was housed in the ornate former presidential palace with interior decoration by Tiffany Studios of New York. Everything the revolution stood against.

Other than the scammer trying to bring a naïve tourist to a restaurant, Nikki had not noticed anyone following her. She continued on her planned route, stopping to sit on a bench in a small park to study her map. That move should help her spot anyone who might be tracking her. She identified one possibility but moved on to the Cathedral of the Immaculate Conception. It was smaller, making it easier to scout out anyone following her without alerting them. At least she hoped so. She paid the fee to visit the church and to climb the bell towers for a view of the city. An old man in the ticket booth took her money.

He handed her the ticket and asked where in Mexico she came from.

"The state of Aguascalientes."

"My son worked at the Cuban embassy in Mexico City. He loved your country."

"I'm glad to hear that. How long was he there?" she asked.

"Six years. Raúl brought him back. My son is still with the government, I'm pleased to say." The man shook his head. "There are so many changes in Cuba these days. One never knows from one day to the next if you'll have a job. We need Fidel back."

Nikki smiled and nodded. "I had not expected so many churches in Havana."

"We're a Catholic country. Very Catholic. Fidel let us worship and attend church. He knew that's what his people wanted. He called us a secular nation, not an atheist one."

Nikki nodded. Hamilton had told them that unlike some other

socialist nations, Cubans could join the Communist Party and not renounce their faith.

"I'm still a member and proud of it."

"That's wonderful," Nikki said. Thanking him, she entered the cathedral and marveled at the ornate neoclassic decoration with beautiful paintings and frescoes styled after Rubens and Murillo. It reminded her of churches she had visited in Mexico as a teenager.

On the stairs of the larger bell tower, Nikki felt someone following her. At the top, heart pounding, she glanced through the belfry opening to gaze upon the city. She turned to look at the man who had ascended immediately behind her. Young and handsome, he was by himself. She'd also seen him at the Museum of the Revolution.

"Magnificent view." His Spanish had a heavy Cuban accent.

Nikki agreed. Uncomfortable, she could feel the bulk of the wig inside the hidden pocket under her armpit.

"It's quite beautiful," she said. "I always thought my country had the most beautiful churches. Now I'll have to say Cuban churches rival the ones in Mexico."

"The Jesuits labored on it for many years before being expelled from the New World in 1767," he said. "Over the years, the interior has been remodeled to its present neoclassical design but the exterior has not changed. It's a UNESCO world heritage site."

"Interesting," Nikki said. "Are you a student of architecture?"

"History is my hobby. I'm a medical student, moonlighting as a tour guide. It's perfectly legal. I'm not a bisnero."

He looked at the plaza below.

Nikki followed his gaze and noticed more people milling around in the square.

Nikki could hire him, but he might be too interested in her activities. He could even report her to the authorities on a trumped-up charge.

"Tourists must still be afraid to travel for fear of the virus variants. Or the quarantine. It's hard to earn a living right now." He handed her a card with his name and phone number. "Let me know if I can be of service."

She thanked him. Looking at the card, she saw his name was Oliver Ortega.

"I understand Cubans have unusual names. Yet yours sounds North American."

"You're right. My parents left Cuba as children, met in Miami, and married there. They were unhappy when I applied to the university here, but I can study, work, and live more economically than I can at home. Though I live much better than the average Cuban."

Nikki's danger antennae started to relax but she knew she had to proceed with caution.

"So you're a US citizen?"

"Correct."

"Yet your Spanish is spoken with a perfect Cuban accent."

"Picked it up at home from my parents. Living here has also influenced my way of speaking."

Nikki glanced at her watch and back at Oliver, telling him she'd enjoyed talking with him.

"And your name?"

"Valentina."

"Be sure to walk along the malecón to see the beauty of Havana Bay known as the old port, Valentina. The Spanish founded this city in 1519. By the 1800s, it had become a leader in ship building and the most important port in the Caribbean."

He explained that Christopher Columbus had landed in Cuba in 1492, thinking he had sailed to Asia, and claimed the island for Spain. After that, Spaniards settled here. Throughout the centuries, Cuba maintained trade, economic, and social ties to Spain.

Oliver continued giving her tips on tourist attractions and things to do in Havana. He recommended that when she returned to the Vedado district, she should take in the beautiful National Hotel, a landmark on the oceanfront. "If you want to people watch, Café El Lucero is good and inexpensive. It's always crowded because that's where a lot of locals go. It's a block from the Museum of the Revolution."

"Whoa, stop. Any minute now you'll present me with an invoice," she said.

"What a great idea. I'll write it up now."

They both laughed.

She descended the stairs and he followed her. In the square, he wished her a good visit and walked away. Nikki's concern returned. The young man had obviously followed her. Was it to earn money, as he said? Or was he following her for more sinister reasons? If so, it would be difficult to shake him off.

Except for Café Lucero, she'd already planned to visit the places he mentioned. To make certain he was not following her, she would walk along the malecón, the wide esplanade with a walkway and sea wall, to the church of San Francisco. Eventually she would retrace her steps to the museum and stop at Café Lucero. That should flush him out or reveal anyone else following her.

If she found no one trailing her, she would walk the malecón in the opposite direction toward the Vedado district until it dead-ended at the Almendares River. The Meliá was still a considerable distance from the river. If she got tired, she'd take a taxi. If she detected someone following her, she'd have to lose the tail. Her primary task for today consisted in confirming she was invisible and squeaky clean before returning to her hotel.

CHAPTER TWENTY-TWO

Urbano sat through the morning's presentations with eyes burning with tears that he couldn't allow to fall. He felt numb. At the lunch break, he asked the Colombian who'd told him of Raquel's death to join him at a nearby restaurant. The two men walked a couple of blocks and went inside a small café. After ordering, Urbano choked up. Taking the napkin, he wiped away his tears.

"Raquel left me a few weeks before I came here. If only I'd known what would happen," he said, still choking up, "I would not have left. I was angry with her for moving out and the timing was right for a trip to Havana."

The Colombian doctor offered his condolences. Urbano could not recall the man's name. But his weeping made things awkward. They had just met, but he felt he could talk to his fellow doctor.

"I'd had a disagreement with my business partner," Urbano said. "So I stopped answering my phone and didn't listen to messages. Raquel and I had a tough time over the last few months. But this, I never expected anything so terrible. They threatened me, but I never thought they'd harm my wife. If I'd stayed there, she'd still be alive."

"You can't blame yourself," the man said.

The waiter set their lunch in front of them, asking if they needed anything else.

Urbano shook his head, lost in thought.

"Do you want to share who threatened you?" the man asked.

"What good would it do? She's gone." He picked up his fork mechanically. "Buen provecho."

"Bon appétit."

Urbano asked if a police investigation had been started, if funeral arrangements had been made, or if he should be aware of any other matters.

"I don't know them, but it's my understanding Raquel's parents are handling everything. I've been told they tried to contact you. Perhaps you should call them."

Moving food around his plate with a fork, Urbano looked up. "If they think I did it, they don't know me as well as I thought. But you're right, I should call them."

Urbano listened intently as the Colombian told him that circumstantial evidence on the case made him look guilty. He pointed out three issues: "Raquel is murdered, you leave town around the same time and travel to Cuba, a country that does not have an extradition treaty with the US. Plus, you've been unreachable by phone."

Urbano squinted at the man. Would a doctor say these things? "Who are you?"

"Carlos Ramírez, Colombian-born doctor now working in Mexico." It sounded memorized.

"No, that must be an assumed name. I want to know who you really are so we can talk honestly."

The man remained quiet. That he was Colombian, Barriga had no doubt. Perhaps he and his guest were considering the same question. And that was whether each could trust the man sitting in front of him.

"I *am* a doctor, neurosurgeon, and Colombian born, as I said. Guess you could say that I'm doing a bit of private investigative work here."

"Who hired you?"

"A friend of yours."

Urbano shook his head. "My friends in Mexico wouldn't have hired you."

"I know people in Miami who know you."

"Is anyone else with you?"

"My wife, Valentina."

Urbano studied him again. The man was clearly holding back a lot of information.

"And you probably think I've committed murder?"

"Have you killed anyone?" the man calling himself Carlos asked.

"I did not kill Raquel. I would never murder anyone."

Urbano then shared the case that weighed on his mind. Last year, he'd brought a young Miami girl, and her parents, to Cuba for therapy. They waited out the five-day quarantine and taken COVID tests together. Then she had her treatment, a regenerative transplant. It went badly. Her parents, especially the father, thought Urbano had been negligent. Despite his efforts to find another donor to save her, it had proven impossible.

"Can you give me the father's name?"

Urbano wasn't sure if the ploy would work, but he'd heard that police had to answer truthfully.

"Are you an undercover police detective from Miami?"

The man laughed. "Not at all. If I were, I'd be in violation of several international laws. I don't believe in asking for trouble."

"His name is Benjamín Ávila. Goes by Benjy. Blamed me for his daughter's death and said he would take revenge. He's Venezuelan. And Raquel's cousin." Urbano looked at the man sitting across from him. "Can I believe you're not working for him?"

"If I were a hired gun, I would have killed you by now. I swear I never heard of Ávila until you mentioned him."

Urbano told him Ávila could not be trusted.

"Would he have killed Raquel?"

Urbano mulled it over. It was possible. But he'd always thought Ávila admired Raquel. He shook his head. A lot of people had admired his wife. He couldn't imagine why anyone would kill her.

The Colombian asked Urbano who else might have been motivated to kill her.

Changing the subject, Urbano asked if the man liked Cuban food.

Glancing at his half-eaten plate, the Colombian looked uncomfortable, maybe afraid of offending his host. "I've eaten worse, but I've eaten better."

Without hesitation, Urbano invited him to his apartment for dinner that night at his house for a better meal than visitors could get at hotels and most restaurants. "And of course, bring your wife."

CHAPTER TWENTY-THREE

Charlotte was waiting for Floyd to return to the office to tell him she'd been unable to find any further information on Spider Candella. The post office box that had been rented in his name for one month was all she'd found. She'd even looked up people elsewhere in Florida with the surname Candella and did not find a single one.

"If you can't find him," Floyd said, "then no one can."

"The connection to the Rodríguez family is there," she said, "It's not a coincidence that Andrea's medicine was mailed to that box right before she disappeared. When Nikki asked me to find Spider Candella, I even stopped by to speak to the pharmacist, but he said he didn't remember anything about it."

"The pharmacist probably wouldn't say anything without a warrant. This Spider Candella is connected to the parents all right. What's the connection to Raquel or Barriga?" Floyd sounded as if he were thinking out loud.

"Candella must be connected to the girl's disappearance," she said.

Floyd whistled. "By god, I think I have it. Spider Candella may belong to the Cuban spy system here in Miami. Otherwise why would he be untraceable?"

"Then JSOC, Joint Special Command Operations, or the FBI could probably find him." Charlotte thought Floyd could make a call to get more information on the guy.

Floyd scoffed. "I'd need more information than that to ask for a favor."

Charlotte suggested meeting up with the guard, Téllez. She could work with him on a composite photo of the woman. From her research, she knew today was Téllez's day off and he'd probably be at home right now.

"Good idea. Look up his address," Floyd said.

Charlotte grinned. "He lives on the west side."

"Then what are we waiting for?" Floyd asked.

Packing her laptop, she followed him outside. From the passenger seat, she tapped the address into Floyd's navigator.

Floyd glanced at the GPS map on his car screen. "Good lord, it's practically the Everglades. Maybe I should call to make sure he'll be there."

"As you wish, but I think surprise is better. It's early and he was probably at the tango club until late last night."

More than an hour later, they arrived at an apartment complex. Floyd knocked on the door while Charlotte stayed in the SUV.

A sleepy and hungover Téllez, dressed in boxer shorts, opened the door.

Explaining why he'd driven out, Floyd emphasized the importance of preparing a composite picture of Raquel's attacker so they could interview her and get closer to locating the killer.

"I don't want to get involved."

"I'll keep you totally out of this," Floyd assured the man. "Go get some pants on so my assistant can come in to work with you."

Floyd and Charlotte waited outside while the guard dressed. Finally he invited them in. Téllez sheepishly apologized for his studio apartment. "It's usually cleaner than this."

"We came to talk to *you*, not your sofa or your stove," Charlotte said, smiling as she looked around. "May I move these dishes so we can sit at the table?"

Téllez piled the dishes in the sink. Then he wiped the table.

"I'll be using software developed in the UK," Charlotte explained. "It's called E-FIT. You'll look at groupings of faces and we'll narrow it down from there. It's easy, fun, and will probably take us an hour to get a good likeness."

"You won't be drawing the face?" Téllez sounded disappointed.

"We use technology now. You've seen too many movies." Charlotte glanced at Téllez. "But I think the FBI still has skilled artists do handmade sketches whenever they can."

"And you're not going to tell anyone that I helped you. Right?"

"You have my word," Floyd said.

Using the app, Charlotte guided Téllez to select facial traits until the composite resembled the person he'd seen. When they were almost finished, he ran his hands over his head to demonstrate her disheveled hair. Charlotte made the final adjustments.

"That looks just like the woman," Téllez said. "You're amazing."

"Thanks," Charlotte smiled. "Glad you think so."

As they drove back to the office, Floyd asked Charlotte to find the bus drivers scheduled on the Deep Sea Cruises neighborhood between two and six p.m. She opened her laptop and started working.

"You didn't ask the guard about Spider Candella," she said.

"The police might interview Téllez, and I'd rather keep Spider to ourselves for now."

By the time he dropped her off at the office, Charlotte had found the driver most likely to have been on the route the day Raquel was assaulted.

CHAPTER TWENTY-FOUR

Floyd parked two blocks away from Deep Sea Cruises and walked to the corner. He stood there for fifteen minutes before he saw a bus. He hoped the guard had been right that the mystery woman had boarded a bus headed toward the city center. Soon he'd start to unravel her identity.

Acting like a passenger at the bus stop, Floyd got on.

"I'm an investigator with a quick question." Floyd flashed his badge to the driver and then showed him the composite of the woman. "Did you see this woman almost three weeks ago?"

The driver peered suspiciously at Floyd. "This is not the place to do this."

"It'll take a minute, unless you prefer to come to my office."

He took the picture from Floyd's hand. "I'll never forget that hair," he said. "Yeah, she got on."

"Did she say anything?"

"When I saw her hair, I thought she was either drunk or a street person. But then I noticed her clothes. Expensive. I asked if she was okay."

"What did she say?" Floyd asked.

"That she was hopping mad and wanted to kill that puta chonga."

"Did she say who that whore was?"

The driver shook his head. He handed the composite back.

"Did you notice anything else?"

Tilting his head to indicate the direction, he added, "She got off the bus three blocks up."

"Anything else?"

He blinked several times, as if he were thinking.

"After she got off, I checked my rearview mirror. She got into a silver sedan. A Nissan Maxima, I think. Plate with the big U in orange and green, the colors of the University of Miami."

"Do you remember any of the numbers?"

The driver shook his head. "Like you said, it's been almost three weeks."

Floyd thanked him and stepped down to the sidewalk. Walking back to his SUV, he called Charlotte, gave her the details he'd obtained, and asked her to do what she could to find that car.

———

Back at the office, Floyd was reviewing reports on other cases. He kept expecting Charlotte to barge in at any moment and tell him she'd found a silver Nissan Maxima with a university license plate. Not wanting to pressure her, he kept busy on other matters. He knew she would find an answer to his request the way she found everything else, fingers flying over her keyboard. And then she'd bring the data to him.

After reviewing the other cases, Floyd called Sergeant Maldonado and asked if the police had found anything significant in the hunt for the missing teenager.

Maldonado told him they'd done an exhaustive hunt for the Rodríguez girl. "We get too many of these cases. It's like a spaceship swooped in and carried her off. Just like other kids who are never found."

Floyd considered pointing out that traffickers often did exactly that, but he let it pass.

"My department can't spend any more time on the Rodríguez case," he told Floyd. "Have you found anything?"

"Nothing so far," Floyd responded, sensing Maldonado was anxious to negotiate. "Are you working the Raquel Álvarez murder?"

"Yep. But we haven't made much progress there either. As a

professional courtesy, would you contact me if you find anything on the Rodríguez girl?"

"Be happy to," Floyd said. "I'd ask you to reciprocate if you get any concrete developments with the murder case."

Completing the call, Floyd grabbed a fresh cup of coffee. Then he dropped by Charlotte's office.

"Have you found anything on the Nissan so far?"

"Working on it." She looked up from her computer. "I've found five cars that fit the description."

Floyd figured she was narrowing the parameters to the most likely prospects.

She told Floyd she was eliminating two that belonged to students. "That leaves me with three cars that meet the description. The only problem is that they're registered to men."

"Our blonde must be married to one of them," Floyd said. "Or she's at least a friend."

Nodding her agreement, she kept bringing up files on her monitor so fast it made Floyd dizzy to watch.

"By cross referencing to another database to get the owners' ages, I've eliminated one last guy. Aha," she said. "It's got to be either one of these two."

She moved a chair closer for Floyd and showed him.

"There's a Steven Mohle and a Fernando Márquez," she said, asking Floyd if he wanted to visit them right away.

"Yep, let's head out now."

Charlotte sent herself a text message with the addresses for the two most probable options and picked up the envelope containing the composite. On their way out, they told the receptionist that they were off to find a person of interest.

CHAPTER TWENTY-FIVE

A man dressed in white shorts and a Tommy Bahama shirt in blue and purple palm fronds answered the door at the first place they stopped.

After identifying themselves as investigators, Floyd showed him the composite picture. He noticed a flicker of recognition in the man.

"We're trying to locate this woman."

"May I ask why?" The man's face reddened.

"She may know something about a crime," Floyd responded.

"What kind of crime?" The man shifted his weight and appeared uncomfortable.

"A woman was found dead in a canal in the Cutler Bay area recently. We've been told the woman in our drawing may have seen her a day or two before she died," Floyd said, holding the composite up again.

The man stared at Floyd, as if he were confused about the people at his front door. "A murder's been in the news, but the name hasn't been released."

"Sir," Charlotte said, "do you know this woman?"

"Is she in trouble?"

Floyd assured the man they only wanted to ask her a few questions.

"She's asleep. She's a nurse and works nights. Can you come back later?"

"I'm afraid not. We need to speak with her now," Floyd insisted.

The man introduced himself as Steve Mohle and invited them to enter and sit in the living room. Clearing his throat, he explained that Yésica, his wife, was the jealous type. He hoped there'd be nothing in the questioning to make her think the matter had anything to do with him.

"Not if you're not guilty," Charlotte said.

Mohle asked if he could stay while they questioned her.

"I'd like to interview both of you, but separately," Floyd said.

"What's going on, Spider?" a sleepy voice asked from another room.

Floyd and Charlotte glanced at each other.

A blonde woman in a teal robe burst into the room. Her hair looked as uncombed as it appeared in the composite picture. She saw Charlotte and frowned.

Floyd stood up. The woman's demeanor softened. He introduced himself and Charlotte, saying they needed a few words with her.

Her husband left the room. They could call him if they needed him.

"We're here to ask you a few questions about Raquel Álvarez," Floyd said. "But first, state your full name."

"Is Raquel going to sue me?"

"I doubt it," Charlotte said. "Dead people can't sue anyone."

"Dead?" the woman repeated. Her expression changed, she looked shocked. Before speaking, she inhaled loudly. "I had a public disagreement with her, but I didn't kill her."

"What did you say your name is?" Floyd asked again.

"Yésica. Yésica Fernández. Honest. I did not kill her." She dropped onto the sofa. "Can you call Spider? I think he went outside. He needs to hear this."

Charlotte left the room in search of Spider. She returned shortly with the husband in tow.

"Spider, did you know Raquel is dead?"

He turned white. Looking at his wife, he stuttered as he asked what had happened.

Floyd told him she had been found dead under a small pier in the canal behind her house. He mentioned that Barriga's partner, from the medical travel business, had also suffered a loss. The Rodríguez child was missing.

Yésica said they knew Delfina's daughter had disappeared. "You don't think the two incidents are connected, do you?"

"Oh my god, I must call Barriga," Spider said. "He should be back in town."

"Actually, no. We haven't been able to find him," Floyd said.

Spider's voice cracked. "You don't suppose he's also—"

"We don't know," Floyd said. "We hope he's safe. Do either one of you know where he might be?"

"He travels to Cuba. Taking people to his clinic in Havana for stem cell treatment," Yésica said. "Could it be that Raquel's cheating caused a murder-suicide?"

Spider jumped. "That's a mean thing to say. You have no evidence she was ever unfaithful to her husband. You can't seriously believe that rumor."

Charlotte looked at Yésica. "When was the last time you saw Raquel?"

"About two weeks ago. No, it's been more like three weeks. Anyway, I went to where she works. A mistake, I know. We . . . had an altercation."

"Explain," Floyd said.

"Spider was getting therapy from her. Twice a week, meditation using sound and music. After those sessions, my husband would get distant. A friend told me Raquel used music and special tea for Voodoo entrapment. She could hypnotize her patients and manipulate them to do whatever she wanted."

"And you believed that?" Floyd kept his tone free of the skepticism he felt.

"A friend told me. I decided to have a talk with Raquel." Yésica hesitated and looked at the floor.

"Go on," Floyd said.

"To demand she leave my husband alone. Our altercation happened in the parking lot."

Spider shook his head in apparent frustration as he listened to his wife.

Floyd turned to Spider and asked him when he'd last seen Raquel.

"About a month ago. The last session I had with her. She's a good counselor, especially for bereavement. My son died last year." He glanced at his wife. "Raquel helped me a lot. Then she and Barriga separated. She was too distraught to continue the therapy. But I continued at home with the process I'd learned from her."

Yésica quickly made it clear Spider's son was from his first marriage.

"My son overdosed and I felt guilty because I'd divorced his mother. If I'd stayed with her maybe it wouldn't have happened. Yésica didn't want to hear about it," Spider said, looking at Floyd. "My son and Yésica did not get along."

"But I told you to go to a psychiatrist, not a Voodoo healer," Yésica said, anger rising in her voice.

Spider protested that the sessions were not Voodoo. Yésica's voice rose even more as she called out aspects of the therapy she thought sounded like some occult practice.

Again Floyd interjected, asking them not to argue or he would have to interview them separately.

Spider and Yésica looked at Floyd. They both nodded.

"Do either of you know who might have wanted Raquel dead?" he asked.

Spider said he had no idea.

Yésica sighed. She shook her head.

Charlotte looked at Yésica and asked for the name of the friend who had called Raquel a Voodoo enchantress.

"My friend Delfina," she responded. "Delfina Morales."

Before leaving, Floyd handed Yésica a business card. "If you remember any details that might help us find Raquel's killer, please call me."

Charlotte chatted with Yésica as Spider and Floyd walked to the front door.

"I want to talk in private," he told Floyd under his breath.

"Call me," Floyd whispered back, handing him another card.

Spider suggested the Juan Valdez Café on Northeast Second Avenue in one hour.

CHAPTER TWENTY-SIX

Floyd had time to take Charlotte back to the office and return to the café. He sat where he could watch the entrance. Spider joined him shortly. A friendly server offered menus, but both men indicated they only wanted coffee.

Not one for small talk, Floyd said it would help if Mohle could explain why his wife calls him Spider.

"It's a childhood nickname."

"Tell me about it."

He explained, that as a kid, he'd been in the backyard, swimming in the pool, with his older brothers. When his mother served lunch one day under an old sycamore, a big spider dropped from the tree onto his plate. He'd started screaming. His family called him Spider after that. "Not a great beginning for my nickname, but I've grown to like it."

Floyd asked if the name Candella meant anything to him.

Spider looked surprised. "It was my father's surname. Dad walked out on us when I was six. My mother wanted to obliterate his memory, so she legally changed my surname to Mohle, which was her surname."

"That sounds German," Floyd said.

Spider nodded. "Mother was Argentine but her father had come from Germany."

"Do you use the name Candella?"

Spider shook his head. "Some people know about it, but I don't use it. When Yésica wants to get my attention, she'll call me Candella."

"What else can you tell me about it?"

"There's not much more to tell."

Floyd nodded. "Tell me why you wanted to see me."

Spider told Floyd he couldn't name a suspect in Raquel's murder, but Barriga had been threatened before he left. It was a man whose daughter had regenerative therapy. The girl died about a month after treatment.

"Why did she die?" Floyd asked.

"Apparently the stem cells were not properly matched. Barriga tried to find a match so the surgery could be redone, but he failed. He felt terrible about losing her."

Floyd asked if Barriga had done the surgery himself.

"No, it's done in Cuba. I understand the surgeons are top notch."

"What's the name of the man who lost his daughter?"

"Barriga never told me. He did say the man accused Barriga of killing his daughter through his negligence, and the man threatened to retaliate."

"As far as I know," Floyd said, "Barriga has no children. Is that correct?"

"That's right. He loves Delfina's daughter. He's the girl's godfather. A couple of times he told me that if he ever has a daughter, he'd want her to be like Andrea."

The comment provided Floyd with the perfect segue to his next question.

"When you rented the post office box and received the medication for Andrea, who did you give the meds to?"

"Meds? I don't understand what you're talking about. I've never had a PO box. Not anywhere."

Floyd told him a box was rented for one month to Spider Candella. Andrea's medications were sent there by the pharmacy, right before she disappeared. "And you don't know anything about it?"

"Not at all. Honest," Spider said, looking uncomfortable.

"It was the post office in your zip code. So if you didn't rent it, who did?"

"I hope it wasn't Yésica. I don't know why she'd do that. Unless Delfina asked her to. But don't you need identification to rent a box?"

"Correct," Floyd said. "People go to UPS for anonymous mail delivery. Name the people who could rent a postal box using your name."

"Besides Yésica, maybe Barriga, maybe Delfina. I can't think of anyone else. Perhaps Rodríguez."

"Ever had an ID under the name Spider Candella?"

Spider shook his head.

"Are you a close friend of Barriga's?" Floyd asked.

"We're good friends. Unfortunately, my wife doesn't—didn't care much for Raquel."

"Why?"

"Woman stuff, you know." Mohle shrugged. "Yésica admires Delfina, and Delfina doesn't like Raquel. Well, didn't like her when she was alive. Delfina can be very convincing. But let me tell you, Raquel was not practicing Voodoo."

Floyd entered Charlotte's office. "This case makes my head spin."

Charlotte told him Nikki had used the same words after visiting Raquel's parents.

"I wish she were here to talk this case through," he said.

When Charlotte suggested using the emergency channel on Nikki's watch or sending an encrypted message on her mobile, he shook his head.

"Too risky."

She shrugged. "Then you're stuck with me."

"How can you be so calm when we keep hitting a wall in this case?"

"It's probably how I'm wired. My parents were addicts. To survive, I learned not to take things too seriously. But when something gets to me, it gets bad."

He'd observed that Charlotte seemed to channel her stress into productivity. Then he thought about Nikki. When stress hit its highest peak, Nikki seemed to calm down.

"Maybe women manage stress better?"

"Aha! The male recognizes women may handle at least one thing better than men," Charlotte said, making him laugh.

Grounding himself back on the case, Floyd muttered out loud that they had another suspect—a man who lost his daughter after regenerative surgery in Cuba.

"Do you think Sergeant Maldonado has turned up as many suspects as we have?" she asked.

Floyd looked at her.

"I figure we have at least six suspects. Barriga and Rodríguez are prime suspects." Charlotte counted them off on her fingers. "Delfina is not far behind. And we can't rule out Spider or his synthetic blonde wife, despite their denials. And then there's the unsub Spider mentioned to you."

"The Rodríguez and Barriga families knew each other," he said. "Raquel's death and Andrea's disappearance happened about the same time. I can't think of one case without the other. But Maldonado is treating them as separate."

CHAPTER TWENTY-SEVEN

To distance herself from the moonlighting student, Nikki walked to the basilica of San Francisco de Asís, but it was closed.

On the way, she saw no one lurking in the bushes, behind a column, or in an outdoor café while pretending to read a newspaper.

She longed to know how Eduardo's day was developing. And she'd like to discuss Floyd's latest findings in Miami. The hardest part of being an investigator was building a case on minimal facts.

Proceeding along the malecón to take in views of the harbor, she diverted toward the Museum of the Revolution to find the café that Oliver had mentioned. She sat outside and ordered coffee and maduros. This would be where she'd flush out anyone following her. Savoring the sweet Cuban coffee and the plantain snack, she scanned for anyone tracking her.

Scrutinizing the wait staff, other customers, and people hanging around the café, she tried to determine if any of them could have her in their crosshairs. If someone did, she did not detect it. She stood to leave.

Then Nikki's pulse jumped. Oliver was leaning against the wall near the corner. He'd donned a floppy hat and sunglasses and looked like a tourist. She watched him as he approached a middle-aged couple sitting at the outermost table. He started talking to them. Still positioned to see her, he waved.

She wondered if Oliver's surveillance could be as bad as it looked. Or were the couple serving as camouflage? Maybe, just maybe, he'd found tourists to guide through Old Havana. Taking the devil by the horns, she walked toward them. Oliver grinned and gestured for her to join them. He introduced Nikki. The couple were from Spain, visiting Cuba for the first time.

Nikki asked where in Spain they lived.

"Somos madrileños," the man answered.

"Madrid, huh?" Nikki said. "Beautiful city."

"Do you want to join us on a walking tour?" the wife asked. "This young man is going to show us la Habana Vieja."

"Did you know he's a medical student?" Nikki asked. The woman glanced at him, showing surprise. "Why are you working? Don't you have to study a lot?"

"Tengo que resolver." Oliver chuckled. "I have to make ends meet."

"You have an excellent tour guide. He'll make your trip memorable," Nikki said. Glancing at her watch, she asked Oliver if he could recommend stores selling Cuban-made goods.

"You don't come to Cuba to shop," he said.

"No shopping? Why then do so many tourists visit?" the Spanish woman asked.

"To see an island frozen in time. The antique cars, la Habana Vieja, the port fortifications. And to enjoy the beaches."

"Frozen in time?" the husband asked.

"Most foreigners don't know that access to the internet and social media only became available in the last five years."

"No internet?" The husband smiled. "That's not such a bad thing. In Spain, we've lost our privacy."

"That's true in most countries." Nikki glanced at her watch once more and told them she had to get going.

The wife smiled and said goodbye.

Nikki walked away at a brisk pace, wondering if that was a genuine encounter with visiting Spaniards, or if it was a setup.

Once she put three city blocks between her and Oliver's tourists, she turned right, paced out two more blocks, and turned right twice more at street corners. She detected no one after her, not on foot and not in cars either.

MISSING IN MIAMI | 125

Feeling safe, she walked up the Taganana Hill to the National Hotel. Two cupolas rose above the roof, giving the hotel an antique feeling. They must have once served for ventilation or to allow natural light into the building. The hill, with its view of the ocean and its outcropping of rocks, contributed to the beauty of the landmark.

At the hotel entrance, she hopped a cab to the Quinta Avenida Habana Hotel. Once there, she found a ladies' room and waited a few minutes before walking six blocks to the Meliá. She hadn't seen anyone even remotely suspicious after leaving Oliver and the Spaniards near the café.

Eduardo was waiting in the suite when Nikki finally entered. He kissed her in greeting and suggested going for a walk. He could hardly wait to tell her about his day. But Nikki wanted to shower first. Eduardo paced the room as she dressed.

After they left the hotel, Nikki told him she'd tired of carrying the wigs and had left them in the chest of drawers. She'd bring them with her again when she had a real mission to accomplish—like once they had actual information on Andrea.

Eduardo took her hand, anxious to update her about Barriga.

"I told Barriga a mutual acquaintance had asked me to tell him something unfortunate. Then I dropped the terrible news about Raquel. He steadied himself against the wall. He seemed genuinely stunned."

"Was he shocked because you came out of nowhere with the news, or was he truly upset about Raquel's death?"

"Both," Eduardo said. "He wanted to know if our mutual friend was Benjy Ávila."

"I haven't heard that name," Nikki said. "What did you say?"

"That I didn't know Ávila, but that I couldn't say who sent me."

"You took a huge risk." Nikki adjusted her purse over her shoulder and asked where they were going for dinner.

"There's more. I thought, what the hell. I asked if he knew about Andrea's disappearance."

"You didn't! Damn it, Eduardo, you've blown our cover." She dropped his hand.

He'd never seen Nikki this angry with him. "I blew mine, but it seemed appropriate to get facts. I'm still using the fake name and he doesn't know you're the real investigator."

"Well, that makes me feel safe," Nikki said sarcastically. "If the DI picks you up, do you think they'll let me keep running around the streets like a tourist?"

They approached a crowded intersection and fell silent. They crossed the street and Eduardo still kept quiet. The roar of an accelerating bus passed them, black smoke billowing in its wake.

"Now that our cover's blown, don't keep me in suspense. Tell me the rest."

Eduardo told her Barriga had looked away without speaking when he mentioned Andrea's disappearance. "When he finally spoke, he said the word Rodríguez. I assumed he meant Rodríguez was our mutual acquaintance, but maybe he meant Rodríguez was at fault for Andrea vanishing."

Nikki coughed. "Maybe he meant Rodríguez is Andrea's last name."

"I told him I'd never spoken with Rodríguez," Eduardo said. "I did tell him that the person who'd told me about Raquel had mentioned the teenager. At that point, he asked me if I was traveling alone or if I had anyone with me."

Nikki pulled on Eduardo's arm, stopping him.

"He needed to know that in case he wants to get rid of you."

Eduardo told her Barriga had been worried for his own safety. He must have thought that whoever killed Raquel was now here to kill him. "And he thought I was the hired gun."

"Then you said nothing about me?" Nikki asked again.

"If I lied, you and I couldn't share a room, walk together, eat together, do anything together. So of course, I told him my beautiful wife was with me. Then he invited us to dinner. A tactic I was going to use. He beat me to it."

Eduardo took a piece of paper from his pocket. "That's where we're headed. To his apartment."

Nikki gasped. "That's dangerous."

"It's as safe as anywhere. Plus he claims he'll give us a better meal than most of the restaurants here."

"It's not the food that worries me. It's hidden cameras and recording devices. I don't want to be hauled off by the DI."

Nikki stopped abruptly.

"He may have murdered Raquel. What if he's setting us up and plans to kill us? Or worse, report us to the police?"

"I'm willing to take a little risk for better food." Eduardo chuckled.

"Don't joke," she said. "I can't defend us. I don't even have a taser with me."

CHAPTER TWENTY-EIGHT

T he offices for SunNSand Getaways were more subdued than
Floyd had expected. Plain in comparison to the Rodríguez
home. Maybe the partners didn't want to display wealth to their
clients.

Floyd waited in the reception area until Rodríguez finished a meeting.
Finally, the receptionist led him down the hall. Rodríguez was typing on a
laptop when Floyd greeted him. He stood and shook Floyd's hand, asking
him to take a seat.

"I don't think you're here about regenerative procedures," Rodríguez
said in a strong Cuban accent, "so how may I help you?"

"Actually, I am here to inquire about a procedure," Floyd responded.
"One that took place about six months ago. A girl was taken to Havana
for treatment. Unfortunately, she died."

Floyd waited a few seconds.

Rodríguez frowned. "Our clients sign waivers that clearly explain
possible complications, including death. The case you speak of was not
my patient, so I don't see the relevance."

Floyd shifted in his chair, studying Rodríguez. He needed to phrase
the request without providing too many details. He told the man that
information about the transplant incident in Havana might help Security
Source bring his daughter home.

"You come here asking about another case. That girl's death had nothing to do with me. What about Andrea?"

Floyd told Rodríguez he needed to speak with the father of the unfortunate girl that died. Not that the girl's father was suspected in Andrea's disappearance, but the man could lead them to people of interest.

"What do you need to know?" Rodríguez asked.

"Details of the young patient's death. What went wrong? How did the parents, particularly the father, respond to her death? How did your partnership handle the family's grievances?"

"The girl sustained spinal cord injuries playing soccer. She lost bladder and stool control and the use of both legs. She lived with a lot of pain. After physical therapy and the best care available in the US, the family decided to take her to Cuba. Stem cell rehabilitation is used in the US, but the transplant they were seeking is not yet approved here."

"Do you know how the father acted toward the soccer coach and the other players?" Floyd asked.

The doctor shook his head and looked away. "All I know is he demanded his money back from us, which my business partner refunded immediately after she died. And even gave him more as a goodwill gesture, or something like that."

"Is that it? Surely, you can fill in some details."

Rodríguez stole a glance at Floyd and sighed. "The surgeon discovered he'd used the wrong stem cells in the transplant. The patient remained in intensive care in Havana. Barriga did his best to find another donor. It's ironic. The lab technician and medical team were to blame. Yet the father took it out on my partner."

"I need the father's name."

When Rodríguez hesitated, giving an excuse of confidentiality, Floyd stared into the doctor's eyes.

"An American child died in Havana after a stem cell transplant organized by a Miami-based travel agency. The police would come with a warrant to obtain the full case files." Floyd paused. "Think about the bad publicity you'd get once it hit the news."

Rodríguez seemed to consider his options. "Benjamín Ávila."

"Address? And give me his business address too."

Picking up the phone, Rodríguez asked the receptionist to give Ávila's personal and business contact information to the investigator on his way out.

"You come here and demand information. You don't even know where my daughter is, do you? And what's happened to the detective working with us?"

"Nikki's in Canada, following a lead."

"Canada? Why didn't you inform us? Do you think Andrea is in Canada?"

"I've kept Delfina informed," Floyd said. "At this point, we're pursuing several leads. We're not wasting time in Canada; I can assure you. The minute we find her, we'll be in touch with you and Delfina."

Rodríguez's expression became somber and sad. "Is she still alive?"

"We have reason to believe she is, but I cannot guarantee anything."

"The police are doing nothing. It's up to you to find her." Rodríguez shook his head. "My wife sits at home depressed, worrying all the time. She can't concentrate. I'm afraid Delfina could lose her job."

Floyd asked Rodríguez about Barriga's absence.

"I don't know where he is. I've told you everything I know. I can't reach him by phone, so I'm in the dark as much as you." Rodríguez shrugged and opened his hands, palms facing up.

Floyd stood. "We're doing everything we can. Believe me, Andrea is our priority."

Even though it was late, Floyd headed for the engineering building on Northwest Sixty-Second Avenue where Ávila worked. On the drive over, he called Ávila's number. It went directly to voicemail.

At the building, Floyd checked in with a guard. A few minutes later, another guard escorted him to the fifth floor to meet Ávila.

A short, stout, dark-complexioned man greeted him. Straight jet-black hair and a prominent aquiline nose gave the man a raven-like appearance. Thick-framed glasses partially hid his small beady eyes. He invited Floyd into his office.

"Thanks for meeting me," Floyd said, handing the man a business card. "I'm here about the surgery your daughter underwent in Havana."

The man said it was about time for an inquiry. The situation had devastated his family.

Picking up on Ávila's willingness to talk, Floyd asked him how events had unfolded.

Ávila spoke with a slight accent. The man seemed understandably emotional as he explained what led to his daughter's death. And there was no doubt he was resentful and angry at Barriga.

"What, exactly, caused your daughter's death?"

"Simple incompetence. They gave her stem cells that did not match. She got so sick. It was pitiful." The man stopped speaking, shook his head, and looked down. "Barriga kept telling us he would find a donor who matched, but he never did."

"No one in your family could donate?"

Ávila shook his head and clamped his lips as if to avoid breaking down.

When Floyd moved the conversation toward Raquel's death, Ávila acted surprised at the news.

"Raquel? Dead? That can't be. Raquel's my cousin." His voice had gone up in volume. He took a few seconds to compose himself. "My aunt told me nothing. When did this happen? I'll tell you Barriga is a Jekyll and Hyde. People close to him always get hurt."

Floyd explained that her body had been found more than three weeks earlier in the canal behind her rented house in Cutler Bay. Police had not released her name pending notification of her husband. And the autopsy was not yet complete.

"Cutler Bay? Did she and Barriga get divorced?"

Floyd provided a few details about the separation.

"Barriga is not only incompetent. He's evil. Probably killed his wife. My cousin was a beautiful woman and she helped so many people," Ávila said. "Have the police picked Barriga up?"

"We don't know where he is. I was hoping you could help us."

"He'd be in Cuba. Yes, no doubt. Cuba. It has no extradition with the US, so he would hide there. He takes Americans and Canadians to get regenerative transplants there. You'll never get him out for prosecution of my cousin's death."

"Let me make sure I understand you. You sound certain that your daughter died because of Barriga's incompetence. Did he perform the actual surgery?"

"No, but Barriga and his partner are so greedy, they take risks with patients. He might as well have done the transplant. The clinic, the regenerative medicine part, moves to his every whim. He lines hotels up where family members can stay, where patients go to recuperate. My daughter never left the intensive care unit after the transplant, but we were there for over a month. I regret we ever took her to Cuba."

"Is there any possibility someone else was at fault. The lab, perhaps?"

"No way. He runs the place. Besides, I know my daughter's death caused friction in his marriage. If Raquel left him, that speaks for itself—she thinks, or rather, she thought his negligence caused my Lolita's death."

"Did Raquel say that?"

"Not in those words. But she talked to me several times, telling me I could find solace by finding God. She said she'd told her husband to find God, too. So she knew he was guilty."

Floyd asked if Raquel practiced Santería.

Shaking his head, Ávila explained some people he knew thought Raquel practiced Santería or even Voodoo. "But Santería is Cuban. Raquel's not—sorry, she *was not* Cuban."

"Would Raquel have believed in her own version of Santería?"

Ávila removed his glasses and rubbed his eyes as he considered the question.

"She helped many people, the grieving, the suffering, and the desperate, by encouraging them to pray. She guided them in meditation and used music as part of the healing process."

"Did you have an argument with Barriga that led you to threaten retaliation against his family?" Floyd asked.

"Who told you that?"

"Let's just say I have ways to uncover facts."

Ávila pursed his lips. "I did not kill my cousin. I was angry and may have told Barriga I'd take revenge for what he did, but I would never kill anyone. Never."

Thanking him, Floyd asked him to call if he thought of anything that might lead to Barriga. Or if he had any idea who could have wanted Raquel dead.

CHAPTER TWENTY-NINE

Nikki, still furious, asked how far it was to Barriga's place. Eduardo told her they should take a taxi to the Almendares River, where the malecón started, and walk from there to Barriga's apartment. They'd turn onto N Street, two blocks before the National Hotel.

Families were out, walking, talking, laughing, and enjoying the ocean breeze along the sea wall. A scrawny dog found a cup and licked the interior.

A band played salsa and Nikki saw people dancing. She moved to the rhythm and soon Eduardo joined her. He took her hand and led her into a triple spin and a single spin, then guided her into a spin by herself. When the piece was over Nikki threw her arms around his neck and kissed him. The dance had melted her anger.

After a few more minutes of watching the spirited crowd, their lively dancing, and the even livelier music, Eduardo took Nikki's hand again. They walked until they saw the National Hotel and they crossed the street.

Nikki slowed to watch a group of girls playing hopscotch. She smiled, remembering childhood games she'd participated in when she visited her grandparents in Oaxaca. It'd been a long time since she'd seen anyone playing hopscotch.

A man walked behind them. Not close, but he seemed to be watching them. He crossed the street after they did. She felt palpitations in her chest. Using their finger messages, she informed Eduardo.

He traced a circle in her palm, meaning they should go around the block. After turning right, Nikki checked. The man had gone straight ahead. They took a second right, a third one, and by then she confirmed no one was following them. When she caught sight of the National Hotel again, Nikki remembered the extra precautions she had taken returning to the Meliá that afternoon. While Eduardo had been at the conference blowing their cover with Barriga.

"We should be more cautious, as Hamilton advised."

"Okay. I goofed up today. But how could I have told Barriga about Raquel and Andrea without revealing some information?"

Nikki sighed. "I'm not sure. But I'm thinking about what we do at his apartment. What if he attacks one of us?"

"If he attacks me, hit him with something so we can get away. And then we go straight to the airport."

Nikki agreed. They arrived at the building and looked for a doorbell. Not seeing one, they took the elevator to his floor and knocked on his apartment door.

A friendly Barriga opened the door. "Carlos. Good to see you again. Do come in."

The aroma of cooking was equally inviting. Lively salsa music came from a speaker on a side table in the dining room.

"Doctor Barriga, this is my lovely wife Valentina," Eduardo said, introducing them.

"A pleasure. Call me Urbano." He bowed slightly.

Nikki wondered if Barriga used music to prevent the conversation from being recorded. Or maybe he just wanted to add a touch of Cuban atmosphere. Regardless, it would prevent their conversation from being overheard.

Their host seemed awkward, as if he were not accustomed to entertaining. He offered them a Cuba Libre, rum and Coke with lime juice. The nonalcoholic option was a malta.

Nikki, being cautious, took a malta. Eduardo chose the rum and Coke. Nikki listened to Barriga explain to Eduardo how to make a Cuba Libre. Her ear was getting more accustomed to the Cuban accent.

Barriga served the drinks.

"I'm going to grill spiny rock lobster. It's different from Maine lobster. I buy it from a bisnero. His shellfish is fresher than the ones from the government stores."

Nikki had heard the medical student use that term and she guessed it meant something like an illegal business.

"You can follow me to the balcony, if you wish to awaken the curiosity of the neighbors," the host announced.

A few minutes later Nikki and Eduardo sat at the table in the small dining area. Barriga served them congrí. He described making it with onion, lots of garlic, bell peppers, chunks of Spanish sausage, mountains of cumin and cilantro, and olive oil in a rice and bean mixture.

"A typical Cuban dish," he said. "When my mother cooked it when I was a kid, we'd stand in line with our ration cards for hours to get the rice and beans. Of course, the Spanish sausage was never available. Ration cards have almost disappeared now. Salaries are still low, and food is government subsidized, except for the dollar stores that have opened in the last ten years."

"A lady who owns a travel agency told me Cuba is changing," Nikki said.

"Cuba may not be changing as much as some anticipate," Barriga said, joining them at the table. "Some want our system to stay as it has been for the past sixty years. Before 2008, all jobs were supplied by the government. There was comfort in a guaranteed job. Now entrepreneurs can make a living with their own businesses. Many hope to improve their lives through the opening of the economy. They want freedom to prevail."

"How will it impact you?" Eduardo asked.

Shaking his head, Barriga looked sad. "I don't know yet."

"You've been able to come and go frequently," Eduardo said.

Barriga stared at his food. "That's my agreement with the government. It's been honored so far, but that could change at any time. I've brought many tourists to Cuba. It's helped the economy a lot." His voice trailed off until the music made him inaudible.

No one spoke. The music continued its lively beat.

"I did not invite you here to be sad. We Cubans are a happy lot."

Then he passed something to Eduardo. Two handwritten notes, one on top of the other. "Instructions," Barriga said, looking at Carlos, "on how to get to a dessert place tonight."

Nikki asked about the music, and Eduardo discreetly read the notes.

They resumed eating. The lobster was indeed different from any Nikki had eaten before. It was bland but nice. The rice and bean dish, by contrast, was spicy and delicious.

"I called my in-laws today. Understandably, they are shattered." Barriga brushed his napkin under his nose, covering his emotions.

Turning to Valentina, he asked if she knew that Raquel, his wife, had been murdered.

Nikki nodded and said she was sorry for his loss.

"I've been told not to leave the country until the new Cuban president provides guidelines on relations between the US and Cuba," Barriga said. "But I'll ask to leave for Raquel's funeral." Anxiety battled with sadness on his face.

Eduardo asked what the chances would be to get the permission granted.

His host waved away the question, instead asking Valentina what she thought of Cuba.

"Havana is beautiful. The historical parts are the most interesting. I went to la Habana Vieja today and it's more picturesque than I'd imagined."

Nikki told Barriga about visiting the museum, the churches, seeing El Morro from across the waterway, and discovering a great café near the museum. She wondered if the topic of conversation took his mind away from losing his wife, or if, like so many men, he avoided showing emotion.

CHAPTER THIRTY

After dinner, Urbano suggested to Carlos and Valentina that they go out for dessert. He'd handed a note with the address to Carlos. The other note was the important one, saying he needed to speak about personal matters.

When they hit the street, Urbano told them they could talk as they walked, unless someone got close enough to hear. "A very good restaurant in the gay district makes the best ice cream in town."

"Gay district?" Nikki asked. "I thought communist countries opposed gay marriage."

Urbano smiled. Outsiders often assumed that all communist countries were alike. "Things are changing all over. Here in Cuba, the gay district has been around for quite a while. Fidel's brother, Raúl, is rumored to be gay. It's not publicly talked about. Maybe out of respect for his late wife, who knows. They had four children together."

Urbano, talking with the man whose name he thought was Carlos, asked him to keep the note with directions to the restaurant. The other one should be torn up, the pieces dropped along the way.

"I have two questions." Carlos tore the note into tiny fragments as he spoke. "Does the Cuban government always approve your departures from the island? And do you hold a green card in the US or are you a citizen?"

Urbano asked if he could be frank in front of Valentina.

"Of course," she said. "I'm not a spy. At least not yet."

He told them about Cuba's economic difficulties after the Soviet Union collapsed in 1991. Russia stopped sending foreign aid, even stopped buying Cuba's sugar. The island was desperate for cash. Fidel called this the Special Period.

"It didn't take Fidel long to realize he had to generate income, and in the mid-1990s, he opened the island to tourism. That helped, but it did not bring in as much money or create as many jobs as projected.

"By the time I graduated from medical school and had acquired a bit of experience, I saw an opportunity. In 2005, I petitioned the Cuban government. If they approved my move to Miami, I would get a green card and open a travel business to bring tourists and people seeking medical care from the US and Canada. Cuba's expertise and treatment options in stem cell therapies are far superior to those offered in the US. You see, I started working in stem cell research from my university days, so I know the field well.

"Fidel bought into the concept. I was granted permission in 2006, the year he transitioned the government to his brother Raúl. The major condition was that I could not apply for US citizenship. And my travel agency was started with Cuban money. It was never spoken of, but if I defected, I'd likely be hunted down and probably killed."

Urbano stopped to let a man pass. At that moment, he noticed that Valentina looked across the street and put a hand to her chest. In a whisper, Urbano asked her what was wrong.

"It's nothing. Just a Spanish couple that I saw at a café near la Habana Vieja. I thought they might recognize me, but they didn't look this way."

When Urbano spoke again, he reminded them that anyone in hearing range might be a spy. "Most Cubans are good people, but you never know when a spy might report something to the police."

Urbano started walking once more.

"I've always had approval to travel back and forth. My stem cell business, and my tourist business, brought in people with money to spend. Even after Raúl took over, my travel to the US was never questioned."

"The only issue now is that you're at the whim of the new president," Carlos said.

"That is worrisome." Urbano lowered his voice. "The travel agency earned a profit from the time I opened. As it grew, I took on a partner and split profits with him.

"In retrospect, I might have done it differently. But defecting in a homemade boat seemed too risky. Especially since my girlfriend had discovered she was pregnant."

"Did your girlfriend go with you?" Valentina asked.

He shook his head. "She married someone else." His guests didn't need to know how much that had hurt.

The street became more crowded. They walked in silence for almost a block. Once they had some distance from passersby, Urbano vowed he'd find a way to return for Raquel's funeral. And if that proved impossible, he would have a memorial service when he could. He'd told his in-laws that if his stay in Cuba was prolonged, they were to do what they wanted to give Raquel a proper burial.

"I loved Raquel. If I'd only known, I would never have left Miami." He lowered his voice again. Telling them he probably shouldn't even say this, he said, "If I'm approved, I'll leave for the funeral and never come back."

As they walked, Urbano noticed that Valentina searched the faces of passersby, as if she were trained in surveillance.

"Are you checking for the Spanish couple?" he asked. "If you see them following us, let me know. But it's getting dark. And here we are, the best ice cream in Havana."

His guests seemed to enjoy their frozen dessert.

Leaving the restaurant, a rugged young man outside was engaged in a confrontation with the maître. The young man's girlfriend pulled on his hand and asked him to take her home. He continued arguing with the maître that Cuba was his country. "If I have the money to eat here, you cannot deny me entrance," the young man said loudly.

His girlfriend was finally able to coax him to leave.

Walking down the street, Urbano felt compelled to explain the scene they'd all observed. He told them that the restaurant where he'd taken them catered to tourists. "Young people, earning money as cuentapropistas, resent that they cannot dine in places reserved for foreign tourists."

Urbano stopped at the next street corner. Carlos thanked him for the home-cooked meal. He added that there was one more topic to talk about. Andrea.

The street was poorly lit, and Urbano was glad they couldn't judge his reaction.

"I also wanted to talk about Andrea," he said. "She's my goddaughter. But it's getting late. Let's talk tomorrow after the conference."

Urbano flagged an empty taxi for his guests.

The car rolled up to the curb. Barriga opened the door for Valentina. Carlos slid in after her.

"Take them to the Meliá," he said, handing the driver a wad of bills. "Don't pick anyone else up. Understood?"

The old taxi roared down the street, spitting fumes that Nikki could smell. She rolled up the window. She was happy when she saw the malecón up ahead.

"An interesting night," she said, and taking Eduardo's hand, she signaled she wanted to take a walk so they could talk.

As the driver started to turn onto the wide boulevard by the seawall, a Lada with flashing halogen lights swerved ahead of them, cutting them off. The taxi driver stopped. "I'm sorry," he said, looking back at them.

Two armed men got out of the Lada and headed toward them.

CHAPTER THIRTY-ONE

Floyd was catching the world news after dinner while Milena cleaned the kitchen. He'd offered to help, but she told him to relax. Then his mobile rang, a call automatically forwarded from the office.

The caller identified herself as Raquel's mother, Carolina Castillo. She'd tried Nikki but got no answer. So she'd called the other number on Nikki's business card. She asked how she could talk to Nikki.

Floyd explained that she was in Canada working on a case. The caller sounded upset, so he asked if he could help.

Hesitant at first, Carolina soon opened up and said she'd spoken earlier that evening to Benjamín Ávila.

"I feel uncomfortable talking about him. After all, he's my nephew."

"Whatever information you have might help find the suspect in Raquel's case. Besides, our conversation is confidential."

"I'm not sure about what I'm going to say. But Benjy was so bitter about his daughter's death that I thought Nikki or someone from your office should interview him. I'd hate to think he killed Raquel to get back at Urbano, but he's always been a bit of a troublemaker. And he'd threatened revenge for his daughter's death."

"Can you tell me what he said?" Floyd heard Carolina sniffling.

"He called to give his condolences about Raquel's death. Then he said that people around Barriga always get hurt. He referred to our son-in-law as the assassin. After a half hour of listening to him, I was in tears." She paused, then went on. Her nephew's adamant blaming of Barriga made her think he was trying to exonerate himself.

Floyd could tell Carolina had broken down and was crying.

"Raquel was Urbano's only family." Carolina broke into sobs again. "How else could Benjy avenge his daughter's death?"

"I'll talk to him," Floyd said. "It may take a day or two, but I'll let you know what I think after I've spoken to him."

When he'd interviewed Ávila the first time, Floyd hadn't considered the man a suspect. Bitter and angry he was, but any parent would have been. Carolina's call made him think again about following that trail. He thought back on his interview and checked the notes on his phone. He'd failed to ask Ávila about Andrea. But the girl wasn't related to Barriga, so he'd seen no need.

First thing tomorrow morning he had an appointment with Delfina. After that he'd talk to Ávila again.

CHAPTER THIRTY-TWO

"Remember, we didn't talk politics or our host's intentions," Nikki whispered to Eduardo. "And we stick to our assumed IDs."

"The dirty bastard turned us in," Eduardo whispered back. "I'm sorry."

"Maybe not," she said, still whispering. "I saw that Spanish couple across the street. There's something fishy about them."

The police approached the taxi. One of them told the driver to get out. The other ordered Nikki and Eduardo out. In the flashing light of the police car, Nikki made out the insignia on their uniforms: the National Revolutionary Police.

Ordered into the small Lada, Nikki handed over her purse. The officer opened it, examined the contents, and pulled out her passport and phone. He threw the purse on the floor of the front passenger seat. The younger man pushed Eduardo against the Lada and frisked him, taking his wallet and cell phone, and requesting his passport. Then he shoved Eduardo into the backseat of the Lada. Both passports in hand, the older man got into the passenger seat. The other one turned the car around.

It was bad that they'd been picked up, yet Nikki was thankful it was by police and not the Information Directorate. She knew the DI was responsible for foreign intelligence. She and Eduardo were too low level to be of interest to the DI. *But why did the police pick us up?*

The car entered a huge square. She recognized the iconic features of Che Guevara, outlined in steel, on the façade of the Ministry of the Interior. A similar steel likeness of the other martyr of the revolution, Camilo Cienfuegos, graced what she thought was the Ministry of Communications. The quotation 'You're doing fine, Fidel' on the outline of the statue's shoulder was legible from a distance. They were in the heart of the government district, Revolution Square.

She reached for Eduardo's hand. She traced an X on his palm, indicating they were in deep shit.

The hot, airless Lada passed the ministries and the national library. To one side, she caught a glimpse of the University of Havana and the National Theater. It was as if the driver wanted to show them the full force of Cuban power.

One more pass took them by the Palace of the Revolution, the seat of the government bureaucracy and the Communist Party.

Finally, the car went down a side street behind the Ministry of the Interior. It stopped in front of a gate at a nondescript gray building behind a wrought-iron fence. The gate opened and they drove in.

The building's drab décor reminded Nikki of other Latin American government offices. She concentrated to keep her teeth from chattering. It didn't feel like a police station. She wondered if it was a DI office.

The officers who had arrested them turned them over to heavyset guards. One was a couple of inches taller than his companion.

They took Eduardo to a desk in a corner of the room. Nikki heard them ask his name, date of birth, occupation, country of origin, and reason for being in Cuba. Then they asked why he went to the private home of a Cuban national. Eduardo endured another pat-down. This time, they took his watch.

The guards took Eduardo down a long hallway. Nikki prayed he'd be placed in an interrogation room, not a cell. She wished the lobby weren't covered by two other guards. She'd use the satellite radio on her watch to notify Floyd. She asked to use a bathroom, but they denied her request. Unable to send a message, she waited.

When Eduardo's guards returned, they ran through the same routine with Nikki, removing her watch too. The taller man took the pendant and the tree of life Eduardo had given her the year before.

"Please. My grandmother gave me that teardrop for my quinceañera."

The tree of life had sentimental value for Nikki. Right now, though, she needed the necklace with the lithium batteries. She hated to think what would happen if the batteries were found.

"I think my granddaughter would like both," he said, pocketing them. "She's a quinceañera too."

Once they finished, they threw her in a cell.

"You're lucky not to be in prison," the taller guard said. "That's some nasty shit."

Nikki looked at the filthy walls. A rust-brown handprint. Some names and dates chiseled into the gray plaster. Fingerprints, done in blood like the handprint. And a bucket in the far corner.

The men smirked, probably in perverse pleasure at her reaction to the blood-smeared walls. They left without saying another word.

How could this be happening? Barriga must have turned them in. Dinner, dessert, and that walk—just a charade to get them arrested. She shivered. The Spanish couple! Could it be them and not Barriga?

CHAPTER THIRTY-THREE

Floyd rang the doorbell at Delfina's house. He'd made an appointment to give her the second update since Nikki left. He hated to admit it, but part of the visit was mainly to keep his client happy. Handholding, and to thank her for the last payment she'd made to Security Source. He wished Nikki were here. She was much better at this kind of customer service than he was.

After Carolina Castillo's call last night, he had a more pressing reason to visit his client.

Impatient, Floyd rang the doorbell again. Could she have forgotten the appointment? Or had she returned to work? Before leaving, he knocked loudly. He'd started to walk away when he heard footsteps approaching the entry.

The door opened a crack, then a little more. Delfina opened the door wider and invited him inside. She apologized for being dressed in pajamas. She mumbled something about being so worried about her daughter that she had resorted to sleeping pills.

And looks like she flushes them down her throat with her favorite alcoholic beverage. Floyd checked the time. It was just past nine a.m.

"The sleeping pills give me a hangover," she said. "I had a Bloody Mary for breakfast."

Floyd asked if they could sit down. He needed a few more facts from her.

Delfina suggested they sit in the kitchen. She thought some toast would settle her stomach.

He watched her prepare two slices. "Can you tell me about the person who handles the clinic in Cuba?"

Buttering toast, she glanced up. "The woman who works with Urbano in Havana?"

Floyd nodded.

"She's very pretty. Her name's Victoria, but she goes by Vicki. What else do you want to know?"

"Raquel's parents tried to reach Barriga there. The Álvarez family thinks he's in Cuba. The woman at the clinic says he's not there. They worry he might be dead."

"Dead? I hope not. Andrea would be devastated," Delfina said.

"Could you tell me who might want Barriga killed?"

She took a bite of toast and told him she had no idea.

"What about Benjy Ávila?"

"Hmm." Delfina swallowed. "I hadn't thought about Ávila. I know he threatened Barriga."

Floyd asked her what she knew.

"Not a lot. His daughter died in a procedure that went badly at the Havana clinic. I've never met the man, but he's Raquel's cousin. The travel company refunded the fee and also gave him a considerable sum of money. To keep him quiet, I guess. He said he'd use the money to get revenge."

"Do you think he could have killed Raquel?"

"Do I think he's capable of killing her?" Delfina nodded. "Wouldn't killing Raquel exact revenge?"

Changing the subject, Floyd asked if the police found anything on Andrea's computer.

"Nothing. And they are not treating it as an active case. They said if you found evidence worth pursuing, they'd take it up again."

Floyd assured her he'd agreed to share important details with the police.

"It's almost four weeks since my gordita's been missing. Are you any closer to finding her?"

"Barriga's travels and your daughter's disappearance are somehow linked. If we find Barriga, he'll likely have critical information to find your daughter."

Delfina groaned. "You think Urbano took my gordita?"

"We're not ruling anything out."

"No," she said, shaking her head, "Urbano would never do that to me. He knows how much I love my daughter. Besides, he can see her anytime."

"But you let her go with Barriga to Cuba once before. Is that right?"

Delfina nodded. "That was different."

"How?"

"Andrea had leukemia. Urbano offered to take her for a stem cell transplant. We couldn't take her because we're exiles. The clinic in Havana was already well established and he offered to pay for the trip, for everything. We gave him a power of attorney."

"A power of attorney even though you weren't here legally?"

"Of course. Urbano had contacts at the Mexican consulate so they provided us with documents for him to take our daughter on a trip. A lot of undocumented workers get them to protect their children in case of their deportation or death."

"Mexican consulate? What did they have to do with a couple of exiled Cubans?"

Delfina shrugged. "Urbano's contacts, not ours."

Floyd told her it would help if she and her husband would be more forthcoming about Barriga's travels. "Why does your husband claim he hasn't been in contact since Barriga left town almost four weeks ago?"

"You'd have to ask him that."

"I'm asking you."

"Yoani has called Urbano repeatedly. He doesn't answer. Do you think he's in hiding? Could he have killed Raquel?"

Floyd told her the police, not him, were investigating Raquel's case. And he said his team had done a lot of preliminary work on finding her daughter. He asked her to be patient and wait for it all to come together so they could bring Andrea home.

CHAPTER THIRTY-FOUR

After an interminable time in the cell, Nikki estimated it must be seven or eight in the morning. The night-long vigil had given her plenty of time to think. At one point, she'd drifted off to sleep, sitting on the floor with her head on her knees. She'd jerked awake, leaning too far to one side. If only the cells she and Eduardo occupied were close enough to see one another. She thought they were locked up in holding cells.

Hopefully, they wouldn't be transferred to a prison. Hamilton had told them Cuban prison conditions were deplorable, among the worst in the world. Even the guards here seemed to think so.

Speak of the devil. A guard appeared. He handed her a piece of paper.

"I can let you out if you sign this," he said.

The charge she was supposed to confess to: subversion of a Cuban national by a foreign person with intent to destabilize the country.

She laughed, handing the paper back. "You must be joking. I'm a tourist. I've never even been involved in Mexican politics. Why would I subvert a Cuban national or pose a threat to your country?"

"But you admit to subverting a Cuban national."

"Not at all. I told you, I'm a tourist from Mexico visiting your beautiful island. I don't understand why you've detained us."

"We watched you with a Cuban national, a *regulado*. You are a danger to our state security and intelligence."

Nikki struggled not to let her terror show. This confirmed her worst fear. They were being questioned by the secret police. The worst bit of news the guard had dropped, whether on purpose or not, was that Barriga was a regulado. Such citizens, suspected of dissident political activities, were not allowed to leave Cuba. As far as she knew, Barriga was not a political activist or a human rights advocate. On the contrary, he brought tourists and patients seeking treatment to the island—endeavors that attracted money and created jobs. She wondered what he'd done recently to be considered a risk. Or could it be, as Barriga suggested, simply the change of leadership?

"Neither one of us would meddle in Cuba's politics. My husband came here for a medical conference. I'm here to see Havana, as a tourist, nothing more."

"If you sign, we'll put you on the next plane to Mexico."

"I told you. I've done nothing wrong."

The guard stared at her with a malicious grin. "Your husband already signed his confession."

"I doubt it. He's as innocent as I am."

The guard told her he'd be back. "If you have not changed your mind by then, you'll be sent to the Havana Women's Prison. After a couple of days there, you will beg to sign this document."

He waved the paper in Nikki's face.

After he left, Nikki felt like screaming. But she had to think of Eduardo. They might be rougher on him. No sooner had she thought it than she heard noise from a corridor perpendicular to hers. It sounded like someone hitting a punching bag. She curled up with her back against the wall. Her head slipped to her knees. Stifling her cries, she let tears of anger and frustration flow. People she'd met flashed through her mind. María, the woman from the travel agency. Oliver, the medical student. The Spanish couple in Old Havana. Had her conversation with María on Cuban politics prompted a call to the police? The medical student had followed her. He's the most likely to have reported them. Or would he? She hadn't talked politics with him. The Spanish couple might have turned them in. Who were they working for? She considered Barriga again. Could he have been so treacherous? She vacillated. Innocent or guilty?

Who besides Barriga could be a regulado? As an American citizen, Oliver would be watched. Maybe he'd become a regulado and couldn't leave Cuba freely now. Even the Spanish couple could be watched, especially if they worked as spies for Cuba. Or maybe they were Cuban with excellent Castilian accents. Regardless, it was impossible to know which of them was a regulado.

Reminding herself she had pushed for this trip, she prayed that Eduardo could withstand the pain and mental anguish she feared their captors were putting him through.

Don't reveal anything, she repeated, as if mental telepathy could reach him.

CHAPTER THIRTY-FIVE

Back at the office after his visit with Delfina, Floyd was reviewing a job he and Hamilton were working together. Deep in concentration, he jumped when his mobile rang.

Spider Mohle identified himself and asked to meet with him at the Juan Valdez coffee shop in an hour.

"I've stumbled across something you might want to look into," he told Floyd.

Floyd said he couldn't make it in an hour but suggested one-thirty instead. He finished the review, placed the charts and notes on Ham's desk, and locked Ham's office. On his way out, he told Charlotte he was leaving.

Floyd drove to the engineering firm where Ávila worked.

The guard in the lobby stopped him. Floyd flashed his PI license and told him it was urgent for him to speak to Ávila. "I'll repay the favor," Floyd said, smiling and rushing through the metal detector.

The guard had alerted the engineer. Ávila was standing in the hall outside his office, waiting.

"Do you have news on Barriga?"

"Not exactly. Let's go into your office."

Inside, Floyd closed the door. "The other day when I was here, you admitted to threats you'd made to Barriga, telling him you'd get revenge for your daughter's death. Can we go over that again?"

Ávila was surprised. "I thought you were coming to tell me you'd found the man."

"What did you say when you threatened Barriga?"

"I don't remember exactly. I was angry and I said something to the effect that I'd get back at him through his family. Said I'd use the money they paid me to get revenge. But I didn't mean it. I put the money into a foundation to help crippled children. You can check their books."

"Just who in Barriga's family were you threatening?"

Ávila held his hands up, as if Floyd had pulled a pistol on him. "Look, I only said that to scare him."

"Answer me, damn it."

"I didn't mean Raquel. She told me her husband was the Rodríguez girl's godfather and that he treated her like family, that they were close. I thought about doing something to scare the kid, but then I found out she had lupus. I felt guilty even considering it. That doesn't mean I've forgiven Barriga. I haven't. He's evil."

"So you kidnapped Andrea Rodríguez? Where is she?"

"No, no."

"Do you know Andrea's whereabouts?"

Ávila narrowed his eyes. "Look, I'm the victim, not the perpetrator."

"Answer me. Unless you want me to call the police."

"I didn't even know the girl was missing."

"Once more, did you kidnap or harm her?"

The engineer looked down. "No. I haven't hurt anybody."

Floyd spotted Spider with a plateful of flattened bread toasted on a panini grill. A whiff of café con leche made him crave one.

Spider immediately started telling Floyd what was bothering him.

"I overheard my wife on the phone with Delfina, who's drinking heavily again. She's upset with her husband. He's been suspended from his university work."

"I thought Yoani was partner in a medical travel agency," Floyd said. "What kind of work did he do at the university?"

Spider didn't know, other than teaching.

Floyd thought back if Nikki had mentioned Rodríguez having university work, but he couldn't remember anything. "If Rodríguez was an adjunct, what could get him suspended?"

"I didn't even know he was at the university until I overheard Yésica trying to calm Delfina."

The server took Floyd's order.

After the young man left, Spider told Floyd he'd also overheard his wife ask Delfina if she thought Barriga was still alive. "From Yésica's response, I could tell Delfina assumed he was dead."

Floyd told Spider he had no reason to believe Barriga was dead. That seemed to perk the man up a little. Then he asked if Barriga had any other family in the area.

Spider shook his head. "He has a sister in Cuba. Now that Raquel is gone, he has his in-laws. He used to be very close to the Rodríguez family. They have fallen out, but I know he thinks Andrea is the most wonderful girl in the world. He used to dote on her, until . . . well, he married Raquel and Delfina didn't like Raquel so she didn't let him take her as often, though Barriga and his wife did take her places."

The server brought Floyd's lunch—crusty grilled panini. The two men dunked their Cuban toast into the sweet café con leche.

Floyd changed the subject and asked Spider about his work. He told Floyd that Barriga had helped him get his job at a boutique hotel chain, Avalon, where he was a general manager.

When they left, Spider thanked Floyd for listening. "And please, let me know if you hear any news on my friend Barriga."

Driving back to the office, Floyd dialed Charlotte and asked her to dig up what had happened at the university to get Rodríguez suspended.

CHAPTER THIRTY-SIX

L ater that afternoon, Charlotte knocked on Floyd's door. Looking up from his computer, he invited her in. She closed the door behind her.

"This looks serious," he said.

"I've dug into Rodríguez as you requested. Besides being handsome, he's deceitful."

"Not to worry," Floyd joked, "he's married."

She told Floyd she'd sent him an encrypted file on the Cuban's extracurricular activities.

"I gather this is more than simple infidelity." Floyd turned serious.

"When you told me that Spider suspected Rodríguez did something serious enough to get him suspended from the university, I brought out my big guns."

"Go on, I'm listening," Floyd said.

"Barriga started the travel agency and still owns half of it. It's going on to four weeks since he's been missing, yet his partner doesn't seem concerned. So I looked into Rodríguez's work at the university."

Floyd nodded.

"He's been teaching at the School of Medicine, primarily a research institution. Rodríguez had a research position at the university in addition to managing his partnership. Guess what type of research?"

"Stem cell. What else?"

Charlotte gave him a thumbs up.

"Though the project had been ongoing for years, Rodríguez made a huge medical breakthrough nine months ago." Charlotte gestured to Floyd's computer. "Details are in the encrypted file. Other researchers did experiments to verify the findings. In the process of testing Rodríguez's innovation, another lab found the original project unethical. Not only that, but possible cyber evidence was left on a server. Details of this great discovery had been transmitted to a foreign government."

Floyd sat up straighter.

"Health and Human Services has supported many of the world's largest research efforts over the years. They've instituted special programs to protect humans and animals when they are used in research."

"I see where you're headed," Floyd said. "No wonder Nikki had trouble finding Rodríguez at the travel agency. If he was doing research, he must have spent the bulk of his time at the university."

Charlotte confirmed Floyd's assumption. "But the university reprimanded Rodríguez for using human embryos in an unethical way. A way that most states have outlawed."

"What was he doing?"

"Taking stem cells from human embryos to use for regenerative therapies in mice." At Floyd's quizzical look, Charlotte went into more detail. "The issue was twofold. First, he removed eggs from women he personally paid. Second, he removed the stem cells, thus killing the embryos he'd created using those eggs. Creating, growing, or killing embryos for research purposes cannot use federal Health and Human Services funding. Using leftover in vitro embryos is legal, but that's not what he was doing."

Floyd raised his eyebrows. "Let me make sure I understand. He was harvesting stem cells from embryos, thereby killing them, while using H&HS funding."

Charlotte nodded. "Along with all the other stuff he did, he placed several women in danger."

"How so?"

"His donors, the eight women selling their eggs to him, donated more often than they should have over a two-year period. Nobody knows the long-term effects of frequent egg extraction. But it can have severe health implications. Think breast cancer or eventual infertility, along with extreme discomfort due to the massive doses of hormones involved."

Floyd's expression grew somber as he listened. "It seems to me the research facility has a serious situation on their hands."

"It's people like this you want to see punished," Charlotte said.

He leaned forward and spoke in a lower voice. "You said something about sending the research to a foreign government? Could that have been to Cuba?"

"You got it." Charlotte elaborated that Rodríguez had not been accused of any type of criminal activity. The university handled it internally, reprimanding and suspending him from teaching and performing research.

"Did you hack the university to get all this information?" Floyd asked, concerned.

She sighed. "Of course not. I relied on my boyfriend. Scott's a doctoral student in regenerative medical research. I thought you knew that."

"I knew he was a doctoral student, that's all. I didn't know his field. He found a lot of information for you. Does he know if it's reliable?"

"I asked him to find out what he could. He accessed files submitted to the university by other research institutions who were verifying Rodríguez's work. He downloaded these files onto a thumb drive."

Floyd looked shocked. "It's that easy?"

"When you're a PhD candidate and you're cleared to work there, you can access files easily. Though Scott mentioned the department is tightening up its security since they uncovered Rodríguez's unethical experiments and information transmissions."

When Floyd expressed concern about her boyfriend getting into trouble for taking the information, she told him Scott had wiped away his digital fingerprints after obtaining the files.

"That's left a digital record of stuff coming to us."

"Not the way we did it." Charlotte elaborated. "Everything's clean. I took care to read on a stand-alone computer. I did not save any of it. After reading it, I created my own files summarizing the information. My files would never serve to legally prove anything."

Floyd thanked Charlotte and told her it would help a lot in the case. Taking out his car keys, he said he was heading to the travel agency. "And don't ask Scott to do anymore cyber snooping."

CHAPTER THIRTY-SEVEN

A t SunNSand, Floyd asked to speak with Rodríguez.

"He's out right now," the receptionist said.

"I suggest you call him. I need to speak with him today."

He waited by her desk to make sure she followed up. When she called Rodríguez, he asked his receptionist to put the PI on the line. Floyd refused, saying he had to speak with Rodríguez in person.

After an hour, the doctor walked into the travel agency.

Floyd followed him down the hall and into his office.

"Is it good news about Andrea?"

"It's not about Andrea at all. At least not directly."

Without waiting for an invitation, Floyd took a seat.

"Are you a green card holder in the US?" he asked.

"You made me return for this? I left an important meeting thinking you had something about my daughter." The man seemed annoyed. He turned to the window as if to calm his anger.

"Answer me," Floyd demanded.

"Yes," Rodríguez said harshly. "I'm here on a green card. What of it?"

"You've never applied for citizenship, even though you are eligible?" Floyd asked.

"I'm extremely busy and have not taken time to start the process. But

I need to. Delfina had started looking into it before . . . when Andrea . . . months before Andrea went missing."

"Isn't it because you don't want to be here?"

Rodríguez stared at Floyd, saying he was proud of his Cuban heritage. And also proud to be an immigrant to the US, adding that the green card basically gave him the same benefits US citizens hold. His wife and daughter wanted citizenship, so he would apply after they recovered Andrea.

"You've given us the runaround," Floyd said. "We're trying to find your daughter. She's been missing for almost four weeks now. And you're playing games with us. Instead of leveling with Nikki and me, you've kept vital information from us. Information that might lead us to Andrea."

Rodríguez appeared shocked.

"I need total honesty," Floyd continued. "You have enemies, even enemies willing to take your daughter. People in Miami, people you deal with through the travel agency, but more importantly, people at the university."

Floyd didn't mention Cuban Americans with citizenship that don't care much for traitors. Even after all the time they've been in Florida.

"It's a gray line and the law is complicated in this country. I'm a scientist, not an attorney," Rodríguez said. He denied any wrongdoing at the university, saying he didn't realize his stem cell project shouldn't have been done with federal funding. "Just for the record, I paid for the embryos out of my own pocket."

"The biggest danger for your daughter is the fact you were sending your research results to Cuba—"

Rodríguez put his hand up, like a policeman stopping traffic. "That's a total misunderstanding. I was sending it to our clinic in Havana. We want to constantly improve our treatments."

Floyd scoffed. He pointed out that the clinic was owned by the Cuban government and staffed by government employees including doctors and nurses.

Rodríguez's expression melted into surprise.

"I always think of the clinic as being ours. It's my mistake, I guess. Maybe that's why the university suspended me."

"Now that you understand, can we talk about who could have been upset enough to take your daughter?"

Once more, Rodríguez's expression changed. Floyd thought the man was showing fear.

"Did you receive threats from anyone?"

Rodríguez shook his head.

"If you're not honest with me, how do you expect me to do my work?" Floyd asked. "You know how to find me if you decide to come clean."

With that, the private investigator stood and walked out.

When Floyd returned to Security Source, he called a meeting with Hamilton and Charlotte, and they discussed the doctor's research shortcomings and his apparent cyberespionage.

"When I confronted him," Floyd said, "he went from arrogant and demanding to total astonishment. He defended his innocence by saying he hadn't known about the funding rules. But I think that's a lie. In his next breath, he told me he'd paid for the embryos out of his own pocket. And you should have seen him when I said we knew he'd sent medical research secrets to Cuba."

"Do tell," Charlotte said.

"Claiming he'd only sent it to his clinic in Havana, he told me there could be nothing wrong with trying to improve therapies for his clients."

Charlotte shook her head. "What an actor. The clinic isn't his. Has he forgotten it belongs to the Cuban government?"

Hamilton rubbed his chin as he listened. "He may be a spy, stealing research for Cuba with the US footing the bill."

"You have a point. We should probably mention it to our friends at the agency," Floyd said.

Hamilton offered to handle it with the CIA and wondered aloud whether they should continue to work for Delfina.

"With Nikki and Eduardo in Havana, we can't drop the case," Floyd said. "It would endanger them."

"Plus, Nikki will risk her life to save that girl," Charlotte added.

Hamilton suggested contacting Nikki.

Floyd disagreed, saying it would be best to wait a couple of days.

"You've opened Pandora's box," Hamilton said to Floyd. "Rodríguez himself could endanger Nikki and Eduardo through his contacts in Cuba."

"He can speculate they might be in Havana, but we've said that Nikki's in Canada."

"In view of that," Hamilton said, "I'll wait and talk to our CIA and FBI friends after we hear news from Havana."

CHAPTER THIRTY-EIGHT

An hour or so after the paper-waving guard left, a grumpy matron emerged from the dark hallway with a tray holding a plate of dry toast and a large mug of café con leche. Without talking, she opened the service hatch and pushed the tray through. Nikki took it.

The woman eyed her. "You better sign your confession before they send you to the women's prison. It's not like this at all."

Nikki looked at the bucket in the corner.

"Worse than this?"

"If you don't believe me, just wait. You'll consider this a paradise." She reversed her steps and waddled down the corridor.

Nikki hated to eat, but the toast wasn't bad when she washed each bite down with coffee. Taking another sip, she realized she hadn't had water or anything else to drink since she'd been locked up.

The stillness of the corridors was interrupted by loud voices. The guards sounded upset. Four or five people, all hollering at once. Nikki couldn't make out the words.

The noise came down the corridor. Four police officers like those who'd arrested Nikki and Eduardo were handling two young men in bloodied clothes. They were thrust into a cell next to hers. Loud voices still echoed through the corridors. She wondered how many more detainees could be in the lobby.

After a few minutes, a man in street clothes arrived with what appeared to be a first aid kit. He was escorted by two guards Nikki hadn't seen. A new shift must have arrived. One opened the door so the plainclothesman could enter where the two detainees were held. Nikki heard him explain to the injured man that despite blood loss, he would be fine.

The caregiver left and the two men in the next cell quieted down.

Angry voices erupted from the lobby again. Shortly, a parade of police officers and guards came into view. Three more cells were opened, and young men who looked as if they had been in a barroom brawl were locked up. A lone woman was placed in a cell by herself. Nikki was grateful they hadn't been put together.

A guard threw two more men into the cell next to hers. The cells were small. She dreaded what the odor, already bad, would be like by the end of the day.

When the guard finished with the new detainees, he opened Nikki's door and asked her to follow him. At the intersection of corridors, another guard had Eduardo by the arm. A side of his jaw looked swollen. She tried to embrace him, but the guard stopped her, keeping his hand firmly around her upper arm.

Nikki's spirits dropped when they entered the lobby. About twelve people, mostly men, some with bloodied clothes, were being interrogated. They must need Nikki and Eduardo's cells to process the new detainees. Would she and Eduardo be sent to prison?

The guard escorted them to a room off the lobby and told them he'd be back.

Nikki tightened her quivering lips to keep Eduardo from seeing her fear. When the man left, she hugged Eduardo.

"I'm afraid they're taking us to a prison," she said.

"That's likely," Eduardo said. "Since they didn't get what they wanted from us here."

"We could sign their blasted confession sheets. That'd get us out of here," she said. Taking a closer look at his jaw, she noticed a large bruise partially hidden by his beard.

A guard returned. He had Nikki's purse, Eduardo's wallet, and their passports, phones, and watches. Nikki was surprised to see both necklaces.

He told them they'd be released as soon as they signed.

Nikki protested, saying she wouldn't sign a confession when she'd done nothing wrong.

The guard held up a fat brown book. A record book, he said, for release. It merely stated that their personal effects were being returned. She held her breath as she signed. Eduardo signed after her.

She grasped the world tree necklace and put it on. Caressing the world tree medallion for a couple of seconds, she felt renewed hope. Next she clasped the teardrop pendant around her neck.

The guard told them they were free to leave. In the lobby, police brought in four more people, these in handcuffs.

Eduardo took her hand as they walked out of the building and down the steps. They could hear a crowd shouting a few blocks over.

"I'm sorry I got you into this mess," she said, looking at his jaw. "Does it hurt?"

"It's not bad. It just feels weird."

"I'm so sorry," she repeated.

"Don't blame yourself. This is not your fault. It was my decision to come on this trip."

When they approached the corner, they had a clear view of Revolution Square. They saw a large crowd.

"It's a demonstration. That's why they've arrested those young people."

Eduardo pulled slightly on Nikki's hand. "Let's avoid the crowd and get back to the hotel. Today's the last day of the conference and I want to attend. To see if Barriga is there."

"Wait, I want a photo," she said, opening her handbag.

They watched a government bus unloading people and handing out Cuban flags. The newcomers lined up on the street, following instructions from a military officer. The group started shouting "Fidel, Fidel," but their voices were drowned out by the original demonstrators, a group far greater in number, chanting "Libertad, Libertad."

"A photo will only get us in trouble with the police again," Eduardo said. He grasped her hand.

Eduardo held tight to Nikki's hand as they walked for several blocks. He'd been miserable the whole night without her. Police were everywhere: on foot and in cars, pickups, and small vans.

"They mobilized quickly," Nikki said.

"Just as Hamilton told us." Eduardo saw a community taxi and flagged it. The car stopped and they piled in.

A few blocks down, the other passengers got out. Eduardo used a few euros to convince the driver to take them directly to the Meliá.

A mess greeted them when they entered their room. The police had been there. Eduardo started to clean up, but Nikki tidied the bed and told him to lie down while she got an ice pack for his swollen and bruised jaw. She left and returned with ice wrapped in a hand towel. When she put it on him, she leaned in to whisper in his ear that she'd awaken him after twenty minutes so he could attend the conference. Eduardo understood. He needed to find Barriga.

CHAPTER THIRTY-NINE

Before leaving, Eduardo made certain the lock to their room still worked and extracted a promise from Nikki not to open it until he came back.

By eleven a.m., he entered the auditorium. He knew he looked awful, and the bruised jaw wasn't the worst of it. After spending a night in what was essentially a jail cell, he felt filthy. Stubble above the top line of his beard needed to be shaved, but since it concealed the bruising, he'd leave it that way. His mustache needed a trim. He wore the same clothes as the day before, the clothes he'd been jailed in. Glancing around the large room, he spotted Barriga midway on the opposite side.

Barriga spotted Eduardo too. He stood and headed for the aisle. Eduardo watched to see if the man would run, prepared to run after him. When Barriga circled around the back of the auditorium to avoid distracting the speaker, Eduardo relaxed.

Barriga took a seat next to Eduardo.

"I was concerned when I didn't see you this morning. Looks like you had a rough night," he whispered.

"Hotel Fidel's hospitality," Eduardo whispered back.

Barriga seemed shocked but tried hard not to show it. "What happened?"

"The taxi you put us in was stopped at the river and two police officers took us to a detention center at Revolution Square."

"The secret police," Barriga said softly.

"One of the guards peppered me with questions about you, and offered to take us to the airport if I signed a confession involving you. When he didn't like my answers, he beat me up."

"Questions about me?"

"They wanted to know what we'd talked about at your house."

Still whispering, Barriga suggested they leave separately and meet two blocks away, along the oceanfront on the way to the Meliá. If police were in that area, then they agreed to meet in the restaurant where they'd eaten lunch.

The beach narrowed in this spot. Eduardo saw security vehicles, their occupants interested only in the streets they were patrolling and not in the empty beachfront. Yet he also thought about the events from the night before, trying to analyze the situation. Could Barriga be innocent? If so, what caused their night of detention? Nikki had told him about the woman at the vacation rental agency, the medical student who offered his services as a tourist guide, and the Spanish couple. Except for Barriga, they'd had very little interaction with people.

The ocean breeze felt good. Almost as good as a shower would feel. He heard footsteps behind him. As he looked back, Barriga caught up with him.

"I'm sorry for the bad night you had. Is your wife okay?"

Eduardo stopped and gazed straight into the doctor's eyes. "Valentina was also detained."

"At least they did not put you in a prison. Tell me what they did."

"First of all, I want to know why you called the police on us."

Barriga denied it without hesitation. "I invited you to dinner at my house, to get to know you a little bit, and see if I could trust you. Then I planned to ask you for a favor. I wouldn't call the police if I want you to help me, would I?"

"So what's the favor?"

They started walking again, the gravelly beach slowing their pace.

"It's about Andrea. But if the secret police picked you up, we may all be in more danger than I thought."

"They asked what you'd discussed with me," Eduardo said. "My wife was in a separate cell. They asked her similar questions. They took our passports and phones, my wallet, and Valentina's purse."

"I hope you got everything back."

"When they let us out, yes. During our detention, they wanted us to sign a confession that we were subverting you, a Cuban national, with intent to destabilize the country. We were threatened with prison if we did not sign. They even sweetened the deal with offers to fly us out if we accused you."

Barriga groaned. "You refused to sign, I hope."

Eduardo told him the secret police released them to make space for the protesters.

"A demonstration? That's against the law."

"It looked pretty crowded to me," Eduardo said. "By the way, did you know the authorities consider you a regulado?"

"Ever since I first went to Miami, I've been watched by the government. But I was never considered a regulado. From what you're telling me, I'm afraid that's changed now. They haven't granted me travel permission this time. If I get out of here, I'm not coming back."

Perspiration beaded Barriga's forehead.

"I wouldn't have made this trip if I'd known Raúl was giving up his position as party chairman. It has the country on edge. Despite living in poverty for over six decades, a lot of people here loved the Castros."

"You keep avoiding the subject of Andrea. Is she here with you?"

Barriga nodded. "I have a power of attorney from her parents. I can explain."

Eduardo waited. When the explanation was not forthcoming, he asked for it.

"I'm thinking how to say this."

"Just give me the facts," Eduardo said.

Barriga cleared his throat. "The day before Andrea 'disappeared'"—he made air quotes and continued—"she called me, sobbing. She was having problems with her father. Rodríguez has a violent temper. To punish her for whatever transgression she'd committed, he killed her puppy. A birthday gift from me a few weeks earlier."

Eduardo interrupted. "My wife needs to hear this."

Barriga seemed panicked. "If the police catch the three of us together, they can apprehend you again. And take me too. Then what would happen to Andrea?"

The beach was devoid of pedestrians. Eduardo convinced Barriga that the police were too busy with the demonstration and asked him to wait for them on the beach.

Eduardo rushed to the hotel to get Nikki. The whole purpose of this trip had been finding out what Barriga knew about Andrea. Now he'd admitted to having the teenager with him. Nikki needed to hear this. As he jogged along Third Avenue, Eduardo counted ten police cars and vans pass by.

Eduardo panicked when he scoured the oceanfront and did not see Barriga.

"Damn, he's disappeared," he told Nikki. "I should never have left him."

Eduardo chastised himself for leaving the man alone. He picked up a rock and threw it in anger. "Our backup plan was to meet at the restaurant where he and I ate lunch. Let's get over there before we lose him completely."

Nikki kept looking up and down the beach. Then she pointed out a ledge and asked Eduardo to walk over with her.

As they approached, the Cuban stood and shook sand off his pantlegs.

"Good morning, Valentina. It's a pleasure to see you," Barriga said.

Before Nikki had time to respond, two police cars, their lights blinking, appeared on Seventy-Sixth Street and Third Avenue, the closest intersection to the Meliá. Barriga threw himself to the ground, urging them to do the same. Eduardo and Nikki watched the cars go into the circular driveway of their hotel. Two policemen swaggered into the lobby.

"They're looking for you. They're here to arrest you," Barriga said, holding his head up from the ground.

CHAPTER FORTY

When Charlotte arrived at the office and turned her bank of computers on, she saw breaking news about the demonstration in Havana. She called Floyd and Hamilton to her office to show them.

Hamilton kept saying he could not believe what he saw.

"We must contact Nikki," Charlotte said.

Instead of rushing to make a call or contact her on satellite radio, Floyd advised caution. "Let's wait a couple of hours and see how this develops. Maybe they'll call us. If they haven't called in four hours, then we'll try them."

"You mean they could be in danger?" Charlotte asked.

"Danger?" Hamilton repeated in a sarcastic tone. "There's no danger in Cuba. The crime rate is low. The only threat comes from those who should protect you."

"Nikki and Eduardo both know when to keep a low profile." Floyd's voice was calm.

Charlotte wasn't so sure about Nikki, who could be impulsive.

"The government will cut internet and cell service to isolate people and to keep news from getting out. And a curfew, they'll institute one," Hamilton said.

Floyd suggested they all get back to work and reconvene at noon.

Charlotte could not get any work done. Her normally upbeat personality had taken a hit today. One of her favorite people in the world might be in grave danger. She couldn't concentrate and spent the next hours checking on the situation in Havana. One newscast said Cuba was experiencing food shortages due to the pandemic. People were protesting to demand vaccinations and better hospital facilities.

Another newscast reported that ships and dock workers were severely impacted by the virus. Small markets, like those in the Caribbean, were getting cut by shipping lines.

And yet another newscaster blamed food shortages on the embargo imposed by the American government. That caused the Cubans to riot, he reported. They cast blame on America to bring world attention to their cause.

Several sites mentioned that lack of tourism during the pandemic had brought the island nation to the brink of collapse. Even though Cuba was open to tourism, the risk of getting sick, the five-day quarantine, and testing discouraged many travelers.

Yet others reported the worst sugar crop in decades had contributed to the problems in Cuba, stating that exports were down significantly.

Videos showing Cuban demonstrators demanding freedom, chanting "Libertad," were broadcast by the stations she had on every monitor.

She stared at the videos, thinking she might see Nikki and Eduardo. The more Charlotte listened, the more worried she became.

CHAPTER FORTY-ONE

Nikki, Eduardo, and Barriga huddled behind the small ledge, staring at the hotel entrance. A police officer leaned against the hood of one of the Ladas. The halogen lights were still rotating on both cars.

"It's time we get you out of Cuba," Barriga said. His voice was trembling. "You can't fly out. They'll have your passports flagged at the airport. I know someone who could get you on a boat to Andros Island in the Bahamas. It's more than twice as far as Key West, but safer."

"What about Andrea?" Nikki asked.

"I'd ask you to take her," Barriga said, his voice still cracking. "I'd already decided to leave the island. The plan was to take her to Andros with me. But they're watching me now and the minute they suspect I'm gone, they will turn the island upside down looking for me. She'd be safer with you."

"Aren't we in as much danger as you are of being arrested?" Nikki asked.

"As tourists you're probably flagged at the airport. But my house is being watched. If I don't return home, they'll search until they find me."

"Outline your plan," Eduardo said.

He explained they'd travel by car to a swampy area on an isolated beach near Puerto Escondido. "You'd go by night. Avoiding the police on the highways and roads, and later the patrols in the ocean are the riskiest parts of the trip. A dinghy would be waiting for you to get you out of Cuban waters."

"A dinghy!" Nikki struggled to keep her voice down. "If the police don't get us, the ocean will."

"It's just to avoid patrol boats. You'll get picked up by a speedboat after you're away from Cuban patrols. The speedboat will take you to Red Bays, on the west coast of Andros Island. You'll be driven to Fresh Creek Airport. From there you can fly to Nassau, where you get a flight to Miami."

"I don't know," Eduardo said, raising an eyebrow. "Sounds pretty risky."

"Leaving through the Havana airport is no longer an option. Not with the police searching for you. You won't get out. Worse yet, if you take Andrea, you'd be accused of kidnapping."

"I want to see Andrea first," Nikki said. She wasn't ready to reveal that they had a passport and ticket for her.

"I'll take you. After the police leave."

"Why did you take her from her parents?"

Barriga cleared his throat. "I thought I was doing the right thing. She suffers from lupus. She needed a stem cell transplant to help control her symptoms, and her father refused to let her have the treatment."

Nikki could not believe what she heard. "You literally kidnapped her, brought her to Cuba without parental consent, and had her undergo surgery? My god, do you realize the charges you'll face in Miami? Unless you don't plan to go back."

Was that his plan? Nikki wondered. *Would he stay in Cuba to avoid prosecution in Florida for kidnapping Andrea?*

"The evening before I took her, she called begging me to get her out of the house. She told me Rodríguez had lost his temper. She was terrified. He killed her little dog, Pepito. Threatened her, saying she'd be next. What father says that to his daughter?"

Nikki recoiled inwardly but kept her face neutral. "Regardless, what you did was illegal." Delfina told her Andrea's dog was in a kennel. The vinegar, the baking soda made sense now. It was masking the smell of death.

Barriga told Nikki that if she knew the full story, she might agree that his taking Andrea to Cuba was the best solution.

"If Andrea was in physical danger from her parents, Child Protective Services from Florida's Center for Child Welfare should have been your option, not kidnapping," Nikki insisted.

"I'd intended to let Delfina know she was safe. But Andrea asked me not to tell her mother. Not the best decision I've made, but here we are. When you get back to Miami with Andrea, you can ask the state to intervene. Right now, I want her out of Cuba for her own safety. I hope to get out someday too."

"I'm curious. How is it that Rodríguez didn't check the airlines and discover you had flown with Andrea?" Nikki wondered why Charlotte hadn't found his travel either.

"We flew Miami to Panama to Havana on Copa Airlines. That's the Panamanian airline. Since I had Andrea with me, I could not leave a trail on the airlines I usually used."

Nikki had never even heard of Copa.

Eduardo asked them to focus on their upcoming travel. He suggested Barriga make the trip with them to Andros.

Barriga shook his head. "I can't go. The authorities would miss me and suspect I was fleeing. Their hunt for me would make me a liability to all of you. I beg you to get Andrea out while we still can."

Nikki asked why he was so concerned about Andrea leaving Cuba.

"The change in government. In the US she can have control of her life. She has her mother, and hopefully she can have a career of her choosing." In Cuba, he told them, many talented people never get the opportunity to reach their potential.

"Andrea obviously doesn't live with you. Where is she?"

He told them she was at an apartment complex with his sister and her children. His sister, Mama-Sonia as she was called by her children and a lot of her friends, had stayed with Andrea at the clinic for almost three weeks. After Andrea's release, Sonia took care of her at the apartment. "My sister already knew Andrea from the first time she'd had stem cell surgery."

"It sounds like you have Andrea's best interest at heart." Nikki tried to soften her criticism. "But you don't have the legal standing to make medical decisions for her."

"I'm her godfather. When she had her first surgery several years back, her parents gave me a power of attorney. It has no expiration date and provides me with the authority to make medical decisions. They are exiles and could not come to Cuba. They asked me to handle it."

"Maybe it's legal in Cuba, but in Florida, a POA does not give you custody or the right to abduct her."

"Of course, Andrea misses her mother," Barriga said. "But she's told us how happy she is here. She doesn't miss the terrible fights between her parents. Her mother's drinking and her father's anger are not good for her. Life in Cuba is not what I want for her either. I fear she'll be so happy here she'll decide to stay."

"That's not her decision, is it?" Nikki asked.

Barriga stared at Nikki as if it were the first time he'd thought about Andrea being underage.

"Oh, look, they're leaving. And they weren't after us." Eduardo gestured to the officers leaving the Meliá with a fellow who appeared to be handcuffed.

They watched as the man was placed in one of the Ladas. The police turned their halogen lights off and sped down the street.

Barriga wiped perspiration from his forehead. "What a relief."

"I still want to meet Andrea," Nikki said. "And take her to Miami."

CHAPTER FORTY-TWO

I t was lunchtime and Charlotte kept watching the news and live feeds of anonymous videos taken in Havana. Her monitors displayed ten different newscasts, including three Spanish-language transmissions.

Without warning, her screens went blank. Almost simultaneously, each newscaster, including one from Mexico, said the feed from Cuba had been lost. The Cuban government had cut internet and announced a curfew in Havana.

She punched Floyd's intercom button and informed him.

When she told Hamilton, he swore over the intercom.

"I'm sorry, Ham, I only wanted to let you know what's going on. Don't kill the messenger," Charlotte said. Hamilton had a calm, fun-loving attitude toward life. Except when it came to Cuba.

Floyd entered Charlotte's office. He asked Hamilton to join them. It was time to decide whether to contact Nikki.

Hamilton pointed out that Cuba would be tracking any type of radio communication, including two-way satellite radios. "They've declared a state of emergency. You know how advanced they are technologically, and they always believe the US orchestrates any expression of dissent. I think we've lost our window of opportunity. Before they turned the internet off, it would have been safer to call Nikki. Now we have no choice but to wait it out."

"It's the same risk if she tries to contact us," Charlotte said. "I haven't prayed in years, but I'm starting now."

"The government may also cut flights in and out of the country for a few days," Ham said. "It will depend on how quickly they feel they have control again."

"They'd really stop air traffic?" Charlotte asked, exasperated. "Looks like Nikki and Eduardo are stuck there."

Floyd reminded her of September 11, when the World Trade Center in New York collapsed after jets flew into them. "All planes flying over US territory had to land at the closest airport."

"I was just a kid," Charlotte said, "but I've read about it. For a country in need of more food and medical supplies, how can Cuba stop all its flights?"

"Those in control, as in all governments, have what they need," Floyd said.

"It's not fair," she said.

"No one said anything about fairness," Floyd said. "Let's get back to work."

CHAPTER FORTY-THREE

T he sun felt warm and the pebbly seashore was inviting. Nikki took her shoes off and dug her toes into the sand. Knowing the police had arrested someone else at the hotel gave her a guilty sense of reprieve.

Not only that, Barriga had Andrea and wanted them to take her back to Miami. She felt an immense feeling of freedom, even if it were only momentary.

"Shall we go to your sister's to meet Andrea?" she asked.

Sounding like a concerned father, Barriga grilled them about Andrea's safety and well-being once they returned to Miami.

"Other than giving you our word to protect her from her father, we can only do what's within the law to keep her safe. What do you expect of us?" Eduardo asked.

Nikki reminded Barriga that they'd been arrested in the course of their stay in Havana. She asked if that wasn't proof enough they were willing to help. They had said nothing to the secret police about Barriga. They could have signed the confessions and boarded a plane out of the country.

"On the other hand," Nikki added, "Andrea has parents in Miami, and legally, we must return her to her home. If Rodríguez poses a danger to his daughter, there are ways to involve Child Protective Services."

"Look," Barriga said, "I've committed no crimes in Cuba. On the contrary, I've helped in the best way I could. That doesn't mean I want to see Andrea live here forever. She's had her treatment and so far she's doing great. She's off antibiotics, though she's still on other medications. My sister makes sure she takes them. But I'm feeling a lot of pressure."

He glanced toward the ocean and shook his head.

"Tell us what's bothering you," Nikki said.

"In the US, I might face kidnapping charges, even if Andrea testifies about begging me to take her away from her parents. I've lost my wife. I may face murder charges, even though I did not kill her. I would never have harmed Raquel. She was a kind and wonderful woman and I loved her." Barriga choked up.

Eduardo said that no matter how dark everything seemed, there was always a brighter tomorrow.

Barriga looked sad and full of self-reproach. "With Raquel gone, Andrea is all I have left."

"You speak as if you're Andrea's father," Nikki said.

"Godfather," he replied. "And I love her like my own."

"What about your sister?" Eduardo asked.

"She's a good woman, and of course, she's important to me, but it's not the same."

At that point, he suggested going to Sonia's house. He wrote the address on a slip of paper.

"Let's go in your car," Eduardo said.

"It's against the law," Barriga said.

Nikki remembered from Hamilton's lessons that Cuban citizens weren't allowed to transport foreigners in their own vehicles. Both parties would be fined if caught. People surely got away with it. But the secret police were already eyeing every move Barriga made. They took separate taxis to his sister's place.

The taxi left Nikki and Eduardo by a small apartment building. They walked up the stairs to the second floor. Barriga had already arrived and opened the door for them. A petite teenager stood next to him. She had her arm wrapped around his waist and he had his arm loosely over her shoulder. The young woman had a beautiful smile. Nikki was surprised at Andrea's small frame. Thin, she couldn't be more than five feet tall. She was wearing the "Be Happy, Be Me" necklace Nikki first saw in the picture in Delfina's office.

When they entered the small living space, they were introduced to Sonia and her two teenagers, a boy about fourteen and a girl about Andrea's age.

Sonia, a petite woman, had a kind and affectionate manner and Nikki could see why she was called Mama-Sonia.

After a couple of minutes of small talk, Mama-Sonia and her teenagers left the apartment.

"Remember the boat trip I'd told you we might take to Andros Island?" Barriga asked.

Andrea nodded.

"These people will take you with them, and back to Miami. They know your mom and will make arrangements for her to pick you up," Barriga said.

Andrea's smile disappeared. "I don't want to go. I'm happy here with you and Mama-Sonia."

"We've spoken about this moment. It's time you return."

"Not without you, Uncle Urby." She threw herself into Barriga's arms.

"I'll get to Miami as soon as I can. We'll work things out with your parents. I promise."

"Not after he killed Pepito." She started sobbing. "I don't ever want to see my father again. Don't forget, he also killed Bonita, my cat."

Nikki and Eduardo exchanged glances.

"Sometimes in life we have to do stuff we don't like. Trust me, I'll get to Miami as soon as I can."

Wiping tears from her face, she stepped away from Barriga.

"Okay, Uncle Urby, I'll do what you ask. But I want to see you in Miami soon. You've promised." She glanced at Nikki. "When must we leave?"

"We'll get together tomorrow to decide on timing," Nikki said.

———

Barriga and Andrea walked Nikki and Eduardo to the street to wait for a taxi. An older woman, scruffy and disheveled, leaning on a cane at every step, ambled in their direction, extending her free hand toward them, palm down, as if giving a benediction.

"Axé, Axé. May the orichá be with you. Yemayá, mother to all of us and ruler of the ocean, will take care of you. Remember to pray to your ancestors before you embark."

Andrea drew closer to Barriga. He peeled a couple of bills from a small bundle of money he drew from his pocket and handed them to the woman.

"Don't be scared, my sweet one," Barriga said to Andrea.

"Uncle Urby, how does she know about our journey?"

"Lucumi practitioners just know things," he responded.

Nikki also handed the woman some money and thanked her for the blessing.

CHAPTER FORTY-FOUR

With trepidation, Nikki entered the Meliá with Eduardo at her side. The young receptionist who had flirted with Eduardo the day they arrived smiled at him and waved as they passed through the lobby. Nikki didn't breathe until they reached the elevator. No police appeared, and she relaxed when they reached their floor and found their room the way they had left it.

Eduardo suggested they shower together. Nikki looked at him in disbelief.

"I get it," he said, "but I still need a hug and a kiss." They embraced, and Eduardo quickly stepped into the shower and started the water.

Damn those hidden cameras and microphones. Nikki couldn't wait to get home.

Nikki nudged Eduardo to awaken him for dinner. She'd seen a small restaurant close to the beach where they'd met with Barriga earlier that day. Of all the meals they'd eaten since arriving in Cuba, Barriga's had been by far the best. Nevertheless, Cuban ice cream was delicious, and she'd also seen a frozen treat shop along the beach close to the restaurant she'd chosen for this evening.

Eduardo reached for her and brought her toward him, rubbing her nose with his and kissing her briefly. "Isn't this romantic?" He laughed. "I guess you're hungry."

They dressed and took the stairs down to the lobby. Again, Nikki felt a twinge of anxiety as they crossed to the main exit. When she didn't spot any uniforms or Ladas with rotating lights, she relaxed and led Eduardo to the deserted beach. Though the city was teeming with police, they were on the streets, not on the beach near the hotel.

"We have to contact Floyd," she said.

"Can't it wait?"

She shook her head. "He needs to know we've found Andrea. And that we may take a boat trip to Andros."

"Tell him not to mention anything to Delfina yet. Andrea has reason to fear her father. You should ask Charlotte to research Child Protective Services."

"Yeah, I'll ask that Charlotte contact them." Nikki then expressed concern over interference from the Cuban spy apparatus if they used the satellite radios on their watches.

"I'll tell you what," Eduardo said, "we'll take a longer stroll after dinner. We will only use your watch. Make your call super short, and then turn your watch completely off so you can't be tracked. We'll still have my watch."

"That woman, the one who gave us a blessing, how do you think she knew we're going to be taking a trip?" Nikki asked, kicking a few pebbles with the tip of her shoe. "Do you think it was coincidence?"

"What else could it be? She was speaking to tourists. She probably does that at the port when the cruise ships arrive."

Nikki conceded that her husband was probably right.

"I'll bet she rakes the money in when the port is full," he said.

Their dinner had been okay. Nothing fancy, but it had satisfied them. The best part had been the fried plantain they'd ordered as an appetizer. Nikki decided she would try her hand at making maduros once they returned to Miami.

Alone on the oceanfront after dinner, enjoying their walk to the frozen treat shop, they stopped to call Floyd. They did not have to search for an isolated spot. People had stayed off the streets tonight. There was no one on the beach either, probably because of the demonstration earlier in the day. Despite the practice they'd done before leaving Miami, it took Nikki about five minutes to figure out how to use her wristband satellite radio and get Floyd on the channel she was supposed to use.

"This will be quick," she told him. She continued in code words. "We bought pork bellies and won first prize at the eating contest," meaning they'd found Andrea and Barriga. "We're anxious to do a contest at home, but we can't leave. Airlines are not operating. Will try to island hop to the beautiful Caribbean music."

She was afraid Floyd wouldn't understand the last sentence. They didn't have a contingency plan involving another island.

Floyd must have understood that there were no airlines they could take. He responded that planes should be flying again in a day or two. "Wait until then," he advised.

"Don't tell mama bear anything. Papa bear has been bad to baby bear and we need to pow-wow before mama hears anything. A welfare counselor bear should meet baby bear first. Over and out."

When Floyd said "copy," she turned the satellite radio and her wristwatch off.

"Took you less than twenty seconds," Eduardo said. "That was good."

"It was complicated. I hope he understood."

Eduardo took Nikki's hand and they strolled along the beach. Getting closer to the water, he stopped and twirled her toward him and kissed her.

"We're here alone," he whispered in her ear.

"No cameras or listening devices." She moved her body closer to his, her curly hair whipping in the breeze. "It's so romantic. Let's make love before the ocean engulfs the sun."

They continued on the beach until they found an even more secluded spot, a ledge like the one where they'd found Barriga. A clump of sand verbena with small purple flowers covered the hill leading up to it.

Kissing her again, Eduardo slowly unbuttoned her blouse. He knelt, cleaned the sandy area of gravel, and gently pulled her to the sand.

Laying down, Nikki reached for him. He opened her blouse, kissing her nipples. She moaned and undid Eduardo's belt, murmuring that they should not undress completely. He unzipped his pants and lifted her skirt.

She wrapped her legs around him. Soon her hips were moving rhythmically with Eduardo's gentle thrusts.

The sun, barely above the horizon, was obscured by heavy clouds reflecting bright red and orange. Nikki nestled into Eduardo's chest. She was just saying that the sunset was as beautiful as any she'd ever seen when a blinking light broke their interlude. She felt Eduardo's arm muscles tighten as he looked over the ledge.

"We have company," he announced.

The light came from the roof of a Lada, a single car parked at the end of the street, which also happened to be the closest point to them. Light flashing behind the officer created an eerie silhouette of a heavyset man. The flashes brought out the drab color of his uniform and the dark, split-second in-between times without light gave him a ghostlike appearance.

They snapped into upright sitting positions, fumbling like teenagers trying to button and buckle up quickly. In her haste, Nikki mismatched the buttonholes, leaving her blouse hanging unevenly. She had no time to redo the buttons before the man was standing above them.

"What are you doing out here all by yourselves?"

"Watching the sunset. We'll be going for ice cream in a bit." Nikki turned and pointed toward the shop near the parked police car.

"No you're not," he said gruffly. "You're coming with me."

CHAPTER FORTY-FIVE

Floyd glanced at his watch. Quarter past seven. He turned his communicator off. Deciding it was time to leave the office, he called Milena to tell her he was on the way home.

Nikki's message had been cryptic. He felt certain he understood the first part. Andrea was indeed in Cuba with Barriga. Nikki had intuited that early in the investigation.

The next bit, papa bear, mama bear, and baby bear, he took to mean there was violence in the household and the teenager was afraid of her father. The important thing was not to inform the Rodríguez household they'd found Andrea. And, if he understood correctly, they'd need to meet with a counselor from Child Protective Services once they arrived home.

The confusing part was about the island hopping. Not certain what she meant, he'd chosen not to ask for clarification to avoid being on the air any longer than necessary. How would they island hop? Were they planning to take a cruise ship in the old port of Havana? Some cruise lines were sailing again. Or would they get a smaller boat? Caribbean music, that had to mean they were going to another island. But which one?

Tomorrow he would share the message with Ham and Charlotte. They were both excellent at deciphering puzzles.

On the way home, Floyd called Spider on the speaker. Spider

answered on the second ring. A television program played in the background.

"Can you talk privately, or should I call again tomorrow?"

"I'm home alone. Yésica is working the night shift."

Floyd asked if he knew anything about violence in the Rodríguez household.

"Rodríguez has a volatile personality," Spider said, adding that a couple of times he'd overheard Yésica talking to Delfina when she was complaining about the difficulties in her marriage.

"Do you know if he's ever hurt Andrea?"

"I don't think he'd injure his daughter, but Delfina has shown evidence of physical abuse."

"Can you explain?" Floyd asked.

"She's always blamed her bruises on falling or hitting herself with a book or a door. Yésica's been trying to talk her into treatment for alcohol addiction." Spider paused. "She might have hurt herself after drinking too much. I'm sorry, but I don't pay that much attention to the Rodríguez family. I can ask Yésica about physical abuse and get back to you."

Floyd told him it'd be best not to bring Yésica into the conversation at this point.

"I've been trying to call Barriga. There's no answer and his voicemail is still full. Have you found him?"

"Not yet." It was Floyd's natural response to protect Barriga at this point in the investigation. "You'll be one of the first to know when we do."

CHAPTER FORTY-SIX

Nikki's heart raced as the policeman walked them back to his vehicle. As they treaded along ahead of the officer, she imagined a prison cell, a space ten times worse than the holding cell, crowded with other women, a few hardened by the system, unkind to foreigners. Certainly, they would not be sympathetic toward her. It would be even worse for Eduardo. Other prisoners would likely beat him up. She broke out in a cold sweat.

The policeman asked them for the second time what they'd been doing, lying on the isolated beach.

"Enjoying the sunset," Eduardo responded.

"Are you aware there's a curfew?"

They both nodded.

"By nine p.m., we'll be back at our hotel," Eduardo added.

"The curfew has been moved to seven p.m. due to the riots this morning," the man glanced at his watch. "In five minutes, you will be in violation."

Eduardo explained that, as tourists, they did not know about the curfew change. "How can we fix this?"

"We can make an exchange." The man's smile was evil. "A few dollars, enough for a bag of coffee at the dollar store, and I'll let you walk back to your hotel. If it's close by, that is. If not, I'll give you a ride."

Eduardo reached into his pocket. "I don't have dollars, but here are some Mexican pesos. Oh, I'll throw in ten euros, too."

The euros alone were more than half his monthly salary.

The man did not thank them. Counting the pesos, he looked pleased and stuck them in a pocket. He looked at the ten-euro bill with obvious satisfaction and placed it in a different pocket.

"Our hotel is right over there." Nikki pointed to the Meliá. The policeman could check where they were staying anyway. "We can walk."

The policeman told them to remember the new curfew time.

Nikki took Eduardo's hand and they marched off.

"I was terrified of getting into the car with that pervert," she said. "We're lucky it wasn't worse."

"The ten euros took care of it," Eduardo said, slowing his pace. "Isn't there a song about money making the world go round?"

"Liza Minelli sang it in *Cabaret*," Nikki said, relaxing. "A fantastic scene."

"And that movie really dates us, doesn't it?"

Nikki smiled at Eduardo. "Maybe it dates you, but I saw it on Netflix a couple of months ago, one evening when you were studying."

Eduardo playfully slapped her arm. "I forget you're five years younger than I am."

"Hey, those five years mean a lot to me." Nikki saw a police van on Third Avenue. She took Eduardo's hand and they picked up the pace.

CHAPTER FORTY-SEVEN

T he next morning, Nikki and Eduardo strolled through the lobby. They planned to take a hotel taxi to Sonia's apartment. They had everything they needed for the trip, including their passports and other documents. They left their suitcases in the room, as if they planned to return.

They'd be ready if Barriga had arranged overland transportation for them to an obscure and swampy beach near Puerto Escondido where they'd catch a dinghy at night. Presumably, Barriga would provide them with false Cuban documents that would make it easier for them to travel the roads out of Havana.

Before they could step into a hotel taxi, Nikki saw Oliver Ortega, the medical student and would-be tour guide, approaching them.

"I have just the tour for you," he said quietly, almost whispering. "I'll take you to Sonia. She's waiting for you."

Nikki stared at him in disbelief.

Oliver lowered his voice even more. "Doctor Barriga arranged for me to pick you up."

"That can't be," Nikki said. "He didn't mention you."

"Explain to me what's going on," Eduardo said, his arm around Nikki.

"Follow me and I'll tell you." Oliver headed toward his car.

Eduardo and Nikki shared a glance before they agreed to walk with him.

Away from the hotel taxi drivers, Oliver explained that Barriga had been arrested. Sonia had contacted him. Barriga had set up a contingency plan with his sister and Oliver.

"What were you doing the day you followed me in la Habana Vieja?" Nikki asked.

Oliver admitted Barriga had asked him to monitor Nikki's whereabouts around town. "When your husband told Doctor Barriga about Raquel's death, he thought you both might be CIA agents looking to snatch him and return him to Miami to stand trial."

"Interesting," Nikki said. "So you were surveilling me."

"Everything I said the day we met is true. I am a licensed guide," he said, defending himself. "I met Doctor Barriga two years ago at the university when he gave a guest lecture on stem cell breakthroughs to my class. He took special interest in me since I'm from Miami. He's a good man."

"Let's pick up where you started. You said Barriga's been arrested," Nikki said. "On what grounds?"

"I've not spoken to him. No one has. But a neighbor at his condo called Sonia this morning telling her the police left with him in handcuffs. And he failed to show up at Sonia's apartment to meet with you."

Concerned about Barriga's arrest, Eduardo inquired if Barriga had known anything about Raquel's death before Eduardo and Nikki arrived on the island.

"To my knowledge, he knew nothing about her murder until you told him," Oliver said.

Nikki told Oliver they'd take a taxi to a park she'd noticed two blocks from Sonia's. Oliver could tell Sonia where to find them.

"I'll have her meet you by the kiosk in the center of the park," Oliver said. "It's secluded, a safe place."

For six more blocks, Nikki and Eduardo walked until they reached the Quinta Avenida Habana Hotel on stylish Fifth Avenue. The streets were almost empty of pedestrians, but they entered the hotel lobby to make certain no one was following them. Ten minutes later, they took a hotel taxi.

Vehicle traffic was lighter than usual. Police presence remained high.

On the way to the park where they'd meet Sonia, Nikki spotted a bell tower. She asked the driver to leave them there, saying they wanted to see that church.

"Do you think Oliver can be trusted?" Nikki asked, climbing the few steps up to the church.

"Guess we'll find out shortly," Eduardo said, "whether it's Sonia or the secret police waiting for us."

At the park, they strolled toward the center, hoping to find Barriga's sister at the kiosk. They passed a small gazebo without spotting anyone.

"Now what?" Eduardo asked.

"Maybe she's also been arrested," Nikki said. "We might have to find Andrea without her help. Then we can either leave by commercial airline or call that number Hamilton made us memorize to get off the island."

"And if we can't find the kid?"

"We'd abort our mission," Nikki said.

"Seriously? You'd never do that."

"You know I don't want to leave her behind. It's a last resort. We know where to find Andrea and hopefully Ham's contact can get all three of us out."

Eduardo pointed to a hunched-over, gray-haired woman in an oversized raincoat trudging toward the kiosk. He whispered to Nikki to have a look. The old woman plopped down on the steps.

"That's all we need." Eduardo sounded frustrated.

"Wait." Nikki examined the woman more closely.

As she suspected, it was Sonia in disguise. She had rigged herself out as a hunchback, probably with blankets tied to her back and shoulders. The DI must still be too busy with demonstrators to monitor Sonia's apartment.

Approaching her, they realized she was breathing heavily.

She took her glasses off. Nikki saw fear on the woman's face.

"My brother, you know, has been taken by the DI. As his closest relative here, that means I'm in danger too, and I'm carrying out his request. He fears for Andrea if she remains here."

"Explain his request," Nikki said.

"You take her with you. She's sixteen. The secret police might use her to make him talk."

"What about your own children?" Nikki asked.

"If I'm taken, they'll go to their father's relatives. They are good people and will look after them as best they can."

"How do we get Andrea if your house is being watched?"

"We'll talk about that in a minute." Sonia handed Eduardo an envelope. "These documents will protect you while you're still in Cuba. Arrangements are already made for the trip. Oliver knows all of Urbano's contacts. He'll make the boat trip with you and return here after you catch the plane in San Andros."

Sonia's expression revealed the sadness she felt.

To comfort her, Nikki said she could visit in Miami once things settled down in Havana. "I know it's sad for you to let Andrea leave."

"I must stay strong for her. I love her like my own, but she will be much safer away from here. My brother asks that you look after Andrea when you get back to Miami. Will you do that? Make sure she's safe."

"I promise," Nikki said. "We'll take care of her."

"Where is she?" Eduardo asked.

Sonia turned. A basketball hoop at the opposite side of the park had one lone person languidly practicing long shots. Sonia whistled loudly. The girl took one last shot and picked up the ball, then strolled across the patchy grass toward the kiosk.

CHAPTER FORTY-EIGHT

Charlotte hadn't slept well since the demonstration in Havana blasted across the internet. Now it was impossible to get news directly from Cuba. She relied on reports trickling out of the island. A news flash from Spain stated that the hardline Cuban government was losing control, with the advent of the internet and mobile connectivity. The Cuban people were emboldened to get news of their suppressed condition out to the world. Shortages of food, medicine, and medical facilities to combat the pandemic had them demanding their rights.

Unfortunately, Charlotte thought, the internet has been turned off, making it impossible for people to send their anonymous videos to foreign news stations.

When Hamilton came into the office, she asked him to check again on the status of the airport in Havana. She stood by his desk while he made the call to a CIA operative. When the operative responded, Ham repeated the words.

Charlotte cheered. "They can take a plane and come home!"

She marched straight to Floyd's office.

"Great news! The airport is open in Havana. My friend John at the travel agency told me it's operational again. Then I had Ham confirm it with one of his CIA colleagues."

Floyd took a hand to his chin, looking pensive.

"Should we risk letting Nikki know?" he asked.

"Why don't you call Eduardo," she suggested. "Nikki called you from her wristband radio. If you use Eduardo's channel, it will be different. Minimizes the risk of getting them in trouble."

Floyd agreed it was a good idea. "Before calling Eduardo, I'll get hold of my friend in Mexico City to confirm the reopening."

"It won't hurt to get a third opinion." Charlotte was biting her nails. She left his office, closing the door behind her.

Two hours later, Floyd's contact called him back and confirmed clearance in Havana. Taking the satellite radio out of the top drawer, he punched in Eduardo's channel.

A few seconds later, Eduardo responded with a strong "good check."

Using their code, Floyd told him the airport in Havana was open. And his contact in Mexico City had verified that Nikki and Eduardo seemed clear if they chose to fly out.

"And our daughter?"

"Clear to fly. Flight fifty-two at martini time."

"Ten-four," Eduardo said.

"Copy," Floyd said, ending the call. He scrambled down the hall to let Charlotte know he'd contacted Eduardo. And he breathed normally for the first time in days.

CHAPTER FORTY-NINE

Finished with the call, Eduardo turned his watch completely off. Leaving the kiosk where Nikki had been talking with Sonia and Andrea, she joined him.

"What's up?"

Taking his glasses off to clean them, Eduardo relayed that the airport was open and they could take the last flight of the day to Mexico City. Unless the schedule had changed, that would be five p.m.

He put his glasses back on and glanced toward Andrea, who was still at the kiosk with Mama-Sonia. They both seemed sad.

Sonia reversed the raincoat to a lively purple color, put her glasses in a pocket, took the wig off, and tied a scarf around her head. She folded and carried the blanket she'd used to pad her back. She looked completely different.

She asked them to wait for Oliver at the park. They would need to coordinate the exit out of the country. Mama-Sonia handed Andrea a paper bag.

"Remember to take your medicine," the woman said, embracing Andrea.

The teenager handed the well-used basketball to Mama-Sonia.

"We'll do everything we can to make Andrea safe." Nikki put an arm around the teenager's shoulder.

"And we'll also do whatever we can to get her Uncle Urby to Miami," Eduardo said.

Andrea nodded, looking down at the concrete around the kiosk.

Eduardo moved closer to Andrea. Quietly, he told her that her Uncle Urby had promised to catch up with them in Miami as soon as he could.

The three of them watched Mama-Sonia cross the park.

Eduardo hated mentioning Barriga's promise. There was no guarantee he'd ever reach US soil. Then again, there was no guarantee any of them would.

Eduardo wasn't sure if Andrea believed anything he'd said. An uncertain future lay ahead of her. Ahead of all of them. In Miami, Andrea had parents with full legal custody, yet he and Nikki had promised to take care of her.

Through the trees and shrubs of the park, Eduardo caught a glimpse of Oliver approaching.

Eduardo walked over to meet Oliver. When they all gathered at the kiosk, Oliver told them everything was in place for the boat trip to Andros Island. Eduardo waited patiently while the medical student explained the plan to leave the city and journey by car to a swamp along the coastline where a dinghy would take them by night to a waiting speedboat.

After dutifully listening, Eduardo asked why they couldn't take an airplane from the Havana airport.

"For one," Oliver said, holding up his index finger, "you don't have a passport for Andrea. At least not one that you can use at the airport. Second, we don't know if your names are on the list of people who cannot leave Cuba."

Eduardo handed him the passport they'd brought with them. Oliver looked as if the wind had been knocked out of him.

"How did you manage it?" he asked, reaching for the passport, and studying Andrea's new identity.

"The same way you got our Cuban documents."

"It looks authentic," Oliver said, running his finger over the embossed photo before returning the passport to Eduardo.

"Back to my question," Eduardo asked. "Which is safer: the airport,

MISSING IN MIAMI | 199

or traveling overland to the swamp, taking a dinghy, and getting away in a speedboat?"

Oliver shook his head. "If the authorities stop you at the airport, I can't do anything."

"On the other hand," Eduardo said, "the entire island is on high alert. Every vehicle leaving Havana will be stopped and inspected. Neither Nikki nor I speak with a Cuban accent. Despite the documents Barriga provided, we'd never pass for Cubans."

"Tough call," Oliver said. He asked Nikki how she felt.

When Nikki agreed that flying out seemed safer, Eduardo volunteered to go to the airport and change their return tickets.

Oliver offered to drop him off. As a registered guide, he was allowed to transport tourists.

———

"If you're not back in three hours, I'll call the office," Nikki said. She hugged Eduardo and whispered that she loved him. Turning to Oliver, she handed him a few euros to pick up lunch on his return to the park after leaving Eduardo at the airport.

"Let's sit in the shade of that tree," Nikki suggested to Andrea. She wanted to get to know this petite yet strong-willed young woman. And she needed to explain a few things.

"You've heard us talk about Uncle Urby being in trouble with the Cuban government, even though he's done nothing wrong. Do you understand why he wants you to leave Havana?"

"He's afraid that people will hurt me to get to him."

"Are you willing to do your part to get us out safely?"

Andrea nodded. Her eyes brimmed with tears.

"You're traveling as Valentina Ramírez, our daughter. We cannot get you out any other way."

Again, Andrea nodded.

"All three of us have been here on vacation."

"Did we visit friends or relatives?" she asked.

"Great question," Nikki said. "It's best not to mention Uncle Urby or Mama-Sonia. We don't want to get them in trouble, so we'll say we didn't visit anyone."

"Did Uncle Urby do anything wrong in Miami?"

"In the US, he took you without your parents' consent. That's against the law in every country."

"But I asked him to take me," she said, looking down with her voice faltering. "My father killed Pepito, my puppy. He said I'd be next if I did not behave."

Nikki's stomach tightened.

"Has your dad been mean like that before?"

"He hits Mama. She's been drinking a lot and it makes him angry, like when she misses work. Sometimes she can't get up in the morning after they fight about her drinking. And a long time ago he killed my cat."

Nikki told her the state of Florida offered services to children if she wanted to live somewhere else.

Andrea frowned. "I'm not a child!"

"I meant you're not yet eighteen. Once you reach legal age, you can make your own decisions."

"I don't want to live at home, and I don't want to live with a family assigned by Child Protective Services, either."

Nikki asked how she knew about CPS.

"I looked it up online. After reading about people who grew up in foster families, I decided it's not for me. Uncle Urby is good to me. He loves me, and I want to be with him."

Nikki reminded Andrea she was underage and she might have to live with her parents until she was eighteen.

"When Uncle Urby returns to Miami, I'll live with him."

Not wanting to argue the point, Nikki let it go.

Eduardo returned, having walked the last four blocks to the park. Nikki ran over and threw her arms around him.

"We have Floyd to thank for purchasing first-class tickets," he said. "Otherwise we'd be stuck here another day."

"We should be okay, since they didn't stop you," Nikki whispered.

He squeezed her closer and whispered that he'd come to the same conclusion.

She told him that Oliver had brought lunch, but she wanted to speak to Andrea about her passport first.

Eduardo called Andrea aside. He showed the passport to her while Nikki explained it would help if she wore the dental device to change her appearance a little to match the photo.

"My hair isn't right," Andrea said, glancing at the passport. "Will they stop me?"

"We have a wig with short hair for you," Nikki said. "When we head for the airport, you can put it on and the dental device can go in your mouth."

They returned to the kiosk where Oliver had left the sandwiches and maltas. They ate quietly, as if everyone understood the momentous step they were about to take.

Eduardo broke the silence. It was time to leave for the airport.

CHAPTER FIFTY

The airport was busy with travelers catching flights that had been canceled earlier that week. Departing passengers, wearing masks, rushed down corridors. Arrivals pulled their luggage toward the exit.

Eduardo handed the passports to the immigration official. The skinny man looked at each passport, checked the photo against the person in front of him, removed the visitor card, scrutinized the computer, and kept the pile of passports until he'd finished. Without a word, he handed them back to Eduardo.

Lounges were available for an extra fee, but Eduardo wanted to wait at the gate for boarding to begin. As first-class passengers, they were called in the first group. The Aeroméxico flight attendant greeted them with a warm smile and indicated the direction of their seats. Nikki and Andrea sat together. Eduardo occupied one in front of them.

Nikki noticed Andrea was still uptight. She gently told her to relax and take a nap.

Nikki checked her watch, trying to be discreet. Departure time passed. Thirty minutes late, then forty-five. No inflight magazines because of the pandemic. Nikki felt anxious. She pulled a small paper notebook from her purse and tried to doodle.

Finally, an hour later, the cabin doors were shut. The prerecorded safety briefing and video were broadcast on the entertainment system.

The plane did not taxi out to the runway. It remained at the gate. After another twenty minutes, the public address system came on. The attendant who had welcomed them on board informed passengers the flight was delayed due to paperwork. Ground personnel needed to complete it before the plane could depart.

The cabin doors opened.

A policeman stepped in and handed the flight attendant a slip of paper. She used the PA to request Valentina Ramírez to identify herself.

Andrea turned to Nikki with a frightened expression. Eduardo stood and asked why they needed his daughter.

The policeman stepped forward. "You did not give us the visitor card for her," he growled.

Eduardo took the three passports from his light jacket. Grabbing the one for Valentina Ramírez, he flipped through the pages trying to locate the card.

The policeman snatched the passport from Eduardo's hands.

"Wait a minute—" Eduardo started to protest.

As the officer opened the passport, the card fell to the floor. He picked it up. Glancing between the passport and the card, he glared at the teenager.

"Remove your mask."

Andrea obliged.

"You seem nervous," he said. "Is anything wrong?"

"I'm always nervous before flying," she responded.

Nikki cringed internally. Andrea's Spanish had a heavy Cuban accent, and at this moment, it seemed more pronounced than usual.

The officer kept the visitor card, returning the passport to Eduardo.

"I hope you've enjoyed Cuba. Have a good trip," he said, changing his demeanor and tone of voice.

Nikki melted into her seat.

The flight attendant thanked the passengers for their patience during the delay and announced the flight would leave the gate momentarily.

Halfway through the flight, Andrea still seemed too nervous to fall asleep. She talked to Nikki about Pepito. She missed her little Chihuahua, and she felt guilty for not being able to save him from her father's cruelty.

Nikki comforted her. To distract the girl, she told Andrea that Chihuahuas were like the dogs that the ancient inhabitants of Mesoamerica loved. Had she ever seen a hairless Mexican dog?

Andrea smiled. "Hairless? Like completely bald?"

Nikki nodded. To her surprise, that made Andrea laugh. She laughed some more. Her eyes glistened.

Andrea's laughter was contagious. Nikki laughed too. They were both releasing tension.

The plane landed at the Benito Juárez International Airport in Mexico City two hours late. Nikki was certain they'd missed their connection. Eduardo glanced at his watch and announced they'd have to sleep in the airport.

"Only if you want the adventure," Nikki said. "As for Andrea and me, we'll find a nice hotel."

Andrea smiled.

They took a shuttle to the airport Marriott. After settling Andrea into her bed, Nikki called Floyd's office phone and left a message. They'd arrive with the teenager at noon in Miami. And Security Source should find someone from Child Protective Services to assess the Rodríguez household. Nikki shared a room with Andrea and Eduardo slept in the connecting room.

CHAPTER FIFTY-ONE

Charlotte waited for the Mexico City flight with the limousine drivers. Seeing Nikki, Eduardo, and the girl with them, a sob rose in her throat.

Sniffling, Charlotte introduced herself to Andrea. Nikki hugged her and thanked her for picking them up. Since they had no checked luggage, they made a quick escape to the parking garage.

In the car, Andrea removed the dental piece and wig.

Now that they were in Miami, Nikki told Andrea their real names. The assumed names had been to protect all of them.

At first Andrea seemed surprised. "You mean like I was Valentina Ramírez for a few hours?"

Nikki nodded.

Eduardo told her she wasn't the only one who'd had to change her appearance. He'd grown a mustache and beard. "Now I'll be happy to shave all this off."

"Are you and Eduardo married?" the teenager asked.

"Yes, that part is true," Nikki said, laughing.

"Now if we can get Uncle Urby out," Andrea said. "And someday maybe Mama-Sonia and her family."

Nikki was glad to see that Floyd had ordered food brought into the office. A homemade welcome sign made Andrea smile.

The girl smiled even more broadly when Charlotte handed her a gift-wrapped package. "It's not even my birthday," she said, unwrapping it to reveal a slim backpack.

"Look inside," Charlotte said.

She pulled a book out and read the title. "*The Book of Unusual Knowledge*. Nice!"

Among the people around the conference table eating lunch was a woman Nikki didn't know. She assumed she represented Child Protective Services. The woman observed Andrea as she described her stay in Cuba.

After lunch, Nikki told Andrea it was time to talk about her parents. The teenager had been smiling and talkative since her arrival at Security Source. Now her smile evaporated.

Nikki led Andrea to her office.

"Please don't send me home. I'm afraid."

"If you're afraid of your father, we should talk to an expert."

"Someone from Child Protective Services?" Andrea asked.

Nikki nodded. She asked Andrea if she wanted to speak with a caseworker.

"I guess."

Nikki called Charlotte on the intercom and asked her to bring the caseworker in.

Terri Acosta introduced herself. She wore black pants and a navy blouse that accented her slender body. She explained that where a minor feared for her life, she could immediately remove the minor from the parental home. She could do this for Andrea and place her with a family where she'd be safe.

"Like a foster family?" Andrea asked.

"It will be a family approved by the state and, yes, they are often called foster families.

"I don't want to live with a family I don't know." Andrea coughed. "I'd rather live at home."

Nikki asked her if she wanted a glass of water.

Andrea nodded. "I need to take my medicine."

Terri asked her if she was sick.

"Only my lupus, but I'm feeling better every day."

Terri asked the teenager why she feared going home.

"My father started getting really angry all the time when I had that lung thing, PSP."

"Why was he angry?"

Staring at the floor, Andrea shook her head. "He was angry all the time. Mama started drinking more."

Nikki asked Andrea to explain what had happened to Pepito, her dog.

When Andrea said what her father had done, she broke down. Nikki hugged Andrea and told her they would work things out so she'd be safe.

Terri offered a solution. "If you're in danger at home, we'll find a good foster family where you can stay for two years. Your parents will have supervised visitation."

Andrea shook her head.

"You're sixteen. You need to tell us what you want."

"I'll give it a try at home."

"Why?" Terri asked.

"I miss my mother."

Nikki intervened and said a foster home would be much safer. She and her husband would be happy to have Andrea stay with them.

"That's not the way it works. We'd have to get you approved as foster parents. But before that happens, I need to do an initial home assessment and talk to Andrea's parents," Terri said. Then she added that she wanted a surprise visit to the home. "That way, I can get a better idea of the dynamics."

Terri looked at Nikki and back to Andrea. "How about if you go home, just for a trial. If things get bad, you can call me and I'll immediately pull you out of there."

Andrea agreed that could work.

Nikki repeated that she and Eduardo would be happy to have Andrea stay with them. Nikki gave Andrea a card with her phone number on it and Eduardo's written in. "Do not hesitate to call us, day or night."

Terri handed Andrea a burner phone and told her that two numbers had already been added—her own and her supervisor's, Mrs. Ballesteros. She suggested adding Nikki's number. The phone was prepaid for three months.

CHAPTER FIFTY-TWO

By the time Floyd drove to Palmetto Bay and arrived at the guard shack at Paradise Point, it was approaching four-thirty in the afternoon. Andrea spoke to the guard, who immediately recognized her. He told them he'd call ahead and let her mother know. When Floyd pulled into the driveway, the front door of the house was open.

Delfina was leaning against the doorframe. Andrea jumped out of the car and ran to her mother. They embraced.

Floyd, Nikki, Eduardo, and Terri got out. Andrea hugged her mother while Delfina smoothed her daughter's hair.

Delfina thanked Nikki and Floyd for finding Andrea. Delfina studied Nikki for a few seconds and told her she looked different.

"I went curly," Nikki said, reaching up to touch her permed ringlets.

Delfina invited them in. She noticed Eduardo and the caseworker and asked who they were.

Terri introduced herself, telling Delfina that circumstances made it necessary for Child Protective Services to make a home visit.

"My husband's not here. Yoani left early this morning for Latin America. He's traveling for business and won't be back for a month."

"I'll come back another time to interview your husband," Terri said.

Delfina frowned.

Nikki introduced Eduardo, saying he had also worked the case. They shook hands and headed inside. Delfina draped an arm over Andrea's shoulder.

Nikki was surprised to find books and clothes spread over the sofa and designer chairs in Delfina's elegant great room. Two suitcases, open and partially packed, rested on the floor.

"Let's go into the kitchen," Delfina said. "It's tidier in there."

In the kitchen, still embracing Andrea, Delfina started crying.

The reunion between mother and daughter felt awkward to Nikki, as if the rest of them were intruding. It was unfortunate the situation called for Child Protective Services to be involved. She felt bad about not insisting on taking Andrea out of the parents' home, yet Andrea seemed very happy to see her mother.

They gave Delfina the space to talk with her daughter. Delfina seemed shocked to learn Barriga had taken Andrea without permission. Andrea defended him, saying she'd asked him to take her to Havana. He'd taken her for the regenerative surgery her father had denied. He still had the power of attorney her parents had given him several years ago.

"And, Mama, I feel good and I'm not taking as many meds as I used to."

Delfina's spirits seemed to crumble when her daughter mentioned Barriga and the stem cell treatment.

"The first surgery gave you lupus. I worry what will happen this time."

"I wanted this treatment, so don't blame Uncle Urby." Andrea put her arms around her mother.

"He had no right to make that decision," Delfina said forcefully. Looking at the others in the kitchen, she told Andrea they'd talk later.

Terri asked to speak with Delfina privately.

Delfina and the caseworker walked down the hall toward the office. Nikki asked Andrea if she cared to take the welcome gift from Security Source to her room. When Andrea agreed, they headed toward the second floor. Floyd and Eduardo followed them out of the kitchen and stayed behind in the great room.

At the landing, Nikki looked back over the great room. If Rodríguez was traveling, it didn't make sense that two partially packed suitcases were left behind. Floyd had picked up a book and was sitting on the edge of the sofa leafing through it. Eduardo stood over a suitcase, peering at the contents.

Andrea's room looked just as it had the day Nikki was there with Delfina. The dolls on the bookcase shelves were lined up the way she'd last seen them. She asked the girl to explain about her collection. Andrea dropped the backpack on the bed.

Nikki stepped in closer as Andrea picked up the first doll and explained what was special about it. She seemed lively and self-assured, making Nikki glad she was settling back into her home. She stole a glance at the ornamental Japanese dolls still on the shelf. To the side, she saw the Voodoo effigy that had upset Delfina so much. Instead of standing, the figure with the lavender cape was lying on the shelf. The pins had been removed.

She brought Andrea's attention to the doll, the one the expert had called a poppet.

With an inquisitive look, Andrea picked it up and turned it over three or four times, studying it.

"I don't know where this one came from. Its dress looks like a blouse I have. But I've never seen it before."

When Nikki asked to see the blouse, Andrea went straight to her closet. She searched hanger by hanger, to no avail.

"I don't know what happened. I left it right here."

"Are you sure?" Nikki asked.

"I know it was hanging in my closet because it was my favorite blouse. Whoever made that doll for me made the dress with the ruffle like my blouse."

"Do you think Raquel might have made it for you?"

"Raquel? How could she? Uncle Urby told me she was murdered."

Nikki explained Raquel could have made it before she'd died.

"She didn't know how to sew. Uncle Urby always had to send clothes out to be fixed, like the hems on his pants."

Nikki knew she was pushing it, but she asked Andrea about Raquel.

"Oh, she was a really nice lady. Mama didn't like her, but I don't know why. I was sad to hear she'd died. And Uncle Urby cried when he told me."

Nikki reminded Andrea that she could call any time and suggested she memorize all three numbers. Terri would be following up soon. Nikki herself could not intrude, though she and Eduardo would not hold back in an emergency. She made it clear they would come and get Andrea if she needed them.

"We'll be happy to help," Nikki assured her.

They joined the two men in the great room. Floyd was deep into a book on Simón Bolívar. He smiled and put the book down. He started to ask Andrea if she had hobbies or special topics that interested her when they heard the caseworker and Delfina returning.

Nikki glanced at Delfina with apprehension. Some of Terri's questions might have upset her. But she looked more relaxed than when they had arrived.

Delfina took Floyd's hands in hers and thanked him profusely for the good work. She turned to Nikki and did the same. She said she was happy to have her daughter back and could now think of returning to work.

"Send me your final invoice," she said to Floyd. "I'll wire the money as soon as I receive it."

Delfina was charming and delightful as she escorted them to the front door. "Come back anytime," she said.

When they drove over the small bridge as they left Paradise Point, Nikki told the rest of the group she found something strange about suitcases with men's clothing when Rodríguez was already traveling.

Terri told them Delfina had said she'd started packing for her husband, but he'd decided to travel light and only took a smaller piece of luggage.

"I'm not sure I believe her," Nikki said. "He's supposed to be on a long trip."

Floyd agreed something did not sound quite right about the explanation.

"Andrea seemed happy to see her mother," Terri said, changing the subject. "In the meantime, you can start the foster home application in case I have to remove her in an emergency." Terri promised she'd stay on top of the case and interview Rodríguez as soon as he returned.

CHAPTER FIFTY-THREE

VILLA MARISTA PRISON, HAVANA

Urbano lay awake, praying his friend would release him from prison. Unable to sleep, he feared his friend might back out or turn him in, for an even worse sentence. He hated to resort to bribery, but it was the only way to get out of the country and back to Miami. He had to do it for Andrea. She needed him.

Urbano watched the faint glow of light that filtered into the corridor. The glow disappeared and he made sure his eyes were open. It was the power outage he'd been promised.

A slight rustle in the corridor filled his chest with fear and hope.

As quietly as he could, he rose from the cot.

In the dark, Urbano could tell it was his childhood friend, the prison warden.

Unlocking the door, the man came into the cell. He handed Urbano a police uniform. He waited for his prisoner to change. The warden took back the standard prison uniform and handed him a cap. The two walked into the corridor. Urbano kept his head down as he'd been told during the warden's visit the night he was apprehended.

Silently, they walked to the warden's office. Urbano couldn't know when the power might return. Using a dim flashlight, the warden returned Urbano's passport and led him to the exit. The prison was totally dark. Just one of Havana's many power outages, but the money he'd given the warden had made this one possible.

Outside, he felt a chill despite the warm weather. The half-moon was partially obscured by clouds. He walked three blocks as he'd been told, slowing periodically to make sure no one followed him. Around a corner, he recognized a car that presumably was waiting for him. Urbano walked cautiously to it. The passenger door opened up and he ducked to glance inside.

"Just get in, man. It's me," Oliver said.

The headlights of another vehicle turned onto their street. Urbano slid down to avoid being seen, and Oliver did the same. After it passed, Urbano peered over the dashboard.

Police van. Urbano held his breath as he watched it disappear around a corner two blocks away. It might have been headed to the Villa Marista, the political prison he'd just escaped.

Oliver eased the car away from the curb with the lights off. Without speaking, he drove slowly for several blocks.

"The one advantage," he said, "we're close to the outskirts of Havana, heading to Santa Cruz del Norte. Wish we could drive the Vía Blanca toll road, but we must take back roads to avoid checkpoints."

"Why Santa Cruz?"

"It's safer than driving to the swamps near Puerto Escondido. Your guy told me the swamps are patrolled day and night for people trying to escape after the demonstrations. We're headed to Jibacoa Beach. The Sargasso seaweed there is keeping patrol boats from getting too close to shore."

"And the dinghy can handle the seaweed?" Urbano asked.

"So I was told."

Urbano turned to the backseat. "Did you bring the briefcase?"

Oliver told him it was on the floor behind the passenger seat. Oliver checked his rearview mirror again and again. Both men fell silent. Urbano spent his time praying. Not a churchgoer, he did believe in a higher power. Now seemed like a good time to pray. If nothing else, it kept his mind occupied.

On a long stretch of road with chuckholes, it was impossible to avoid hitting them in the dark. By the time the parking lights shone on one, it was too late for Oliver to swerve. Urbano saw the back of a police car ahead of them, and Oliver saw it at about the same time. He maneuvered the car onto a side road.

"Hide in the bushes," Oliver said.

They got out and Oliver lifted the hood of the car as if to fix the motor. Urbano told him to disconnect the battery in case he had to play it up with the police.

Sure enough, the police doubled back.

Urbano hid his briefcase, then crouched in the underbrush.

The patrolmen strode up and asked Oliver why he was driving despite the curfew.

Oliver pulled his documents from the glove compartment.

"My girlfriend called," he said. "You know how women are when they get it in their heads they need to see you."

One patrolman laughed. The other one, more aggressive, asked for Oliver's license and car documents. Using a flashlight on the papers, he said Oliver could lose his tour guide permit.

"I hope not," Oliver said meekly.

"You're in violation of curfew. All I have to do is write you up and your tour guide license will disappear. Poof, just like that."

"There's surely a way to avoid that," Oliver said. Urbano imagined he was showing them a few Cuban pesos.

"It's one way to fix things. If you add a few dollars it would work better." The more aggressive one said, apparently not satisfied with Oliver's offer.

Oliver must have pulled out some dollar bills.

"You'll have to do better than six bucks. You're from La Yuma and I want more Yuma dollars," the same greedy fellow said.

Oliver offered something else, saying that's all he had.

"Fifty works." The patrolman said. Then, "I have to pee."

The man went behind the bushes. Urbano could not move for fear he'd be detected. The second man decided he needed to visit the bushes too.

As the patrolmen left, they wished Oliver good luck with his woman.

Urbano crawled out from the bushes and picked up his briefcase. Oliver was under the hood reconnecting the battery.

"Coño," Urbano said, standing up. That was a close one. "My pant legs, socks, and shoes are wet."

"Could be worse, hijo de puta," Oliver said. He laughed so hard that he had to steady himself against the car. "You're lucky. You're still a free man."

"You should leave the country," Urbano said. "If they find out you helped me escape, they'll throw you away for life. Take it from one whose been in prison here, it's a fate worse than death."

"But you got out all right," Oliver said.

"Through a childhood connection who risked his life if they find out he helped me. And paying bribes to these poor people who live on less than twenty dollars a month. It's no wonder they turn to bribery."

"Don't you have any love for Cuba?" Oliver asked.

"For the country and the people, yes. Not for the government."

They were approaching Jibacoa Beach. Oliver skirted the town completely to avoid attracting patrols, if any were out, either on land or in the ocean. He handed a compass to Urbano to find the coordinates where they were supposed to wait for the scout who would take them to the dinghy. Next, they looked for a place to hide the car. The clouded sky gave them barely enough moonlight to see the mangroves.

Urbano watched as Oliver took documents from the glove compartment and stuck them into his beltline, covering them with his shirt.

"Will there be room for me on the dinghy?" Oliver asked, keeping his voice low.

"I assume so. I paid for a seat for Andrea so you can take that one."

They waited over half an hour before Urbano heard the trill of a male Cuban hummingbird courting a female. Once he'd made certain it was their scout making the bird sound, they both stood. The scout hugged Urbano. Another childhood friend, Urbano told Oliver.

Walking for another half hour over smooth sand, they stayed close to the mangroves whenever they could to avoid being spotted.

"The clouds are covering the moon, but we must still be careful," the scout whispered.

They were walking west along the edge of the mangrove forest. After a mile or so, the scout stopped and imitated more bird songs. Two other men arrived and said they were ready. Five minutes later, they scrambled aboard a rowboat. It had a small outboard motor attached at the rear, but the men handed oars to the new arrivals. The bird caller pushed the boat out and all four men started rowing. Finally, the bird caller jumped in.

CHAPTER FIFTY-FOUR

MIAMI

Floyd had promised them a vacation of their choosing. Instead of a romantic destination, Nikki and Eduardo stayed in Miami, the city they'd recently moved to and had not yet explored. They planned to spend their vacation taking advantage of the Everglades, museums, beaches, tours, and other activities Nikki had on a list.

Three days after taking Andrea to her mother, Nikki and Eduardo started their vacation. They'd walked out of their condo building and gone next door to the Faena Hotel. Nikki wanted to see the installation in the patio called *Gone but Not Forgotten*, a gilded woolly mammoth skeleton contained in a glass cage. The valet attendant at their building had mentioned the installation the morning Nikki found the dead alligator on her car.

A doorman opened the door for them to enter.

Beyond the lobby, the golden skeleton glistened in the sunlight on the patio.

They walked outside. Reading the plaque on the installation, they learned the glass case was hurricane proof.

"The mammoth is safer in a hurricane than we are," Eduardo said.

"Too bad they're extinct." Nikki was not impressed and was ready to move on.

Breakfast was on the patio of a hotel two buildings down from the condo. They were enjoying freshly squeezed orange juice when their server arrived with eggs benedict. Nikki told Eduardo there was no place she'd rather be. The love in his eyes reflected what she felt for him.

They had started eating when her mobile rang.

Eduardo placed his hand on hers. "Please don't answer. We're on vacation."

She glanced at the caller ID. It was Delfina. "I must," she said. "Sorry."

"Please help me," Delfina whispered over the phone. She sounded as if she'd been crying. "I'm afraid my husband took Andrea . . ." her voice trailed off.

"When did he return?" Nikki asked, grabbing her purse.

"I don't know. Maybe Andrea called him and he came back for her."

"I'll leave now and be there as soon as traffic permits. Call me if you hear from her." Something nagged at Nikki. Andrea feared her father. She wouldn't call him, would she?

Eduardo frowned at her.

"Floyd and Hamilton are out on an investigation this morning. There's no one else to handle it." She put her earbuds in and dialed Charlotte.

"Oh, no," was all Charlotte could say.

Nikki ended the call and gave Eduardo a kiss.

"Do you want me to come with you?" he asked.

"I'll be fine. I need to figure out what's going on."

"From now on, I'm going to trash your phone whenever we're on vacation," he said. "This happens every time. When you find her, bring Andrea to our place."

Nikki didn't hear him. By then, she was jogging toward the door leading to the Miami Beach Walk. She dodged cyclists, pedestrians, and dogs on leashes in her rush to the condo's garage.

The toll roads and freeways were jammed. Nikki decided to take Route 1 to Palmetto Bay. On the way, she called Floyd to let him know where she was headed.

"Did Andrea strike you as ready to run off again, especially since her father is traveling?" Floyd sounded skeptical.

"Not at all," Nikki said. "She's a very sensible young woman. But I'm worried. Delfina said she thinks the father came back for her. But those suitcases we saw looked like someone was packing, not already gone. Terri Acosta wouldn't take Andrea to foster care when Andrea said she missed her mother. And Andrea assured me she'd call if she got scared."

Floyd reminded her to be careful and let him know what she found out.

Traffic was worse than she'd expected. Nikki's mouth went dry with panic at the thought of Rodríguez taking Andrea. She tried focusing on her breathing, but it wasn't enough to make a difference.

When she finally arrived, Delfina opened the door, with narrowed eyes.

"Why did you ask my daughter about the Voodoo doll that woman made?"

Nikki took a step back. "I don't understand."

"The day you brought her home. You asked my daughter who could have made that doll for her."

"I was curious why you'd still have it there when it upset you so much when we found it. That's all."

"It's caused a rift between Andrea and me," Delfina said.

"I'm sorry, but Andrea was showing me her doll collection. It was still there and I asked a reasonable question."

Every light in the great room was turned on, casting harsh shadows on Delfina's angry face.

Nikki felt a lump in her throat. "Let's talk about where your daughter might be."

"She'd still be here if you hadn't planted doubts in her mind," Delfina said.

CHAPTER FIFTY-FIVE

Exhausted and stiff in the filthy police uniform he'd worn for the last forty-eight hours, Urbano nudged Oliver awake. "We've landed."

A bleary-eyed Oliver looked out the window before glancing at his watch. "Coño, it's early." Oliver stretched. "It feels good to come home."

Urbano pulled his briefcase from under the seat and stood in the aisle. He could smell his own body odor despite his mask. A woman in front of him turned and stared. He'd buy clothes in the terminal to change into after a shower in the airline lounge.

In the terminal, he thanked Oliver and paid him. He also gave him two hundred dollars in cash for the taxi fare home.

When he paid for his new clothes, Urbano asked the salesclerk to cut the price tags off every item. The hot shower invigorated him. He looked at himself in the mirror after dressing, adjusted the collar on his shirt, and threw the uniform into the trash. He transferred his green card to his wallet and put a folded sheet of printed test results in his pocket. The tests had been done in Havana. Satisfied he'd taken care of everything, he headed for long-term parking, where he'd left his car when he and Andrea had left Miami.

Urbano unlocked the car and jumped in. He drove to West End at Three Lakes, best known as the Miami CIA office.

"Look, Delfina, if you think I had anything to do with Andrea leaving, you're mistaken. Let's sit down and strategize where to find her," Nikki said.

"I'm going to strategize, all right." Delfina stepped toward the console table in the entry. "You led my daughter to believe I did something wrong. She practically accused me of killing Raquel."

Nikki's attempts to calm the woman were getting nowhere.

"If that's what you think, you're wrong. Do you think I would have brought Andrea home to you if I thought you'd killed Raquel? Or anyone else for that matter." She moved toward Delfina.

"Keep your distance."

It was impossible trying to talk sense to Delfina. Nikki suggested Floyd could come to take her place. She turned to leave. Delfina opened a squeaky drawer on the console. Spinning around, Nikki found herself facing a handgun.

Floyd excused himself from the meeting when he saw Spider Mohle's ID on his mobile. Worried about Nikki, he'd left it where he could see the screen.

"What's up, Spider?"

Spider said he hated to bother Floyd, but Delfina was acting strange. "She dropped Andrea off at our house—"

"Andrea is at your house? Delfina brought her there?"

"Yeah. My wife, she works nights. Yésica had just returned from her shift when Delfina arrived, asking us to take care of Andrea for the day. She told us she had a score to settle. But she . . . I hate to say this, she had a crazed look about her."

"Listen, thanks. Call me immediately if anything else happens."

Floyd dialed Nikki.

No answer.

Considering the few facts he had, he dialed the police department in Palmetto Bay. Before they answered he'd already made it a three-way conference call with Charlotte. He asked to speak to Sergeant Maldonado.

"Sergeant," Floyd said, when the man answered, "I have an urgent favor to ask. My assistant, Charlotte, is also on the line. I'm calling about Nikki Garcia, whom you met when she found Raquel Álvarez. She should be at the Rodríguez house right now. My agent may be in danger, grave danger. Can you send a couple of patrol cars out there? Immediately. Break in if you have to. I'll meet you there in about forty minutes. Charlotte will give you the address."

The sergeant indicated he would get right on it, telling Floyd he would call once he found out what was going on.

Floyd told them he'd also drive to Delfina's house. Ending the call, he ran to the elevator and pressed the button to the parking garage.

Charlotte provided the address. She stayed on the phone with the sergeant long enough to mention she had an app open that showed the location of Nikki's car. It was parked in front of a client's house, Delfina Morales, at the address she'd given him. "Is there anything else you need?"

Maldonado thanked her.

Charlotte ended the call and felt sick. She wished she could do more to make sure Nikki was safe. Her heart was beating so loudly, she could hear it.

CHAPTER FIFTY-SIX

Delfina held the gun so tightly that Nikki could see the woman's knuckles had turned white.

"Besides questioning my daughter about Raquel and the blouse, how could you have gone to Cuba without letting me know? I was told you were in Canada. I resent that.

"I hired you and you should have answered to me. I'm her mother. Andrea told me how her 'Mama-Sonia' stayed almost three weeks in isolation at the clinic with *my daughter* to take care of her after the transplant."

"You hired me to find Andrea. What does it matter if I went to Cuba? Your daughter is back. You would not have been able to . . ." Nikki's voice trailed off. "Are you angry that I went to Cuba? Is that why you're pointing the gun at me?"

"Shut up, bitch."

"If I didn't keep you informed, it was for Andrea's safety."

"Andrea told me you became friends with Urbano."

Nikki's phone rang. The purse was over her shoulder.

"Don't answer it. Or I'll kill you right now," Delfina said, cocking the hammer.

Nikki was too far away to dive toward Delfina and overpower her. Throwing her purse at Delfina wouldn't work either, for the same reason.

Using the gun, Delfina made a sweeping motion pointing at Nikki's head and chest.

"Where do you want the bullet? Your heart?" Delfina asked with a macabre laugh. "Or your head? Maybe I won't kill you, just leave you a vegetable for that good-looking husband."

"Stop this if you don't want your daughter to turn completely away from you."

"Shut up."

"Think, Delfina. If Andrea suspects you killed Raquel and now you kill me, she will have nothing to do with you."

"For the last time, shut up." Delfina kept the gun pointed at Nikki, her finger on the trigger, and ordered her to move toward the patio.

Nikki's baby Glock was in the hidden compartment in her purse, but getting it was impossible right now. Nikki racked her brain for ways to distract Delfina as she took slow steps toward the patio.

When she set foot on the slate floor of the patio, Nikki thought she'd heard a knock at the front door. She hoped anyone, a neighbor or Floyd or a gardener, would arrive to stop Delfina. *If only Eduardo were here.*

The sinister silence was broken by Delfina's raspy voice telling her to get on her knees. Since the gun was already cocked, Nikki obeyed. As she kneeled, she turned toward the great room. Had someone knocked? Or was it wishful thinking? Maybe she could tell Delfina someone had arrived. But what if that didn't work?

Nikki's mouth was so dry it hurt. Then she saw movement inside. The light was so bright that at first she thought her eyes were playing tricks on her. But then she clearly saw three uniforms—Sergeant Maldonado followed by two officers.

Guns at the ready, all three men looked around. One started down the hallway, but stopped abruptly. She thought he'd seen her. Nikki's heart thumped in her ears.

Nikki was paralyzed with fear. She could feel the pressure of the barrel against the back of her neck. *If Delfina sees them, she'll kill me.*

Maldonado and his men were moving silently against the wall of the great room. Nikki felt her heartbeat accelerate.

Delfina moved the barrel against Nikki's head.

A shot rang out.

And then, deafening, a second shot.

CHAPTER FIFTY-SEVEN

The guard at the reception desk in the CIA building asked Urbano if he had an appointment.

"No, but I have something the CIA will want."

The guard eyed the battered briefcase and made a call.

Half an hour later, Urbano passed through the metal detector. He figured the unrest in Cuba helped him get through so quickly. The guard opened his briefcase and ran his hand around the inside, checking for false compartments where an explosive device could be hidden.

"Your case has seen better days," the guard said, closing it. "Hardly anyone carries one anymore."

Finally, Urbano sat before a field operative who looked to be about twenty-five. The name plate on his desk read Frank.

Urbano explained he had proof of medical espionage by the Cuban government that resulted in critical research being transmitted to the island nation. He opened his briefcase and pulled out a stash of documents and two thumb drives, placing them on the operative's desk.

"Your proof is in these documents?"

"Yes. In exchange," Urbano said, "I want American citizenship."

"No promises. We need to take a look at what you've brought us," Frank said. He set the thumb drives aside and shuffled through the documents to assess what was being offered.

"Over what period of time was this happening?"

"What the documents will clearly show are the last four years. But I think this operation was going on for much longer. The thumb drive labeled Exhibit 1 details what occurred this past year. The other one shows older files."

Frank took the loose papers and thumb drives and told Urbano to wait.

CHAPTER FIFTY-EIGHT

From her knees, Nikki spun around with force, hitting Delfina and knocking her to the slate floor. The gun fell within Delfina's reach and she stretched to grab it. She got her hand around it just as Nikki jumped up, kicking it away.

Maldonado and his men rushed toward Delfina, who was still on the ground. The sergeant moved in to prevent her from getting up. One of the officers handcuffed her, helped her to a standing position, and had her take a seat on a patio chair. The third officer took a position near Delfina.

Nikki felt stunned. She watched the sergeant photograph the ground near the flowering bushes where the gun had landed. When he finished recording the scene on his phone, Nikki heard him mirandize Delfina and formally arrest her. The two policemen took her into the great room, apparently to hold her there until they took her to the station.

Thoughts were racing through Nikki's mind. She knew there were things she needed to prioritize, but she felt bewildered after the assault. If only she could focus.

Then it came to her. Andrea! The girl would need a place to stay. She and Eduardo needed to start the process to become foster parents.

The sergeant stayed on the patio with Nikki. He picked up Delfina's gun with gloved hands and placed it in an evidence bag. He looked for the casing and bagged it too.

"You only found one casing." Nikki held up two fingers. "But I heard two shots go off."

"You're right," Maldonado said. "I shot the first one down the hall to scare Delfina so she wouldn't kill you."

Nikki sighed. She was too tired to think about the consequences. What if that first shot hadn't startled Delfina? She'd think about those details later. Right now it was time to call Floyd.

Updating her boss, she told him she was in good shape despite the harrowing encounter. He told her he was on his way to Delfina's house and he asked to speak with Maldonado.

She passed the phone to the sergeant.

Maldonado told Floyd he'd arrested Delfina for aggravated battery with a firearm. "It could have ended tragically if you hadn't called when you did."

He passed the phone back to Nikki.

"We have to find Andrea," she said. "We don't know if Rodríguez took her—"

Floyd interrupted to tell her the teenager was safely at Spider and Yésica's place. Delfina herself had taken her there earlier that morning.

Nikki felt sick. How could a mother do that? "Another one of Delfina's lies."

"It's worse than that. She really did intend to kill you," Floyd said.

EMTs arrived, interrupting Nikki's phone conversation. "I'll call Eduardo to tell him what's happened," she said before ending the call.

Nikki saw through the window that one EMT stayed inside to check Delfina. The other walked to the patio.

Nikki's vital signs were good, except for her blood pressure, which was higher than normal. She protested that she didn't need anyone fussing over her. The sergeant probably needed a statement from her, or she would have already left.

Maldonado, still holding the evidence bag, agreed he'd need her statement.

The EMT noticed blood on her left sleeve and asked her to roll it up.

"Good grief, you were lucky," Maldonado said, looking on.

"Fortunately, the bullet barely grazed your upper arm," the EMT said. "Didn't this hurt?"

"I didn't even feel it. Now that you've brought my attention to it, yes, it stings."

"It'll sting more when I clean it, but really, it's just like a big paper cut," the EMT said.

The EMT cleaned it right there on the patio. She told Nikki to keep it clean to prevent infection, and to see her doctor if it did get infected. She gave Nikki extra bandages and a tube of medicated ointment.

"I'm fine. Really," Nikki said. "And my husband's a doctor."

That reminded her. Nikki called Eduardo to let him know what had happened. He said he was thankful she was okay. Nikki told him that Delfina had lied and taken Andrea to Spider's house.

"We promised Barriga we'd take care of his goddaughter. Do you want to apply to be foster parents?"

"I was thinking the same thing," Nikki said. "Of course, we'll have to ask Andrea."

CHAPTER FIFTY-NINE

When Frank returned, he ushered Urbano into a small conference room where two other men were waiting. Introductions were made around the table.

Urbano started by telling them how he originally came to the US with the full cooperation of the Cuban Communist Party during the last year Fidel was fully in control of the government. He showed them his green card.

"If you've been a resident for so long, why didn't you apply for citizenship?" Sam, a gray-haired operative asked.

"As I told you, I opened a travel agency with money supplied by the Cuban government."

"Everything you've said makes it tough for you to break your deal. They'll hunt you down unless the new leaders show clemency. So far, the new president is hard-core, like Fidel. He's reversing Raúl's modest policies to modernize Cuba and open the economy."

"Did you send almost all the money you earned back to them?" Frank asked.

"They let me keep the profits from the travel part of the business. Their cut was all the money from the medical procedures. They did a lot of stem cell work. That pays well."

"I'm still confused," Sam said. "Why did you take a partner?"

"Rodríguez married the woman who'd been my girlfriend in Havana. She was pregnant with my child when I left. Afraid she'd be a single mother, she married Rodríguez despite my assurances I'd get her out of Cuba once I was established here. Later, I helped bring them to this country and find jobs. She would not leave her husband. She was afraid of him, she told me. Still, I wanted my daughter here, even if I could not openly be a father to her."

The operative scoffed. "How convenient. We get rid of your partner and you get the old girlfriend back. Is that your plan?"

"Not at all. I'm here to report a man who has been stealing medical research and sending it to a foreign government. I'm no longer interested in the old girlfriend, to use your term. But I'd like to get custody of my sixteen-year-old daughter."

Sam asked if Urbano had been involved in gathering and sending research to Cuba.

He vehemently denied any involvement. "I've only recently discovered Rodríguez is a spy for Cuba."

"How did you find out?" Sam asked.

"I accidentally ran into him in Havana. As the exile he was pretending to be, he could not have entered Cuba. I asked a doctor I trusted at the clinic, and he told me Rodríguez visited Cuba three to four times a year. He even had an intimate relationship with one of the women at the clinic. He told them not to ever tell me he visited."

Sam questioned Urbano for two hours while the other two men listened, occasionally taking notes.

"Can you prove the teenager is in fact your child?"

Urbano pulled a folded paper from his pocket and pushed it toward Sam. "This test is from Havana. It proves I'm Andrea's father."

Sam opened the test results.

"I'll need a new identity," Urbano said. "And one for my daughter, if I get custody."

Sam repeated questions throughout the interrogation. Urbano knew the gray-haired man was trying to trip him into making mistakes. Feeling tired, he remained as alert as he could, hoping not to make any.

"I'll review this. Are you available for further talks?" Sam gathered the documents and the thumb drives.

"Of course. I'll keep a low profile though. I've not been in contact with my Miami office and I intend to keep it that way. I purposely kept my voice mail full so I wouldn't get messages this past month. If I don't answer, keep calling till you get me."

"And if you need anything, give me a call," Sam said, handing Urbano a card.

Urbano glanced at the card. Sam Hurtado, principal in a real estate consulting firm.

CHAPTER SIXTY

After Delfina had been taken to the police station, the sergeant took Nikki's initial statement. When Floyd showed up, Nikki thanked both men for saving her life. Floyd immediately told her the real person to thank was Spider.

Maldonado told Nikki he was very impressed with her reaction in a tough situation.

"I've had a bit of practice," she said.

"Call me anytime you need help," he told her.

"Now may I explain why you need to thank Spider?" Floyd asked.

Nikki nodded.

"Spider called to say Delfina had dropped Andrea off at his house. You were already on your way here, so I called Sergeant Maldonado. I knew she was out to hurt you."

"Still, without your instinct and the sergeant's quick response, I wouldn't be here," Nikki said.

Floyd asked Maldonado what would happen to Delfina.

"She'll probably be tried for aggravated assault with a deadly weapon."

Nikki's phone rang. It was Eduardo calling to say the guard wouldn't let him enter Paradise Point.

The sergeant took the phone from Nikki and told the guard to allow Eduardo through.

When Eduardo arrived, Nikki stepped outside to meet him. "Don't say a word. I know it was brash of me to come here alone."

He took her into his arms. "You're okay," he whispered into her ear. "That's all that matters." He lifted a corner of the bandage and took a peek. "You'll be fine."

They joined Maldonado and Floyd inside the house. The sergeant was taking pictures inside the great room.

Eduardo noted that the luggage was gone.

"That's exactly what I told the sergeant," Floyd said. He introduced Eduardo to Maldonado.

"You've missed most of the excitement." Maldonado turned to the rest of the group. "I'll take a couple more pictures I need in here. Then we can wrap things up for today."

Nikki volunteered to inform Charlotte of the latest happenings.

"That leaves Andrea," Floyd said. "I'll visit Spider and call Child Protective Services from there."

"We'll go with you," Nikki said.

Floyd shook his head. "Not necessary. Go home and relax."

"We'd like to become her foster parents," Eduardo added.

"Let me handle it," Floyd said. "I'll call if the caseworker needs to talk to you. I'd like for both of you to go home and take it easy."

Nikki shook her head. "You know there's too much going on and this is really my case. We need to make certain Andrea is safe."

Floyd looked at Nikki. "Okay. If you insist on helping, I'd like for you to visit Raquel's parents. I hadn't mentioned it, but Carolina called a few days ago to say she was concerned that her nephew, a fellow by the name of Benjamín Ávila, might have killed Raquel to get at Barriga."

"Hey, that's the guy Barriga mentioned," Eduardo said. "When I first met him, Barriga thought I was a hired gun sent by Benjy Ávila."

"Barriga thought that? Well, there's no doubt Ávila holds a grudge against Barriga," Floyd said, "but I'm convinced the man did not kill anyone. Besides, all the evidence points in a different direction. You can tell Carolina that I interviewed Ávila twice and have concluded he did nothing more than verbally threaten Barriga."

Eduardo looked at his wife and said he'd take his car and drop it off at Security Source and then they'd go in hers to see the Álvarez family.

Nikki was hesitant.

"Carolina feels comfortable with you," Floyd said. "It'll be better if you tell her."

Nikki agreed—but only if Floyd would keep her informed about Andrea. "And I'll take you up on the offer to stay home and relax. On Monday."

CHAPTER SIXTY-ONE

Urbano knew he should probably go straight to a motel and not go to his house. But he figured the Cubans were too busy to be looking for him just yet. Needing clothes, he decided to take the risk. He'd only stay a few minutes.

The guard was happy to see him. They chatted before Urbano continued to his house. He opened the garage door and drove in. Careful to bring the door down again, he went inside. The kitchen looked the same. Nothing appeared out of place. In the primary bedroom, he felt lonely and sad. Andrea and her safety had been occupying his mind, and he hadn't let himself grieve for Raquel. He sat on the king-sized bed and wept. He'd come to love his wife very much. Only too late, he'd realized. He'd spent years longing for Delfina. When he'd arranged for Rodríguez and Delfina to get into the US, she refused to leave her husband.

A year later, Urbano asked Delfina to leave Rodríguez. This time she suggested waiting another year, until their daughter was old enough to grasp the situation. He was living with Raquel, but he would have left her if Delfina had agreed to marry him.

Delfina met him once a week at a rendezvous hotel in Miami Beach close to the hospital where she worked. Yet she always found excuses not to leave her husband. The year she used the excuse that she feared

Rodríguez too much to leave him, Urbano gave up and married his live-in girlfriend. Once he married Raquel, he was never unfaithful. Not with Delfina. Not with any other woman.

He went to the sink and washed his face. Almost by accident he glanced at himself in the mirror. The face that stared back at him looked old, ragged, and sad.

He stuffed some clothes into a suitcase that had belonged to Raquel. Heading for the chest of drawers to get socks and underwear, he heard a noise.

Listening, he heard it again. Light footsteps, as if someone were in the house.

He looked around the room and grabbed a metal reproduction of Rodin's *Thinker* off the dresser. He turned on the shower, hot, and closed the opaque shower door. Then he wedged himself behind the door to the bathroom, leaving it open. If anyone was out to kill him, he wanted to strike first.

He waited. And waited. He heard nothing more and was about to return to his packing when he heard a rustling from the bedroom.

In the foggy mirror, he saw a figure. He gripped the reproduction's base harder. The intruder might have seen him halfway hidden by the door if not for the steam. He watched the reflected image as the man crept closer.

Urbano had to strike if he were to survive.

The man stalked through the door, a bat at the ready. Urbano stepped forward, hitting him in the forehead. The baseball bat crashed into the vanity. The intruder wobbled and fell to the floor, banging his head against the door frame.

"Oh my god. It's Rodríguez." Urbano was shaking. Rodríguez's head was bleeding. The doctor looked for the carotid pulse and found him still alive, though unconscious.

Urbano's first instinct was to call paramedics. Then he saw a half-used roll of duct tape around one of Rodríguez's wrists. He needed to protect himself. Urbano used the tape to secure Rodríguez's wrists behind his back. Next he taped both legs tightly. Once he finished, he turned his erstwhile partner face up again.

He started to step over the body when Rodríguez opened his eyes.

"Coño," Urbano said. Still holding the roll of tape, he stopped and ripped another piece off to put over Rodríguez's mouth. Neighbors were always out strolling or jogging, and Urbano didn't need him to scream and be heard outside.

With a sigh, Barriga took his phone from a pocket and dialed Sam, the gray-haired CIA field operative.

CHAPTER SIXTY-TWO

The Mohle household welcomed Floyd as if he were a member of the family. After a few minutes of small talk, Floyd told Spider he needed to speak privately with him. Yésica took Andrea to the backyard, under the sycamore where Spider's nickname originated.

"I'm sorry to say I've got bad news," Floyd said.

"Barriga?" Spider asked.

"Your friend Barriga is alive. Four days ago he was jailed in Cuba."

Spider groaned.

"There's worse news yet. It's Delfina." Floyd explained how Delfina would have killed Nikki if the police had not arrived in time.

Spider looked at him in disbelief. "We'll keep Andrea here."

Floyd grimaced. "I wish you could keep her. The circumstances require Florida's Center for Child Protective Services to be involved. They'll place her in foster care. A caseworker, Terri Acosta, is already assigned and has made an initial visit to the Rodríguez home."

"That's too bad," Spider said. "She's gone through so much."

"My investigator, Nikki Garcia, and her husband also offered to take Andrea. First, I need to call Terri. I suggest we let her sort out where Andrea will stay. Now we should tell Andrea the sad news about her mother."

Spider went to the backyard to bring his wife and Andrea inside while Floyd spoke to Terri and provided directions to the Mohle house.

As they waited for the caseworker to arrive, Floyd summarized for Andrea, as best as he could, what happened at her house earlier that day. She sat up stiffly.

She looked at Yésica and then at Spider. "Mama's left me homeless." Tears streamed down her face. She wiped them with the back of her hand. "What will happen to Mama?"

"There will be a trial, and if the jury finds her guilty, the judge will sentence her." Floyd's chest felt tight as he delivered the awful news. He asked if she had any questions.

"Will Nikki be okay?"

"Fortunately, yes," Floyd said.

"Please tell her I'm sorry," Andrea said.

Floyd was amazed that she could be so stoic and thoughtful.

Terri Acosta arrived. The case manager, Mrs. Ballesteros, a plump woman with a serene manner, came with her. They gathered the information they needed with compassion. Floyd was impressed.

The teenager kept quiet and only looked up when they asked her a question.

Yésica asked if Andrea could stay with them instead of going to a foster family.

Terri said it was possible if Andrea wanted to remain with them and if they were related.

Shaking her head, Yésica explained that Andrea's mother was her best friend.

Floyd told everyone that the investigators from his office who'd brought Andrea home had also offered to take her. He didn't want to add complexity to the decision, but he had to mention it.

Spider reiterated that they'd love to have Andrea stay with them if that worked out.

Terri looked at Yésica and then at Spider, telling them that state licensing would be required before either family could have the teenager live in their home.

"That includes fingerprint-based criminal background and child abuse checks, a home inspection, and a home study," the caseworker said. "You also have to attend foster care education. We can speed some of it up, but permanent approval hinges on the background checks."

Mrs. Ballesteros smiled at Andrea, telling her that she was in a wonderful position where she had a choice to make. And that she didn't have to make it right now if she preferred to think on it. "Perhaps we can leave you temporarily with people you know until we obtain formal licensing approval."

Andrea looked up with a hint of a smile that spread across her face. "That's very nice of Nikki and Eduardo. But I've stayed with Yésica and Spider before and my school is close by. It's best if I stay here. Maybe I could spend a few weekends with Nikki and Eduardo." Turning toward Yésica, she said, "We'll need to pick up my meds at the house and more clothes. Oh, and my computer and the *Book of Unusual Knowledge*."

Spider glanced at his wife. "Are you ready for this?"

"It's best for everyone. I love the idea. I'll take vacation time and I'll request a day schedule at the hospital."

CHAPTER SIXTY-THREE

Urbano glanced periodically out his bedroom window while keeping an eye on Rodríguez. When two cars pulled into the driveway, he ran downstairs to open his three-car garage.

Sam and two federal agents from the FBI followed him upstairs. The agents immediately went to work on Rodríguez. He yelled obscenities when they ripped the tape from his mouth. An agent told him to pipe down or he'd tape his mouth shut again. When he'd made sure Rodríguez was coherent, he handcuffed him. The other agent bagged the baseball bat, metal reproduction, and the roll of tape.

The agents carried Rodríguez down. Sam picked up the evidence bags. Despite the restraints, Rodríguez kept jerking his torso and knees to get free. With some effort, they got him to the garage. Laying him down on the backseat, they strapped him securely into the car.

Urbano was amazed when they unrolled a blanket-type bundle and covered the man in the backseat. The bundle in reality was a disguise. Rodríguez now looked like a shaggy dog, sprawled out and sleeping. That would get them past the guard at the entrance.

Sam popped the trunk and deposited the evidence bags. Then the federal agents left with Rodríguez. Sam stood with Urbano as they drove off.

"Seems like I misjudged Rodríguez," Urbano said. "I didn't expect him to move on me that quickly. I should have known better."

Sam didn't smile. "So far, we've managed to keep your identity a secret. Not even Frank at the office suspected you of being undercover CIA. But now you'll have to go into hiding. And I'll have to find a replacement for you. Someone with ties to the Cuban embassy in Mexico City."

"I still want custody of Andrea," Urbano said.

"We'll see what we can do. We don't know if Rodríguez was acting as a jealous husband out to get his wife's former lover," Sam said, "or if this is related to espionage."

Urbano told him it was likely espionage.

"If it is, then it's in the FBI Counterintelligence ball court. But I'll keep a finger in it."

Urbano nodded.

Sam advised him to rent a car and leave his BMW in the garage. "To hide, you need to blend in with the people no one looks at twice. Rent a cheap car, get a room in a rundown motel in the Redland district, and wear ordinary clothes. We'll arrange to get money out of your account. Make it look like you withdrew it from Seattle or San Francisco. Then you'll have cash. Don't use your credit cards. And don't look up friends or anyone you know. Not even Andrea. Understood?"

Again, Urbano nodded.

"I was wondering if you know what kind of car Rodríguez drives."

"A late-model gold Mercedes. In his wife's name. Everything they own, except the partnership, is in her name. I should have suspected him much earlier. If he got caught spying, the assets would be registered to her."

No one would look for him in the farmland between Miami and Everglades, Urbano thought. He packed some jeans and old sweatshirts. Satisfied he had everything, he took the suitcase downstairs and called a taxi.

At the car rental, he took out the forged ID he'd used once before, to

244 | KATHRYN LANE

rent a post office box. Glancing at the driver's license, he felt a twinge of guilt about impersonating his friend. Requesting the smallest car they had on the lot, he drove toward Redland to find a rundown motel.

CHAPTER SIXTY-FOUR

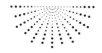

Nikki brought Eduardo with her to debrief Carolina and Alejandro, Raquel's parents.

"Did your boss follow up with Benjy, my nephew?" Carolina asked.

"That's why I'm here. Floyd interviewed your nephew twice. He's certain that Benjy didn't harm anyone." She explained that yes, Benjy was still angry at Barriga. But that didn't make him a killer.

"We want closure, but I'm relieved it wasn't Benjy," Carolina said.

Alejandro nodded. "It would've been a terrible family predicament if he'd killed our daughter. Is there anything else you can tell us?"

Nikki shook her head. "Only that the police investigation is ongoing." She asked if they had any other questions.

"Will we ever find out who killed Raquel?" Alejandro asked.

"No guarantee," Nikki said, "but we hope so."

The four of them chatted for a few more minutes. Nikki told them she'd let them know whenever she learned more. As they prepared to leave, Carolina gave Nikki a hug.

Nikki reminded them to call her anytime.

Charlotte stared at her alert system. "I can't believe it," she said aloud to no one but herself. With a couple of clicks of her mouse, she got a hit on a query she'd put out.

She dialed Nikki. Eduardo answered on speaker and told Charlotte that Nikki was in the car.

Charlotte told them she'd found an interesting detail on a computer search. It gave her a tiny thrill to prolong the suspense.

"Something good, I hope," Nikki said.

"Some dude rented a car in Spider Candella's name." Charlotte smiled, anticipating what Nikki would ask next. "I'll send you the rental agency and the license plate."

"You're amazing," Nikki said. "I'll check it out. And if you'd ask Floyd to call me about Andrea when he gets a minute, that would be great."

Nikki asked Eduardo to drive to the car rental. The attendant who handled the car arrangements for Mr. Candella was reluctant to give out information. Nikki pulled her PI license and flashed it quickly to the young woman, who opened up more once she saw the license. She told them he'd asked for the cheapest, smallest car on the lot.

"Tell us what he looked like," Nikki said.

When the attendant described him, they both knew who he was.

Nikki called Charlotte to ask her to resend Barriga's home address and asked Eduardo to take a detour to Barriga's private community.

Nikki's stomach tightened when she saw the guard. The same guy had denied her access the first time she'd been here. When Eduardo stopped at the shack, the guard told him Mr. Barriga had returned home, but he'd left in a taxi a couple of hours later. He added that several visitors, including Mr. Barriga's business partner, had been to see him. The guard appeared perplexed. He looked at his roster and back at them. "Rodríguez might still be at his house."

"May we go in to see him?" Eduardo passed the guard his driver's license.

The guard recorded their names.

"I think I'll keep you as my chauffeur," Nikki said. "The guard let us right in."

To be cautious, Nikki asked Eduardo to park a block away on a cross street near Barriga's house. They walked up and rang the doorbell. And rang it again. Nikki tried the knob. It was locked. Eduardo knocked loudly. Still nothing. They walked to the backyard. The place was deserted.

"I don't see Rodríguez's Mercedes," she said.

They returned to their car. After driving two blocks, Eduardo stopped. "Do you think he also parked out of view of the house?"

"Good point." She asked him to drive the nearby streets.

Eduardo took a section three blocks away and drove around slowly.

"Oh, my god. Stop," she said. "That's the Honda that was following me." She took photos.

"Are you sure?"

"Let me send the tag number to Charlotte for confirmation and get the owner's address."

Charlotte confirmed it in less than three minutes.

Eduardo headed into traffic again, muttering something about the great way they were spending their vacation.

"I'm back on the clock. And guess what? You are too!"

Nikki called Maldonado to ask if he could do her a favor.

"You name it," he responded.

"Can I text you a license plate of a rental car? If you could let me know if anyone finds it, that would be amazing."

"That's all?"

"Yes, I'd like to speak to whoever rented it, if possible." As an afterthought, Nikki asked how it was going with Delfina.

"She's sulking. I'll be interrogating her on Monday. And, of course, she's lawyered up."

"If there's anything you can share from what she has to say, I'd really appreciate it. I've always thought the Raquel Álvarez murder is related to the Andrea Rodríguez case."

"Sure thing," Maldonado said.

Nikki's phone rang again. She put Floyd on the speaker.

"Charlotte told me you're anxious to learn about Andrea," he said. He told her the case manager had assessed the situation and authorized Andrea's stay with Spider and his wife. Andrea seemed very comfortable with that decision.

"That's good," Eduardo said, "especially since the guard at Barriga's community told us that Rodríguez is in Miami."

Nikki brought Floyd up-to-date on Barriga's renting a car in Spider's name. They hadn't found him at his house, but while they were inside the gated community, she'd recognized the car that followed her several times.

"We're on our way to check out a student who might have loaned that car to Rodríguez."

Nikki ended the call and relaxed as Eduardo drove through Miami traffic to the address Charlotte had given them.

"I could fall asleep," she said, yawning.

"I could, too."

Nikki sat up straight. "You can't, you're driving."

Eduardo laughed.

The GPS informed them their destination was ahead on the right. Eduardo eased into the parking lot of a large apartment complex. He drove around the buildings until they found the one where the student presumably lived.

"Look over there," Nikki said, pointing to a gold-colored Mercedes. "They must exchange cars—"

"Whenever Rodríguez doesn't need to impress anyone," Eduardo added.

"You finished my sentence perfectly." Nikki laughed and kissed him. "I love working with you."

When they knocked on the walk-up apartment door, a tall, thin blonde about thirty answered.

"We're looking for Jordan. Is he available?" Nikki asked.

"That's me," the woman said.

"Oh, sorry! We assumed . . ."

"Happens all the time," she said. "What can I do for you?"

"We're here to ask about the gold Mercedes that belongs to Dr. Rodríguez."

The woman turned white. "Did something happen to him?"

They told her they were only confirming she had the doctor's car.

Jordan's expression had gone from neutral to appearing concerned.

"The car's in Yoani's wife's name. Delfina Morales. If you're bill collectors, go see her."

"No, we're private investigators." Nikki flashed her license.

The woman's expression changed to fear. "I don't want any trouble."

"Don't worry, you're okay," Nikki said. "We needed to confirm the location is all."

"Is Yoani in trouble?"

"Not that we're aware of," Nikki said, trying to keep a straight face. "The dealership sent us because they suspected the car had been stolen, so I recommend that you not drive it."

The woman nodded. "But Yoani has my car. How am I going to get to work and to the university?"

"I'd suggest taking public transportation," Eduardo said.

"My work requires a car."

Eduardo suggested she rent a car for a week.

"I can't afford that. I need my car." The woman backed away, frowning. She spoke into her mobile phone. "Call me, Yoani, I want to know what's going on." Then she slammed the door closed.

"Guess we're not welcome," Nikki said.

Before they left, Nikki took photos of the Mercedes.

"Since I'm working the case again and it's Friday," Eduardo said, "I'm clocking out. And ordering pizza."

"Add champagne too," Nikki said.

CHAPTER SIXTY-FIVE

Nikki had told Floyd she'd take Monday off. But by noon, she could think of nothing but Andrea's case. "Let's go to the office," she told Eduardo.

"I knew you couldn't make it through the day," he said, chuckling.

She went to see Floyd and waited in the hall while he talked to the accountant. She guessed he might be asking the finance guy how much of the Rodríguez case was going to be written off. When he'd finished the call, she stepped inside his office.

"I overheard you with the accountant. Are we going to write off a big chunk on that job?"

"She paid everything I'd billed her, plus she transferred more the night before she tried to kill you."

Floyd's mention of Delfina gave her a chill. "Part of her game. She wanted to appear innocent."

Floyd shrugged. "She'll still owe a small amount, but we're not going to bill her. I want this case to be over."

"She'll be paying a ton to her defense attorney."

"I thought I'd kept you safe by nixing Hong Kong, but this assignment turned out dangerous. I'm sorry," he said.

"It's all part of the job," Nikki said. "In fact, it was interesting up until

Delfina went berserk. I'm happy we brought Andrea back. She's a sweet kid."

"And she was worried about you when she learned what her mother did."

"I hope you didn't tell her about my arm."

Before Floyd could answer, Nikki was called on the office intercom. She picked up in Floyd's office. A new hire, a young woman fresh out of college, told Nikki she had a phone call and would transfer it to her office.

Returning to her desk, Nikki was delighted to find that the caller was Maldonado.

He asked about her wound and Nikki laughed. "It's nothing."

He told her he shouldn't, but he would share a couple of details, confidentially, colleague to colleague, about his interrogation of Delfina. "You're right that her daughter's disappearance was related to the corpse you found in the canal."

"I'm listening," Nikki said, biting her tongue to avoid saying, 'I told you so'.

"Delfina admitted she placed the alligator carcasses at the canal victim's home and on your car. She also admitted to sewing the dress on the Voodoo doll, but she vehemently denies killing anyone. Claims she only tried to scare people."

Nikki asked about the blouse on Raquel's body.

"Said she doesn't know how the dead woman got that. Of course, she might be lying."

"You told me she'd lawyered up," Nikki said, "so if she's implicated in the murder, she's been advised not to admit it."

"She hired a damned good one. He'll try to get her out on bond."

"If she didn't kill Raquel, then who did?" Nikki asked.

"That's the sixty-four-million-dollar question."

"It could have been someone who knew about the blouse and had access to it," Nikki said.

Eduardo knocked, then walked into Nikki's office when she beckoned. Maldonado continued. "A sheriff's deputy was called to stop a fight at a hotel in Redland. He noticed the license plate you wanted. Let me warn you, it's a rough area. Don't go there alone."

She wrote down the address he gave her. Thanking Maldonado, she ended the call. Turning to Eduardo, she asked him to drive again.

They headed to Redland, passing through Little Havana. Nikki pointed out a restaurant, Juancho's. "Let's eat there sometime."

"Cuban food? Didn't you get enough in Havana?"

"Outside of Cuba, Cuban food is excellent. But that place serves Spanish food. Tapas, paella, stuff like that."

"Tapas? Huh, I'll go for good tapas," Eduardo said.

It took Eduardo and Nikki more than an hour to find the shabby place in Redland. Sure enough, a white Chevrolet Spark that had seen better days was parked there.

"How do we find which room he's in?" Eduardo asked.

Nikki was already out of the car, heading for the office. Eduardo started to get out, but she turned and held her hand up telling him to stay put.

A wrinkled, gray-haired woman shuffled out from a side room to the registration counter. "How many hours you want the room for?"

Nikki asked for Spider Candella, the man with the white Chevy Spark.

The woman opened a large book and traced her finger down a page to find the correct entry. "Number 21 upstairs."

Nikki thanked her. Outside, she signaled for Eduardo to join her.

They knocked. No one answered, but Nikki detected a slight movement behind the curtain, as if Barriga were checking out who'd knocked on his door.

The door opened a crack. It was Barriga all right.

"What are you doing here?"

Eduardo said they'd come to talk with him.

"How'd you find me?"

"If you'll let us in, we'll tell you that and more," Nikki said.

The door opened further but Barriga stood behind it.

Once they entered, he seemed like the man they'd met in Havana, the man who entrusted Andrea to them. He was hiding, he told them, because he'd come face-to-face with a killer on Friday afternoon.

"We thought you were jailed in Havana," Eduardo said.

"I was. A childhood friend and a bundle of money got me out. How's Andrea?"

"She's fine, but there's been a change to her living quarters."

Barriga looked concerned. "Not foster care, I hope."

"Not at all," Nikki said, "she's temporarily staying with your friend Spider Mohle and his wife. Child Protective Services granted an exemption until they're approved for foster care to keep her."

Barriga could not contain his shock. "What's happened?"

"Delfina was arrested," Eduardo said.

"Coño," Barriga said. "What did that woman do?"

Nikki told him. Barriga shook his head as she described the ordeal.

Eduardo said they'd both used aliases in Havana. He gave him their real names and told him Nikki was a private investigator Delfina hired to find Andrea.

"I suspected you were working under assumed names," Barriga said.

"And still you trusted us," Eduardo added.

Barriga nodded. "You've had a rough time of it. I never thought Delfina would come to this. I'm glad it wasn't worse."

"It could have been," Eduardo said.

"When I was younger, I was hopelessly in love with Delfina. When I helped them come to the US, I expected her to leave Rodríguez. She wouldn't." Barriga shook his head. "But the minute I married Raquel she got jealous, insanely jealous. She must have killed Raquel."

Ah, Delfina was the pregnant girlfriend he'd left behind in Cuba. So is Andrea his daughter? "An investigation is ongoing," Nikki said. "It might help bring out what really happened to Raquel."

"Now we want to hear how you got out of jail and made it here," Eduardo said.

"My story is very simple." Barriga apologized for not having anywhere for them to sit. "A childhood friend is the warden at the prison where they took me. He arranged my escape, from sparking a power outage to coordinating with Oliver to pick me up. Oliver came back to Miami with me."

"So Oliver knows you're in hiding?" Eduardo asked.

"No. I don't want anyone to know. I'm shocked you found me."

"Nikki's one good investigator," Eduardo said.

Nikki assured him they wouldn't reveal his whereabouts. "But who tried to kill you?"

"The Cuban government," Barriga said. "Who else?"

"You can't hide forever," Eduardo said.

Barriga sighed. "I know." He focused his gaze on the opposite wall.

"I'll have to come up with a plan. The most important issue is not endangering Andrea. I can't even contact her at this point. She mustn't know I'm here."

Nikki could tell the man was nervous despite his calm exterior. "What can we do for you?"

"Don't tell anyone I'm here."

Eduardo drove toward home. Nikki dialed Floyd and Hamilton on her secure phone to update them on Barriga.

"That's impressive," Hamilton said. "Escaping from jail and making it over here so quickly is almost impossible."

"The pictures you took on Friday of the Mercedes and the Honda give me a good reason for calling my friend Sam at the CIA," Floyd said. "Of course, there's the more pressing issue of Rodríguez's espionage."

"I'm concerned with Rodríguez being in Miami. Andrea's safety could be in jeopardy. And Barriga thinks Delfina could have killed Raquel," Nikki said.

Floyd told her he'd already spoken to Spider and Yésica about calling the police if Rodríguez showed up.

CHAPTER SIXTY-SIX

Hamilton joined Floyd in the soundproof conference room to make a call to Sam at the CIA and, if necessary, to the FBI. Both men had excellent relationships with Sam. In fact, he'd mentored them at different periods. Though Sam was older, Floyd was closer to Sam's age. Ham was in his mid-thirties.

When they'd reported the locations of the cars, Sam told them he was glad to find the Honda that Rodríguez had driven to Barriga's house. They'd also found the Mercedes. And the FBI said that Rodríguez and Jordan, the woman who owned Rodríguez's loaner car, were involved in a love affair. "Not a surprise."

Floyd updated Sam on the wife's case. Delfina Morales had been arrested on Friday for aggravated assault on Nikki.

"Do you think Delfina's also an agent?" Sam asked.

"We doubt it. She's unreliable and a bit unstable," Hamilton said, "not the type that Cuban intelligence would keep."

"Rodríguez will be put away for a few years on charges of economic espionage. So far we've uncovered that Cuba's national health system recently patented and trademarked products developed from the research Rodríguez stole in the US. They'll only be effective in Cuba, but it lets us prove a foreign government has benefited from the research Rodríguez stole." Sam paused for a couple of seconds. "He'd been passing secrets for much longer than we first estimated. He'll be locked up while the trial is pending. It's a complicated case."

Floyd said he was glad the fellow would be punished. Thinking of Barriga, he asked what the CIA was doing about him.

"Barriga? We've moved him again, changed his car, done about everything we can so your PI cannot locate him unless we tell her where he is," Sam said.

"Don't be so sure," Ham said, chuckling. "Nikki's a really good PI."

"What about the child?" Sam asked. "Really Barriga's child, we think, though we need to redo the paternity test."

Floyd explained that Andrea was staying with a friend of Barriga's.

"We should move quickly to establish paternity so Barriga can get custody," Sam said.

"Isn't that tough, since Barriga's in hiding from the Cuban government?" Hamilton asked.

"Ham, you know the CIA has ways of moving the process along. The intel Barriga gave us is immensely valuable. The FBI will use it to put Rodríguez away. We'll make sure Barriga is safe and gets custody of his daughter."

Remaining in the conference room, Floyd dialed Maldonado and asked him to make sure the judge in Delfina's case knew her husband was jailed, pending trial, for economic espionage.

"Delfina has told us she packed her husband's bags so he could leave the country at a moment's notice when he thought law enforcement was closing in on him," Maldonado said. "She can be considered his accomplice. At the very least, she's a flight risk to Cuba where we can't bring her to justice. Bond is not going to be granted. Nikki should be happy about that."

Floyd thanked the sergeant.

"Oh, there's more," Maldonado said. "Delfina has asked to speak to Nikki."

"That's interesting," Ham said.

"She's already placed Nikki on her approved visitor list. If Nikki wants to speak with her, she'll need to register first."

"I'll pass the message on to her," Floyd said.

CHAPTER SIXTY-SEVEN

Nikki shuddered when the metal doors clanged shut behind her. Eduardo had insisted on driving her to the detention center. He'd reminded her that her last visit with Delfina had not gone well and he wanted to be available, even if that meant waiting in the parking lot, should Nikki need his support.

"The guards won't let anything happen to me. Besides, there will be a glass partition between Delfina and me."

The guard escorting her told Nikki to sit until the prisoner was brought out. He informed her that an audio and video recording would be made of the visit.

Nikki waited. Then Delfina was brought to the other side of the partition.

Delfina raised her hand in a half wave as she sat and reached for the telephone. Nikki followed suit.

"I want to apologize."

Nikki nodded.

"I was under a lot of stress and handled it badly. I don't know where to start, but I'll tell you I was terrified of Yoani. My husband forced me to lie about a lot of things. He'd found out through Raquel that Andrea was not his daughter. That was the night before she ran away. In a fit of anger

Yoani killed Pepito, her dog. My daughter said that was why she asked Urbano to take her away.

"That night, quite by accident, I discovered he'd killed Raquel. After the mess he made with the dog, I was going to clean it up, but there were no cleaning supplies anywhere in the house. I used hydrogen peroxide and vinegar to disinfect and get rid of the odor. For several days I could smell the blood.

"After he fell asleep, I checked the inside of the Mercedes. I found nothing. When I opened the trunk, I saw blood-covered clothes and cleaning materials. I thought the pants and blouse belonged to Raquel. I did not touch them, but four days later, I looked in the trunk and it had been thoroughly cleaned.

"That's when I called Security Source. I was afraid Yoani might have harmed my daughter.

"When Yoani sensed the CIA, FBI, or police were closing in on him, he told me you were responsible for it, that you had reported him.

"I did not find out he was sending research to Cuba until that day, the same day you brought Andrea back." Delfina stopped talking and sniffled. She leaned against the shelf of the partition.

"I was packing his bags when you arrived with Andrea. He hid in the bathroom. He left that night after Andrea was asleep. He never saw her. Not even to say goodbye. That's when he told me he was abandoning me and returning to Cuba. Claimed he would never be accused of killing Raquel, that I'd be the one to pay for the murder because all the evidence pointed to me. I lost it after that. I couldn't think clearly. I'm sorry for what I did to you."

Nikki looked at Delfina through the glass without responding.

"Yoani told me he had the Information Directorate in Havana pick you up. At the time, he was having Urbano followed. That's how he found out you and Eduardo were in Cuba."

Delfina paused as if to gain control of her emotions.

"For being stupid and jealous, I've lost Andrea."

Nikki felt sorry for her but was not about to show any emotion to the woman who had nearly killed her.

"I don't want Andrea to see me in jail. But I will write to her. They may let me send her videos. But please tell her I'm sorry and that I love her."

A guard on Delfina's side of the partition opened a door and told her the visit was over.

Nikki nodded, adding that she'd give Andrea the message.

At the car, Nikki was glad that Eduardo got out to give her a hug. She needed that. He opened the door for her, but before he drove off they talked about the visit. She told him Delfina said Rodríguez had found out Andrea was not his daughter.

"So Barriga is her father," Eduardo said.

"Looks that way."

On the return drive to the office, Nikki called Floyd and Hamilton to debrief them. She told them they were on speaker and Eduardo was with her.

"As manipulative as Delfina appears to be," Ham said, "I hope you didn't say much. Her attorney can use the video to their advantage."

"I put on Floyd's school-of-not-showing-emotion face," she assured him. "But thinking back to when I first discovered the corpse, I'd called Delfina and she immediately assumed the body was Raquel's."

"She obviously *knew* it was Raquel," Eduardo said.

"Has the FBI continued to interrogate Rodríguez?" Nikki asked.

"They had a baseball bat that had his fingerprints and DNA all over it. First he claimed Barriga had tried to kill him with it, but his interrogators told him there was no indication Barriga had ever touched it," Ham said. "When they told him it had traces of Raquel's blood on it, he confessed to killing her. He must have figured they had a tight case on him."

"The Cuban government planted him here," Floyd said. "So he was never an exile. He was a spy from the time he arrived."

Nikki ended the call. She turned to Eduardo, telling him how much she appreciated his help on the case. She then asked if he thought Barriga could be a CIA field operative.

"Hmm, interesting thought. I guess he could be. Regardless, he caught someone who was no good and turned him over to the authorities."

CHAPTER SIXTY-EIGHT

Three weeks later, Nikki and Eduardo picked Andrea up at Spider and Yésica's house. They asked her to pack for a trip to the Everglades with them. A nice surprise awaited her there. The man Nikki called CIA Sam, because she'd never met him, had made special arrangements for them to take Andrea to reunite with Barriga now that a paternity test had confirmed she was his daughter.

Nikki wasn't sure how it all happened, but either the CIA or the FBI or both had brought the custody case before a judge, who ruled in favor of the biological father. With both Delfina and Rodríguez in jail, awaiting trials, it apparently had been easy to grant custody to Barriga. She and Eduardo had made depositions that were used in the case. But they were not called to testify in a court of law. She'd have to ask Floyd how it had all transpired.

She sat in the backseat and played a computer game with Andrea. Every time one of them won a round in the game, it played a little jingle.

When Eduardo complained about the noise, Nikki told him she could drive and he could play. He stopped the car and Nikki moved to the driver's seat. She delighted in hearing Eduardo laugh every time he won and Andrea cheer whenever she took a round.

After driving for a good while, Nikki pulled onto a dirt road and followed it until she saw a boat fitting the description she'd been given. She parked the car and the three of them boarded the boat. For half an hour it meandered along a saltwater estuary in the red mangrove forest. Birds waded in the mangroves, calling for a mate or complaining about the intrusion of the boat. Andrea pointed out an alligator floating in the river, looking like a submerged log except for its eyes and snout.

Andrea was interested in everything. Nikki had the feeling Delfina and Rodríguez had never taken her out much.

Finally the boat pulled up to a larger one. A man on the deck of the big boat threw a Jacob's ladder overboard so the passengers could climb up.

Andrea went first. When she got to the top, she saw her Uncle Urby. In her excitement to climb onto the bridge to hug him, she almost fell off. He pulled her up onto the deck.

Nikki steadied her purse over her shoulder before getting on the ladder. She saw how happy Andrea was to see Barriga. The two other men on the boat went into the cabin to allow Barriga and his guests to talk privately.

Nikki told Barriga they would stay until everything was explained to Andrea.

Barriga beamed upon informing Andrea he was actually her father and custody had been granted to him.

Andrea hugged her dad. "I'd already figured out that I'm your daughter."

"How?" Barriga asked, looking intrigued by Andrea's comment.

"For one, we both had PSP and collapsed lungs, and second, I have the same Italian notch on my left ear that you have." She pulled her hair away from her earlobe to show him. "It's an inherited feature."

"Italian notch? I didn't know I had one," he said, touching his earlobe. "You're right!"

Andrea giggled.

"I never told anyone, but I provided the stem cells for your transplants."

"And I'm much better," she said, smiling at her father.

Barriga wanted to make certain she was willing to move away from Miami. They would go somewhere that had a good school she could attend and buy a small house. Barriga would find a job, under an assumed name. To be safe, they would have a new surname.

When Andrea realized she was not returning to Spider and Yésica's house, she thought she should call and thank them for letting her stay with them.

"Great idea," Nikki said, explaining the new rules of using a phone. "Your Uncle Urby . . . I mean your dad could be in danger from the Cuban government if they find him."

"It's terrible they can hurt him even here," Andrea said.

Eduardo nodded. Handing Andrea a new phone, he told her about its security features. Location and caller ID on all calls were permanently off. When he finished, he asked Andrea for her old phone.

"Remember, you can never, ever tell anyone where you are. It's for your protection as well as your dad's," Nikki said.

Barriga said it was true. They discussed the situation Delfina and Rodríguez were in. Andrea might not be able to speak to her mother for several years. Her father asked her once more if she felt certain about moving with him. The other alternative would be for her to continue to live with Spider and Yésica. She said she was more than certain she wanted to be with him.

"I'll miss Mama, but I'll wait until you tell me I can visit her," Andrea said, looking at her dad.

"I hope it won't take too long," he said.

"Can I call Spider and Yésica on my new phone?" Andrea asked.

Barriga glanced at Nikki.

"Yes, you can. They should know by now that you won't be coming back."

Yésica answered. Andrea thanked her for taking her in when she did not have a home.

Yésica told the teenager she was happy for her but missed her. "You've made me realize how much I'm missing out in life. Spider and I loved having you. We've decided to adopt a baby now that you won't be living with us."

Barriga spoke to Spider, who wished him the best in their new life. He and Yésica hoped to visit them in France, he said.

"We look forward to that day." Barriga looked perplexed.

He asked Nikki to step aside for a quick question.

"Are we going to be relocated to France?"

"That's a cover the CIA used when they contacted Spider. His wife and Delfina are close friends. Even I don't know where you will be settled. Oh, and I have a question left from Havana. Why is it that you never answered messages left for you at the clinic?"

Barriga grimaced. "I never got them. Vicki, the woman who managed the operation for us at the clinic, was Rodríguez's mistress, and he'd instructed her not to give them to me."

"Mistress in Havana? I thought Rodríguez could not get into Cuba."

"That's what I thought. Until I accidentally ran in to him at the clinic. He thought I'd left the island that morning. Another person told me Rodríguez and his mistress had schemed to cut me out of the business. Of course, now the entire US operation will be closed."

"Rodríguez was quite the ladies' man," Nikki said. "Did you get any messages on your mobile regarding Raquel?"

"I had purposely left my voicemail filled to capacity before I took Andrea to Cuba. The only person whose calls I'd intended to answer was Raquel. She never called. By then, she'd been murdered, but I thought she was still angry with me." Barriga sighed. "I thought she'd miss me and we'd get back together. Unfortunately, it was not meant to be."

"Shall we rejoin them?" he asked. Eduardo and Andrea were engaged in a game on Eduardo's phone.

Nikki and Eduardo wished them good luck. She pulled a gift-wrapped box from her purse and handed it to Andrea. In typical teenage style, she ripped the paper off and discovered a book, *Klara and the Sun*.

Andrea hugged Nikki. "I love reading. Thank you."

Eduardo told Andrea how much he'd enjoyed playing computer games with her.

After saying their goodbyes, Eduardo helped Nikki onto the ladder and followed her.

Once they were in the little boat, the boatman eased away. They looked up at Andrea and Barriga waving at them.

Nikki blew kisses and Andrea did the same.

"It's nice when there's a happy ending to a case," Eduardo said, waving back.

"After I make a call to update Raquel's parents, I'll ring the office to tell them we saw a happy teenager reunite with her father. Then I'll let you hide my phone."

"No phone interruptions?"

"Not on this vacation." Nikki leaned in to kiss him.

A NOTE FROM KATHRYN

Thank you for reading *Missing in Miami*. If you enjoyed it, I would very much appreciate a review on Amazon, BookBub, and Goodreads so others may also find Nikki Garcia.

If you'd like to learn about my new releases, please sign up for my newsletter at kathryn-lane.com.

— Kathryn Lane

WAKING UP IN MEDELLIN

CHAPTER ONE

If only Manuel Del Campo would speak to me, I could be on my way.

I sat in Del Campo's plush office near Medellín, Colombia, waiting for him to answer a few questions. Fidgeting with my nails, I was having second thoughts about the job, but it was too late. Now that I was on-site, it was better to get on with it.

It was exasperating to wait on him. The man's bombastic voice gave final instructions to a subordinate in the hallway at my back.

"Tell them we can ship to Singapore and have it there in six weeks. Or they can pay for air freight if they want it sooner."

I twisted in my seat and saw Del Campo standing outside the double doors of his office. The molding of the oversized doorway framed his muscular and impeccably dressed physique. He wore a crisp, highly tailored, bone-white suit—appropriate to the climate, yet contrasting conspicuously with the concept of steel mills.

I'd flown in last night. A weather delay before I left Minneapolis, plus the five-hour flight to the José María Córdova Airport in Medellín, gave me ample time to think about corruption in Latin America—corruption so widespread that individuals across the workforce, from police on the street to low-level government officials in back offices, supplemented their incomes inappropriately. When dishonesty exists so openly, it emanates from the top and permeates all of society. In countries like Colombia, drug-related crime adds layers of complexity. To their credit, the Colombian people had fought against traffickers. And I was fortunate not to be investigating the trade. I was only here to probe into possible mismanagement of a steel mill.

I turned toward his desk again. A photo of Del Campo, wearing the same bone-white suit he sported today, stared back at me from a gilded frame. Suddenly the man entered the room, lowering his voice to apologize for his delay.

"I have time," I said, thinking he probably kept business appointments with men promptly.

He walked behind his carved mahogany desk, preceding our meeting with pleasant Latin platitudes as he flipped open a cherrywood humidor, his initials engraved on the top, and selected a seven-inch Churchill. He cut the cap with a double guillotine cutter and lit a narrow strip of Spanish cedar with an old-fashioned butane lighter he retrieved from the top drawer of his desk. Cigar in mouth, he slowly rotated it in the spill's flame as he pulled air in gentle puffs to ensure an even burn. The spicy-sweet aroma of good hand-rolled tobacco mingled with the scent of the burning cedar, making me crave a cigar. But Del Campo was not about to offer one to a woman, certainly not to a lowly auditor. The man could ignore the ban on indoor smoking that worldwide headquarters in Minneapolis had issued. After all, Medellín is a long way from Minneapolis.

He rolled the cigar between his fingers. Without lifting his eyes, he abruptly turned the conversation to the purpose of my visit.

"So you're here to investigate me." His voice hardened.

"I'm here to investigate allegations of wrongdoing reported to headquarters," I said.

"I'm completely transparent about managing this company." Del Campo puffed on his cigar. "Everything here is on the up-and-up, like in a fencing bout."

"Fencing? What does that have to do with managing a company?"

"You don't go for perfection," Del Campo said. He puffed on his cigar, blew out three smoke rings, and stared at me as the rings slowly dissipated. "You just go for solid returns."

"I don't know much about fencing. But let me ask a few routine questions about the mill."

"Women would understand business if they learned the art. In the context of fencing, it's all about the frame you set up." He angled the photo of himself so it sat straight ahead of me.

"Frame?" I asked, confused.

"Let me explain. If you tell yourself your opponent is weak, you create a psychological advantage. On the contrary, if you are afraid of your opponent, you will see yourself ambushed."

"That sounds true to life. In the weeks to come, you can explain fencing to me. Right now, though, I need to get some information from you about the company."

"I'm at your service," he said, leaning back in his chair.

For the next hour, I asked a lot of questions. He lit up a second cigar. The more he spoke, the longer he drew on each puff. He held the Churchill between his thumb, middle, and index fingers, clearly an aficionado. I continued probing. He continued blowing smoke rings.

"If everything is aboveboard, as you say, why did your employees call the corporate security office to report misappropriation of company assets?" I asked.

He switched the cigar to his left hand. The inch-long ash fell in one piece on the highly polished mahogany. His right hand, fingers cupped, pushed the ashes across the desk in a semicircle and onto the floor in one sweeping motion.

"It's probably a disgruntled employee trying to discredit me. Or a competitor," he said.

"You think one disgruntled employee would be so persistent?" I asked, my voice firm.

"Why believe a caller who won't give his name?" Del Campo asked, his tone playful.

Almost immediately, he swiveled his chair, moved forward, and looked me straight in the eye.

"Look, Ms. Corporate Auditor Nikki Garcia, I'm tired of your insinuating questions. I find your tone accusatory. If corporate headquarters is not happy with my performance, they can fire me. They can trust me and stop this goddamned investigation, or they can fire me. You tell them that."

His voice heated and his face reddened. He looked at me as if it was all he could do to control his anger. If I'd been a man, I think he might have taken a swing at me.

"I thought fencing was about dealing psychologically with the opponent," I said.

He took what remained of his cigar and crushed it against the ashtray with such force I thought it would break. His face purple with anger, he stood, signaling our meeting was over. As I got up, his demeanor relaxed. He escorted me out of his office, smiling like a man accustomed to getting his way through temper tantrums. He cleared his throat, as if the cigar had irritated it.

"If you need anything while you're here on assignment, Nikki, just speak with my assistant. She'll arrange it for you. We want to make your visit to Medellín as pleasant as possible." He closed the door to his office, officially ending our conversation.

I stood by the door, once again livid with the corporate policy of informing high-level executives when they were the object of a review for fraudulent activity. No one ever told lower-level employees when they were the target of an audit, a tactic that ensured they didn't have time to cover up or destroy evidence. *So why inform executives?*

That man, manipulative as he seemed, had been president of Amazonia Steel for twelve years. He had taken control of a small company that manufactured for the Latin American market and grown it into a vast enterprise that exported around the globe. And he had been relentless in building his empire. His name had been tossed around at headquarters as a successor to the aging worldwide CEO, but Del Campo himself had taken his name out of contention, preferring, he claimed, to live in his native country.

I looked at the lavish furnishings in the office Del Campo's administrative assistant occupied. I'd met Theya, his assistant, that morning before she left at noon for personal reasons. The entire building was impeccable, but the elegant setting of the executive suite made me feel as if I were in upscale offices in New York.

I walked to the window to calm my anger at corporate policy before I talked with anyone else. Five floors up, I had a splendid view of an artificial lake that sparkled in the sunlight. Feeling queasy, I moved slightly away from the window, where I could better appreciate the view.

A bridge curved gracefully over the lake, ending at a small, tree-lined parking lot near the front entrance to the building. Trees shaded a path around the lake. Beyond the lake and across the highway were low, rolling hills. The vacant land, lake, and neatly tended lawns around the company gave the entire complex a country club atmosphere. The steel mills were tucked out of sight half a mile away.

Amazonia Steel was one of the most profitable affiliates in the Globan family of companies. Globan International, where I worked, had worldwide holdings in steel, mining, energy, and large-scale construction. I'd been sent to "la ciudad de la eterna primavera," City of Eternal Spring, after the Globan corporate security office received fifteen anonymous phone calls on the Sarbanes-Oxley hotline claiming the president was defrauding the company.

Sarbanes-Oxley was the law that resulted from several large accounting and fraud scandals in corporate America, including giants like Enron, Tyco, and WorldCom. Though the law is complex, multinational companies instituted telephone hotlines as part of their internal policing function to comply with a small part of the legislation. Employees could report malfeasance anonymously on these hotlines.

Calls to Globan's corporate security office hotline gave few details on the accusations against Del Campo. *I could be chasing a hoax.* Yet that thought quickly evaporated as I focused on the man's behavior at our meeting. Still gazing out the large window in Theya's office, I glanced at my watch. It was time to call it a day.

My driver maneuvered slowly through the evening rush-hour traffic. I appreciated having a chauffeur, leaving the driving to him while I organized my thoughts. I pondered Del Campo's responses to my questions, the same routine I go through with employees suspected of deceitful practices for personal gain. The most prevalent frauds involve accounts payable or accounts receivable supervisors who add themselves, under fictitious names, as vendors or suppliers and send fraudulent invoices to the company. Or shipping and receiving clerks, where internal controls aren't enforced, caught stealing merchandise or supplies. The most classic fraud of all is perpetrated by payroll managers who pad the number of employees while collecting the salaries of nonexistent personnel.

This particular assignment was in another league. The president was being investigated. The benefits of being president—the seven-figure salary, cash bonuses, stock options, and perks—are not usually risked by getting involved in scams or swindles. At least, reasonable people wouldn't risk it. But I had seen corruption many times, including at high executive levels.

We arrived at the Intercontinental Hotel, an old property in the prestigious El Poblado area in southeast Medellín, which had been recently renovated. A garden with flowering shrubs and trees graced the driveway leading to the spacious portico, like an old Southern mansion. The lobby was open and airy, typical of hotels in temperate climates, with flowers everywhere in colorful ceramic pots. I could even imagine Rhett Butler lounging by the bar, sipping a mint julep. But glancing over at the lobby bar, I didn't see any interesting men. I wondered where Colombian men hung out. Before that thought evaporated, a tall man in uniform, his thick biceps bulging through crisply ironed shirt sleeves, handed me a long-stemmed red rose.

"I'm Juan, the concierge," he said. Surprised, I stared into his dark-brown eyes. "This is my card. Call me if you need anything during your stay."

I thanked him and continued on my way. The fragrant aroma of cut flowers arranged in elaborate vases followed me across the lobby to the elevators. My suite was compact yet cozy. I kicked off my high heels even before I locked the door behind me. Taking the computer out of its case, I locked it in the safe inside the closet, a practice I'd followed for several years now. An extra stash of three disposable mobile phones was also stored in the safe. And the one I always carried, my secure phone—a petite model with a high-powered battery, good German encryption software, and a GPS system. But I always used a throwaway for local calls.

I could reach Ian McVey, head of corporate security, with the touch of a button any time, day or night. Even Sarah, my assistant at headquarters, was accessible to me twenty-four seven. Paul Harris, my boss, was vice president of the audit department, but I worked much more closely with McVey from security, a man who styled himself my unofficial mentor.

I dialed Sarah from my secure phone and left a voicemail telling her all was quiet in Medellín. In the middle of the room, I stretched up on my toes and back down several times to relieve the pressure from the spiked heels, all the while craving a good cigar. Healthier thoughts soon took over, and I slipped into my swimsuit.

Small waves, created by three children playing in the water, rippled along the width of the pool, breaking gently onto the mosaic tiles of the pool's rim. The scene brought to mind images of Robbie, my son. He had loved to swim. By the time he was twelve, his coach told me Robbie was Olympic material. And then his death. It was over six years ago now, but the pain was as sharp as if it had happened yesterday. My nightmares persisted, interrupting my sleep with horrifying images. Malevolent figures snatched Robbie out of my arms. I could hear his screams, and they would wake me. Then I'd realize they were my own screams, which left me sweating, shaking, and sleepless.

After Robbie's death, I'd found solace in the swimming pool. We'd talked a lot as I drove him back and forth to swim meets. People told me time heals everything, but I was still mourning. I'd buried my head in work, becoming a workaholic. To counter the long hours, I took up exercise, training at times as if I were preparing for a triathlon.

Diving into the pool, I took up a butterfly stroke. The sweeping movement of both arms coming out of the water and moving toward both thighs with my legs close together as I kicked created a soothing wave effect throughout my body. I focused my mind on swimming and forgot the rest of the world.

After showering, I ordered dinner at the open-air café and savored a margarita while focusing my thoughts on the job at hand. McVey had asked me, on short notice, to perform the review in Colombia. It meant I'd not had adequate time to prepare, so I would have to intuit my way, especially at first. McVey thought this job would be easy, and I'd be home in a week. McVey also knew I enjoyed working in exotic locations. But I'd had second thoughts about this job. I hated being in a country that still produced and exported cocaine and other illicit drugs. My feelings against them were so strong, it was almost a phobia.

While I mentally worked on a strategy for this assignment, my waiter offered me limoncello instead of coffee after dinner.

"Señora, it's the perfect digestivo to follow the osso buco and risotto you enjoyed. An Italian meal must be finished off with an Italian liqueur. That way, everything is complete, a la Italiana."

I agreed to the drink with a nod, but his suggestion sparked an idea. I couldn't rely on my sixth sense alone for finding fraud. I needed reason, too. My waiter had given me the answer when he paired an Italian liqueur with Italian food. I was investigating a steel operation, so I should review the steel manufacturing process instead of focusing exclusively on financial data.

At Amazonia, there were two mills, side by side. One produced steel, and the mini-mill rolled steel and made specialty products. From the little bit of research I'd had time to do before leaving Minneapolis, I knew Del Campo was tripling the size of the plant. Construction projects often provided opportunities for fraud to occur, but the steel mill's processes would be my primary focus.

Now I had a plan. I leaned back into my chair and enjoyed the rest of the limoncello.

"Buenos días, señora." My chauffeur greeted me with a warm smile.

"Good morning," I said.

We drove several miles without conversation. I gazed out the window, noticing how densely populated and disorganized the city was compared to Minneapolis. We drove through busy city streets, then on highways leading to industrial parks beyond the suburbs. People teemed everywhere —walking, waiting for buses. Desperate folks competing for rush-hour taxis, others riding bicycles or motorbikes, and the lucky ones in cars, honking at every obstacle that threatened their foot on the gas pedal.

By contrast, the company's administrative office building, where Del Campo's office was located, sat opulently in the middle of the meticulously landscaped campus, with the artificial lake and bridge that I'd viewed yesterday from Theya's window. This sumptuousness was precisely the show of wealth that headquarters did not approve of. A line of trees, set back at least a quarter of a mile on the left side of the property, partially obscured the large steel mill from view. The additional steel processing plant was needed to meet the demand for the Asian export market, Del Campo had told me yesterday. I could see construction cranes towering over the site.

After passing the guard station, my driver stopped the Mercedes sedan at the main entrance. He jumped out and briskly walked around to open my door. At the reception desk, I presented my temporary pass to the security detail. She phoned Theya to inform her I was on my way up. Instead of taking the elevator, I made my way through the five-story atrium to the spiral staircase, a graceful curved sculpture that echoed the opulence leading to the main entrance. The staircase connected the ground floor with the wide mezzanines of each of the four floors above, all open to the lofty atrium. Some employees stood around, while others, engaged in animated conversation with their coworkers, sat in the open café on the ground floor, sipping coffee before taking the elevator to their offices to begin their work for the day. Everything was serene and beautiful. It was difficult to believe I was here on a high-level investigation. As I entered my temporary office to set up my computer, Theya walked in with coffee and biscotti.

"The biscotti are baked on the premises, different flavors every day. They're delicious," she said.

Theya—a tall, attractive woman in her mid-thirties—dressed, looked, and spoke like an executive. She had been hired by Del Campo when he came on board. She spoke several languages and had moved to Colombia when she married. Her Spanish was flawless, and her English was spoken with an elegant British accent, a status symbol for Del Campo. What did not make sense to me was why a woman of her education and polish was an administrative assistant when she could have been an executive herself.

"Thanks, Theya. Do you have a minute?" Without waiting for an answer, I added, "I interviewed Señor Del Campo yesterday afternoon. When I finished, I lingered in your office to enjoy the view. It's magnificent. Especially the rolling hills across the highway. Is there any plan to use that land in the future?"

"Señor Del Campo likes to look at those wooded hills from his desk, so I doubt it, but you should ask him. He's the one who makes those decisions."

"You know, Theya, I was wondering why you're working as his

administrative assistant. Your boss should recognize your abilities and place you in marketing or public relations."

"Funny you should say that. He's tried to promote me, but it's my choice to stay where I am. You see, I have a son who was born with CP."

"CP?"

"Cerebral palsy. It's difficult with all the medical attention and therapy he requires. Señor Del Campo gives me the time off I need to take care of him. In fact, that's where I was yesterday, taking him to the neurologist. We have a full-time nanny, but I'm the one who takes him to doctor appointments. My husband travels with his job, and I want to be home every evening with my son. This job doesn't require travel, but as soon as I move to an executive position, travel becomes a must. I can't say I'm not tempted to have a more exciting career, but I'm a mother before anything else."

"How old is he?"

"Twelve. We celebrated his birthday a couple of months ago. He was so beautiful and so perfect when he was born. We didn't notice anything wrong until five months later. That's when he showed signs of something wrong. It was devastating."

"I can imagine your pain," I said, thinking of Robbie.

"We've adjusted. Now I wouldn't know what to do with my life if it were not for him," Theya said. "Thanks for your concern. Regarding work, is there anything I can do for you today?"

"Yes, I'd like to see the mill director, if you could arrange a meeting for me."

I dunked the biscotti in the coffee. It was delicious, as promised.

She returned almost immediately with a young man, maybe late twenties, with jet-black hair, brown eyes, and a winning smile. His smile reminded me of the way Robbie beamed at swimming meets he'd just won.

"This is Luis Ceballos. He'll escort you to the mill and introduce you to our plant director, Ramón García. Also, here's Señor Del Campo's mobile phone as well as my own number, in case you need us," she said.

Theya walked us to the president's private elevator. Luis and I took it down to the ground level, walked outside, climbed into a golf cart, and headed toward the mill.

"Is this your first visit to Amazonia Steel?" Luis asked as he drove the cart across the manicured lawns toward the mill.

"Yes. I'm looking forward to working here for a few weeks. I'm certainly enjoying the warm weather. Minneapolis is such a cold place. Even our summers are too short," I said. Changing the subject, I added, "How long have you worked here?"

"Eight years," Luis said. "I started straight out of college, although I'd done a summer internship before I graduated, so I knew that it was a great place to work."

I took advantage of the ride to input Del Campo's and Theya's phone numbers in my throwaway mobile.

The mill director, Ramón García, was a short, stout man with glasses that slipped down his bulbous nose. He had assembled, on short notice, a small army of people for me to meet. They were amazed I was fluent in Spanish. I explained that, growing up in Minneapolis, I'd spent the summers with my grandparents at their small ranch a couple of hundred miles south of Mexico City in the state of Oaxaca. My abuelita tutored me in Spanish, and my abuelo taught me to ride horses. What I did not mention was that at age sixteen I'd lost my parents in an auto accident. I lived with my grandparents in Oaxaca for two years before they sent me back to Minnesota to study at the University of St. Thomas.

With the exception of Ramón, none of the assembled personnel were fluent in English. Ramón had pulled together a formal slide presentation, complete with video clips, probably from one he'd given recently. He was going all-out for the meeting. I would have preferred a less formal approach, without the dog-and-pony show, but it was part of the game. It was the price of their cooperation with my audit. And it gave me a chance to see the group interacting.

"When was the decision made to add the mini-mill?" I asked. Someone had enough strategic vision to have complementary mills operate side by side.

The manager for the specialty products started to answer, but Ramón, adjusting his glasses with the middle finger of his left hand, cut him off in mid-sentence.

"When Señor Del Campo was hired as presidente, he brought in the concept of the mini-mill. The specialty products are very lucrative, so it's been a very wise decision."

"Tell me what you make there?"

"There's normal rolling of plate, but custom engineered products, proprietary tank or vessel requirements, bring in the money. We work with orders from water treatment facilities that are upgrading or repairing their equipment," he said.

Again, his middle finger propped up his glasses into their proper position. He did this several times while he talked.

"The tank and vessel products are also used in the petrochemical industry. Worldwide, these markets are worth billions of dollars. We're already an important player in the Americas. We are positioning Amazonia to become the leader in servicing these worldwide markets ten years out. That's the reason for the expansion project."

"Tell me about the expansion," I said.

"It will triple the size of the mill. We will have the construction complete by the end of this year."

"Who is the contractor? I asked.

"Zambrano Construction Company," Ramón responded.

"Why aren't you using an affiliate of Globan for construction?" I asked.

"We received a better bid from Zambrano. It's the biggest construction company working in Colombia. They are also the most reputable. Your corporate offices vetted them and approved them before we signed the contract." He sounded defensive.

After an hour of more questions, Ramón conducted a tour of the mill. It was an impressive operation. Robotics and automation were so prevalent that only twenty or so employees worked in each of the production areas. Mills are mills. They aren't the cleanest operations around, but this mill was spotless.

"The engineering offices are equipped with the latest technology," Ramón said. He adjusted his glasses again.

We walked through a wing of product design and planning offices. Then Ramón instructed Luis to conduct the rest of the tour and bring me to his office when we were finished.

The mill was enormous. It took over an hour for Luis to show me the remaining sections, including the manufacturing floors, where I wanted to see a few details the director had not shown me. Nothing of what I'd seen so far seemed out of the ordinary, but I had a gut feeling that, contrary to what McVey thought, this job was not going to be easy.

Back in Ramón's office, I told him I'd start running computerized audit programs the next morning.

"I'll need a technical person to work with me to pull reports off the computer system. I'll also need temporary office space."

"Luis can help you," Ramón said. "He's very knowledgeable on the accounting and procedures of operations. He knows the flow of production, and he's practically an expert on our computer system. I'll make sure he's assigned to assist you."

I noticed a hint in Ramón's attitude, courteous as he was, that he felt this female auditor in her mid-thirties posed no threat at all. If I had assessed his attitude correctly, I would use it to my advantage. I knew every step I made, every action I took, and every word I said would be reported to Manuel Del Campo.

The next two days slipped like sand through my fingers. I became familiar with the company's processes and procedures. I relaxed into a routine. Luis was an excellent assistant, and we worked effectively together. For production reports on raw material used in the manufacturing process or documentation for a quality assurance inspection, he showed me how to pull the information from the computer system. When I requested an overly long report to be printed, he suggested doing it overnight. He volunteered to come in early and pull the supporting documentation.

"Let me look at the report first thing after I arrive tomorrow, and I'll select a sampling of items," I said.

I wanted Luis to assist, but I did not want to provide opportunity for documents to be destroyed, altered, or instantly produced. Also, I intended to check the items I selected all the way through the production batches into inventory and through the shipment process to customers. I also wanted to trace the raw materials back to receiving reports confirming the arrival of the raw material lots at the factory.

On the job the next day, every single item I selected from the computer reports checked out to original documents or procedures. I was beginning to feel I had fallen into a perfect make-believe world, where errors never occurred.

Finally, it was Friday—the conclusion of the first week on my assignment. No discoveries of wrongdoing, no suspicious transactions, nada. Nothing except for Del Campo's aggression toward me in his office earlier in the week. I thanked Luis for his help.

"It's been a pleasure to help you, Ms. Nikki. Feel free to call if you want a tourist guide to show you the city." He handed me a business card with his personal phone number handwritten in.

I packed my computer and dialed Theya.

"I just want to let you know, my driver is already at the mill to take me to the hotel. I'll coordinate my pickup on Monday with him if I'm going to have the same driver next week."

"I'm so glad you called," Theya said. "I was just going to call you. Señor Del Campo is having a dinner party at his home tomorrow night, and he would like for you to join them. He has a friend who's a sculptor, and it might be nice for you to meet him. We'll send the driver for you at seven p.m. And yes, Tomás will be your driver the entire time you're in Colombia. He will even be available on the weekends, if you need him."

Del Campo, inviting me to a dinner party at his home? I was flabbergasted. My first thought was to decline the invitation, even though it sounded like a command performance. I could turn it down, being an invitation to the home of the person I was investigating. On second thought, he probably calculated it as part of his psychological fencing strategy. I'd be able to see where he was headed with the frames. From a work perspective, I'd have a firsthand look at the lifestyle of this individual —an opportunity not to be refused. Lifestyle analyses cost tens of thousands of dollars, and I was being offered the chance to obtain one totally free.

"Theya, thanks, I'd love to meet a Colombian artist," I replied. I thought Del Campo was probably attempting to help a starving artist by introducing him to people in the community who might purchase his work. I just hoped I was not expected to buy a piece of art. "What is proper attire?"

"A cocktail dress."

"Cocktail dress?" I asked. I was unable to hide my surprise at the apparent formality of the event. "I don't bring cocktail dresses on assignment. I'll need a boutique where I can buy one."

"I will have Tomás pick you up tomorrow morning, say ten-thirty, and take you to a couple of nice places. I'll call tomorrow afternoon to make certain you found a dress you like. If not, I'll take over two or three of my own. We are about the same size," Theya stated in a polished, professional voice, as if she were dealing with a head of state.

The lush gardens behind the hotel, beyond the pool, tennis courts, and open-air café, were as beautiful as any I'd seen. I needed to check in with McVey. What better place to do it than among the colorful flowering shrubs and aromatic orange and lime trees. Besides, it seemed like a very safe place to call from. No bugging devices dangling from rosebushes. McVey answered on the second ring.

"How's it going?"

"Not much to report. Del Campo got angry when I questioned him, but as far as the records are concerned, everything I check is absolutely perfect," I said.

"Angry? About what?"

"Well, he said corporate should review his record and decide if they want to keep him or fire him."

"And you haven't found anything wrong?" McVey asked.

"No, but that makes me feel uncomfortable. For a fraud auditor, it's a dead end. I need errors, exceptions, problems, or strange items requiring further investigation."

As I spoke, I plucked a little blossom from the orange tree where I stood and almost dropped my secure mobile phone.

"Are you ready to come home, or do you want to spend another week there?" McVey asked.

"I think I should check a few more things out."

"Yeah, good idea," McVey said. "It's probably nothing more than a jealous competitor or disgruntled employee falsely accusing Del Campo. You can wrap the job and fly home early."

Did McVey say disgruntled employee or jealous competitor? Funny, Del Campo had used those exact words.

Tomás was waiting for me outside the hotel when I came out after a leisurely breakfast at the poolside café. He opened the door for me. He was an efficient driver, well-mannered and well-dressed. He had a distinguished look about him. In fact, he was much more distinguished looking than the mill director. Probably in his late thirties, he was in excellent shape. He looked as if he worked out regularly. We had exchanged a few pleasantries during the week as he drove me to the company and back to the hotel. Now it was time to find out more about my chauffeur.

"How many years have you worked for the company?" I inquired.

Tomás expertly maneuvered the car from the quiet hotel grounds into the heavy street traffic.

"I've been at Amazonia longer than Señor Del Campo himself. I've worked here for sixteen years. It's my second home."

"Who hired you?"

"Mr. Sweeney, an American who was president before Señor Del Campo. Mr. Sweeney set up the original plant. Mr. Sweeney was a great manager."

"Do you know anything about the party at Señor Del Campo's home tonight?" I asked.

"It's a reception for Señor Pacheco, one of our famous sculptors," he said. "You see, Señor Pacheco lives in Spain and only spends three months a year in our country. Señor Del Campo has a party for him every year. Pacheco is not quite as well-known as our other famous sculptor, Botero, the one who does the fat people."

This conversation was already proving to be useful. The guest of honor was no starving artist. To host a world-famous sculptor was quite a feat for the president of any company. I was relieved not to be obligated to buy something.

Back at the hotel after a marathon of trying on dresses and shoes, I looked at the charges on my credit card slips and was amazed my full attire had cost over six hundred dollars. More money than I would have liked to spend, but I needed to dress the part. I also knew that my attendance would cause rumors to fly around the company on Monday morning that the auditor was being bought out by Del Campo. Not a bad thing, as long as someone at the company approached me on the strength of those rumors. I had no leads yet, no evidence at all of any wrongdoing, so I had to take a bold step—in a six-hundred-dollar dress.

The phone rang.

"Did you find a cocktail dress?" Theya asked.

"I did. Royal blue georgette with an accent of sequins and little cut crystals along a V neck."

"I just wanted to check that you felt comfortable with your attire," she said.

"Comfortable? The dress is a bit sexier than I'm accustomed to wearing."

"You'll look beautiful. Besides, you're in Colombia. Women dress much sexier here than in the States."

CHAPTER TWO

T he lights of Medellín glittered as if decorated for one of the many festivals that had made it a favorite tourist destination in recent years. Though still overcoming a bad reputation from the days of Pablo Escobar—the drug lord who became one of the world's richest men—Medellín was a modern city with universities and a lively cultural scene. It was also a top producer of steel and exporter of flowers, products so different from the coffee and gold that made it prosper before the Medellín drug cartel threw the city into chaos decades ago. I asked Tomás about the industries in his city.

"In my youth, I never guessed Medellín would become a leader in pharmaceuticals and health care. I should have studied chemistry or become a lab technician," Tomás said. "That's where the jobs are."

"So what did you study?"

"History. I have a master's degree, but I earn more money as a driver for Amazonia than I would as a high school teacher, so I continue as a chauffeur, the job that paid for college."

The night air was cool. Medellín's subtropical, humid climate, high elevation, and surrounding wall of blue-green mountains made the weather more temperate than other cities at the same latitude. Tomás drove past Botero Square, a large downtown park permanently displaying twenty or so large sculptures donated by its namesake. He was the most prestigious of Latin American sculptors, far better known than the one I was meeting tonight. I had once seen about fifteen Botero sculptures in a temporary exhibit running the length of the Magnificent Mile in Chicago, where the sculptures had appeared out of place and the massive proportions of the bodies rather grotesque.

I had googled Pacheco and his work so I could converse intelligently with the famous painter-turned-sculptor. In New York, I realized I had seen Pacheco's monolithic steel sculptures—a few with straight beams rising out of the ground with angular crossbeams, others with polished curved surfaces like giant wombs. My own taste ran more toward Pacheco's modern pieces than those obese people molded in bronze by Botero.

"We have arrived, señora," Tomás announced.

I was unprepared for what I saw. If the company was in an opulent setting, this was an even more impressive site. On a smaller scale, of course, but that human scale was precisely what made it more attractive.

At the entrance, four guards stood by a two-story house that looked more like a wooden Swiss chalet than a guard shack. Inside the grounds, the driveway curved and wound around the property like a maze. Tomás drove me slowly through the gardens, where purple, orange, and red flowers planted next to dark-green shrubs grew in carefully planned landscaping, like a scene from an English countryside. He continued past an artificial lake, encircled by graceful verawood trees covered in orange-yellow flowers. A dramatic, cascading waterfall reflected the last rays of sunlight at the farthest end of the lake, where the terrain rose into a gentle hill. In the middle of the lake, a Pacheco sculpture sat imposingly on a tiny island. The steel structure was wrapped in the golden light of a fading sun, making it appear in harmony with the surrounding nature. We drove past three splendid homes as we made our way to the mansion.

"What are these other houses on the grounds?" I asked.

"That first house is for Señor Del Campo's parents, and the second one for his in-laws," Tomás explained. He pointed at two brick homes. "The third one in the back is a guest house. The stables and an equestrian field, where la señora practices dressage, are beyond the guest house, at the back of the property. Señor Del Campo's stables are considered the finest in the country."

"What types of horses does he own?"

"Thoroughbreds, señora. That's what makes his stables famous. Señor Del Campo has told me his horses have pedigrees traceable to three stallions imported into England in the 1600s and 1700s. That bloodline was introduced into Colombia in the late 1800s. He races them. And he breeds for other disciplines—show jumping, dressage, and polo. He exports polo ponies to Argentina, England, and Dubai. He's crossbred his Thoroughbreds to have a line of quarter horses that he also exports."

"How does he have time to devote to such a complex activity?" I asked.

"Señor Del Campo has ten or twelve employees who care for the horses, including a full-time veterinarian."

"Is it a profitable enterprise for him?"

"That I cannot say, señora, but Señor Del Campo tells people that horses are his passion."

"Quite a hobby," I said. I was looking for the stables, but instead I saw a helicopter.

"Does the señor own a helicopter?" I asked, pointing toward it.

"Oh, sí, señora. It is a Sikorsky S-76C, a beautiful machine."

I didn't know much about helicopters, but I did recognize Sikorsky as a major manufacturer, the one that builds the Black Hawks used by the military.

"Does Señor Del Campo deliver fillies in the chopper?" I asked.

"Fillies?"

"Sorry, Tomás, bad joke. Where does he fly it?"

"He doesn't fly it himself. He has a pilot," Tomás said.

"And where do they fly?" I asked again, trying to sound indifferent.

"I don't know. To call on customers, he says."

This evening, thanks to my driver, had turned into an informative one, and it was just beginning.

We arrived at the front entrance, and Tomás opened the door of the Mercedes so I could step out. He took my arm, and we climbed the steps to the extra-wide double doors. He continued to politely hold my arm until we stepped inside a grand vestibule with marble floors. A bronze Botero sculpture, dwarfed only by the size of the foyer itself, was placed in the center of this show hall, and a grand piano was offset against the farthest wall of the two-story atrium. Twenty or so guests were standing around, engaged in conversation in groups of two or three. Manuel Del

Campo himself stepped forward to greet me as my chauffeur doubled back to the car.

"Welcome, welcome to my home," he said with a smile.

Del Campo, reframing himself as the charming host, placed his arm around my shoulder, as if I were an old friend. His wife approached, and he introduced us. I had seen photos of her in my brief research into the man and knew her name was Clara Iglesias.

"Manuel told me you grew up around horses," Clara said.

"Only in the summers, when I visited my grandparents. My grandfather was an avid horseman, so yes, I grew up loving horses."

I had not mentioned a word to Del Campo about horses. That rumor had filtered up from my meeting at the mill with Ramón and his management group.

"We have stables, and if you'd like to ride, you're more than welcome to come out while you are in Medellín," she said.

"Thank you, Clara. I haven't been on a horse for almost seven years," I said.

I thought back on the last time I rode a horse. We were on vacation in Colorado, a few months before Robbie died. Robbie had loved horses, too.

"There's always time to start again," she said.

"And I'm looking for a person to manage my stables," Del Campo said. "I need someone with an international business background and language skills." A small grin emerged on his face, as if what he said was humorous.

Looking away and pretending to ignore the suggestion, I made small talk with his wife, but Del Campo put his hand on my arm. He maneuvered me around the vestibule, as if I were a filly on a short rein, introducing me to a businessman and his daughter, a neurosurgeon with a wife young enough to be his daughter, and several other couples. We moved through another set of oversized double doors into a well-appointed parlor, where five people gathered around a distinguished looking, gray-haired gentleman. I recognized him from my internet search. Del Campo guided me right up to the famous artist, ignoring the other guests.

"Francisco, this is Nikki Garcia. She's visiting us from the States. I promised her that you'd take her around the house and show her my art collection," he said, interrupting Pacheco in mid-sentence. "And don't forget to show her my collection of fencing equipment in the library."

Pacheco smiled and excused himself from his admirers.

"Será un placer. Let's start with the Renoirs in the dining room," he said.

A waiter in a tuxedo stopped us and offered me a glass of champagne, which I was glad to accept, although my head was already spinning.

"Our host appreciates Renoir's diffused palette, although I personally prefer bolder statements and definition of line, like Goya or Velázquez. Or Picasso, to name a more modern painter," Pacheco said as I followed him.

The dining room had nineteenth-century French cherry and walnut burl cabinets with ivory inlay and gilt bronze details. A grand mahogany table was formally set for dinner, surrounded by four smaller round tables, also set for tonight's dinner. The wall directly across from where we stood had four floor-to-ceiling windows overlooking the lake, which was resplendent in artificial light as the encroaching darkness surrounded it. Long brocaded curtains accented each side of the window frames. The Renoirs, four of them, brought a sense of serenity and quiet elegance to a room that could easily have been overdecorated.

I had hardly uttered a word, other than the usual pleasantries during introductions.

"Are these real?" I asked out loud.

"Most definitely."

"Where did he purchase the Renoirs?"

"From the Impressionist auctions at Christie's and Sotheby's in New York," he answered. The artist selected a chicken liver wrapped in bacon from the tray of hors d'oeuvres offered to us by another tuxedoed waiter.

Not liking chicken liver, I took a miniature cheese puff. Pacheco suggested we move to the next room to see the Monet water lilies.

"The water lilies are his favorites," he stated.

"Monet's water lilies? Really? I like those, too," I said, trying not to sound flabbergasted or stupid, the way I'd sounded over the Renoirs.

Next we visited the library. Two life-sized mannequins in full fencing regalia stood on wooden stands. Each mannequin was encased in a Plexiglas bubble, like those in museums covering antique pottery or other valuables, only these enclosures were large enough to cover the mannequins.

Pacheco pointed toward one of the fencing figures.

"Look at those hideous mannequins. How can you not see them? They dominate this room. I guess he's proud of the fact he was an Olympic fencer."

Then Pacheco steered me toward two rather large, brightly colored paintings displayed on the only wall space not covered by volumes of books, arranged on built-in bookcases.

"These are the most worthwhile assets Manuel owns—two of my original paintings. Early work. Look at the vibrancy of those colors."

Listening intently as he described his own art, I commented on how the near photorealism of his oil paintings differed from his modern abstract sculpture.

"Styles change over time," he explained. "It would be boring to work the same themes in the same style for too long. Like a man married to the same woman all his life. Can you imagine how dull that would be? It's the same in art. You have to keep reinventing yourself."

Since he appeared to be by himself at the party, this led me to believe he was between wives or women friends. Changing direction in the conversation, I asked him how long he had known Del Campo.

"Oh, for the last eight or nine years. He contacted me for advice on purchasing art. We hit it off. We work together on my favorite charity here in Medellín. As you know, he has a lot of influence in the business community of this country."

I wondered to myself if Del Campo had inherited great wealth, but it was not a question to be asked here. It would have to wait until next week, when I was back at the company.

We walked and talked our way through two more roomfuls of exquisite art, including a Degas ballerina. We returned to the foyer, where a quintet of mariachis was finishing a rousing rendition of Mexican music. The mariachis and their Mexican folk songs seemed out of context in the elegant surroundings. Pacheco must have seen my perplexed look.

"Mexican music and soap operas are very popular in Colombia. Everybody listens to mariachis, and all the women, rich and poor alike, watch the telenovelas," he said. I sensed a facetious tone in his voice.

Continuous lines of waiters in matching tuxedos still offered wine and champagne, as well as the tasty hors d'oeuvres. Over the murmur of voices engaged in small talk, I began to hear soft music, either a violin or another string instrument, streaming in from the dining room. The soft melody was far more appropriate to the ambiance than the earlier mariachis had been.

Del Campo, with Clara standing next to him, requested that his guests join them in the hotel-sized dining room. Name cards had been placed above the plates. Pacheco found my seat with his name at the next place setting.

"I know a gentleman here who is far more interesting for you to sit next to than this old man," he said, looking around.

I started to protest, but he was waving his hand at a very handsome man I hadn't seen until now. The stranger approached us.

"Eduardo, this is Nikki Garcia from the US. She's here on business, and I think she would be much more interested in hearing about your charitable foundation and your research department than listening to this viejo carry on about the inequities of the art world," Pacheco said.

I was embarrassed by the switch in companion, but I reached my hand out to the stranger. He took my hand in his and smiled.

"Eduardo Duarte." He followed up very quickly with the usual, "A tus órdenes." Repeating "At your service," he pulled the chair out for me to sit down.

The first course, seared tuna on a bed of greens, had already been served prior to the guests being seated. When everyone was settled, Del Campo and his wife picked up their forks at the main table. All guests, including me, followed suit. Such formality is inconceivable today in the United States, except for state dinners at the White House, perhaps. I suspected that, with the exception of very formal events, it is not seen often even in the finer homes in Colombia. Not many people anywhere lived the lifestyle the Del Campo family obviously enjoyed.

The same tuxedoed waiters from earlier were now serving wine, taking away dishes, bringing the main course, and offering bread rolls with the precision of the robotics I'd seen at the mill. They seemed programmed to bend in stiff formality at the same moment. It felt surreal, out of a science fiction script. Was Del Campo an obsessive-compulsive man who orchestrated the robots at the mill? Demanded the inconceivable cleanliness of the mill's floors? And still had time to command the performance of telerobotic waiters serving us, or at least controlling them through carefully devised instructions for attending to his guests? Could he really have his nose in everything?

Eduardo sat to my left. To my right was the neurosurgeon I'd met earlier, conversing with his young wife. That was fine by me. Eduardo was far more interesting. A harpist played soft music from the back of the room. Eduardo mentioned that South America produces a lot of modern music for the harp, and the piece being played was written by an Argentine composer.

The main course—filet mignon in a delicious wine sauce, mashed potatoes, and five or six giant asparagus tied, like a bundle of logs, with a strip of red pepper—was so good that I ate every morsel. I passed on dessert in a feeble attempt to save my figure after having stuffed myself with all that continental-style food. Four waiters with carts moved effortlessly around the tables, tending to each guest individually. I'd seen this in restaurants but never in a private home. The waiters offered a selection of cheese, both local and imported, and served the cheese and crackers with coffee, poured into dainty demitasse cups. I could tell I was getting tired because the waiters were beginning to resemble penguins in their tuxedos. Or perhaps I was feeling the effect of the wine and the altitude.

"May I ask what plans you have for tomorrow?" Eduardo's tone was formal.

"I'm working for a while, and then I'll swim an hour to get rid of the calories I've put on tonight."

"Work? Really? On the weekend?"

"It's typical for me to work on weekends," I said.

"Would you consider a better offer?"

I simply stared at him. My hands gripped the napkin in a nervous gesture. I hoped he hadn't noticed.

"I'd like to take you on a tour around Medellín," he said. "If you want to swim, then we'll go to my house. I can grill a steak or seafood. You can work in the morning, and I'll pick you up after lunch."

"Don't you need to check with your wife before you invite me out?"

"I don't check with her now that she's divorced me," he said. "How about you? Are you married?"

"No, I'm divorced, too."

"What time would you like for me to come by?" he asked.

I'd enjoyed talking to him over dinner. He was handsome. He was charismatic. But as a Latin man, he was probably a notorious womanizer. I didn't need trouble, but maybe he could offer insights into Del Campo's background or social standing that might prove useful.

The sunlight was bright around the outer edges of the draperies I hadn't bothered to close properly last night. I looked at the clock radio on the nightstand and was startled to see it was almost nine-thirty. I jumped out of bed, went to the bathroom, and turned on the shower. My mouth tasted awful. So tired last night I'd gone to bed without brushing my teeth, I brushed them while the shower warmed up. Comforted by the spray of warm water, I stepped out, rubbing the towel vigorously over my body. I put sweats on over my swimsuit and headed downstairs to swim those laps I'd promised myself.

Lingering over coffee at the poolside café after breakfast, I analyzed the extravagant lifestyle Del Campo and his family maintained. It's customary in Latin America for business executives to have chauffeurs, a house full of servants, and other luxuries. It's also customary for various members of a family to live in a compound with several homes, but the attention-getter was the lavish lifestyle Del Campo and his family enjoyed. The helicopter, complete with pilot, the exquisite art collection, the first-rate stables with accompanying equestrian field, the full-time veterinarian on the payroll—all these extras were definitely over the top.

But there was more. I had a gut feeling a lot more was under that luxurious veneer. *How could Del Campo run everything with such a tight rein that robots seemed to surround him during his lavish entertaining? Why did employees of the company seem to act on cue and not of their own free will? What about the way he tried to intimidate me at his office and then turn around to treat me as a longtime friend at last night's party? And his stupid offer of a job at his stables? And his comments on the art of fencing? What did all that mean?*

Tomorrow I'll phone Sarah, I thought as I waved at my waiter to bring me fresh coffee. My assistant was very efficient at running the office and attending to the requests of junior auditors when I was on assignment. She was also excellent at following up on the most unusual requests I often burdened her with while I was performing a special review, such as this one. This job was going to require delicate investigative work, and for that, I would have her contact the private detective firm we had used on several occasions. Security Source, based in Miami but with international pull, would be able to dig up whatever Del Campo was trying to bury.

Back at the desk in my suite, I opened the computer and listed the items for Security Source to work on:

1. Search for bank accounts in US, Canada, Caribbean, Panama in Del Campo's name
2. Search for bank accounts in US, Canada, Caribbean, Panama in Clara Iglesias's name
3. Investigate Zambrano Construction Company for corruption
4. Investigate possible related party links between Del Campo and Zambrano Construction Company

A second list contained items for Sarah to investigate, such as helping me put together a lifestyle analysis on Del Campo.

Inflow:

1. Compensation, cash bonuses, stock awards, stock options
2. Investigate any special benefits or deferred compensation plans where he received advances
3. Stables—income—I will follow up and submit data to you

Outflow:

1. Personal home, paid in full or mortgaged?
2. Household expenses, including full-time gardener, groundskeeper, housekeeper, and staff
3. Helicopter—Sikorsky S-76C, paid in full (how much) or mortgaged?
4. Helicopter—Sikorsky S-76C, operating expenses for a year
5. Helicopter—pilot salary and benefits for one year
6. Stables—expenses—I will follow up and submit data to you
7. Art collection—investigate sales of Impressionist art sold to

Latin Americans through Christie's and Sotheby's websites and catalogues, especially the works of Monet, Renoir, and Degas —go back 10 years

I finished a memo to Sarah, instructing her to purchase the catalogues from all auctions of Impressionist paintings held in New York and London for the past ten years and overnight them to me. With physical catalogues in hand, I might identify, during moments of leisure at the hotel, specific pieces of art hanging on Del Campo's walls. If we could prove the authenticity of the works through his accounts at auction houses, we could include the millions he'd spent on art. It was obvious to me there would be a colossal gap between his known income and his expenditures. I was not a forensic accountant. I would need additional help, especially since we'd be doing it without Del Campo's knowledge or cooperation. We would have to rely on estimates in a few areas. I'd personally handle the stables through Security Source and have Sarah plug that information in later to complete the analysis.

Just a casual observation of how that man lived convinced me there was wrongdoing at the company. His abrupt change in attitude toward me also made me suspicious. Apprehension stirred in my stomach. I'd have to be cautious in everything I did, even in submitting files to Sarah. I should not send sensitive data from the company premises, and I suspected that transmitting from my hotel room was not safe, either.

The phone rang, interrupting my thoughts. I wasn't expecting a call on the room phone from anyone. I answered, thinking it might be housekeeping since I'd spent most of the day in the room and the bed remained unmade. Instead, it was Eduardo, apologizing for calling early.

"The weather is so beautiful, I thought I could pick you up an hour earlier," he said.

The scent of flowers wafted through the lobby thirty minutes later, reminding me I was in the flower capital of Latin America, and Eduardo walked toward me the minute I stepped out of the elevator. His arms open in the traditional Latin embrace he was about to give me, he blew a kiss on the side of my face. He was wearing white pants, a yellow polo shirt, and men's Prada wrap-style aviator sunglasses. Several people in the lobby turned to look at us as we walked out.

The weather was indeed gorgeous. Eduardo opened the door to his Audi R8 for me. Driving with the top down, the warm breeze felt good through my hair.

"There was a time when we could not drive a car like this because of the drug cartels. We've made so much progress in the fight against illegal drugs that we have transformed our country," he said with obvious satisfaction.

"It seems to me that Colombia only exported its drug cartels to Mexico," I said. I hated to dismiss his gratification about his country's war against drugs, but it was the truth. "Colombia may feel it won the war, but drugs are just as plentiful now as they were in the 1980s and 1990s. The violence Colombia experienced then has gripped Mexico this past decade."

"Unfortunately, you're right. Colombia is safer, but Mexico is suffering," he said.

"And the use of illicit drugs continues unabated, causing innocent people to die, whether it's by gang warfare or overdoses."

"How much of the city have you seen? I don't want to waste time on what you have already visited," he said, tactfully changing the subject.

"My chauffeur, Tomás, gave me a tour of the business district and Botero Square."

"Then we'll head to Nutibara Hill to get the full view of the city and continue on to the top so you can see a replica of a typical Colombian village called Pueblito Paisa. We'll return to see the cathedral and the historic part of the city. Then we'll go to my condo, and I'll cook dinner for you."

"To save time, why don't we just return to my hotel and grab a salad or a sandwich? That way I can get a little more work done tonight," I said.

"If that's what you prefer. Would you allow me to change dinner to a restaurant that serves typical Colombian fare, instead of eating at the hotel? That way you can experience how the other side of Colombia lives. I'd hate for you to return to the US with the idea that all Colombians live the way Manuel does." He stopped at a traffic light, took off his Prada shades, and looked at me.

I laughed, out of nervousness. "Very few people anywhere in the world live as lavishly as he does. I know his lifestyle is not your typical Colombian household. How long have you known Del Campo?"

"About seven years, when he helped Niños del Parque, the nonprofit foundation I started. He has served on our board of directors. He's donated both time and money to bring street children into orphanages," he said.

I seized the opportunity. "Does Señor Del Campo come from a wealthy family?"

"Not real wealth, not the kind of wealth he has now. He comes from an upper-middle-class family, though. Why do you ask?"

"Just curious."

"The auditor in you is assessing his lifestyle?"

"Well, yes. You have to admit, it's a bit extravagant," I said, trying not to show my surprise at his question.

"To my knowledge, he made money in a joint venture before he joined your company. He sold his interest to the other party, and rumor has it that it was for a very tidy sum of money. At least that's what he tells people."

I was about to ask that, if Del Campo had made so much money, why was he working as president/general manager for a multinational conglomerate when he could have a company of his own, or merely live the life of a philanthropist? But the curvy, windy road to the top of Nutibara Hill gave way to a lovely, typical little Spanish town, with whitewashed walls and red tile roofs. I was too distracted to pose the question.

Eduardo parked and rolled up the top of the Audi. We strolled down the main street in Pueblito Paisa, open only to pedestrian traffic. I felt as if I were floating on air, like a cotton candy princess, light and fragile, unable to feel my legs as I walked the cobblestoned street with this handsome man.

In the city for dinner, Eduardo ordered arepas, unleavened cornmeal patties, as an appetizer and the most typical Colombian food, bandeja paisa, as the main dish. It turned out to be a stew with meat, beans, rice, egg, sausage, and plantain.

"The word paisa is slang for peasant or folksy," he explained. "But the people from this region are also called paisas. A lot of the local culture incorporates the word paisa, like the village we visited and the stew we just ate."

I was anxious to inquire more about Del Campo but decided not to raise suspicions. Eduardo must have read my mind.

"I guess you're here investigating Manuel. And I know he probably looks guilty by the way he lives, but keep in mind that anyone who is as successful as he is abounds in enemies as well as friends, even enemies that pose as friends."

I smiled. "So you invited me out this lovely afternoon to pick my brain about the assignment that's brought me to Colombia. All this time I thought it was because you wanted to show a foreigner your beautiful city."

Eduardo leaned toward me. "Well, first of all, I don't know if he is guilty or not, though I would prefer to think he's innocent. I'd hate to lose my biggest contributor to the foundation."

"He's your biggest contributor?"

"As we say in Spanish, 'no voy a meter las manos al fuego por él,'" he whispered. "I'm not going to put my hands into the fire and defend him. You want to know the real reason I invited you out? Well, I'm trying to find out why an attractive woman like you does this type of work."

"You don't approve of my work?" I asked, nibbling on another spoonful of the Colombian stew.

"That's not it. It's all about your personal life. What kind of life, what kind of personal relationships can you build if you're always traveling from one country to another, working your life away?"

"I love to travel, see new places, experience new cultures, and meet new people."

"Meet new people? Really? You don't have time to meet people when you work weekends."

I smiled at him. No man was going to pry into my life. In defense, I flipped it over.

"Why don't you tell me about yourself," I said.

"What do you want to know?"

"Why did you start a foundation for street children? How do you spend your leisure time? Do you have time to do your own research when you're also running a research department?"

"Wait a minute," he said. He laughed, but his eyes were smiling more than his lips. "I'll have to invite you to dinner during the week to answer all those questions. Is Tuesday good?"

"Actually, Wednesday is better. I have plans on Tuesday."

"Dinner on Tuesday?" he asked. The grin faded from his lips. "Who's the lucky guy?"

"Two guys. The local CPAs in charge of the Amazonia account. The external auditors," I said.

"Then I'll settle for Wednesday night. I'll come by your hotel at six o'clock. There's more of the city I'd like to show you."

We both ordered fresh fruit for dessert and lingered over coffee, talking much more than I'd planned. Eduardo spoke of his childhood, of losing his father when he was young. He also talked about his scholarship to Harvard Medical School. He promised to tell me, at our next outing, how he got the idea for the foundation for street children.

———————

I brushed my teeth and got ready for bed, reflecting on my afternoon with the Colombian philanthropist. Medical doctor from Harvard, masculine and handsome, founder of a charitable organization to save street children in Medellín, Eduardo was quite a guy. He could stand to lose about twelve pounds, but it was evident he exercised.

Why did he invite me out? Not that I had low self-esteem, but really, why had he taken the trouble to take me out? Was his humanitarian side feeling sorry for a woman, all alone in a foreign country, carrying out an investigation? Or was it the worst-case scenario, that Del Campo had asked him to distract me from the job? In time, perhaps I would know the answer.

CHAPTER THREE

That blasted wake-up call. It always came too early, especially after a night when I'd slept so badly. I'd struggled to fall asleep after a nightmare. Monsters stole Robbie away again. Between the lack of sleep and the hangover of regret and fear caused by the nightmare, I didn't feel well. I'd set the call half an hour earlier today because I needed the extra time to phone Sarah and submit my files to her.

I wanted to avoid using my own suite, in case the place was bugged, and instead use a separate room in the hotel. As I engaged in debate about this with the front desk clerk, Juan, the concierge, walked over.

"Can I help you?" he asked.

"The phone in my room is not operating properly, and I'd like to borrow an empty room so I can make a rather urgent phone call," I said.

I looked at his muscular physique, wondering how Juan could keep himself in such great shape when he worked all the time.

"Our business center is available, or my office is at your disposal," Juan informed me.

"But I need privacy, and I only need a room for a few minutes," I pleaded, biting my lower lip, a nervous habit I'd tried many times to break.

Even though the files were encrypted, if my phone line was tapped, they could hear my conversation with Sarah. Also, I feared they could retrieve the transmitted files and, to my mind, the encryption we used was not foolproof. Too many technical articles indicated that a lot of off-the-shelf encryption really wasn't.

Juan told the clerk to give me a key to a vacant room. He also told her to have maintenance check out the phone lines in my suite. I ran upstairs, grabbed my computer, and went to the loaner room. Working as fast as possible, I connected to the net and accessed email to submit the files I'd prepared yesterday with Sarah's to-do lists. I signed off and, using my calling card, I dialed Sarah at the office and kept my fingers crossed she would answer. Her voicemail greeted me. I left a message, informing her "the weather was chilly," code words we used so she could inform McVey I had a hunch a cover-up might be occurring, a cover-up I could not yet confirm.

McVey had developed the codes so we could talk without raising suspicions over telephone lines. With the codes, I could also call him directly, twenty-four seven, and in an ordinary and innocuous conversation, let him know the status of the job, including if I felt in any danger. It was a backup method to be used when not communicating over a secure line or if there were other people present.

I closed the door to the loaner room, took the elevator to the lobby, dropped off the key with the front desk clerk, and walked outside to my waiting car.

Theya welcomed me with a big smile. "How was the dinner party?" she asked.

"Magnificent," I said.

"I can imagine. Señor Del Campo knows how to do things right." Then Theya added, "Señor Del Campo will not be in the office today. He's calling on customers in Bogotá."

I decided to take advantage of Del Campo's absence. Lunch with administrative assistants might prove more productive than the routine work I'd planned. Meeting other staff members might be helpful, too. Luis could run reports I'd formatted, print them, and give them to me midafternoon. He had proven to be such a good worker, I thought I'd approach him, once this job was complete, for a job rotation in the States. His fluent English and attention to detail, in addition to being an accountant with expert knowledge in computers, would make it easy for me to recommend him for the rotation program. That he reminded me of my son also made it easy to think of offering him opportunities to further his professional development.

Late morning, I took a stroll down the impressive, open mezzanines that served as hallways around each of the four floors that were open to the full five-story atrium occupying the center of the building. Steel railings on the inner rim around the circumference of each mezzanine kept absent-minded employees from falling off the edge to the ground floor five levels below. Still, I kept my distance from the railings. Fear of heights made me instantly dizzy if I got too close.

Looking around as I walked down the center of the mezzanine, I noticed for the first time a large number of paintings in various sizes and themes hanging on the spacious walls. On the floor along the walls, oversized, colorful glazed urns contained white and purple orchids, streaming profusely over the sides of the urns. The open, airy spaciousness of the mezzanines, the abundance of colorful orchids, and the paintings exhibited on the walls contributed to a relaxing atmosphere, which resembled an upscale Miami art gallery rather than an office building in the middle of an industrial park in Medellín. Del Campo's office suite looked more New Yorkish, but the mezzanines looked like Miami's best design. Del Campo, without a doubt, had good taste.

My plan was to meet a variety of employees. They needed to see me and know I was accessible, if they chose to talk. This tactic had worked for me at other operating companies. An important key to unraveling fraud at a company was having an insider talk. I had not yet found any leads, so my hope was to find a whistleblower. Or could it simply be, as Eduardo stated yesterday, that Del Campo had enemies who might be trying to sabotage him? *Was I jaded by other fraud audits and looking for culpability where none existed? Was I on a witch hunt?*

As I walked down the mezzanine on the fifth floor, I headed for the office of the chief financial officer, a man I had met at worldwide meetings but who was currently out on medical leave. He had undergone major surgery for lung cancer the week before I arrived and was not expected back for at least two months. I walked to his office to speak to Elena, his administrative assistant. She was plump, mid-forties, and wore her black hair, accented by a few gray strands, in a swirl pinned at the back of her head with a decorative comb. Bright-red lipstick matched her bright-red fingernails. I asked her if she had any lunch plans.

"I brought my lunch from home and plan to eat at my desk today," she said.

"Well, I'd like you to join me for lunch in the cafeteria instead. I also want you to ask a couple of other administrative assistants."

I could tell from the perplexed look on her face that she thought my invitation was strange. She repeated my request to make certain she had not misunderstood me.

"Yes, that's correct. I want to have lunch with administrative assistants because, you see, I started out my career as a secretary," I lied. "And at every company, I like to keep in touch with that line of work, in case I get tired of working at what I'm doing." I must have sounded convincing because Elena now had a smile on her face. "What time do you normally go to lunch?"

"One o'clock."

"Is that the time most people go to the company cafeteria?" I asked.

She nodded affirmatively. Good. I wanted to be in the cafeteria during the peak hour to have as many employees as possible see me at lunch with the assistants.

"Fine. I'll return here, and we'll walk down together," I said.

Like a seasoned politician, I walked all the way around the oblong mezzanines on all four floors waving, smiling, stopping to shake hands, and speaking with as many employees as I could. I was still walking around, introducing myself and talking, when I realized it was time to return to the fifth floor to meet my group of administrative assistants for lunch.

Elena had invited only one other woman to join us. Claudia was tall and attractive, with curly brown hair that fell to her shoulders. An accounting clerk from the finance department, she was young and had worked for the company for two years.

When we approached the cafeteria, heads turned. And more so as we took our place in line and got our lunches. Then we sat down at a table in the center of the cafeteria where everyone could see us. I asked each of the women to tell me a little about themselves, but they were more interested in knowing how I'd learned to speak Spanish if I lived in the US.

"My parents left Mexico City and moved to Minneapolis when they got married. They were seeking a better life. We spent our summers in Southern Mexico with our grandparents. My dad reasoned we would have a competitive advantage as adults if we spoke both languages fluently, so we spoke Spanish at home. And he's been proven right. I wouldn't have this job if I didn't speak Spanish."

I did not mention that my brother and I lost our parents when we were teenagers.

I told them a couple of stories, to break the ice, about getting the languages confused with comic consequences when I was a kid. I wanted the two women to feel perfectly comfortable with me. Soon they were laughing at my anecdotes, and employees at surrounding tables could see we were having fun.

I asked them what they liked about their jobs, and when Elena asked me the same question, I had the opening I was hoping for.

"I'm a CPA with an auditing background. At corporate headquarters, a group of junior auditors report to me that perform work at our US companies. A predictable routine without much excitement. Two supervisors assist me because I also perform fraud investigations," I said.

"Fraud investigations?" Claudia asked. Her eyes were wide, and she moved closer to me, as if eager to hear more.

"Yes. Last year I was in South Korea, reviewing our affiliate there. Top management at the Korean mill was involved in a fraudulent scheme. I was able to crack the case because two of the local South Korean employees talked to me about what was going on."

"What happened?" Claudia asked.

"We fired them," I said.

"You fired the employees who talked to you?" Claudia asked. Her voice whispered in horror as her shoulders rounded, as if to hide within a protective shell.

"No, no, they still work at the company in Seoul," I answered. "It was the executives involved in the fraud who were fired."

"Oh, okay," Claudia said. Her shoulders straightened a bit.

"I've also done several fraud investigations of high-level executives in the US and Europe," I added. I wanted to make certain the word would be out, beyond doubt in anyone's mind, that I was here investigating top management. I also hoped it would serve to counteract the effect of rumors that were probably raging in the hallways that I had attended a party at Del Campo's palatial home.

Elena looked around the room. The cafeteria was clearing as people returned to their offices.

"I must get back to my desk," Elena said. "My boss had a radiation treatment today, and I promised his wife I'd call to get a report on how it went."

Elena lingered at the table and looked over her shoulders. She moved a few inches closer to me.

"I think my boss got cancer because of the stress Señor Del Campo puts on him. Señor Del Campo asks my boss to cover up things," she said in an almost inaudible whisper.

"What sort of cover-up?" I asked.

"Look, I really must go," Elena said. Her lips quivered ever so slightly, and she stood up abruptly and left the table.

I asked Claudia if she could stay a little longer. It seemed to me from her body language that she wanted to open up. I made small talk until employees in the cafeteria had essentially cleared out, at least all the tables around us. Then I took a direct approach.

"Claudia, do you have something you want to say?"

"No, not really. But you should know that not everything is as wonderful here as it appears to be," she said.

"Can you explain?" I asked.

"What I mean is that the company may not be such a wonderful place to work as some people try to make it out to be."

"Are you unhappy here?" I asked.

"It's hard to get good jobs in Colombia, even when you are very qualified, so I want to keep my job." She fidgeted with a bracelet on her left arm.

"If I could assure you that you will keep your job, even if you tell me what's on your mind, would you trust me?" I asked.

Claudia was now looking at the top of the table and running her right index finger in little circles or figure eights over the ceramic top.

"It's just that I'm afraid walls listen," she said.

"That's not going to happen. I always keep confidential the names of people who supply information to me. I have corporate behind me. I will make certain you don't lose your position."

"I don't know that there was anything wrong, but I think it was strange, the way things happened."

"About what?" I asked.

Claudia looked around the room. Then she looked straight at me. "All I can say is that a friend of mine, a coworker, Oscar Fuentes, died here."

"Died?"

"Yes. It was an accident. That's what the company said. They had an investigation, and that's what the investigators said, too."

"But you don't think it was an accident?" I asked.

"It's hard to tell. I don't know, but I have always been suspicious that it wasn't." Claudia looked around again, her nervousness apparent.

"Can you tell me more?" I asked.

"It's all I can say. Maybe you can investigate it, but promise me you won't do it today or tomorrow because everyone saw me having lunch with you today. I need my job." She looked very tense.

"Can you at least tell me how he died?"

"He fell at the mill."

"Fell?" I asked.

"Yes, from the catwalk."

I kicked off my high heels as soon as I opened my hotel room door. Then I put the computer bag on a chair, took the Mac out, and locked it in the safe where my extra throwaway mobile phones were stashed. I was trying to sort out my thoughts on the information Claudia had given me.

A death at the company? He fell to his death from the catwalk? What was he doing that caused him to fall? Could foul play be involved? Claudia's nervousness certainly pointed to it. Elena had insinuated a cover-up in the financial data, but that was a small deal compared to the bombshell Claudia had laid out that a death had occurred. One that might not have been accidental.

After twenty minutes on the treadmill and a few laps in the pool, I returned to the suite for dinner. The phone rang as I picked up a dessert spoon to scoop up my first bite of ripe, red raspberries. Hesitating slightly, I popped the raspberries in my mouth before picking up the receiver.

Sarah's voice greeted me with a cheerful, "Your number one, handy-dandy assistant is calling."

In reality, this was the code to let me know she had received my first email message, the one I'd sent that morning from the borrowed hotel room.

"The Miami Dolphins had an excellent practice this week," she said in code, confirming the private detectives from Security Source in Miami had been instructed to search for bank accounts and investigate Zambrano Construction. "They will practice for two full weeks before the playoffs."

I interpreted her words to mean it would be two weeks before we might have any news from the detectives on the success or failure of their search for overseas bank accounts Del Campo might have. Obviously, their investigation would track large or unusual flows of cash.

"Is the weather still chilly?" Sarah asked.

"Enough to need a light wrap when I go out at night." Words to let her know the status of the job—suspicions and minor leads, but nothing concrete. I purposely did not mention anything about a death at the mill, not on the hotel telephone she had called me on. We chatted about a couple of routine office issues before we said goodbye.

Sarah's call was the only one I received. I'd hoped to hear from Eduardo, but that was wishful thinking. I was kidding myself if I thought he was unattached. I was kidding myself even more if I thought he was interested in me in a romantic sense. But it was fun to dream.

CHAPTER FOUR

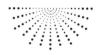

Most of Tuesday morning I spent at a computer terminal at the mill, checking various items I'd marked for review from yesterday's online reports. I decided to pay a visit to Isabel, the filing clerk, and request several files—just to appear busy until I was able to investigate Claudia's lead on the accidental death at the mill.

"Come in, señora," Isabel said. She spoke Spanish with the soft accent of the northern coastal area of Colombia. She looked to be in her late thirties with a beautiful olive complexion, green eyes, and thick, wavy, brown hair that swept across her forehead in a stylish cut. She wore a gold chain with two dangling fourteen-karat-gold profiles of children. Traditional among many Latin mothers, these silhouettes announced how many children they had. She was responsible for paper files, which still constituted a warehouse of paperwork, despite the ability to go green. Many government export documents were still handled in hard copy, and companies stored them for legal and tax purposes.

After we exchanged a few pleasantries, I provided her with a list of original documents I wanted to inspect—customs forms, export paperwork, and receipts from the trucking companies used to transport the finished product. To be thorough, I would check for domestic deliveries as well as international ones. I was hoping to stumble across suspicious items, though I was also creating busywork to avoid anyone thinking I was here spending corporate money to take a break from the cold climate in Minneapolis.

Isabel said it'd take five minutes to get the files I needed. I glanced at my watch. Almost one o'clock. After I returned to my office, files in hand, I asked Marisa to bring me a sandwich so I could review the files over lunch. While I was eating, the phone rang. It was Theya, who asked me to return to the main building. Del Campo, back from his trip to Bogotá, needed to have a word with me.

"I'll jump in the golf cart and be there in fifteen minutes," I said.

Entering the administrative building, I walked up the spiral staircase because it provided an opportunity for me to remain visible to the employees who were now walking down to lunch. Once past the second floor, I started experiencing vertigo, even though I was holding the hand railing, so I moved to the middle of the wide staircase to steady my nerves and avoid letting the dizziness get a stronger hold on me.

I'd been fighting vertigo since that night in Minneapolis at the Abbott Northwestern Hospital, on the sixth floor. I had been standing near the wall of windows, overlooking the lights of Minneapolis, praying for Robbie's life, when two doctors came to speak with Robbie's father and me. Robbie was dead, they said, and my whole being fell into a dark chasm. I started screaming, hugging and scratching the wall of glass. Beyond the windows, the city lights flickered like a thousand candles, all lit for Robbie.

My eyes had caught sight of an ambulance approaching the emergency entrance, like the one that had brought Robbie here. From this height, its flashing lights were a harbinger of death, not a hope for life. My mind was swirling, caught up in the red and white flashes, and the sudden impulse to hurl myself through the glass to the gyrating lights six levels below was overwhelming. My life wasn't worth living without my son. Like an earthquake, my body started trembling. The building itself had started shaking all around me. I was sick to my stomach. My head was spinning. Then everything went black.

When I awoke, I was on a stretcher in a room behind the nurses' station. The faces of the two doctors, the ones who had broken the news to us, loomed above me. They were asking me what my name was.

"I'm Robbie's mother," I had sobbed. "Robbie's mother."

Walking into Theya's office in a daze from the memories of that night when I'd lost Robbie, my head was still spinning, but her voice grounded me in reality again. The door to Del Campo's suite opened, and he stepped out with a short man of dark complexion with piercing, jet-black eyes and graying hair around his temples. Del Campo, cigar in hand, walked straight over, gave me the cheek kiss, and introduced his companion.

"This is Roberto, my pilot. He's worked for me for eight years. Before that, he flew helicopters for the Colombian Department of Defense, when the war against drugs was being fought so hard in the mountains. He'll take you up for a ride sometime. He's also a good fencing partner."

I extended my hand to Roberto in greeting, but he hardly acknowledged me. *An odd attitude for a Colombian man, not to be more attentive upon meeting a woman.* He shook my hand limply, nodded, turned, and left the room without uttering a word. I checked the front of my blouse and then touched my hair, wondering if there was something wrong with my appearance.

Del Campo motioned for me to follow him into his office suite. After small talk about the party, he asked how the investigation was proceeding.

"There's nothing to report," I said.

"You're not going to find anything," Del Campo affirmed, taking a long puff of his cigar. "I've already told you, I manage this company with complete transparency and high ethical standards."

"And I'm just doing my job," I said. I surprised myself, sounding like a bureaucrat.

He returned to small talk about the party. "I noticed you and Eduardo seemed animated in conversation during dinner. My wife and I are taking the helicopter up to Cartagena this weekend. I have a fencing match. Clara suggested we invite you and Eduardo to come along with us. We plan to rent a yacht on Sunday."

"You know I'm here to work. How can you expect me to jet-set around, having a grand old time, instead of doing my job?" I asked. I could only imagine the rumors that would fly through the company if I toured Cartagena over the weekend with Del Campo and his wife.

"We're just trying to keep you from being bored," he said, smiling. "And the weekend should be your time."

"You know corporate headquarters would not approve."

"You can always take the job at my stables," he said in a serious manner.

What the hell was that? Was he trying to insult me? If he was using fencing psychology, what was he trying to achieve? Undermine my self-confidence? I pretended to ignore it, as I'd done at his home when he made a similar remark. Instead, I decided to go on the offensive.

"While I'm here, let me ask you a question. Why do you need a helicopter?" As I waited for his answer, I pushed my right shoe off with my left foot and stretched the toes of my bare foot.

"It's a convenient way for me to travel around the country to call on customers without wasting time in airports. I also use it to fly to Venezuela, where we have significant pipe sales to the government and the oil industry there."

"I understand it belongs to you personally. Yet you use it for business purposes."

Del Campo looked surprised. "Ah, yes," he said. "I purchased it and hired Roberto. I rent it out on days when I'm not using it, which pays Roberto's salary. I get reimbursed for the business use of it, just as you get reimbursed for car mileage in the US. You're the auditor. Check the records yourself."

"Thanks. I will," I said.

I slipped my shoe on and stood up to exit the room, but I was seething. *How could that man invite me to join them for a weekend at a resort? Was Eduardo a willing accomplice to this?* The whole trip smacked of bribery. And that offer to work in his stables was ridiculous. Even if Del Campo wasn't an embezzler, he had an attitude that he could buy anyone.

Perhaps he was assuming too much because I'd accepted the invitation to his house. I noticed my teeth were clenched as I walked down the spiral staircase, but I told myself it wasn't worth getting so upset. Instead, I breathed slowly to calm down. Still not sure what game Del Campo was playing, I realized that, so far, he had managed to set up plenty of tension for me.

I was still on the stairway, almost at ground level, when a woman's scream echoed through the atrium. I froze, clutching the railing. Yelling erupted from the top floor—first a woman's voice, then several tumultuous voices, nervous and horrified, shouting orders, all overtaken by hysterical crying coming from one person. An alarm sounded, then a siren.

The screams and the siren brought back my pain of the night Robbie died, but I was not the one screaming this time. Instinctively, I started running up the stairs toward the commotion.

Paramedics with a stretcher got off the elevator near the office of the chief financial officer. I ran down the hallway to where people gathered. The paramedics, four of them, were ordering people to move away. A defibrillator in hand, one of them started working on a body sprawled out on the floor. A decorative comb and long, black hair that had come loose lined the carpeting near the downed woman's head.

Elena—what happened to her? My heart pounded so fast I thought it would rip my chest open. Two paramedics kneeling over her stopped working and placed her on the stretcher; three of them picked it up, while the fourth medic moved toward the elevator.

By this time, coworkers who had gathered were completely silent. Manuel Del Campo walked up. He asked people to remain calm, pray for Elena, and await further notice of her condition. He informed everyone he would personally contact the director at the hospital where she was being taken, and he would join Elena's family at the hospital.

I lingered for a little while, taking in the scene. Elena's desk seemed normal. A busboy arrived to retrieve the tray of unfinished food.

"What happened to Elena?" he asked.

"No news on her condition," I said, "but news travels fast."

"Ms. Theya called to have the tray taken back to the cafeteria," he said.

A young man with humped shoulders came up behind me, cleared his throat, and asked me to excuse him. He leaned in toward Elena's computer and turned it off.

I walked to Theya's office, and she was standing in the doorway.

"What happened?" I asked.

"We don't know," Theya said, "but Elena suffers from a heart condition. She may have had a heart attack. We won't know much until she's evaluated at the hospital."

"Is she even alive?" I asked.

"I don't know any more than you do. I'll notify you as soon as we have an update."

"Why did you order the food tray removed and the computer turned off?" I asked.

"To keep things tidy. The computer for security purposes," she said. "Is there anything wrong with that?"

"No, just wondering," I said.

Outside, I jumped in the golf cart I'd driven over, turned the key, gripped the steering wheel as if I were in heavy freeway traffic, and headed toward the mill, wondering whether Elena was still alive. Glancing across the acres of manicured lawn and grassy hills, I guessed Del Campo was not a golfer. Otherwise, he'd already have put in an eighteen-hole golf course on company grounds—the way he controlled everything. It was beginning to look as if he even controlled life and death at the company.

Could Elena be one of his victims? If so, what kind of beast would want to kill an employee like Elena?

Continue reading *Waking Up in Medellin*

ALSO BY KATHRYN LANE

Waking Up in Medellin

Danger in the Coyote Zone

Revenge in Barcelona

The Nikki Garcia Mystery Series: Box Set

Backyard Volcano and Other Mysteries of the Heart

AWARDS AND PRAISE FOR
KATHRYN'S BOOKS

WAKING UP IN MEDELLIN (A NIKKI GARCIA THRILLER)

Waking Up in Medellin was named "Best Fiction Book of the Year—2017" by the Killer Nashville International Mystery Writers' Conference and also won Killer Nashville's "Best Fiction—Adult Suspense—2017." It was also a finalist for the Roné Award—2016.

DANGER IN THE COYOTE ZONE (A NIKKI GARCIA MYSTERY)

Danger in the Coyote Zone won first place in the 2018 Action/Adventure Category of Latino Books into Movies Award, named a finalist in the Thriller Category at the 2018 Killer Nashville International Mystery Writers' Conference, and a finalist in the 2018 Book Excellence Awards.

REVENGE IN BARCELONA (A NIKKI GARCIA MYSTERY)

Revenge in Barcelona won first place in Latino Books into Movies-Latino Themed TV Series Category 2020; won the Silver Medal in the Mystery Category 2020 by Reader Views Literary Awards; Finalist in the Eric Hoffer 2020 Book Awards; Finalist for Silver Falchion in the Best Suspense by Killer Nashville; Finalist in the Suspense Category by Next Generation Book Awards; Finalist in the 2020 International Latino Book Awards; Awarded Five Stars by Readers' Favorite

BACKYARD VOLCANO AND OTHER MYSTERIES OF THE HEART (SHORT STORY COLLECTION)

Backyard Volcano and Other Mysteries of the Heart was named "Best Short Story Collection —2018" by the Killer Nashville International Mystery Writers' Conference.

ACKNOWLEDGEMENTS

I am indebted to countless individuals, many of them from book clubs I have visited, who express the desire to read more Nikki Garcia adventures and to offer suggestions of future locations for Nikki's investigations. Their recommendations provide an impetus to continue writing Nikki's story. The list runs too long to include them all. Those who contributed directly to *Missing in Miami* are listed below:

My incredible husband, Bob Hurt, who not only supports my writing but also participates in many of my writing activities. Coincidentally, he happens to be my most enthusiastic fan.

I am deeply indebted to James M. Olson, Professor of the Practice, at Texas A&M University's Bush School of Government and Public Service, and former CIA Chief of Counterintelligence, who generously discussed various topics on Cuba and suggested books for my research.

My former boss from my corporate career, Alberto Perez, and his wife Nancy Borges, both Cuban Americans, who came to the US and, believing in the American Dream, have built a beautiful life in their adopted country. Over the years, they have inspired countless people, including me, with their joy of life. Through them, I learned first-hand accounts of life in Cuba.

I am grateful to Dr. Joseph Burckhardt for reading and reviewing *Missing in Miami* to make certain the medical descriptions contained in the novel do not mislead my readers.

My incredible team of expert readers—David Hart, Pattie Hogan, Jorge

Lane, Ann McKennis, and Nancy Miller—I appreciate the edit recommendations.

A friend I met at the Killer Nashville International Mystery Writers' Conference, Robert Selby, who encourages me to keep writing better and better books.

Dr. Lowell Mick White, who generously guided my early efforts to write.

To my Houston Writers' Group—thank you.

Special thanks to my editor Sandra A. Spicher, Heidi Dorey for the beautiful cover design, Danielle Hartman Acee for the book interior and, more importantly, for her valuable technical expertise, and Maureen Donelan for the Tortuga Publishing, LLC logo.

And to my readers, friends, and fans—I could not do it without you!

ABOUT THE AUTHOR

Kathryn Lane is the award-winning author of the Nikki Garcia Mystery Series.

In her writing, she draws deeply from her experiences growing up in a small town in northern Mexico as well as her work and travel in over ninety countries around the globe during her career in international finance with Johnson & Johnson.

Kathryn loves the Arts and is a board member of the Montgomery County Literary Arts Council. Kathryn and her husband, Bob Hurt, split their time between Texas and the mountains of northern New Mexico where she finds it inspiring to write.

Kathryn's Website
Kathryn-lane.com

amazon.com/~/e/B01D0J1YES
bookbub.com/authors/kathryn-lane
goodreads.com/kathrynlane
facebook.com/kathrynlanewriter